Sara Charles
is the pseudonym
of a well-known writer.

SCHOOL
FOR SCANDAL

Sara Charles

CORGI BOOKS

SCHOOL FOR SCANDAL

A CORGI BOOK : 0 552 14130 5

First publication in Great Britain

PRINTING HISTORY
Corgi edition published 1994

Set in 11½pt Monotype Bembo by
Phoenix Typesetting, Ilkley, West Yorkshire

Corgi Books are published by Transworld Publishers Ltd,
61–63 Uxbridge Road, Ealing, London W5 5SA,
in Australia by Transworld Publishers (Australia) Pty Ltd,
15–25 Helles Avenue, Moorebank, NSW 2170,
and New Zealand by Transworld Publishers (NZ) Ltd,
3 William Pickering Drive, Albany, Auckland.

Reproduced, printed and bound in Great Britain by
Cox & Wyman Ltd, Reading, Berks.

To Averil and Linda —
Daughters may think what they wish,
but there's no substitute for experience

Contents

1

New Girl

The new girl stumbled and said, not bothering to lower her voice, something that sounded like, 'Oh, screw it to hell!'

Julia Hastings was amused.

The first thing she had noticed about Kate McNamara was her legs. They were just too perfect for words beneath her short summer skirt: long, slim and beautifully tanned. The 'sinistrals' – Latin for left-handers, and St Clare's code for lesbians – in the Upper Sixth would have her marked down as prey – 'fresh meat' as the jargon went – before she got her trunk unpacked. Especially Dutch Paula, who wasn't Dutch at all but South African, with a Boer surname. And who gave a whole new meaning to the fable of a Netherlands town being saved from flooding by a finger being put in a dyke.

Paula had a penchant for tall blondes, and Kate fitted the bill.

Julia wondered if Kate, two strides ahead of her on the broad staircase of Churchill House, was 'that way inclined'. Most of the prettier teenies, the thirteen- to fifteen-year-olds, went through a spell of it at one time or another, with crushes on older girls or younger mistresses. But, except for a handful, their love affairs with their own sex never went much further than running errands for the objects of their desire or mooning at them, cow-eyed, from a distance. The handful took it much further and for much longer, getting up to disgraceful antics after lights out. Girls up to and including the Lower Sixth slept in dormitories, but the Upper Sixth shared two-bed studies. Someone had remarked that the groans and moans emanating from a few of them after midnight reminded her of a bad night in Scutari, though Julia had had to have the joke explained to her. Still, it remained a fact – and an instant expulsion offence if caught – that, even now a one-hundred-year-old tradition at St Clare's had been broken, with a number of boys being admitted to the sixth form, there were some girls who preferred their own sex.

Julia wasn't one of them, having been frightened nearly half to death two years earlier when propositioned by the hockey captain, whose incipient five-o'clock shadow would have won her an audition for *Miami Vice*.

Of course, as Julia would have been among the first to admit, not all of the sinistrals were candidates for the England rugby team, or linebackers for the Chicago Bears. Some of them were sylph-like, pure gossamer. But they were not for her and, thankfully, it was an unwritten rule that, if an attempted seduction was rebuffed, nothing more was said, no offence taken.

Julia occasionally wondered how the former hockey captain, now up at Oxford, was making out these days. Perhaps she'd taken up tennis, where she was much more likely to find acceptance.

Kate McNamara was a year older than the official limit for teenies: sixteen, as Julia was, and only time would tell what her sexual inclinations were. Julia would have wagered that she was strictly hetero, more a target for the male students and a new object of fantasy for Bulgy Algy, the gardener's boy, who spent much of his leisure time and most of his working day, it seemed, within shouting distance of the tennis courts, pretending to mow or weed or hoe but, as was well known, playing with himself while he watched the girls practise. He was nineteen or twenty, Algy, but with the mind of a ten-year-old. And the generative equipment of an Aberdeen Angus, rumour had it, which Julia had to take on trust.

Some of the Upper Sixth and, for that matter, some of her own year, the Lower Sixth, teased him provocatively from the safety of the wire netting that surrounded the courts, while pretending not to be aware of his presence.

He was reputed to walk around sporting a permanent erection, which was why he was known as Bulgy. And there were always stories that this girl or that girl had gone the whole hog with him, or at least fished out his cock and toyed with it until it was stiff enough to measure. But no-one ever identified these mythical trollops.

Like most girls of her age and generation, Julia

put names to sexual acts and bodily functions that would have shocked her grandmother. Perhaps not her mother, who was a child of the Sixties, but certainly her mother's mother. Though still a virgin – even if it had been a damned close-run thing with Teddy Hedges in the village churchyard during the summer holidays, and would have been closer still if the bloody fool had remembered the condoms – Julia reckoned that she and her contemporaries had invented sex. What she had found out already, and was continuing to find out, she imagined was unique in the history of the world. Logic frequently dictated otherwise, but it was impossible for her to imagine that her mother, let alone her grandmother, had experienced the thrills and the exquisitely dirty-minded fantasies she often did, especially when they concerned Mr Penrose, who taught English Lit. to the Upper Fifth and throughout the sixth form. And as for her father unzipping himself to her mother and gasping the sort of words Teddy Hedges had, apologizing for forgetting the condoms but begging her to do something to relieve him, that was impossible.

OK, she'd done as Teddy had pleaded. That is, she'd done *one* of the things he'd urged her to. His first request she'd turned down flat, and his second. She wasn't ready to risk an unwanted pregnancy, and his suggestion of oral intercourse didn't appeal to her even though he protested that he was willing to play his part. He'd have to settle for what was on offer, which he did.

It wasn't the first time and it wouldn't be the last

and, in a way, she'd revelled in the power she had over him while he was lying back and her closed fist was working enthusiastically on him. Well, perhaps it wasn't totally enthusiasm. Partly it was malice because he'd forgotten the bloody condoms, just when, on this last day of her vacation, she was ready to surrender her virginity. But partly, too, she was excited by his helplessness. If she'd removed her hand, said that was enough, she wasn't going any further, he would have burst into tears. Equally, as his eyes began to glaze over, she knew she could have asked him to do anything there and then – rob a bank, jump from the church spire – and he would have agreed to it.

But she hadn't removed her hand, and a curious thing happened to her when she recognized, by the rapidity of his breathing and the noises he was making, that she'd better keep her dress well away from him: Teddy's face became Mr Penrose's. If she shut her eyes, which she did, she could easily imagine that it was her English master who was moaning incoherently.

It was one of the best moments of her summer holidays and she was glad, now, that Teddy had forgotten the condoms. When she lost her virginity it should be to someone like Mr Penrose, if not Mr Penrose himself, who had once been married, so rumour had it, but who was now estranged or even divorced. Whichever it was, he lived on the school premises.

Of course, she knew she wasn't alone in thinking Robert Penrose to be one of the most delicious-looking men she had ever set eyes on, and even though he was approximately twice her age, she often felt that he didn't view her, and her alone, as a schoolgirl.

Whenever he invited her to his study – to which the door always remained open, school rules, when a male teacher was in the company of a female student on a one-to-one basis – to discuss an essay or some other aspect of her work, she sensed he would like their relationship to be more than that of master and pupil. Well, time would tell. There were ten whole beautiful weeks between now and Christmas.

Kate McNamara was almost on the landing at the top of the staircase, and Julia, still a stride or two behind her, felt a sudden twinge of envy. Kate also would be taking English from Mr Penrose this Michaelmas Term, and there was no way Julia could compete in terms of looks. Julia knew she was attractive enough, more so than average though dark where Kate was blonde, but the new girl was a stunner. She hoped and prayed that Mr Penrose was not partial to blondes. If the truth proved otherwise . . . Well, that was in the future.

Kate paused on the landing and glanced over her shoulder.

'Come on, slowcoach, left or right?'

'Left.'

Kate had already been welcomed by Mrs Gordon, the headmistress, and Julia was now taking her to see Mrs Clinton, the head of Churchill House. Michaelmas Term proper did not begin until the following day, but boarders, eighty-five per cent of the school, had to return the evening before.

'Who's that ghastly old dragon?' asked Kate, pointing to an oil painting of a severe-looking woman of indeterminate years.

'The Founder,' answered Julia. 'Lady Elizabeth Hooke, wife of Sir John Hooke. There's a portrait like it, or a copy of that one, in each of the Houses.'

Kate remembered the name from the literature St Clare's had sent her parents when they were looking for a new school.

'Ah, yes,' she said. 'Hookers.'

Julia asked how Kate knew of the nickname, having only just arrived.

'A friend of my mother's was here twenty-five years ago.'

The wife of Sir John had founded the Lady Elizabeth Hooke College for Ladies in 1880, and for the first sixty years or so of the school's existence the students had been known colloquially as Hookers, upper case. Then, some time just before or during the Second World War, when it was learnt that hooker, lower case, was American slang for whore or prostitute, the governors quickly changed the name to St Clare's. The nickname refused to go away, however, and all St Clare's students were still known as Hookers. Whether the speaker emphasized the upper or lower case, however, depended very much on the morals of the girl being addressed or discussed.

'I'd like to have been a fly on the wall when the name change was being discussed,' said Kate. 'Who was St Clare, by the way?'

'St Clare of Assisi, founder of the Order of Poor

Clares, who believed in the doctrine of perfect poverty.'

'How very apt,' said Kate. 'You should have heard my father yelp when he saw the fees.'

'Where have you just come from, Kate?' asked Julia. 'I mean, where were you at school before here?'

'Choate,' answered Kate. 'In Wallingford, Connecticut,' she added when Julia looked blank. 'You know, America? Big place a bit west of here? My father's job took him over there for two years, and he decided it would be good experience if I went with him.'

'Him?'

'Them, then, he and my mother. He was transferred back to the UK in June, which is why I'm here.'

America, thought Julia. That explained a lot. There were a couple of other Americans in the school, real Americans, and they were much more sophisticated than their British counterparts. Little wonder Kate McNamara seemed a very confident sixteen-year-old.

'Here we are,' said Julia, 'Mrs Clinton's study.'

'What's she like?'

'Nice. Heaps younger than the Gorgon. Mrs Gordon,' Julia explained. 'That's what we call her. You'll probably be about fifteen, twenty minutes. Mrs Clinton doesn't go in for long welcoming speeches, but she'll brief you on House rules and you'll get a line or two on sex.'

'Oh, Christ,' said Kate.

'It's nothing to worry about. It doesn't go much further than preaching *virgo intacta* if it's still intact,

16

and not treating the male students as potential mates if it's not.'

Julia paused, the obvious question remaining unvoiced but an answer being solicited anyway.

Kate smiled.

'I'll have to know you a lot better before I start discussing *that*.'

Julia returned the smile.

'While you're in there, I'll nip down to the porter's lodge and make sure Dobbs isn't rifling your trunk. I'll meet you back here in, say, half an hour. Show you the ropes.'

Julia skipped down the staircase. Behind her Kate knocked politely on Mrs Clinton's study door. A pleasant contralto voice invited her to enter.

Outside Churchill House other girls were arriving for the start of Michaelmas Term. Some were delivered to the front door by car, others, whose parents were abroad or who lived too far away, were picked up from the local railway station by the school bus, which ran a shuttle service on the day before the first day of term, and deposited them at their respective Houses after their heavy luggage had been dropped off at Dobbs's lodge.

Some girls greeted each other like the old friends they were, and went into huddles to discuss the events of the summer holidays; others watched the arrival of each car and mulled over past feuds. Others still milled around like refugees. These, like Kate McNamara but younger, were newcomers, first-years, none of them older than thirteen. Some would have been to boarding school before and knew what to expect. For the rest, it was their first time away from home.

You could always tell them. They clung to their parents like glue, a few in tears. Many of them carried teddy bears or some other kind of stuffed animal.

On her way to the lodge, Julia waved to Jocasta Petrillo, who was just alighting from a red Lamborghini, driven by her mother whose looks were those of a film star and who could have passed for Jocasta's elder sister. Jocasta's mother was English and her father Italian, and in the peculiar manner of English public schools of giving nicknames to anyone whose forename or cognomen seemed to invite it, Jocasta was known as Jocasta Pasta.

The Lamborghini which brought her was not driven by her mother out of a desire to impress. The other cars the Petrillo family owned were a Porsche and a Rolls. And a couple of Range Rovers for getting round the estate, for Signor Petrillo owned a chain of Italian restaurants in the United Kingdom and Europe.

'My father's all right,' Jocasta often confided. 'He started out as a dish-washer and built up his chain from there, and he's not ashamed who knows it. My mother, though – now there's a different bowl of minestrone. When we used to play Monopoly as a family when I was a child, she would never, even if she had the opportunity, buy any of the utilities. "My dear, I wouldn't dream of being associated with anything so common as a *waterworks*".'

'I'm on an errand,' called Julia. 'Catch you later.'

Jocasta Pasta waved back.

Apart from Churchill, St Clare's had six other Houses. Churchill was the newest, in honour of the wartime prime minister, and the others were named after famous military leaders. Respectively they were Nelson, Wellington, Frobisher, Drake, Napier and Hawkins. Napier was the smallest and housed the male sixth-formers and a handful of bachelor teachers, while Hawkins was for the eleven- to thirteen-year-olds and was nicknamed Cry-baby Corner by the older pupils.

Few of the girls thought it odd or complained that, in this day and age, there were no Houses dedicated to famous women, no Nightingale or Sackville-West or Woolf. (Start that, many of them argued, and before we know where we are we'll have a Greer House or even a Julie Burchill House. God forbid!) Most of the students accepted that they were there for five or six years at the outside, before going on to Oxbridge or elsewhere, and that life was too short for jousts with authority on such pettifogging matters. Just as important, St Clare's had a tradition going back to 1880, which extended to school uniform, magenta in the main, being worn by all students below the Lower Sixth.

To reach the porter's lodge Julia had to pass Napier House, where some of the male students had already unpacked and were sitting on the Napier steps or lounging against the front of the House. 'Sizing up the talent,' as Richard Carson put it, 'the most important part of any academic year.'

Which meant establishing if there were any new

female sixth-formers or if there were any old hands who, during the long vacation, had finally surrendered their virginity and were now up for grabs.

'Believe me,' he said to those in earshot, 'once they've tasted pork they find it hard to give it up.'

Carson was in the Upper Sixth, studying French, German and Spanish with the object of going on to read Modern Languages at Oxford. He was far from being the best-looking male in the Upper Sixth, but he seemed to have an enviable success rate with the female students. And older girls from the nearby town, for that matter. At least, that was his story and, although he never named names, none of his cronies saw any reason to doubt his prowess.

'How can you tell?' asked Ben Fisher, polishing his spectacles with a handkerchief to get a better look at Julia as she passed. Apart from being mildly myopic, Fisher was tall and gangly with red hair and a face and body that sprouted freckles when exposed for more than a few minutes to the sun. He would have given a lot to acquire the sort of light Mediterranean tan Carson had, and to that end spent huge sums on branded browning oils. To no avail. He still looked like a stick of celery that someone had crowned with a radish. Which was a pity, because he was otherwise quite handsome. 'About them no longer being virgins?'

'Easy, old son. It's all in the eyes. That and the way they walk. Take Julia there, for instance. I'd say she still is, though I'd also wager she's fed up with Lady Hymen still hanging around.'

'Doesn't that make her ripe for plucking?' asked someone else.

'Probably, but she'd never leave you alone if you were the plucker, once the plucking was over. Could get embarrassing. Remember Hugh McDermott?'

They all did.

Just before last Christmas McDermott had fallen head over heels for a girl in the Upper Fifth, Helen Baker, who had recently turned sixteen and was therefore legally available regardless of what the school rulebook said. McDermott's infatuation was reciprocated by Helen and, sure enough, they'd consummated their passion one November night in the hockey pavilion. All went well for several weeks, though McDermott started looking paler and thinner by the day, damn near by the hour. In contrast, Helen blossomed.

'Bloody woman can't get enough,' McDermott told his friends. 'My work's going to hell. Wherever I am, she turns up. If I tell her I'm tired or have to study, she just grabs my joint until I'm no longer tired. I tell you, it's costing me a bloody fortune in condoms and ginseng.'

'Give her the shove,' someone advised. 'Tell her it's all over.'

'Are you *crazy*?' said McDermott.

November became December. McDermott and Helen continued their affair. Then, a few days before the end of term, before everyone went home for the festive season and with clandestine parties going on in all the dormitories and studies via smuggled sherry and wine, McDermott and Helen were discovered drunk as owls and totally naked going at it hammer and tongs in the middle of the Nativity scene the Lower Fourth had created. They were sent home as soon as they sobered up, neither tail nor whisker of them ever seen again.

'Which,' said Richard Carson, 'gave a whole new meaning to the concept of getting laid in a manger. Believe me,' he added, 'virgins who don't want to be virgins are dangerous.'

'I wouldn't give a stuff,' said Ben Fisher, with feeling. 'Any port in a storm.'

'I take it,' said Carson, 'that the summer didn't go as planned.'

'It was a summer of cold showers and worshipping Onan.'

'Say no more,' said Carson. 'Hey, Julia,' he called, 'come over here and see the elephant.'

Julia blushed and hurried on. Bastards, she thought. She'd fallen for that elephant trick when she was fourteen. 'Do you want to see the elephant?' she'd been asked. 'Yes, please,' she'd said, wide-eyed.

Then the boy in question had turned his trouser pockets inside out, so that they resembled ears, unzipped his flies, and produced the tail of his shirt through the opening, to represent a trunk.

She'd fled in tears, gales of laughter ringing in her ears. There was no way she could report it to someone in authority, aside from the fact that that would be called sneaking. What could she have said? Well, Miss, this boy asked me if I wanted to see an elephant. *Yes, Julia, African or Indian?* He didn't say,

Miss. *But surely, Julia, you know there are no elephants on school grounds?* It wasn't a real elephant . . .

No, better to forget it, as she had done.

Her heart skipped a beat when she saw, outside Dobbs's lodge, Mr Penrose alighting from a taxi. He had obviously been somewhere exotic during the summer, for his face and arms were brown from a sun not normally in evidence in England. Feeling she looked a fright, not even having had time to brush her hair since being deputed to look after Kate, she tried to duck out of sight. But she was too slow. Mr Penrose spotted her.

'Hello, Julia, have a good summer?'

'Yes, thank you, sir. And you?'

'Excellent. Six weeks in the Dordogne.'

I wonder who with, thought Julia.

'Looking forward to the new term?' asked Mr Penrose. 'Lots of hard work for the next two years if you want that Oxford place.'

'I'm looking forward to it, sir.'

'I'm glad to hear it. I'll be seeing you.'

Little doubt about that, dearest Robert, thought Julia before going in to see to Kate's luggage. Little doubt about that.

2

Once Again Assembled Here

Lavinia Lee, late of Magdalen College, Oxford, taught French and German to the Upper Sixth. Twenty-eight years old, five feet five inches in height and ash-blonde, she had been carpeted by the headmistress during her first term, two years earlier, for wearing skirts that were deemed too short to be modest.

Mrs Gordon had said, 'Miss Lee, I know in this enlightened day and age young women wear clothes that would have been considered egregious when I began teaching, but many of your male students are seventeen and eighteen. I would prefer their concentration to be exclusively on the knowledge you are trying to impart.'

Lavinia Lee took the point and bowed to the head's edict because she needed the job. Oxford, however, had taught her independence of thought, and the hemline came down only to knee-level. Everyone was satisfied, not least the male students under her guardianship, who had heard the rumours and were sorrowfully expecting her to reappear in something down to her ankles instead of her usual skirt and stockings.

There were nine boys and five girls taking A-level languages. Figuring an average length of six inches of penile tissue per boy, and excluding Henry Morton, who couldn't seem to work out whether or not he was gay, Richard Carson reckoned there were four feet of solid dick in evidence every time Lavinia Lee hiked herself up onto her desk, legs crossed, and taught from there.

It became bloody difficult to concentrate on Zola or de Maupassant or Goethe or whoever when Miss Lee was tarted up in her finery, and Carson considered she was responsible for more masturbatory fantasies than some bootleg photographs of a young Britt Ekland that were currently doing the rounds. Among the younger male students, the fifteen- and sixteen-year-olds, she was an icon in mutual masturbation sessions, and that was rated only slightly higher than self-abuse. Though, hell, to any healthy sixteen-year-old, orgasms were orgasms, whether in a Kleenex or a hot-dog bun.

The Upper Sixth had originated a scale of sexual values from one to ten, with doing it to oneself scoring lowest. Masturbation by another boy earned a two, while the same action with a girl rated anything between three and five, depending on the girl. The good-looking ones got the five, while the double-baggers, those whose heads you had to put two Safeway carriers over to prevent yourself being too disgusted, received the three. Straight sex in the missionary position was either a six or a seven and, curiously, oral sex earned a nine. Even more curious, simultaneous fellatio and cunnilingus scored one lower at eight, while cunnilingus alone didn't rate at all, being all put and no take. By general consensus, though only three of the boys in the Languages stream of the Upper Sixth had, or claimed to have, experienced it, the ten was achieved by sex in the horse-and-mare position.

If an eleven had existed, it would have been screwing two or more women at the same time. Twelves and above went into dreamland, involving such sex objects as Madonna and Julia Roberts. Minus scores were sex with Kylie Minogue or any female member of an Australian soap.

One thing about Lavinia Lee that Carson knew but had not told a living soul was that she used, or at least owned, a vibrator. Why anyone who looked like her had to use artificial stimulation was beyond him, and the reason he had not shared this juiciest of gossip was that he hoped, one day, to turn the knowledge to his advantage. Not by threatening to reveal to the world at large her secret unless she humped him; that was a bit too far-fetched for even his colourful fantasies, though she was right up there with Madonna and the other 'twelves'. No, in some other manner yet to be fathomed.

She was a smoker in the privacy of her own study, and one afternoon last term, before the long vacation, during a one-to-one tutorial – the door open as per the rules – she shook an empty packet, tutted in annoyance, and asked him to get her a fresh one from her desk drawer, he being nearest.

'Top right.'

That was another thing about her, her lovely mellifluous voice, slightly husky like that actress he'd seen in a few old black-and-white movies. What was her name? Lauren Bacall, that was it. It was not hard to imagine Lavinia Lee murmuring to some lucky stiff, *'Give it to me now, darling. Oh, Christ, give it to me now.'*

He had opened the top right-hand drawer, and there was the vibrator lying on a velvet sheath that was evidently its normal housing.

A thought, delicious in its prurience, struck him: had she been using it just before he arrived for the tutorial? Was that why it was out?

It was huge, nine inches at least, and shaped like a male cock. A six-year-old could have divined its purpose, and he, Richard Carson, had seen enough of them advertised in skin magazines.

Another thought occurred, this one less appetizing: did she use the giant vibrator because no mere man could satisfy her? Not pleasant, that. He, at any rate, could not compete with something that would not have been out of place in the hands of a baseball player.

'Sorry, top left, I mean,' she corrected herself when he did not immediately produce the required cigarettes.

Too late, of course, and he later wondered: Freudian slip?

He dwelt on it for days afterwards. Had she, subconsciously, wanted him to see it? Even more exciting, had she *consciously* wanted him to know it was there? If he'd said, 'They're not here, Miss Lee, your cigarettes, but what's this?' would she have responded, 'Close and lock the door, Richard, and come over here. And by the way, you can call me Lavinia,' and then spreadeagled herself on the sofa, short skirt raised indicating the road to Shangri La?

The thought that she might gave him many private moments of exquisite pleasure during the summer holidays, the image of her writhing beneath him much more erotic than any *Mayfair* or *Penthouse* centrefold. His girlfriend back home, Mary, with whom he enjoyed a regular if rarely earth-shaking sex life, was surprised by his ardour. Little did she know that it was Lavinia Lee he was humping in his frenzied brain.

These somewhat blasphemous thoughts occurred to Carson in the school chapel during the traditional early-morning service held on the first day of term, when he observed Miss Lee, late, slip into the service during the fourth verse of number 576, *Hymns Ancient and Modern*, 'Lord, Behold us with Thy Blessing' . . . Ironically, in view of what he had been thinking, the opening line to the fourth verse was *Break temptation's fatal power*, and the fourth line, although the congregation, led by the choir, had not reached it yet was *Safe from sloth and sensual snare*.

Because he was a senior boy and supposedly responsible, Carson, like senior girls, was permitted to occupy one of the two or three rear pews in the chapel, and was not forced to sit, as junior years were, near the front, grouped in Houses in order that House prefects could monitor presence and absence. Like most English public schools, St Clare's held great store by the House system. Although members of all six Houses were mixed for lessons, in matters of worship and dining and games Napier prayed or ate or played with Napier, as Churchill did with Churchill and so on. Being right at the back of the chapel, therefore, and on the aisle-side of his pew, Carson saw Lavinia Lee come in.

He looked at her questioningly and indicated that he would move up a space. She smiled gratefully but shook her head, and joined a pew of other masters and mistresses on the opposite side of the aisle. Damn, thought Carson.

'Hard lines, Richard,' said Ben Fisher.

In the opposite pew, Robert Penrose moved up a touch and handed his open hymn book to Lavinia.

'Five seven six, fourth verse,' he said.

'Thanks,' she said, but didn't sing. She knew the hymn by heart and was aware that it was near its end.

'We all thought you weren't coming back when you didn't appear last evening,' said Penrose.

'Car trouble in London,' said Lavinia. 'By the time the garage people said they couldn't fix it until the weekend, I'd missed the last train. I telephoned Mrs Gordon and told her I'd take the first one down today, which, unfortunately for me, left at five-thirty a.m. The next one wouldn't have got me here until after midday. Then there were no damned taxis at the station. I'm worn out already and we haven't even started yet.'

Fifty per cent of Lavinia's story was a lie. She had certainly telephoned Mrs Gordon and also caught the 5.30 a.m. train, but her car hadn't broken down and neither was it in a garage. She had missed the late train because she was having a titanic row with the man she lived with when not in school, and by the time it was over she was too drunk to even start her car, let alone drive it.

Bastard, she thought about Peter Hennessy. No-good lousy bastard.

The previous day had started promisingly enough. Because it was her last before returning to St Clare's, they'd had a light lunch in Highgate – one gin and tonic apiece and a bottle of wine between them, no more – and planned to spend the remainder of the afternoon in bed. Or rather, because that was how they both preferred it, in bed or on the sitting-room carpet or across the kitchen table or anywhere else that took their fancy. He usually preferred to take her only half dressed – *her* only half dressed, that is: one of her short skirts and medium heels, no underwear. Sometimes, again wearing nothing under her skirt but naturally something around her upper half, they would walk the streets until they found a quiet – but not too quiet, that was part of the thrill – alley, and then he would lift her skirt and fuck her against a wall.

The afternoon went wonderfully. They'd laid off further alcohol but each smoked a couple of joints, good Mexican stuff, and screwed each other to near exhaustion. At five o'clock she still thought, in spite of the joints, she would easily be able to drive down to St Clare's. But then, as the saying had it, the shit hit the fan.

Peter was in the bathroom when the telephone rang. The answering machine was on so Lavinia didn't bother picking up the receiver. However, the amplifier was also on, and Lavinia was shocked to hear a woman's voice saying, 'Peter, darling, have you taken that silly bitch to the station yet or is she driving down? Give me a call when she's gone. I'll be waiting.'

He'd denied it at first, of course, even when the message was replayed, but there couldn't be too many men named Peter who had a girlfriend leaving London that day either by train or car, which was what they'd agreed the alternative arrangements might be, depending on how she felt.

Finally he admitted that he had been seeing someone else while she was away at St Clare's and, occasionally, again while she was out of town, during the summer holidays. By the time this confession was made, however, she had polished off the best part of half a bottle of brandy and was weeping huge tears. *Why, why, why?* she wanted to know. They'd been seeing each other, living together when circumstances permitted, since the previous Christmas, almost nine months. Although she still paid her portion of the rent on the South Kensington flat she shared with her sister, she hardly ever stayed there any more. They'd been together almost as man and wife, certainly as an item.

'I'm sorry, Vin,' he apologized, his voice as unsteady as hers since he was demolishing the half of brandy she wasn't – on top of, for both of them, a couple of powerful joints. 'It's just one of those things. Apart from the occasional weekend, you're away over thirty weeks a year. I'm not a monk, you know. Besides, we never agreed that we were a permanent fixture. I'm sure you've had the odd master's leg over you while you've been down there.'

She shrieked at him and threw the nearest throwable object, a heavy ashtray. It missed him by six feet but sailed through a glass panel in the door.

Never, never, never, she told him, had she had someone's leg across her, as he so delicately put it, during the time she'd known him. Hadn't he ever heard of AIDS, for fuck's sake?

Which reminded her.

'I hope your new girlfriend's clean,' she wept, 'because if I catch something I'll know it came from you and I'll cut your balls off.'

She wanted to know the name of his new girl. He wouldn't give it and, the brandy by then finished, she started on vodka.

He sat and took it, not even fielding her abuse or riposting. Drunk or not, high or not, he'd been through scenes like this before and he knew that to be combative would just make matters worse.

Later, it seemed like only a few minutes had elapsed, but it was close on nine p.m. before she was cried out and shouted out. Shortly after that she passed out.

When she awoke, still in the chair, Peter had gone. A note by the phone said that it was probably better for all concerned if he spent the night away from the flat. No doubt she'd be gone by the time he returned and, doubtless too, she'd want to move her things out. He wouldn't rush her on that, but he would appreciate it if, as she was likely to be out of London for most of the time between now and Christmas, she would arrange for her sister to do the removals.

After cleaning her teeth she still had enough wit to call Mrs Gordon and give her the cock-and-bull story about her car and the garage, and then phone her sister, who drove up to Highgate immediately. Between them, they packed what was portable into her sister's car, and she spent the night, or what was left of it, in South Kensington. Her sister promised to pick up Lavinia's own car as soon as possible, before it was clamped or towed away, and the major items of Lavinia's wardrobe shortly thereafter.

Bastard, bastard, thought Lavinia, as the choir led the congregation in Psalm 95, *'Venite, Exultemus Domino'* – 'O come, let us sing unto the Lord'.

Further down the chapel, as accorded with their status, four members of Churchill House Lower Sixth sang lustily, though a few of them, too, had thick heads. Maybe not as bad as Lavinia Lee's, but bad enough.

Julia had only partaken of two glasses of the heavy Italian wine Jocasta Pasta had smuggled in, but Jocasta herself, Kate McNamara and Amanda McDonald, known affectionately as Amanda Panda, had polished off the rest of the three bottles. Discipline was usually lax the evening preceding a new term, although prefects and House monitors knew full well what was going on because they, when they were that age, had done precisely the same. Some girls brought in alcohol, others cigarettes – frowned upon in general, forbidden in the dorms except on that first evening, but tolerated in the sixth-form commonroom – and yet others, usually the new, young and, for the present, emotionally disorientated, brought mountains of chocolate. Kate had also brought, from the United States, several hardcore porn magazines, which all four girls, but especially the three who were attacking the wine with such gusto, gazed at with awe.

'Nothing that size is ever going in me,' mumbled Amanda Panda, perusing a page where a white stud with a gigantic erection was about to enter a recumbent woman. The next photograph showed him with the tip just inside, and the series thereafter depicted both man and woman in the various stages leading up to mutual orgasm. 'I mean, God, how can she *absorb* all that? I'd have trouble getting it into the boot of my mother's Ford.'

'It's trick photography, it has to be,' opined Jocasta. 'They take a photograph of an ordinarily endowed man and then an artist touches it up.'

'Something's certainly touching *her* up,' giggled Amanda.

'I don't think so,' said Kate, slurring her words slightly. 'I must confess I haven't seen anything *quite* like that on my travels, but I don't think it's faked.'

'Confession time?' queried Julia, remembering her unanswered question concerning Kate's virginity earlier in the day.

'No,' answered Kate, 'I'm a voyeur.'

Sixteen-year-old girls are normally very protective of intimate relationships with their own sex, viewing newcomers with suspicion if not downright hostility, and it was therefore somewhat surprising that Kate McNamara had been accepted with such alacrity by the old-established triumvirate of Julia-Jocasta-Amanda. But accepted she was. The trio had become a quartet. Possibly Jocasta's wine and Kate's skin magazines had something to do with it.

'What I can't understand,' said Amanda, 'is how any woman, never mind the size of that damned thing, could allow herself to be photographed in the act. Are they whores, or what?'

'Hookers,' chuckled Jocasta.

'No, I'm serious,' persisted Amanda, taking another slug of wine directly from the neck of the bottle. 'Are they tarts or do they get paid huge sums of money or what?'

'Druggies,' said Kate. 'At least I suppose they are,' she added hastily. 'They get a heroin habit, can't afford to pay for it, and do this to raise their next fix.' She shrugged. 'That's one theory, anyway.'

'But imagine,' said Amanda, 'that one of these girls gets married one day, this girl, for instance. What is she, about twenty? She gets married without telling her husband what she got up to before, and then, one day, he's looking through a magazine like this and sees her photograph, getting laid by Cleopatra's Needle.'

'Girls like that don't get married,' said Julia. 'What would be the point after experiencing something like that? Every other man would probably pale into insignificance.'

'Julia!' said Amanda sharply, shocked. 'There has to be more to marriage than just – well, just *that*.'

Amanda was right, of course, thought Julia, coming back to the present with the lines *O come let us worship and fall down: and kneel before the Lord our Maker.* Amanda was absolutely right. She, Julia, wouldn't care what size Mr Penrose was, though she would prefer it to be not too little and not too much. But just perfect, she giggled to herself, like the baby bear's porridge.

'How the hell much longer does this go on?' muttered Kate, next to her. 'My head's spinning.'

'Not much longer.'

In actuality it was twenty minutes longer, but finally the service came to an end and the congregation trooped out, led from the back by the headmistress, other masters and mistresses and senior boys and girls. The teenies were last to leave.

Outside Julia was irritated to see Mr Penrose talking to Miss Lee. She was beautiful, Miss Lee, there was no doubt about it, though she looked a little under the weather this morning. Mr Penrose had hold of her by the elbow, blast her. It wasn't a too intimate gesture, but it was more than that of just colleagues. Julia wondered what he was saying to her and how soon she could get him to herself. Not at all, she soon found out, as Penrose led Miss Lee away. What he was actually saying, although Julia couldn't hear him, was, 'You look as if you could use a cup of coffee before facing the madding crowd.'

Lavinia allowed herself to be led. She was in no state to argue.

'What happens next?' asked Kate, taking deep gulps of the marvellous September morning air.

'Not a lot,' answered Julia. 'We go to our respective classrooms to see what the term's timetable is, and we have the afternoon off – to do all those things we didn't manage to get done yesterday.'

'We're allowed into town if we wish,' added Jocasta.

'Not me,' said Kate emphatically. 'I'm going to finish my unpacking and then rest, sleep. I take it that tomorrow things start in earnest.'

'You can bank on it,' said Julia, 'although I think you'll find the whole term will be pretty dull. They usually are.'

Apart from one attempted murder, a suicide and a sex scandal that rocked the school to its foundations, Julia was right.

3

A Very Minor Scandal

As Julia Hastings had predicted, Paula van der Groot set her cap ('her little Dutch cap,' as Amanda Panda later put it) at Kate McNamara as soon as she saw the new girl, the evening of the first day of term.

Kate had come across lesbians at Choate and elsewhere in the States, but the American variety of the species tended to look the part: strapping creatures at home in black leather astride Harley Davidsons. 'Diesel' or 'bull' dykes they were known as over there. Nothing about Dutch Paula conformed to the stereotype. Quite the opposite. She was no taller than five feet three, weighed around seven and a half stone, and was almost elfin in appearance. Her dark curly hair was cut short but not unconventionally so, and her brown eyes contained a hint of laughter. Her smile was mischievous rather than menacing, and for all the world she resembled the archetypal Girl Who Saved the Day from an edition of *Schoolfriend*. Kate was caught off her guard. No-one had warned her about Paula's sexual preferences.

It was approaching six o'clock when she appeared

in the doorway of the dormitory. Julia, Amanda and Jocasta had not yet returned from their afternoon excursion into town, and Kate was lying on her bed, fully clothed apart from her shoes, alone in the dorm apart from one other girl whose head was buried in a book while listening to a tape on her Walkman. Kate had been dozing most of the afternoon and had only just woken up. She was debating whether to take a shower and change before the dinner bell at six-thirty when Paula came over.

'Members of the Upper Sixth are supposed to ask permission before entering Lower Sixth dorms, so I expect I should do that. May I come in?'

Paula's accent, though far from heavy, indicated her country of origin.

Kate eased herself up and sat cross-legged on the bed. The weather being far too hot for jeans, she had donned a short tennis skirt, which was riding high on her tanned thighs. If she noticed the South African eyeing them lustfully, and the wisp of blond pubic hair that was peeking from beneath her white cotton briefs, it didn't register.

'Looks as if you are.'

Paula perched herself on the edge of the bed and extended her hand.

'I'm Paula van der Groot. Yes, I know, I sound like a small cigar from Holland, but I'm stuck with it. You're Kate, I believe.'

Kate held out her own hand.

'That's right. Kate McNamara. How did you know?'

Paula smiled, showing wonderful teeth.

'Oh, I make it my business to check on all newcomers.'

'Are you a prefect?'

'Hell, no! Mrs Gordon's got too much sense to appoint someone like me to a position of responsibility. Not that I'd accept, in any case. I don't like being restricted. You're just in from America, I understand.'

'Well, not just, but that's where I last went to school. Do you know the States?'

'I've been on holidays there, but not Connecticut.' Kate raised her eyebrows.

'My, my – your sources of information *are* good.'

'As I said, I make it my business to check on all newcomers. Besides, it doesn't take a genius to work out that you didn't get that tan in England.' Kate didn't follow the logic of that at all, and Paula didn't give her the opportunity to query the statement. 'It is a wonderful tan, Kate. Is it all over?'

'Not quite.'

'Ah, just the tits but not the bottom half, is that it?'

'Something like that. Look, is there something I can help you with? If not, I should be thinking about a shower before the dinner bell.'

'Do you know where they are, the showers? I can show you if you don't.'

'I was shown them last night, thanks.'

'Just trying to be helpful. It comes from being South African. We usually get a bad press, but not all of us want to shoot a kaffir before breakfast, drink gin like lemonade, and have affairs with other women's husbands.'

Paula smiled winningly, ran the fingers of one hand through her short hair and shook her head. Later, Kate was to think she must have been sleep-sodden or unusually thick not to have spotted she was being chatted up, but, at the moment, she accepted Paula at face value. Even the remark about her tits didn't alert her. No doubt her mother would be outraged at the way teenage girls talked nowadays, but that's how it was.

'What are you,' asked Paula, 'sixteen?' Kate nodded. 'Then I don't expect you have had much experience of affairs with married men?'

'No,' admitted Kate.

'An overrated pastime, I can tell you.'

'Sound as if you know what you're talking about,' said Kate cheekily.

'Let's just say I read a lot,' said Paula. 'Do you smoke, Kate, drink?'

'A little of both sometimes, when the mood takes me.'

'A woman after my own heart. A little of both – *sometimes* - is what life is all about.'

'I thought it was frowned upon here at St Clare's, smoking and drinking,' said Kate.

'Drinking is, certainly,' said Paula, 'though the Upper Sixth, in the privacy of their own studies, can often get away with things others can't. That's worth bearing in mind. What I mean is, if you ever feel stressful and need a drink or a smoke of something a little more exotic than tobacco, if you follow my meaning, you can always call on me.'

'I'm not sure I do follow your meaning,' said Kate,

though she knew perfectly well what Paula was hinting at. At Choate, pot and hash were readily available, and she suspected it wouldn't be too different at St Clare's. It was something to know for future reference, but she wanted the South African girl to spell it out. Just so there was no room for error.

Paula edged up the bed until she was next to Kate. She nodded in the direction of the girl with the Walkman.

'Let's not tell everyone.'

She leaned forward to whisper in Kate's ear. As she did so, her hand brushed against Kate's inner thigh.

'Forbidden substances generally obtained from the hotter parts of the planet.'

Paula's fingers ran up Kate's thigh, under her skirt, until they brushed against the visible wisp of pubic hair.

Paula's eyes glazed over.

'Oh, Christ,' she said. 'I'd give anything to fuck you.'

Twigging at last, Kate shot off the bed as if touched by a live wire. She made sure the bed was between her and Paula, but that didn't fool the South African girl. An experienced seducer, she knew instinctively that Kate had enjoyed at least part of the experience.

'I don't think so,' said Kate, blushing furiously.

Paula was not in the least put out. She smiled and winked.

'You don't know what you're missing.'

'And I'm not going to find out.'

Paula glanced at the girl with the Walkman, who

had evidently noticed nothing. Not that it would have mattered to Paula if she had.

'One day soon you will, I guarantee. Before the end of term you'll be knocking at my study door. Don't be scared of it. You'll love it. Men were given dicks so they had something to hold on to when mummy finally threw away the teddy bear. They know so little about a woman's body it's almost criminal.'

'I'd like you to leave now,' said Kate, conscious of how ridiculous the line sounded.

'Of course,' said Paula.

When the South African girl had gone, Kate found that she was shaking. She had to sit on the bed and hug her knees until the shakes went away.

Damn the fucking bitch. How dare she. *How dare she!* How dare she suggest 'one day soon' and 'before the end of term.'

Part of her recognized, however, that she had been, again partly, electrified by the South African girl's touch. If, intellectually, she had denied that possibility, the dampness she felt in her vagina would have told her otherwise. Not since what she privately referred to as 'those other incidents' while she was in America had she experienced such immediate arousal.

Jesus, she thought, I'm turning into a dyke.

She tried to push to the back of her mind the unpalatable thought that Paula's words – *Oh, Christ, I'd give anything to fuck you* – were as exciting as Paula's touch. But they wouldn't go away. The last person to say that, apart from the Choate diesels – *Hey, kid, I bet you got the most welcoming snatch underneath all that finery* – was Adam, from Harvard.

'Kate, you beauty, if I don't get my joint inside that delicious British cunt of yours right now, I'm going to explode.'

She'd let him, of course, and he wasn't the first. She'd enjoyed it too, even if, at six feet four and lettered in football, she'd expected his cock to be larger. It just wasn't true, as she'd believed since she was fourteen, that big men with big feet had big cocks. Some did, some didn't, it was as simple as that.

She hadn't been anywhere near coming until she'd said, 'Ask me to fuck you hard. Tell me to come over your big strong dick.'

He'd been shocked – she could see it in his eyes. It was all very well for him to talk about her 'British cunt'. That was a nineteen-year-old's way of being macho, dominating. But he hadn't expected to hear similar words from her.

'Go on,' she'd urged. 'Ask me to come like I've never come before. *Force me, for Christ's sake.*'

He did it, naturally. And as his excitement mounted, so did hers. Then she was coming like crazy and didn't give a damn who was giving it to her.

Something like that had happened when Paula said, *Oh, Christ, I'd give anything to fuck you.* But it had taken Paula a couple of seconds. It had taken Adam, even with prompting, a lot longer.

Maybe I'm bisexual, thought Kate.

Maybe I just like dirty talk.

No, it wasn't either. She simply liked sex, and sex, like God's domain, had many mansions.

She needed that shower now. Even thinking about it all told her that she couldn't go to dinner with her underwear in the state it was.

Julia, Amanda and Jocasta came in before she had time to strip off and don her robe, grab a towel. They were talking loudly and were hot and sweaty from their afternoon's exertions. Kate decided that attack was the best form of defence. Otherwise, Paula fucking van der Groot might soon be spreading rumours that Kate McNamara was there for the taking.

Which she wasn't. Definitely not. Any taking, she'd do it. And if – just *if* – Paula happened to be involved, then she, Kate, would be calling the shots. She'd tantalize the little cow, make her beg to come.

One thing Choate – well, America, really – had taught her was not to let anyone walk all over her. Do that, and they'd be back for more.

'You bitches,' she said, hissing the words. The dorm was filling up as its other occupants came back from their afternoon out.

Jocasta glanced at her companions.

'Something we said? Deodorant not working?'

Jocasta had a carrier bag from an expensive local store dangling from her fingers. Julia clutched a toy giraffe. Amanda Panda was eating a chocolate bar.

'Paula bloody van der Groot.'

'Ah, yes,' said Julia, 'you had a visit?'

'I was damn near raped! You might have warned me.'

'Sorry about that,' said Jocasta.

'Only "damn near",' tutted Amanda. 'That doesn't even qualify for discussion since you've been here twenty-four hours. Last term Paula seduced three new girls the first night boarders returned. Christ, look at the time! Last one in the showers has to buy condoms for Bulgy Algy. I hear you can hire the Goodyear blimp for a reasonable sum.'

Bulgy Algy, thought Kate. Now who the hell is he? I'd better, she decided, establish where all the dangers lie ASAP. Her parents would go insane if she were 'asked to leave' another school.

Clean and refreshed and while towelling down outside the shower stalls, Julia explained who Algy was and who, among the Upper Sixth sinistrals, not to be caught alone with. Apart from Paula, the names didn't mean anything to Kate, and Julia promised to point them out when the opportunity arose. Though Kate, thought Julia, was likely to be propositioned many times between now and Christmas.

Naked, as she now was, working the towel between her thighs to dry the last of the water, the former Choate girl was even more stunning than fully dressed. Her breasts were large but perfectly firm, her waist trim, her hips designed for clinging outfits. And as for those legs, they belonged on a showgirl.

It wouldn't only be Paula and her coterie chasing Kate. The sixth-form boys would go mad for her.

Julia took a sidelong glance at her own breasts in the steamy mirror. OK, but no prize winners. Still, she was better off than poor Amanda Panda who was still carrying puppy fat where even a puppy didn't have it.

As if reading her mind, Amanda sucked in her tummy and turned sideways to the mirror.

'Shit, I've put on ten pounds during the summer.'

Jocasta, dark wedge of pubic hair glistening with moisture as she dried her back, and Kate's equal in looks if your preference was for Gabriella Sabatini rather than Kathleen Turner, said, 'And it'll be another ten if you don't give up the chocolate. You'll be the size of an elephant before half-term.'

'I'm compensating for lack of parental affection,' lamented Amanda. 'OK, so I'm not. I'm a natural pig.'

Like many girls of her age not blessed with outstanding looks, sporting prowess or dizzying academic ability, Amanda made up for it by being a clown, a comedian. Her hair was neither dark nor blond, but a rather insalubrious shade of mouse. 'And a pretty sick mouse at that,' she often commented. Her nose was broad but snubby, her face freckled, and she wore glasses for study. On the hockey field, the major sporting activity during Michaelmas Term, she was frequently face down in the mud within minutes of bully-off, and during Trinity (St Clare's used the Oxford nomenclature of Michaelmas, Hilary and Trinity terms, where other schools would use Christmas, Easter and Summer), when athletics, tennis and swimming were enforced, she would, more often than not, be last in each running and jumping event, be beaten six-love, six-love on the courts, and sink like a rock in the pool after fifteen metres.

For all that, however, she was popular with her peers, though, speaking for herself, she could have done with a lot less popularity and a bit more skill.

Her favourite fairy tale, as a child, had been *The Ugly Duckling*, but she had long ago recognized that she would never turn into a swan.

'Anyway,' she added to Jocasta, 'who the hell wants to look like you or Kate? Who needs an Oxbridge First, a successful marriage to a man who's both handsome and rich, and her picture in magazines wearing Paris originals? It all ends in tears. I've read Jackie Collins.'

'I've actually met Jackie Collins,' said Kate, putting on her robe. 'And Joan.' She could have bitten her tongue off the second she opened her mouth. She had been out of England too long, and the English, unlike the Americans, didn't go in for name-dropping. On a plane or train an American would give you his whole life story, produce a photograph of the wife and kids, and hand you his business card before take-off or departure. The English, she recalled, winced at such familiarity.

'Where, how?' chorused the other three with one voice.

'Through my father,' said Kate, 'in Hollywood. He's in finance, not films, but nowadays film-makers raise money wherever they can and someone from the investment side is usually around to make sure no-one is going over budget. He took me to a couple of parties.'

'What's Joan like, close up?'

'You'd have to say beautiful,' answered Kate.

'I hate her already,' said Amanda.

In the distance, the first dinner bell rang out. That gave them five minutes to be there.

'I'm going to eat three helpings of whatever's going this evening,' said Amanda, puffing heavily while trying to keep up with Kate's long strides, 'just to show La Collins that I've got something she can never have.'

'Youth?' queried Kate.

'No,' said Amanda, 'blubber.'

The rest of that first, short week passed uneventfully, though Lower Sixth English groaned when Mr Penrose revealed the syllabus they would be required to cover between the present Michaelmas Term and Trinity, two summers hence, when their Advanced Level examinations would take place. Shakespeare, Pope, Hopkins, Auden, Defoe, Thackeray, Marlowe, T.S. Eliot, Chaucer, Jane Austen, Trollope, to name only a few. And that was in just one subject. All of the students were taking at least three, and some of the brightest four and five.

'I know it seems like a lot,' said Mr Penrose, 'but it's nothing compared with what you'll have to face at university. And I'm always available outside normal study hours if you have problems.'

Julia made a very careful note of *that*.

'And a word of advice,' went on Penrose. 'Don't think for even a moment that two years is a long way off, that you can cruise through this term and maybe the next and make up the time later. You won't be able to. Start today. Obtain the required texts and start reading them. I'll be monitoring progress week to week, and I'll be coming down very heavily on anyone who, in my opinion, is falling behind.'

Yes, *please*, thought Julia. You can come down on me as heavily as you like.

'It's impossible,' said Amanda as the weekend approached. 'I couldn't read that much in two years even if I thought I was going to enjoy it, which I know I'm not.'

Being in the Upper Sixth and, in any case, studying languages other than English, it took Richard Carson until Friday of the first week to accost Kate McNamara, although he had been trying since he'd first set eyes on her. She was really something, in his view, and obviously much more accessible than the Lavinia Lee of his fantasies.

Kate didn't see her accessibility in that way, and when he stepped in front of her as she was about to enter Churchill House, she attempted to go round him. But the way she went, he went. Three times.

'I'm better at the foxtrot than the quickstep,' he said.

'Corny,' she riposted.

'Yes, you're right. Put it down to nervousness.'

He moved to one side to let her through. Kate hesitated. OK, give him points for quick thinking and a new approach. Not many boys of eighteen admitted to being nervous in front of girls, even if it was a line.

'Why should you be nervous?'

'Isn't it obvious?'

'No.'

'You're going to make me say it?'

'You must say what you like, but please do it quickly. I'm in a hurry.'

'OK, quickly it is. In case no-one's told you, we're allowed out of school grounds until eleven on Saturday. Upper Sixth and Lower Sixth, that is. Would you like to go somewhere? A film, something to eat, a walk?'

'I don't think so.'

'Just this Saturday or every Saturday?'

'I don't even know your name.'

Carson told her.

'I'll think about it,' said Kate, who had no intention of doing any such thing. 'Now, I really am in a rush.'

She genuinely was.

Since her earlier rejection of Paula van der Groot's advances, Kate had observed the South African girl regularly in the company of a fourteen-year-old teeny, Phoebe something-or-other, a newcomer to St Clare's and Churchill House. What fascinated Kate was that Phoebe was a younger clone of herself: tall, blonde, blue-eyed, tanned, and with an incredibly mature figure for one so young. What astonished Kate was the viperish speed with which Paula had struck. And what amazed her and – it had to be admitted – slightly shocked her was the blatant manner in which Paula made her attentions obvious.

Several times Kate had spotted Paula hand-in-hand with Phoebe, though admittedly when there were no staff around and very few other girls. Once, she had seen Paula with her arm around the youngster's waist, with Phoebe in no way objecting. Paula had also noticed Kate on this occasion, and had had the audacity to wink broadly. 'Plenty more fish in the sea,' the wink implied. 'I'll get Phoebe to tell you in Technicolor detail what you're missing.'

Kate was determined to find out for herself, and with that in mind she had been surreptitiously tailing Paula. A few minutes earlier she had seen Paula and Phoebe enter Churchill House. They were not holding hands or even walking side by side. Paula was a dozen yards ahead, which immediately aroused Kate's suspicions. If Paula was about to seduce Phoebe, she wouldn't want to make it obvious.

The timing was right. Classes were over for the week, it was a fine evening, dinner was two hours away, and most girls were taking advantage of the afternoon sunshine. Few of them would be heading for their dorms or studies until at least five-thirty. Churchill House would be virtually empty, and it was a copper-bottomed certainty that Paula would have warned her study-mate to keep out of the way.

Phoebe was the perfect victim, if victim was the word unqualified adjectivally by 'willing'. First week at a new school, possibly first week ever at a boarding school. Young, away from her parents, disorientated.

Kate was aware that she could be accused of humbug virtue and, if she were honest with herself, she was less concerned about the homosexual defloration of young Phoebe than she was pruriently intrigued by catching Paula in the act.

She sat on her bed in the dorm and gave them fifteen

minutes. That should be enough. Paula wouldn't want to hang around if the most she had was an hour. Besides, the spadework to the seduction would have been accomplished earlier in the week, the subtle replacement of Phoebe's real mother by Paula's ersatz mother figure. Moreover, no-one built like Phoebe, fourteen or not, could have escaped the attentions of boys. Maybe she was still a virgin, maybe she wasn't, but she was probably well advanced sexually.

Which didn't mean, of course, that she would welcome an approach by a lesbian. Didn't mean she wouldn't, either, sniffed Kate.

Paula's study was one floor above the Lower Sixth dorms, along a corridor towards the rear of Churchill. Kate went up the stairs cautiously, a book and notepad in her hands. If challenged unexpectedly by a member of the Upper Sixth – for it was forbidden to be on their landing without permission – she'd say she was looking for a member of the Upper Sixth English stream to explain a particularly troublesome piece of Christina Rossetti.

But she met no-one before she was outside Paula's door, which was closed but not locked. Locks were not permitted, by edict of Mrs Gordon, on sixth-form studies or, for that matter, on any of the dormitories. Ostensibly, this was because, according to the Gorgon, 'None of my girls steal,' though it was suspected by many, largely correctly, that bolts and Yales and the like were discouraged to make more difficult the sort of encounter Kate suspected was now taking place beyond the woodwork. Obviously any sexual activity would be thought about twice if there was a possibility that the door could be flung open at any moment, and the same rule applied to the Upper Sixth boys. The proper form was to knock and await an invitation to enter.

It was absurd for Kate to consider knocking and, self-evidently, she couldn't simply barge in. If she was wrong about Paula and Phoebe – or, if not wrong in general but wrong about timing – and all the two girls were doing was taking tea, she would be in deep trouble, Christina Rossetti notwithstanding. Kate wasn't sure what the punishment was for invading the Sixth Form landing, but she'd lay odds Paula would invoke it. Because Paula would know precisely why Kate was there.

She felt a bit of an idiot. What had she hoped for? Sounds of unbridled passion emanating from the study? If that had been so, and it wasn't as far as her ears could tell, she could certainly have blustered in. Paula would not dare complain if caught *in flagrante delicto* and Kate would have a hold over the South African, to use as and if she chose.

She should retreat down the stairs, back to her dorm. The longer she stood there like a ninny, the more likely a member of the Upper Sixth would collar her. If that happened, being out of bounds would be the least of her worries. She could be accused, rightly, of being a voyeur, a Peeping Thomasina. On the other hand, she'd come this far.

Taking a deep breath and feeling her heart pounding as if it were trying to escape, she put her hand on the doorknob and turned it, easing open the door, praying that it wasn't one of those that squeaked.

She opened it a foot. Any more, regardless of what Paula was up to, and the movement would be spotted, leaving Kate in the effluent.

But the gods smiled on Kate. At least, whoever controlled luck in the Pantheon did. A quite different deity, Aphrodite, was overseeing the activities of Paula and Phoebe.

Upper Sixth studies were some fifteen feet by fifteen. Each contained two desks and chairs, two single beds, two wardrobes. Armchairs and other extras could be brought in by the girls if they would fit. All studies had double side-opening windows which overlooked various areas of the school grounds. The curtains in Paula's study were drawn.

Paula's bed, or at least the one she and Phoebe were using, was within Kate's eyeline. They were both wearing skirts but were naked from the waist up. Phoebe was sprawled against the pillows. Even in the semi-darkness Kate could see that her eyes were closed and the expression on her face one of rapture. Paula was leaning over her, her back to the door which, in her rising excitement, she hadn't noticed opening. One of Paula's hands was beneath the young girl's skirt. Kate could see the material moving and didn't need two guesses to know where the centre of attention was. Paula's other hand was massaging some kind of body lotion onto Phoebe's breasts, squeezing, kneading, concentrating on the nipples, already erect.

Kate felt herself growing hot. Some warning voice

inside her screamed at her to leave, but she couldn't. She was transfixed.

Paula said, her words barely audible and coming in staccato gasps, 'Are – you – enjoying – that?'

'Oh, yes, yes,' said Phoebe. 'Please don't stop.'

'I've – no – intention – of – stopping. Wouldn't – you – like – to – do – the – same – to – me?'

'Show me how.'

Paula abandoned her massaging temporarily, seized Phoebe's left hand and guided it under her own skirt.

Phoebe said, 'Oh, how lovely!'

'Let me,' said Paula. 'Oh, yes, that's good. That's – very – good. You have a natural – Oh, Christ – aptitude for – this – my – dear. Move your fingers slightly. That's it. Just – like – that. Feel the ridge? Just like yours. No, leave them there. I'll move for both of us until I tell you otherwise.'

Paula's hips began to buck. Her shoulders and head started to shake. Kate could stand it no longer. She didn't even close the door fully, although she did pull it to, before she retraced her steps along the corridor and down the stairs.

When she reached her dormitory she flung the Rossetti onto her locker and threw herself on the bed, burying her head in the pillows. Without doubt that was one of the most erotic sights she had ever seen outside bootleg stag films in America, and she was ashamed to discover, most unexpectedly because she hadn't touched herself, that she was in the throes of a violent orgasm within seconds of lying down.

She shuddered from head to foot, unable to stop the spasms, unwilling even if she'd been able. She had to bite the pillow hard to prevent herself crying out.

When it was over and her limbs stopped quaking, she glanced around fearfully, relieved to discover she was alone in the dormitory. Not that the presence of the entire Lower Sixth wielding camcorders would have repressed her coming. It had been involuntary, and it scared her.

It took her a while, until long after dinner, to rationalize; a dinner during which, near the head of table, Paula was grinning like a Cheshire cat. Further down, below the salt as befitted teenies, Phoebe was barely eating. Her adoring gaze hardly left Paula.

It wasn't that she had dykey tendencies, Kate decided, *it wasn't*. Her reactions would have been the same, surely, if she had witnessed Paula, or Phoebe, having sex with a man.

It was just the sexual act *per se* that had aroused her. She was a healthy sixteen-year-old, and it was too long since she'd been laid. Maybe she'd better take up Richard Carson on his offer, though not yet, for God's sake. She couldn't enter St Clare's one week and have sex with a virtual stranger before that week was out. She knew what boys were like. Carson would be bragging in no time. 'Piece of cake, that Kate McNamara. Goes like a train.' She'd have a reputation as a slag before half-term. Christ, why was life so difficult at her age?

She also wondered, if only momentarily, if she

should tell anyone in authority what she had seen – Mrs Clinton, head of House, for example – before dismissing the notion as absurd.

Please, Mrs Clinton, I found Paula van der Groot and Phoebe thingummyjig masturbating one another in Paula's study.

Really, Kate? And what were you doing on the Upper Sixth landing?

Looking for someone to explain a piece of Christina Rossetti to me.

So, you knocked on Paula's study door and Paula bade you enter, in spite of the activity she and Phoebe were engaged in?

Not exactly. I sort of pushed open the door and there they were.

Phoebe was struggling to free herself from this assault, naturally.

Well, no. And it wasn't exactly an assault.

I see. But you immediately ran to tell someone, another senior girl or mistress?

No, Mrs Clinton. Actually, I watched them for some time. You see, Paula had this body lotion . . .

Spare me the details, Kate.

Very well, Mrs Clinton. Anyway, I ran down to my dorm and had this most terrific orgasm . . .

No, thought Kate, it wasn't as if Phoebe had been *forced*. On the contrary, she'd appeared more than willing, and a victim she was not.

Kate opted to keep her own counsel, not even telling Jocasta, Amanda or Julia. Phoebe wasn't Paula's first and wouldn't be her last. If Paula was

Phoebe's first, Kate doubted that she'd be Phoebe's last.

Maybe Mrs Clinton knew about such goings-on but elected to ignore them rather than provoke a scandal. It was, after all, a very minor incident.

4

Lavinia's Anguish

Lavinia Lee couldn't concentrate.

Christ, she thought, the second week of term, the first Monday, and already I'm looking forward to Christmas.

She should dismiss Peter Hennessy from her mind, that was the first item on the agenda – if only it were that easy – and she had been a fool to dash back to London yesterday, Sunday.

Of course there was nothing in her contract, unless she were on duty, to prevent her doing that. And she'd had a good excuse, if only to herself, that she needed to collect her car and clear everything, all her belongings that her sister hadn't managed to move, from Peter's flat.

So far, so good. She could have debated her entitlement to such actions in the Oxford Union and won her case hands down, even if her opponents were militant feminists who'd cut the balls off a man rather than bend the knee.

This House supports Lavinia Lee's right to make her own decisions.

The Ayes would have it, no question. Trouble was, she had not expected her sister, Rebecca, to be so efficient. Every stitch of clothing – every dress, coat, set of underwear, stockings – had been removed. Every personal ornament, book and knick-knack. She only found this out when she saw Rebecca, having been unable to gain access to Peter's flat.

'I thought that's what you wanted,' said Rebecca. 'If you'd telephoned before you took the train, I'd have told you.'

'I didn't think,' said Lavinia.

'The story of your life, sister dear.'

Rebecca didn't add that Peter had had the temerity to make a play for her during the removals.

You know, you're even better-looking than your sister.
Forget it.
I'm merely paying you a compliment.
I know where that sort of compliment ends.
Well, if you're ever free.

No, thought Rebecca, better to keep that little incident to herself.

Actually, Lavinia decided, she *had* thought, at least subconsciously. She had thought that she needed an excuse to return to Highgate. For Rebecca to tell her, during a phone call, 'No, everything's been moved,' would have eliminated the excuse. Her presence on his doorstep would have been seen, by him, for what it was: she would have been crawling back, begging him not to abandon her. After a drink or two, or a joint, she would probably have said it openly. He could have his other women. She wouldn't try to restrict him. But please could they still fuck each other when the opportunity arose?

She hated herself for even thinking it, but there it was.

He was a hell of a lover, that was the problem, and there were too few of them around. She'd slept with enough men to be able to judge. He wasn't perfect technically, but that was part of his charm. She'd been to bed with the so-called 'artists', those who'd read every textbook and knew the precise location of the clitoris and what to do with it. Painting by numbers. Exciting, yes, sure, a pleasant change from the fumblers who thought that Clitoris was a Greek island somewhere near Kos. But . . . but too regimental. Drinks seven-thirty, flowers already on the table. Dinner eight-thirty to ten-thirty, lingering over the last of the coffee like some blasted TV ad. Back to one flat or another, usually his. A brandy, maybe champagne. A hand on her thigh, gently, outside the dress – feeling, as they always did, to find out whether she was wearing stockings, self-supporting or otherwise, or tights. Another hand on her hair.

You have the most beautiful neck.

It was always the neck, far away enough from the more obvious erogenous zones, but close enough to the lips and ear lobes.

I would dearly love to make love to you.

Well, why not?

Then the undressing, then the bed, then the sex. Twelve minutes' foreplay, guaranteed within sixty seconds either way, eight minutes on her back, a few minutes sixty-nine, a few minutes dog-on-bitch.

Orgasms, sure. Multiple occasionally. But never any skull-blowing thrills. She could damn near see them turning the pages in their rather stupid heads.

When it was over, she half-expected some of them to sit up and declaim, 'Was I not superb?'

It was in their minds whether they said it or not. They were more concerned whether she'd give them five stars in her diary than with anything else.

She'd been to bed with men who had big cocks, small cocks, intermediate-sized cocks. But Peter, who belonged in the latter category, did something for her.

If he'd read a textbook, it didn't show. If he cared one jot about her orgasm, it wasn't obvious. He fucked her – in bed, across tables, in public parks and streets – because it pleased him. And in pleasing himself he delighted her.

They weren't easy to find, men like Peter. A woman couldn't start an affair with a man and then say, 'I'd rather like to go out with no underwear on this afternoon. If we can find a convenient spot, I'd like you to have me then and there.'

Of course she *could* say that, and many men would jump at the opportunity. But that would mean her taking the lead. She wanted to be led. Not because she was weak or submissive – though for the life of her she could not understand what was wrong with sexual submission if that's what turned one on – but because it was, well, exciting.

He was going to be damned hard to replace, Peter

Hennessy, but replaced he would have to be, and soon. Otherwise that damned vibrator would be working overtime and she'd thought, except for emergencies, that she'd given up sex with battery-powered objects. But if she didn't get her regular quota – or know it was available after a fast run in her car – she would go raving mad long before the end of term. Either that or she'd start propositioning the older males in her French and German classes.

Maybe that's what she needed. If Peter was *auf der strasse*, in the street, out of her life, an uninhibited youngster might fill the gap, as it were, and to hell with her career. Sex was everything. The rest was propaganda.

Uh-uh, she thought, coming out of her reverie. I haven't quite reached that stage yet.

She crowbarred her mind back to the present, to the subject under discussion – Goethe. She saw Richard Carson, three rows back, staring at her legs, and she quickly and surreptitiously checked that, during her day-dreaming, her skirt hadn't ridden up and that her legs were together. If she was to allow her mind to wander like that, she'd better make sure she did so while standing or sitting behind her desk, not perched on it as she now was. She was almost certain Carson had spotted her vibrator that afternoon before the end of Trinity Term, and she didn't want to give him ideas. Give *any* of them ideas, for that matter, though God knows they were only a few years younger than herself.

She eased herself carefully off the desk, smoothed

her skirt, and checked her wristwatch. Only a few minutes to go before the end of the morning's double German period, and a well-earned cup of coffee and a cigarette in the staff room. Time for a little game with the lascivious Master Carson, to see what he was made of, even though this particular piece of Goethe wasn't in the syllabus.

'Richard,' she said, *'Kennst du das Land, wo die Zitronen blühn? Im dunkeln Laub die Gold-Orangen glühn, Ein sanfter Wind vom blauen Himmel weht, Die Myrte still und hoch der Lorbeer steht – Kennst du es wohl?'*

Translated it meant: Know you the land where the lemon trees bloom? In the dark foliage the gold oranges glow, a soft wind hovers from the sky, the myrtle is still and the laurel stands tall – do you know it well?

Some of the words had double meanings. In the dark foliage, for example, and: the laurel stands tall.

Lavinia had no doubt Carson could translate – he was an excellent student – but she was sure he wouldn't know *Wilhelm Meisters Lehrjahre*. And therefore couldn't know the next lines.

She was wrong.

'Dahin! Dahin,' he quoted. *'Möcht ich mit dir, o mein Geliebter, ziehn!'*

In English this line read: There, there, I would go, O my beloved, with thee.

Lavinia had thought she was too old and experienced to blush at anything an eighteen-year-old boy could say, but to her horror she felt a flush coming to her cheeks. Carson was making it patently obvious that he was not simply quoting Goethe, that it was in her dark foliage – blond, rather, in her case – he would like his own laurel to stand tall.

Carson, too, wondered if he had gone too far, though he was secretly delighted with his pun. He managed a weak smile while the remainder of the class, understanding the words though not necessarily the reference, giggled self-consciously, male and female alike.

To cover her embarrassment, Lavinia turned the episode into a joke.

'Well,' she said, 'as soon as we can find some orange or lemon trees in this country, it's a date.'

'There are some at Kew, I understand,' said Carson.

Lavinia was not about to allow him to get away with that.

'*Entbehren sollst Du!*' she said. '*Sollst entbehren! Das ist der ewige Gesang.*'

In English this translated as: Deny yourself! You must deny yourself! That is the song that never ends.

But Carson had evidently been studying his Faust also.

'*Ich bin der Geist der stets verneint. Zwei Seelen wohnen, ach, in meiner Brust.*'

I am the spirit that always denies. Two souls dwell, alas, in my breast.

A few of the class members applauded. Carson stood and gave a mock bow from the waist. Lavinia spread her arms in a gesture of defeat.

'OK, OK, game, set and match to you. My French class I'll see this afternoon, the rest of you tomorrow.'

In the staff room Lavinia helped herself to a cup of coffee from the table, shunned the biscuits, and sank into an armchair. A cigarette was between her lips and alight before the first sip of coffee. She checked her cigarette packet, which had been full, a new box, when she woke up. There were now fifteen left, and it was only ten-thirty a.m. She recalled smoking one with her early-morning tea, one directly after breakfast and she had one in her hand. That left two unaccounted for. For the life of her she couldn't remember smoking them.

Not every teacher used the staff room unless they had business there. Heads of House usually retired to their own rooms for a little peace and quiet. Mrs Gordon, who taught Latin and Greek to the classicists in the sixth form and intermediate Latin to the Lower and Upper Fourth, almost never appeared. Eight, perhaps ten, was the usual complement.

You could generally depend upon the happily named Mr Chippendale, who taught junior English and history, to put in an appearance. Nicknamed, inevitably, 'Chips', he was sixty if he was a day, a bit clueless and a poor disciplinarian. He could be relied upon to snaffle, furtively, all the ginger snaps that were going and then curl up in a corner with the *Daily Telegraph*.

Mrs Greatorex taught maths and physics to Upper Fifth level. Forty-fiveish, she had returned to teaching three years ago, her children having become old enough to look after themselves. Although St Clare's gave beneficial terms to the offspring of staff members, Mrs Greatorex's two were day pupils at the local comprehensive, and Mrs Greatorex herself lived at home, not on school grounds.

Miss Bartlet, rising thirty-five, unmarried and showing no inclination to change her state, taught Games, capital G. For that matter, Miss Bartlet ate, drank, breathed and slept Games. All Games, but her favourites were hockey, tennis and cricket, for which she had been awarded a Half Blue while an undergraduate at Somerville College, Oxford. She was also a demon skier and invariably the mistress in charge during the annual skiing trips in January. She was cricket coach to the sixth-form boys for those who were interested, who were few. No boy who was sportingly inclined would apply to be admitted to St Clare's. As yet, there were not enough of them to form any kind of side for competition.

Miss Bartlet never walked into a room, she bounced. Depending on the season, and therefore the sport, she wore either tennis or hockey clothes, or a tracksuit. Naturally she never drank coffee, only juice or milk, and she frowned on anyone who smoked. Lavinia was not one of her favourites, and Miss Bartlet took great care to sit as far away as possible, near an open window.

Mr Hobday was the archetypal chemistry master, though he taught sixth-form physics and maths also, taking over where Mrs Greatorex left off and frequently unhappy with the academic standards bequeathed to him. The pair spent much of their time arguing about arcane matters. Hobday's gown, even in these enlightened days of personal computers and individual

VDUs, was invariably covered in chalk. Which puzzled everyone, since no-one could remember seeing a piece of chalk on school premises for years. There were blackboards – or, rather, whiteboards – to be sure, but on these marker pens were used.

Miss Heilbron was a shy, dark-haired twenty-four-year-old, new to St Clare's last Trinity Term, to sit in with the retiring mistress who taught junior French and German prior to taking over her classes. Because Lavinia would eventually inherit Sybil Heilbron's students, Lavinia had tried to get to know her. Without much success. Sybil hardly ever originated a conversation but waited to be asked questions, which drove Lavinia mad. In the staff room her custom was, as it was this morning, to take a cup of coffee, carefully break a biscuit in half, leaving one half on the table, and find a quiet corner to do her *Times* crossword. This never gave her any trouble, it seemed.

Apart from Robert Penrose, who came in as Lavinia was halfway through her cigarette, the only other staff member present that Monday break was Mrs Felicity Coggan, who was form mistress of the Lower Fifth and taught geography throughout the school at all levels. Mrs Coggan was a good-looking woman in her late thirties who liked her whisky and smoked as much as, or even more than, Lavinia. Given to figure-hugging suits and heels high enough to nudge her close to six feet, she had a coarse sense of humour, a fund of particularly dirty jokes which she'd tell at the drop of a hat, and was rumoured to have gone through a spectacular divorce, somewhere in the north of England, ten years earlier. No-one had ever been able to dig up the precise dirt, but the legend was that she'd been caught in bed by her then husband with a much younger man.

Lavinia liked to believe it was true. There was certainly a twinkle in Felicity Coggan's eyes that suggested it *could* be, though it had to be doubted if Mrs Gordon would have hired her if it was. And Lavinia had heard not a whisper that she spent her off-duty hours seducing the males of the Upper Sixth.

Still, that meant nothing. The lucky lads were hardly likely to spread it around and no-one at St Clare's knew much about her, Lavinia's, private life, either. No-one would guess what she and Peter used to get up to around the streets of Highgate.

Robert Penrose dropped into the armchair beside Lavinia's.

'Do you mind?' he asked

'Feel free. As long as you don't expect me to make intelligent conversation.'

'Ah, I'm afraid that's what I'm here for. On the other hand, I can talk and you just listen. Fair?'

'Fire away.'

'*A Midsummer Night's Dream.*'

'I can give you mine without my brain getting out of first gear. A schooner somewhere in the Mediterranean skippered by a young Peter O'Toole. A case of champagne and no-one under the age of eighteen anywhere in sight.'

'I meant the play, though your version sounds better. We're doing it for the end-of-term project. You know, showing the proud parents how talented their little darlings are and how St Clare's brings out the best in them. "Sign here for next term, please, major credit cards accepted."'

'An odd choice for a Christmas play, but good luck to you,' said Lavinia.

'Not that odd, actually,' said Penrose. 'My Upper Sixth English stream are beyond redemption, and Lower Sixth have *Richard II, Hamlet, Antony and Cleopatra* and *The Merchant of Venice* as prescribed texts. I doubt any of them will want to act any of those out as well as read them. But my nose tells me *MND* will be cropping up again on the syllabus in a year or two and this seems as good a time as any to put on a production, seeing as how we have to do a Christmas show anyway. Most of the moderns are out because the casts are too small. Not enough students get a chance to perform. *MND* has twenty or so decent parts. Add in understudies, stagehands, painters, wardrobe, electricians and so on and we can keep forty or fifty of the little beggars occupied.'

'I'm not sure I like the way you said "we",' said Lavinia, sensing a trap.

'Well, I simply thought . . .' began Penrose.

'No,' said Lavinia firmly. If she had been standing she would have stamped her foot by way of emphasis. 'Absolutely not. Forget it. From what I recall of the play, I hate it. Fairies and characters within characters and mistaken identities . . . No, no. I hate amateur dramatics even more, having been compelled to participate when I was at school. I was Eunice Gardiner, would you believe — "famed for sprightly gymnastics and glamorous swimming" — in a cobbled-together version of *The Prime of Miss Jean Brodie*, nothing to do with the Maggie Smith film. I was seventeen and ghastly. To direct or produce, or whatever you call it, others with my sort of Thespian talent is my idea of hell.'

'Some of them aren't bad,' said Penrose. 'One or two might have a future in the theatre. Besides, I'll be doing the producing. What I need is someone to help with the auditions and at rehearsals. It's no more arduous than supervising prep.'

'Why me?' asked Lavinia. 'I'm a linguist, I know nothing about Shakespeare. You're senior English master, true, so I guess you're stuck with it, but Chips is junior English. Why not him? He's done it up to now. He did it last year, anyway, as I recall.'

'Look at him,' said Penrose, lowering his voice. 'He's counting the hours until retirement. Besides, he's a bachelor and you have to keep your eye on him.'

'Oh yes?' said Lavinia, interested. 'Expand.'

'Last year he spent an inordinate amount of time hanging around the girls' dressing areas. The younger girls, that is. There were a number of complaints. Fourteen-year-olds, half-dressed, having their backsides patted and urged to "gee up".'

'If his weakness is pubescent females, he's likely to take exception to being overlooked this year.'

'Not him. He's already hinted obliquely that he doesn't want to be considered, apparently because he doesn't think he can keep his hands off the little darlings' bodies, though naturally he didn't say that. However, one whiff of scandal and he's out on his ear. Goodbye pension, hello probation officer.'

'It's not really for me, Robert . . .'

'Think about it,' pleaded Penrose. 'The evenings are light now, but it won't be long before they start to draw in. It'll give you something to do, the occasional weekend too as we get closer to a performance.'

I'm afraid my weekends are fully booked, Lavinia was about to say until she realized they no longer were, not even the free ones.

Lighting another cigarette, earning daggers from Miss Bartlet, Lavinia studied Robert Penrose through the smoke, wondering if he wanted her as his assistant as a means to finding a way into her pants. What was he, thirty-two, thirty-three? He was handsome in a kind of muscular, tennis-professional sort of way, and she knew from eavesdropped gossip that some of the younger girls found him devastatingly attractive. But he wasn't really her type. Still, who knew where it all might lead? Even if nowhere, doing the play would help take her mind off Peter.

Penrose sensed her weakening.

'Please.'

'All right,' said Lavinia, 'I'll give it a shot. But don't blame me if you live to regret it.'

'Excellent,' said Penrose. 'I'll let you know when I'm holding the first auditions.'

'One proviso,' warned Lavinia. 'Hands off my Upper Sixth language set. I haven't made up my mind who's going yet, but a handful are certain

73

to be taking the Oxford entrance examination at the end of November. I don't want them spouting "Ill met by moonlight, proud Titania" when they should be remembering what they've learnt about *Der Hauptmann von Köpenick*.'

'Oxford,' said Penrose, who recalled that Lavinia had graduated from Magdalen College. 'I've noticed in the past that you hardly ever seem to mention Cambridge when trying to place your brighter students.'

'We never talk about the Other Place,' said Lavinia lightly. 'You were Durham, I believe.'

'Yes.'

'Ah,' said Lavinia.

Coincidentally, the Oxford entrance examination was also under discussion in the sixth-form common-room during the morning break, though it was dropped when Richard Carson said he was bored with the subject.

Far from bored, however, he was worried about his date at England's premier university in less than three months. Although he was fairly sure Lavinia Lee would encourage him to sit it, she had not yet handed out the Oxford application cards, which had to be returned to the Admissions Office by 15 October at the latest. Fair enough, there was still bags of time, but Miss Lee, not wanting her academic reputation sullied at her old university, would not be sending the no-hopers. He was a long way outside that category, but he would have to be careful not to cross swords too often with the delicious Lavinia for the next few weeks. No more smart-arsed cracks about wanting his laurel standing tall in her foliage. She didn't seem the type to hold a grudge, but she could easily mark him down, tell the Gorgon his work was falling off, that it would be a waste of time him sitting the exam, if he became too bold. He'd have more than enough opportunities for further sexual wordplay after he'd passed the papers with flying colours.

Time to play it cool.

The sixth-form commonroom was shared by Upper and Lower Sixths, and was strictly speaking two rooms, one leading off the other. Several copies of each quality British newspaper were available daily and periodicals weekly or monthly. There were chairs to sit in, tables to work at − noise level permitting − and coffee, tea and soft drinks were on tap during breaks and in the early evening. (These were charged for under 'miscellaneous' on each term's bill whether students drank them or not, St Clare's not being a benevolent institution.)

But mostly the commonroom was a place for friends who perhaps shared the same dorm or House, but not the same classes, to gossip. The head girl, Fiona Acland, was in this morning, a rare visit from a *rara avis*. She was sipping orange juice by a window overlooking one of the quadrangles, holding court with members of her coterie and a few hangers-on anxious for a kind word or a smile.

Although head girls were appointed by Mrs Gordon, Fiona would have been elected by acclamation had it been otherwise. (There was no corresponding head boy, their numbers being too few.) She was the most popular girl in the school, and one of the prettiest. Apart from an IQ in the 170s, which she never flaunted, she was captain of hockey and tennis. Her parents were members of the nobility and she had a private income even at the age of eighteen. She drove a vintage Lagonda, which she was allowed to keep on school grounds as one of the perks of her headship, and was destined to read medicine at Cambridge the following year. A brilliant career was predicted for her.

She was, in short, enough to make any mere mortal female spit.

'I see Queen Fiona is granting audiences,' said Amanda McDonald, halfway through a snack, obtained from the tuckshop downstairs, that would have solved the hunger problem on the sub-continent for a month.

'Would you like a saucer of milk to go with that, dear?' purred Jocasta.

'Well,' pouted Amanda, 'it's obscene for anyone to own that much talent.'

'Talking of obscene,' said Julia to Kate, 'that's one of the sinistrals I warned you about, talking to Dutch Paula. Don't bend down in the showers if you drop the soap should she be anywhere near you. Otherwise, goodbye Mademoiselle Hymen.'

'Julia!' spluttered Amanda, face full of bun.

'She is fortuitously named Sally-Anne Peters,' went on Julia, ignoring Amanda. 'SAP, get it? Her nickname, naturally, is Sappho, she of the island of Lesbos. Pretty nifty, huh?'

Though nifty Sappho Peters certainly wasn't. Hefty would be more apt, thought Kate, Wagnerian even.

Twelve stone if she was a pound, fair hair in bunches, six feet tall, and shoes you could paddle the Atlantic in. While it was relatively easy for Kate to imagine Paula in bed with Phoebe thingummy – well, she'd witnessed it, hadn't she? – it was difficult to visualize such an outwardly pixie-like creature as the South African making love, or whatever the terminology was, to someone as huge as Sappho.

Though that was nonsense, of course. There was no reason why Paula and Sally-Anne Peters, even if similarly inclined sexually, should fancy each other. Far more likely they both wanted Phoebe.

Kate shuddered involuntarily.

'Someone walking over your grave?' asked Jocasta.

'Something like that. What's next period? My mind's a blank.'

'Double English with Penrose.'

Goody, thought Julia.

'Did anyone see what's for lunch?' asked Amanda.

Across the commonroom, parked on the window seat opposite Ben Fisher, a pocket chessboard between them, Henry Morton was feeling very much alone, even surrounded by so many people. No, *especially* surrounded by so many people, he decided.

A scrawny eighteen-year-old who'd started life as a premature five pounds six ounces baby, he'd been a scraggy kid, always beaten up by older kids, and a skinny adolescent. Now he was just scrawny.

He accepted he wouldn't grow much taller than his present five feet five, or ever weigh more than nine stone. He accepted that his eyes were bad, compelling him to wear spectacles that made him look like a Jap sniper in a John Wayne movie. He knew he couldn't compete at games with any hope of success, or shine academically. He was in the same languages set as Richard Carson, but he would not be one of those chosen to go to Oxford in November. With luck, he might matriculate to a redbrick, graduate, and find a quiet teaching job somewhere.

He could accept all of this.

What he could not accept was that he was a homosexual.

If he was.

He liked girls, that was the trouble. The concomitant trouble was girls didn't like him, didn't want him pawing them, laughed at him. His solitary experience with a girl, two years ago, had proved disastrous. Like him, she was no oil painting, but it was a case of any port in a storm. Except it had taken him ten minutes to get her bra unfastened, by which time she was ready to knee him in the balls, and another five, four and a half of which were hers, to get her undressed. Then:

Nothing.

Limp dick.

Brewer's droop, except he hadn't been drinking.

All there for the taking, and he had been unable to take.

She'd glared at his genitals.

'Well, it looks reasonable, from my angle, but I'm fucked if I'll wait for a fuck.'

She was his mother's au pair, and she left the same week. Lame explanation.

'I've been offered a better job, Mrs Morton.'

A better jobbing, more likely.

You didn't have, um, anything to do with that young lady, did you, Henry?

No, Mama.

Truth, now?

Of course not. If only . . . if only.

Well, I thought not. Goodness me, the girls these days.

Then came Alan, his own age, from the village. A recent copy of *Mayfair*, pilfered by Alan from his father's stock. Up to the copse, there to gaze upon the beauties they could never have, never fuck. Erect dicks in hand, own hand on own dick.

Jesus, said Alan, I'd give a lot to fuck her.

Me too.

Because the centrefold was forever out of reach, somehow – and Henry still didn't know how – they masturbated each other while looking at the girl in the magazine.

Bet I come first, said Alan.

Bet you don't.

It was about a draw, and they often went amongst the trees with a magazine. Until . . .

One day Alan said, 'You're queer. You're a plonker.'

'I'm not, you bastard. If I am, what does that make you?'

'Not a homo, that's for sure. If I wanted, I could fuck your mother.'

Henry hit him, and Alan beat Henry to a pulp.

See, I knew you were queer.

'You're going to be in deep shit with that knight

of yours unless you move it,' said Ben Fisher.

Henry moved his knight.

'Jerk,' said Fisher.

But why, thought Henry, did I get an erection with Alan looking at filth, why did we masturbate each other, with great satisfaction, and why is he not gay but I may be? Why did he have the absolute confidence that he could . . . do that . . . to my mother, and believe he could, while I couldn't do it to his mother?

I don't understand.

'Mate in two,' said Ben Fisher. 'Unavoidable.'

At the end of the Lower Sixth English class that followed the morning break, Penrose announced that he would be auditioning shortly for *MND*.

'Names to me before you leave, please.'

Julia put her name down.

5

Games

Amanda Panda stretched for one of Kate's sizzling backhands that was way out of reach, missed by a mile, and went sprawling.

'Bugger!'

Jocasta, partnering Kate, creased up with laughter as Amanda's racquet left her hand like a guided missile, cannoned into the wire netting surrounding the court and practically took Amanda's head off, on the rebound, as her chubby little bottom bounced across the grass.

'Oh, yes, highly amusing,' scowled Amanda, skidding to a halt.

Richard Carson, her partner in this game of doubles, helped her to her feet. Carson was no great shakes as a tennis player, but he was taller and stronger than any of the girls and that was some compensation.

'You OK?'

Amanda brushed some of the grass stains from her backside, glancing over her shoulder to see how she was faring.

'Yes, thanks. Damned court's too damned wet.'

Although it had turned out to be a fine evening, it had been raining for part of the day and the court was still slippery.

'Not that it would make a blind bit of difference to my game if it were bone dry. I think Monica Seles can rest easy for another season.'

'Don't put yourself down,' said Carson. 'You're doing all right.'

He went over and retrieved Amanda's racquet, which he handed to her.

Amanda tested the strings.

'We're six-two, five-three and thirty-love down,' she said. 'If that's what you call doing all right, I'd hate you to see me when I was having an off day.'

'It's only a game,' said Carson.

'That's what Nero used to say to the Christians shortly before he let the lions loose.'

'Well, it is. Win or lose, it'll be forgotten by tomorrow.'

Amanda wasn't accustomed to encouraging words from boys even of her own age, let alone one almost two years older, and even though she suspected why they were being uttered – for Richard to show Kate that he wasn't an oik, that he had qualities not always apparent – she appreciated them, and smiled shyly.

'I'll try to remember that.'

Julia was usually the fourth member of doubles games, but this evening she was reading her audition piece from *A Midsummer Night's Dream* for Mr Penrose and was unavailable. Carson had got to hear of this and, having checked the court bookings, had turned up at the appropriate hour dressed to play. He had offered his services before Kate could hunt around for someone to replace the absent Julia. To his surprise, Kate hadn't objected to him partnering Amanda.

At first he had wondered if she was softening towards him, until he saw the strength of her game, which was of a very high standard. Not unexpected, he supposed, when he remembered the time she'd spent in America, where they took tennis much more seriously, even in schools.

After her first few serves whistled past his ears, he was forced to reassess her reasons for allowing him to participate. She was out to teach him a lesson.

Very well, there was only one way to react since he and Amanda couldn't hope to beat her and Jocasta: with dignity and humility. Take it on the chin. If he demonstrated pique, he could kiss goodbye to any chance of a relationship with Kate McNamara.

'Come on, you two,' called Jocasta, whose serve it was.

Carson prepared to receive. Jocasta was nowhere near as good as Kate, but Carson wasn't sure whether he should try to play his heart out and take the match to another game, thus having at least another few minutes on court, or fluff it, allow Jocasta to serve to Amanda for what would undoubtedly be game, set and match, and then attempt to get Kate on her own.

As it transpired, he wasn't allowed options. Jocasta mis-hit her serve completely. What she had intended as a flashing ace down the centre barely bobbled over the net. Carson was prepared for the ace, however, and therefore caught on the back foot. The ball bounced twice long before he could reach it.

Jocasta had the good manners to apologize.

'Sorree,' she trilled.

'Forty-love,' called Kate.

'It would have to be me receiving, wouldn't it,' complained Amanda, 'on match point.'

She moved to the backline to face service. Carson moved forward, as did Kate.

'Fancy another game after this?' asked Carson.

'I don't think so,' said Kate, not unfriendlily. 'Amanda's right, the court's too wet.'

'A walk around the grounds, then. There's still plenty of daylight left.'

'Perhaps – if you win the set.'

'Oh, come on,' protested Carson.

'The game, then.'

'We're forty-love in arrears. Make it the point and it's a deal. If we get to forty-fifteen, you and I go for a walk.'

'I think you've just guaranteed me an early night.'

'Have you two quite finished?' demanded Jocasta impatiently.

'Give me a second,' said Carson.

He ran back to Amanda.

'Come forward a few yards,' he said. 'She'll bobble it again, but you'll be in a position to reach it. Bobble it right back, at Kate's feet. I'll do the rest.'

Please, Lord, he prayed, returning to his place.

'No more bobbles, now,' he called out, just as Jocasta tossed the ball high in the air.

A more experienced player would have voided the serve, accused her opponents of gamesmanship, and insisted on re-serving. But Jocasta wasn't more experienced. Carson's voice startled her, made her take her eye off the descending ball for a fraction of a second. Instead of it booming off the face of the racquet, it hit part strings, part handle, and described the gentlest of looping trajectories. By this time Amanda was on her way to the net, which she reached as the ball did. A child of six could have walloped it, and Amanda knocked seven bells out of it with a forehand volley. It landed nowhere near Kate's feet, but it did land in court.

'I won a point, I won a point!' shrieked Amanda.

'So did I, so did I,' grinned Carson.

'Cheats, cheats!' squealed Jocasta. 'I demand a recount!'

'No, let it ride,' said Kate, thinking, Well, he must really want that walk, so let's see how he operates.

Carson managed to return the next serve to make it forty-thirty, but Jocasta made no mistake with the following one, acing Amanda.

Six-two, six-three, match over, shake hands.

The four went over to their towels and sweatsuits, which were piled on chairs in one corner of the court. Unseen behind the rhododendron bushes, Algy, the gardener's boy, watched the girls towel themselves down. In particular he watched Jocasta, whose dark Italian looks fascinated him, whose white knickers under her short tennis dress excited him when she bent over to unlace her shoes, whose tanned legs, browner even than the blonde new girl's, he wanted to touch, stroke, caress.

He wasn't too worried that someone might see him. He had business here, after all, didn't he? Wasn't it his job to look after the grounds surrounding the courts? Wasn't it also his job to repaint the white lines when they became faint? In any case, he wasn't stupid, though he was aware many of the girls thought he was. Didn't he know that they deliberately showed off their bodies when they suspected he was watching them? Hadn't he even heard one or two of them say, raising their short dresses and adjusting their knickers as if they were in private, 'Bet Algy would like a peek at what's in here,' and others answer, 'It'd be more than a peek he'd want, dear'?

Well, that was true enough. Already he could feel himself almost fully erect. If only the dark girl would let him touch her. If only she would touch *him*. He would give her every penny he had.

The ladies of St Clare's were wrong about Algernon Hicks having the mind of a ten-year-old, though it had to be admitted that, at nineteen, he was backward, only partly literate and barely numerate. They were not wrong in suspecting that Nature had compensated him sexually for robbing him intellectually, even if no-one knew precisely how the rumour had started.

Algy could have told them that it began two years earlier, at the end of Trinity Term, when examinations were over and, before the fretting about results became endemic, partying was universal if clandestine.

Jane Barker she was called, though Algy never knew

her surname. She was eighteen, an effervescent brunette. Due to leave St Clare's in a few days and certain she had done well in her exams, her university place secure, she was also fairly drunk, having consumed three-quarters of a bottle of sherry and two glasses of rough red.

Her friends were egging her on.

Be you wouldn't, Jane. You wouldn't have the nerve.

Who wouldn't?

You wouldn't. He's watering the rhodos if you're serious. At least, he was twenty minutes ago.

Right, but no-one's to follow.

A chorus of disapproval.

But how will we know if you go through with it?

You'll know.

Because it was midsummer the nights were light until ten o'clock, and it wasn't yet nine. But because it was almost the end of term, virtually everyone was in their dorms or studies, getting drunk for those who were old enough, keeping out of the way of term-end pranks for the teenies, who more often than not found themselves being fed nauseous concoctions such as honey and Marmite in giant spoonfuls, or chucked in the swimming pool by their seniors unless they were quick on their feet.

Algy was hosing down the rhododendrons, which were almost out of bloom but still had another week or two in them if sufficiently watered, which could only be done when the heat of the sun had gone. He saw Jane weaving her way in his direction, and he wasn't that dumb that he didn't know she'd been drinking. Still, he didn't pay her much attention. Some of the girls occasionally said 'hello' to him, or 'good evening'. Jane wasn't one of them.

He was therefore surprised when she stopped nearby, a few feet away.

'Hello, Algy,' she said. 'Still very hot, isn't it?'

'Yes, miss,' he managed, remembering then that he'd heard other girls call her Jane.

Because of the heat he was wearing only shorts and plimsolls.

'I must say you keep these grounds looking a rare treat,' said Jane, 'especially the rhodos. They really set off the tennis courts.'

That was true enough, and Algy was quite proud of his work, although he didn't bother to point out that he merely did as he was told by the head gardener. Still, the rhododendron bushes completely surrounded the tennis courts, shielding them from the remainder of the school grounds and the various Houses and classrooms. Even in winter no-one from the other side could see into the courts, while in the summer, with the heads in full bloom, it was like a private little world here.

Jane sat down on a grass verge, apparently unconcerned that her summer skirt had ridden up. If he changed his angle slightly, thought Algy, he would be able to see beneath it.

It was then that he spotted Jane was carrying a bottle, wine it looked like, half full.

'Take a rest a second, Algy, and come and sit next to me. Have a swig of this.'

'I don't think I should, miss . . .'

'Oh, come along, no-one can see us.'

Well, that was true at least.

He sat down, accepted the bottle, and took a long swig.

Then things started to happen that would get him into terrible trouble if he was found out but which he was powerless to stop.

How old are you, Algy?

Seventeen, miss.

You have the most amazing shoulder muscles. She touched them, kneaded them. *And thigh muscles.* She touched those too, high up. To his horror he felt his cock stiffening.

Uh, miss.

Don't mind me. Have another drink.

He did so, and while he was drinking Jane slipped her hand inside his shorts.

Jesus Christ, he heard her say.

Miss, he began, hardly recognizing the voice as his own. It was no sort of a protest anyway. Nothing like this had ever happened to him before, even though he had dreamt of it, and he didn't want her to stop.

Shut up and lie back.

He did so, half dazed. She brought her hand from beneath his shorts and unzipped his fly. His cock leapt out and rose in a lazy arc until it was fully erect.

Jesus Christ, he heard her mutter, *I've never seen anything like it in my life.*

Her hand began to work on him and then, because one hand wasn't enough, she used two. He tried to push his own hand under her skirt, but she brushed it away angrily. And all the time she was talking, whispering really, partly to him, partly to herself.

You've got the biggest cock I've ever seen. And the hardest. It must measure — Christ, I don't know — yards. Come for me, Algy. Come for Aunty Jane. Let's see if there's as much on the inside as there is on the outside. Come on, Algy. Come on.

Her hands worked faster and faster, and soon he couldn't have stopped himself coming for a million pounds. He mumbled something that even he didn't understand, and then he was shooting all over the place. It seemed to go on for ever and he let out a gigantic groan. So did she, he thought he heard, but all he actually made out was, *Christ, Algy, Christ oh Christ, some girl one day is going to get one hell of a surprise.*

When it was over she wiped her hands on the grass and suddenly appeared very sober.

Don't tell anyone, Algy, never tell anyone.

To himself he vowed he wouldn't, but before he could promise her, she'd gone.

In the study where the end-of-term party was being held, the girls gathered round Jane when she got back.

Did you do it, did you do it?

You bet I did.

What, what?

But the experience had, as Algy had spotted, sobered Jane considerably. She wasn't about to give them a blow-by-blow account. What was thrilling in private was, for her, demeaning in public.

Oh, just measured it. Roughly only, of course.

And?

Huge, of traffic-jam proportions.

One or two of the girls were more observant than the others. They pointed to fresh stains on Jane's skirt, unmistakable discolorations to anyone who had been that route, which, at eighteen, all of them had. The Goody Two-Shoes of St Clare's would not be at a party like this.

Jane, you horny bitch!

What was it like?

I don't know what you're talking about.

It had been the best time of Algy's life, one that was never to be repeated. He saw Jane Barker in the school grounds several times over the next few days, but she ignored him and he suspected it was more than his life was worth to approach her. She was a rich young lady, he was a gardener's assistant. Although he couldn't read very well he knew from those who could, boys he met in town, who read the Sunday newspapers, that the rich often sent the poor to prison for sex acts they wanted at the time but later regretted.

Within a week Jane had left St Clare's for ever.

Jocasta looked a lot like Jane in many ways, he thought, watching her slip on her sweatsuit pants. If only, if only . . . If only she would do to him what Jane had done. If he could touch her, be *inside* her. She was so beautiful.

The ache in his groin became unbearable, and he slipped away to relieve it in the only way he knew how.

'Ready?' queried Amanda, shouldering her racquet.

Carson looked at Kate.

'Richard and I are going to cool off with a walk,' said Kate.

Amanda stared at her.

'When did all this happen?'

'When they were talking at the net, dumbo,' said Jocasta. 'We'll see you later.'

'And if you're not in by midnight your father and I are stopping your pocket money,' Amanda called back.

'Where to?' asked Carson.

'Oh, let's just walk and see where it leads,' said Kate airily, not intending any double meaning.

They set off, Kate making sure she kept several feet between herself and Carson. OK, he thought, I'm not going to rush you.

An hour earlier, Julia had dressed herself to kill: a tight Lycra top which showed off her breasts (and which could be removed, she thought with a *frisson*, without difficulty by a man with experience), loafers, and a black Lycra skirt that just about covered her knickers (which could also be removed with ease, and permission).

She gave a couple of twirls before the cheval glass at the door of the dormitory.

Not bad.

She couldn't hope to live in the same league as Kate and Jocasta, but not bad.

Penrose had better watch out.

Not that she was sure what she was going to do,

if anything. Rather, she was hoping he would make the first move. She was merely putting the items, temptingly, she hoped, on display. It was up to him to buy.

Her heart beat faster at the thought. Would he? Even if he did, would she be able to go through with it? It was one thing to fantasize, another to 'go the distance' as current jargon had it.

Yes, damn it, she would. She was sick and tired of being a virgin when others of her age most certainly were not, walking around with those self-satisfied smirks. Kate she was almost sure about, though Kate had yet to confirm it. Jocasta she knew had lost her virginity when she was only fifteen, and had scored a series of conquests since then. It was a club she craved to join, especially if her sponsor were Robert Penrose.

There was, of course, the small matter of birth control. Had she not been concerned about that, she would have allowed Teddy Hedges to be the first. On several occasions during the summer holidays she'd considered approaching her family doctor with a request to go on the Pill, or at least fit her for a diaphragm. But, nice and modern though she was, Dr Morrisey would have insisted on talking to her mother first, which was out of the question. Her mother would have turned blue at the notion.

Parents were funny like that. They did not want their children, especially daughters, getting up to what they themselves had got up to in the sixties, and for the life of her Julia couldn't understand why.

Jocasta took the Pill – with her mother's approval, she said, though not her father's. Jocasta also insisted on lovers using a condom, a wise enough precaution in these scary days of AIDS. The Pill alone was only relied upon in long-term relationships 'when I'm sure the bugger isn't screwing half of Hampshire'.

Unfortunately, the Pill wasn't transferable, like borrowing someone else's Veganin if you had a headache or PMT. You couldn't simply take two and know that all would be well.

But Robert was bound to have the necessary. He was an experienced man, you only had to look at him. A man like that would carry a supply in his wallet, or wherever it was men carried them.

She had prepared her audition piece with care. Robert had told her, told all the auditionees, that they did not have to memorize the lines. He would be satisfied with a reading. For now, he just wanted to get an idea of what everyone could do, before making his final choice.

She was willing to accept any part in the play, but she wanted that of Helena and had studied one of her long speeches in Act 1.

How happy some o'er other some can be!
Through Athens I am thought as fair as she.
But what of that? Demetrius thinks not so;
He will not know what all but he do know.

Di-dum-di-dum.

Love looks not with the eyes, but with the mind;
And therefore is wing'd Cupid painted blind.
Nor hath love's mind of any judgment taste;
Wings and no eyes figure unheedy haste.

And then her big finish.

Pursue her; and for this intelligence
If I have thanks, it is a dear expense.
But herein mean I to enrich my pain,
To have his sight thither and back again.

She was word perfect, she knew, but she'd take her
Shakespeare anyway, and read from it for a while, just
in case she appeared too pushy.

She checked her reflection in the cheval once more
and, satisfied, popped the Shakespeare in her briefcase together with a notebook and pen. This done,
she tripped lightly down the stairs, out of Churchill
House and across to Napier, where Robert Penrose
had his rooms and also his study.

As always when a female student entered Napier
(the same applying in reverse whenever a male student
wished to enter any of the girls' Houses), she had to
ring a bell and wait in the hall until a duty master or
senior boy came to see who wanted what.

It took only a few moments before Ben Fisher came
bounding down the staircase. The senior boys took it
in turns to answer the bell, because it was hardly ever
rung unless a girl was on the premises.

It took a moment for Fisher to recognize Julia,

though of course it wasn't the first time he'd seen her dressed up. But this evening she looked cracking.

'Hell's bells,' he whispered under his breath. 'Hi,' he said aloud.

'Hello,' said Julia. 'I've got an audition with Mr Penrose.'

'Oh, right. Do you know the way?'

'Of course,' said Julia, in her best Lady Windermere voice.

It was customary for whoever met the incomer to escort her to her destination, but the broad staircase to the upper floors in Napier was quite steep, and Fisher wasn't about to miss his opportunity of watching the short-skirted Julia ascend.

'I'll leave you to it, then.'

It took Julia half a dozen steps to figure out why Fisher wasn't accompanying her, that he was staring after her, waiting for a glimpse of thigh.

Silly boy, she thought, even though he was two years older. Still, she held her briefcase behind her in both hands, denying him his cheap thrill.

Christ, thought Fisher, eyeing her until she disappeared round the top of the staircase, now *that* I would dearly love to lay.

He recalled Dick Carson's observation the first evening of term, that Julia Hastings was probably still a virgin but anxious not to remain one. Well, the same went for him.

He would have to start cultivating Miss Hastings. What was this damned play they were doing, *A Midsummer Night's Dream*? He hadn't put his name down when Penrose had come around scouting for boys to play the male parts, but he might have to rethink that. Sure, acting was a sissy pastime, but what the hell?

He knew the play vaguely and he had a copy of Shakespeare in his study. He raced off to find it.

Julia stopped outside Penrose's study door, checked her clothing, squared her shoulders, and knocked.

Penrose bade her come in. Julia took a deep breath and entered.

Her face fell.

Sitting opposite Penrose, in a second armchair, was Lavinia Lee.

Julia almost wept with frustration. All her preparations — having a long soak in the bath, washing her hair, choosing her most seductive clothes — were a waste of time. She might just as well have worn an old sweater and jeans. Damn it to hell, didn't he know, couldn't he see, that she wanted him desperately?

Afterwards she was sure she'd failed the audition. She fluffed her lines several times, even with the book open, and her rendition of Helena's impassioned speech had been colourless. Here was a woman, Helena, willing to give up the man she loves, Demetrius, to her friend Hermia, and she had made it sound like a reading of the railway timetable.

All Penrose said, when it was over, was, 'OK, Julia, not bad, but it will mean a lot of work if you're to be cast as Helena. Anyway, we've still got lots of people to see, so we'll let you know.'

We'll let you know. Julia was green in the ways of the theatre, but she'd seen enough movies about aspiring actresses to be aware that the four most dreaded words for auditionees were *We'll let you know*. In other words, fuck off, get lost, don't give up your day job.

The ignominy of it! Worse, the royal 'we', not even '*I'll* let you know'. Robert and Lavinia were auditioning as a team, and God knows what else they were doing in private. If she had thought, right at the start of term, that competing with Kate for Robert's affections would stack the odds against her, she stood no chance against the voluptuous Lavinia, whom she now hated with Carthaginian loathing.

Which, Julia being Julia, would probably last for all of two days.

Ben Fisher was waiting for her at the foot of the staircase. Halfway down Julia saw him and, in a fit of self-defeating rage, turned her back to him, bent over so that her skirt rode high, and wiggled her behind. Fisher's eyes damn near popped out of his head. He swore, later, that he grew two extra freckles, and not on his face.

Julia brushed past him.

'There,' she spat, 'satisfied now?'

'How did it go?' he called after her.

'Piss off,' she tossed back.

'That good, huh?'

He looked at the copy of Shakespeare he had unearthed. So much for that. Maybe not, though. Maybe he'd still have a crack at an audition piece, because Julia could well get another part if she'd failed the one she'd read for.

Moreover, he'd had a quick flick through the

dramatis personae. There were eight female parts and, as it was doubtful that Penrose could dig up enough boys to play the dozen or more male parts, some females would have to play those also.

He'd never thought of it in that way before, but acting was a bloody good way to meet girls.

'Well,' said Lavinia, the moment the door closed behind Julia, 'that little lady was dressed to kill. Somebody should have told her that the play we're doing is *A Midsummer Night's Dream*, not *The Best Little Whorehouse in Texas*. You're lucky I was here. You'd have had two hours of bliss followed by ten years of reaping what you'd sown in Wandsworth or wherever the equivalent is in this part of the world.'

'You surely don't think . . .' began Penrose before Lavinia interrupted him with a raucous laugh.

'Come on, Robert, don't be naïve. She was ready to throw herself at you. How many girls have we seen yesterday and today? Ten, fifteen? And how did they dress? Like normal teenagers free of the constraints of classrooms, in any old thing. Some of them smelt as if they'd been mucking out stables, but young Julia Hastings must have poured a bucket of Givenchy over herself. And don't tell me you didn't get a whiff of it.'

'Well, yes, of course,' admitted Penrose.

Lavinia studied him curiously.

'What would you have done if you had been alone and she'd leapt on you? She's a pretty little thing.'

'She's also sixteen years of age.'

'And affairs between masters and teenage students

never happen, of course? Well, you're going to have trouble with her in the future whether you give her a part or not. She's in your English stream.'

'What did you think of her reading?'

'Allowing for her nervousness, and probable shock when she saw me sitting in, not at all bad. Streets ahead of some we've seen.'

'So you think I should cast her, as Helena or someone else?'

'That's up to you, I'm just the assistant. If she'd been hopeless, I'd have said no. But she's well on the plus side of borderline. Unless Vanessa Redgrave or Glenda Jackson walk through the door before we've seen everyone, I'd be inclined to chance it.'

'It's going to be – awkward – though, isn't it, if what you say about her vis-à-vis me is accurate? Rehearsals, close contact outside school hours.'

'Oh, it's accurate, believe me. And look at it this way: you can't escape her because of your classes. If you don't give her a part, that adoration or crush or whatever it is will soon turn to hatred. Then you'll really have problems. Besides' – Lavinia smiled mischievously – 'I'll be at rehearsals to hold your hand.'

'I'll think about it,' said Penrose. 'As you said, Vanessa Redgrave might suddenly appear.'

Penrose sighed and stretched, and glanced at the clock on the mantelpiece.

'Well, that's the last of them for today. What about a drink?'

'Town or village?'

'Town's too far, but we can walk to the village in fifteen minutes.'

'To hell with that, it's also fifteen minutes back, most of it uphill. We'll take my car.'

'Drinking and driving?'

'A pint and a half isn't going to send the breathalyser into orbit.'

'OK, if you're sure.' Penrose hesitated, unsure whether to confide in Lavinia. 'I get my licence back next May.'

'I thought it might be something like that, seeing as how you don't have transport on school grounds. What happened? No, sorry, I'm being nosy.'

'I'll tell you when we're behind those pints.'

On the drive down to the school gates, they passed Carson and Kate. Although they were still walking apart, Kate was laughing at something Carson had said, and it was evidently more than a casual meeting.

'That's new, isn't it?' said Lavinia.

'Well, she's a pretty girl.'

Lavinia chuckled.

'Robert, they're *all* pretty girls. If I were a man I'd go mad. All those goodies in the sweetshop, money in my pocket, and forbidden by my doctor to eat sugar.'

'It's the same for you, surely, with the Upper and Lower Sixth boys?'

'Women are different, Robert, didn't anyone ever tell you?'

It occurred to Lavinia that Robert, in spite of those tennis-player looks, was perhaps not quite so experienced as she'd first thought.

Interesting.

Fiona Acland's unmistakable Lagonda was in the pub car park. There were no rules at St Clare's forbidding anyone who qualified, by virtue of age, from visiting pubs, providing they behaved themselves. Nevertheless, Penrose said, 'Oh, hell.'

'Why? We're not doing anything wrong.'

'Agreed, but you know how gossip travels.'

Yes, very interesting, thought Lavinia, curiouser and curiouser. Surely he hadn't had a fling with Queen Fiona?

Lavinia found a vacant table while Penrose ordered the pints. Fiona was playing darts with some of the locals and hadn't seen them yet. She appeared to be winning, too. Captain of hockey and tennis and now a budding darts champion. Quite a games-player.

Penrose returned with the beer. They both drank deeply.

'Much better,' said Lavinia, dabbing her mouth with a tissue and fishing out her cigarettes. She offered one to Penrose, who shook his head.

'Not for the moment, thanks.'

Lavinia lit up.

'You were going to tell me about your run-in with Plod while driving,' she said, not being discourteous or inquisitive, but merely trying to put him at his ease. He seemed distinctly edgy.

'Last Easter. A few too many whiskies after an acrimonious meeting with my estranged wife. Next thing, flashing lights and a couple of hefty policemen slamming me in a cell. Stupid, but there it is.'

Amazing, thought Lavinia. I've been here two years, hardly passed more than the time of day with Robert Penrose throughout that, and in twenty minutes I've discovered he's separated from his wife and banned from driving.

'Mrs Gordon knows,' added Penrose, 'and a few others, I suppose, but I'd prefer you to keep it to yourself. The driving thing, that is. No-one knows about the estrangement.'

Wrong, thought Lavinia, who'd heard rumours.

'Of course,' she said. 'Goes without saying. Queen Fiona's coming over.'

And for this relief much thanks, she thought. She didn't want to hear about Robert's wife, estranged or otherwise. They weren't close enough by a long chalk for those kind of confidences. Before long she'd find herself telling *him* about Peter Hennessy, and *that* episode in her life she emphatically wanted to keep to herself.

'Hi, there,' said Fiona in her beautifully modulated upper-crust tones, looming over them. 'Don't fret, I'm not going to play gooseberry. Just taking a breather from this marathon darts match I seem to have become involved in. My team's winning, in case you're interested.'

'*Your* team?' said Penrose.

'Fiona's Fletchers, fletcher being the generic term for arrowsmith.'

'We did know that,' said Lavinia.

'Of course you did, natch. But I had to explain it to my chaps when they elected me captain.'

'I hope you're not drinking too much,' said Penrose.

Fiona was slightly flushed, but that could have been because the pub was hot. She wasn't drunk by any means, but she wasn't on orange juice, either.

'And risk a scene with Johnny Law, not to mention denting my beautiful Lagonda? No chance, guv. I'm on my second pint, 'onest Injun, and that's an end to it. But thank you for being concerned, Robert.'

Lavinia was intrigued by the familiarity. It wasn't unusual for sixth-formers to address the younger members of staff by their first names, and for the head girl it was practically *de rigueur*, but there was an intimacy here beyond the norm.

'Take it easy, anyway,' said Penrose.

'You bet.'

'Come on, Fiona, you're up,' shouted one of the locals.

'Up,' said Fiona. 'Such curious things they say. However, my public awaits. See you.'

The other players made way for her at the dartboard, adoring subjects sprinkling rose petals at the feet of their monarch. And indeed, thought Lavinia, she did rather resemble royalty visiting the workhouse. Designer trousers at over two hundred pounds. Top from Armani, one hundred and fifty. Gucci loafers – the genuine article, not clever fakes – another two-fifty. Bits and bobs on her wrist, fingers and around her neck – a couple of thousand minimum.

'She'll be OK,' Lavinia said. 'The unpalatable side of life never touches people like Fiona. If otherwise, all the earl or viscount or whatever her father is has to do is call the Chief Constable. Problem solved. Finish your drink, I'll do the next.'

'No, let me.'

'These are the nineteen nineties, Robert,' said Lavinia with mock severity. 'I think I can make the bar, pay for two pints, and return with them safely without being molested. But,' she added, imitating Fiona's dulcet timbre, 'thank you for being concerned . . . *Robert*.'

At the bar, waiting for the glasses to be filled, Lavinia suddenly felt wickedly curious about Fiona Acland's relationship, if any, with Robert. Fiona was only a few feet away, chatting to a young man with a beer belly who obviously worshipped her.

'Excuse me,' said Lavinia, tapping Fiona on the shoulder, 'may I have a word?'

Fiona turned.

'Have two, Lavinia, have six.'

'Far from you playing gooseberry, I hope I'm not treading on anyone's toes, being out with Robert Penrose, innocent though it is. Your toes, specifically.'

'I can't think what you mean.'

'Really,' bluffed Lavinia, 'give me credit for a little intelligence.'

Fiona hesitated. 'Did Robert tell you? He had no right, not that it matters now.'

'It wasn't Robert, though I can't tell you who it was.'

'Mrs Coggan, I'll wager.'

Lavinia made a mental note of that, but grunted noncommittally.

'Mrs Coggan, of course,' said Fiona, taking the grunt as confirmation. 'Anyway, it was all over ages ago, more than a year. It was only a casual fling, in any event. We didn't do it more than half a dozen times. Innocent or not, he's all yours, my dear, every inch.'

Well, well, thought Lavinia, making her way back to the table, well and absolutely *well*.

Back in the school grounds, although the light was fading now, Mrs Bartlet had the junior netball team – thirteen- and fourteen-year-olds – still practising. Whistle in hand, for her darkness always came too soon.

'Come along, Jennifer, pay attention, *do!* Angela, I don't know how many times I have to repeat myself, but this is not basketball. You are not allowed to *run!* Phoebe, you're day-dreaming again.'

The netball court was open-sided, but male passers-by were not encouraged to dawdle by Mrs Bartlet. Few did anyway. In spite of Mrs Bartlet's privately held belief that all boys over the age of twelve were prurient in thought, word and deed, that they would all be much more healthy under a regimen of cold showers twice a day and five-mile runs before breakfast, only one or two thought the sight of pubescent girls heaving a ball at one another erotic. From the lofty heights, for the male sixth-formers at St Clare's, of being seventeen and eighteen, youngsters of thirteen and fourteen were invariably sweaty, red-kneed and runny-nosed.

There were exceptions, of course. Phoebe, for one. And Jennifer Langley, another newcomer teeny, a delightful redhead with exquisite freckles and breasts that threatened to burst out of whatever was constraining them, on court or off.

However, there were no boys around this evening. There were, though, a handful of sixth-form girls, among them Paula van der Groot and Sally-Ann Peters, standing alone.

'God,' said Sappho, 'just looking at them makes me feel as horny as hell.'

'Anyone in particular?' asked Paula.

'Phoebe, of course, naturally. And I must say you're being particularly mean, keeping her all to yourself.'

'She's young, Saff. I've only had her myself a couple of times. It's early days yet. Let's not bring her along too fast or we'll frighten her off.'

'Well, OK – but let's not take for ever, either. Have you mentioned anything to her about Jennifer yet? And if I find you're screwing her too but keeping quiet about it, I'll throttle you.'

Paula laughed.

'No, I'm not screwing Jennifer, much though I'd like to. Both at the same time, for that matter. And I've only *casually* mentioned to Phoebe that she might care to invite Jennifer along to one of our little sessions. She didn't respond positively. A touch of jealousy there, I think. Phoebe prefers to believe that I picked her out specially, which is true enough, and that I'm a one-woman woman. In any case, my intuition tells me that Jennifer's going to be hard work. I'll start with the friendly approach, take it from there. God, will you look at those tits. What I wouldn't give to have those rubbing up against me.'

'And Phoebe?' queried Sappho.

'Obviously I don't want the green-eyed monster rearing its ugly head, because right after that there'll be tears. A day later I'll be standing in front of Mrs Gordon, and the day after that I'll be on my way home. I don't want to lose Phoebe, anyway . . .'

'*We* don't want to lose Phoebe . . .'

'OK, *we* don't. She's got to keep me warm and satisfied throughout the winter. I might try Jennifer with a joint if I can get her by herself.'

'And talking of joints,' said Sappho.

Paula sighed.

'I guess it's the only kick we're going to get tonight.'

In their study, Paula said, 'Stick a chair under the door handle, just in case. I'll do the windows.'

Both girls kicked off their leggings and tops, and stripped to their underwear.

Paula's stash was hidden, wrapped in greaseproof paper, at the bottom of a cornflakes packet. She reckoned she had enough to keep them going, plus a reserve for any partying that might take place, until half-term, when she could stock up with her London supplier.

They shared a thick joint of Moroccan leaf, their conversation concerning Phoebe and Jennifer growing more lustful the more the hash took hold. After half an hour they were both as high as kites. Sappho put a hand on Paula's bare thigh.

'Oh, come on, Saff,' protested Paula.

They had been lovers once, but not for close on a year, both of them now preferring younger girls.

'Pretend I'm Kate McNamara,' said Sappho, eyes bright.

'Christ, yes,' said Paula, 'I've been forgetting about her since that first evening.'

'So, make it a fantasy. I'm Kate.'

She stroked Paula's thigh, causing the South African to give a little whimper.

'There is a difference, you know, between you and Kate.'

'I know, I'm large and she isn't.' Sappho worked her fingers under Paula's briefs, feeling warmth and dampness there. 'There's also another difference. I know what I'm doing and she wouldn't. Please. I haven't had a taste since we came back, and the thought of Jennifer Langley's driving me mad.'

'I get it. You're Kate, I'm Jennifer.'

'You can be anyone you like. Please, Paula. You won't have to do a thing. Just lie on your bed.'

'They'll be doing rounds soon.'

'They won't dare come in here. Anyhow, who gives a fuck? Come on, Paula. You're ready. I can feel you're ready. Keep the joint. You can smoke it while I go down on you.'

Paula clenched her thighs around Sappho's hand. *Yes, yes.*

She unclasped her bra.

Sappho caressed her breasts, squeezing them lovingly, running a forefinger across each nipple until both were hard.

'Remember how I used to hump you from behind with the thing strapped to me?' she said. 'How I used to hold your tits as you were coming, crush them until you screamed? I could do that now.'

'No, no,' pleaded Paula. 'You said you'd go down on me. You *promised*.'

She tried to slip out of her knickers. Sappho stopped her.

'Let me,' she murmured. 'Lie down and let me take them off. You used to love that, remember?'

'Yes, yes! Do it, do it!'

Wide-eyed with desire Paula scrambled to her bed and spreadeagled herself on it, dragging heavily on the joint. Sappho tore the knickers from Paula's body and hurled them to the floor. Astride Paula, her own legs straddling the supine girl's, she teased Paula's vulva with her fingers.

'For God's sake fuck me!' moaned Paula. 'Do something!'

'Patience, my darling, patience. Raise yourself.'

Paula whimpered.

'My, my,' said Sappho with honeyed tones, 'you are in a hurry. Jesus, I'd kill for a body like yours. Do you want me to tie your hands to the rail?'

'No, damn you, you bitch. Just let me come, make me come.'

'You're almost there, darling. There, feel?'

'I'll kill you, you cow.'

'Or I'll kill you, as you're coming.'

'Anything, anything.'

'You always did like the words, didn't you? Now, just lie there, leave everything to me. You don't have to do a thing.'

Paula tossed the joint away, not caring where it landed, as she felt Sappho's tongue lick the inside of her thighs before probing for the heat. With both hands now free, she gripped the back of Sappho's neck, pulling her deeper.

Oh, Lord, Lord, she thought frenziedly, thrusting her wide-open vulva at Sappho's mouth and seeing, in her mind's eye, Kate McNamara's head down there, feeling Kate's tongue driving her out of her mind. Then it was Jennifer Langley's.

She felt herself coming, slowly, deliciously, on a roll with nothing to stop it now, and she put one hand in her mouth to reduce her screams of pleasure. Then she was there, and jerking her hips faster and faster, pushing her vagina upwards towards Sappho's rapidly flicking eager tongue.

And as the juices poured out of her into Sappho's waiting mouth, and she threw her head from side to side, in ecstasy, not caring now who heard her, moaning, 'Fuck, fuck, fuck,' she vowed to have both Jennifer and Kate before the term was over.

Carson walked Kate back to Churchill House. Other girls were heading towards the main doors, anxious to book in before lock-up. A few looked at the pair curiously, but there was nothing in their demeanour to suggest anything other than an evening stroll.

Nor was there anything. Carson had made Kate laugh a few times with jokes and anecdotes, but he hadn't even held her hand.

Beyond the lights which illuminated the entrance

to the House was the relative darkness of some hydrangea bushes, still in full flower. Without appearing to, Carson manoeuvred Kate in that direction. Kate allowed him, though she was perfectly aware of what he was doing.

'Well, that was very pleasant,' said Carson, 'thanks.'

'Thank *you*. I enjoyed it.'

'Then perhaps we can do it again, or more. The cinema I offered you last time, or a meal.'

'Perhaps.'

'Is that a yes?'

'It's a probable yes.'

Kate held out her hand, to shake Carson's.

'No, this is silly,' she said, and leaned forward to peck him on the cheek.

He misread the signals and sought her lips, which she permitted to happen until he was seeking her tongue with his. A moment afterwards his right hand was clutching her left breast.

She pushed him away, not angrily.

'Don't spoil it, Richard.'

He accepted her rejection.

'No, you're right. I don't want this to be just another game.'

6

Open Day

Whereas Speech Day was held in the summer, towards the close of Trinity Term and, naturally, all parents were invited to the Christmas play, a series of Open Days were held throughout the academic year. This was less due to Mrs Gordon and the school governors actually wanting to meet mothers and fathers and guardians, thus disrupting the flow of school discipline, than canny business acumen. With boarding fees at St Clare's now £3,000 per term, it was considered only prudent that the people who signed the cheques receive an opportunity to meet their little darlings' mentors. After all, Mrs Gordon reasoned, long before the end of Michaelmas Term the bills for Hilary Term (money up front, please, or find a state school) would be sent out – to arrive before Christmas, before parents had a chance to book that Bahamian winter cruise or trade in the Rover for something more sporty.

Michaelmas Open Day, therefore, was held during the first week of October, and all staff were carefully briefed to be on their best behaviour. Smile, please. Circulate. Praise the intellectual ability of Emma,

Charlotte and Sara. Anyone caught overdoing the sherry would be offered a blindfold and a last cigarette. It was only for a couple of hours, after all, and doubtless the parents were as anxious to get away as the staff were to have them leave.

Classics scholar or not, Mrs Gordon knew the price of a pound of fish. And, like a barker outside a fairground booth, she knew she was not doing her job if the crowd drifted by to another show.

Roll up, roll up! St Clare's will fit your daughters, and sons, for the world outside.

Also, since St Clare's was a corporation in perpetuity, it was hoped that, when the present parents became grandparents and the pupils mothers and fathers themselves, the next generation would wend its way towards the school's portals and not Roedean or Cheltenham. And if anyone wanted their name in lights via founding a new science block or mainframe computer, why, that would be most acceptable.

For two hours it was hard sell.

'God, I hate these bloody things,' Jocasta Petrillo confided in Kate, examining her reflection in front of the dormitory cheval glass, an hour before the main event. Although on a normal day sixth-formers were not required to wear uniform, and could attire themselves more or less how they pleased providing they were neat and tidy, for Open Days jeans were banned and so were dresses or skirts that were deemed 'unseemly', which meant anything shorter than knee-level. Makeup was to be minimized and hair under control, ribboned if necessary. For two hours the girls resembled extras in an early Judy Garland movie. *Hey, kids, let's put on a show and save the school!* 'I wish Mrs Gordon would simply ask my father to write her a cheque for a new library or hockey pavilion or whatever she's after this year, and leave it at that. He'd probably be happy to rather than suffer all those glasses of sherry. He's strictly a red-wine man, Italian, of course. "Eh, signora, ousa abouta glassa vino, notta this Spanish shitta?"'

Kate giggled.

'He doesn't really talk like that, does he?'

'No. He's actually quite sophisticated – for a Wop.'

'Jocasta!' scolded Amanda, trying hard to damp down a wayward strand of hair. She'd washed it earlier and, foolishly, allowed it to dry by itself instead of using a hairdrier. Now her damned mop wouldn't behave. 'That's racist.'

'It's OK me saying it. I'm a half Wop, a kind of Woppetta. Are your parents coming?' Jocasta asked Kate.

'Not sure.'

They had been invited, formally with a 'stiffy' by Mrs Gordon and the governors, but she hadn't spoken to either of them for a week. She expected they would put in an appearance. She hoped so, anyway. She rather wanted them to meet Richard, to show them she was settling down if for no other reason.

Her relationship with Carson was progressing steadily. They had been out together half a dozen times since that first evening walk after the tennis match: for meals, going Dutch, to the cinema, once on the river, and once to the village pub, where Richard had had beer because he was old enough to buy and she had stuck to mineral water.

Physical contact had advanced, too. Open-mouth kissing was now par for the course, and he'd had her bra off the last two times, which she'd found exciting if not earth-shattering. (How could it be, she asked herself? She'd been the route, and more.) But so far and no further. His hand was not allowed to wander under her dress, not even beyond her knee. She knew her own weaknesses. Let him get that far and she wouldn't be able to stop him going further. Before long he would be screwing her blind and, as she'd promised herself from the start, she was not going to be termed a slag.

Maybe they'd get laid when she knew him better. The sexual heat certainly hadn't gone away. For now, though, what she had was enough, even if, when she'd felt his erection pressing against her, and he'd been trying to guide her hand towards it, she'd been tempted to dig out his cock and show him what it was all about. He was reputedly experienced, Richard – those were the rumours she'd heard – but she knew his experience didn't come within a mile of hers.

It would be self-defeating, anyway, to masturbate him. That too, of course, would earn her a slag's label, but there was more to it than that. With his cock in her hand, it wouldn't be long before it was in the rest of her.

She'd settle, for now, for things as they were, and obtain sexual relief by her own methods, in private.

No doubt Richard was doing the same thing. Such a waste, but there it was. She'd also keep well away from Dutch Paula, who was making it quite clear she hadn't given up, and Sappho Peters.

'What about your mother?' Kate asked Jocasta.

'There,' scowled Jocasta, 'I knew someone would have to make a bad morning worse.'

'Did I say something?'

'Jocasta's mother,' piped up Amanda, 'alights from her Lamborghini . . .'

'It could be the Rolls,' interrupted Jocasta.

' . . .with a display of leg that would send the Pope disavowing his vows, if that's English, and chasing the nearest nun. Or priest. Or goat, for that matter.'

'Do you mind,' said Jocasta, though clearly she was kidding, 'but this is the woman from whose loins I sprang.'

'I doubt that,' said Amanda, releasing, for a moment, the recalcitrant strand of hair, which immediately sprang up like a question mark. 'I very much doubt that. Your mother wouldn't do anything as vulgar as lie there with her legs wide apart while giving birth. You were doubtless launched by simple splitting, like amoebae or whatever they are.'

'True,' grinned Jocasta. 'If Mama had known what having a child was like before becoming pregnant, she'd have had the vapours. *Sweating* is not in my mother's vocabulary. Nor are stirrups unless around a champion hunter.'

'She sounds very formidable, if you don't mind me saying so,' said Kate.

'I don't mind. She *is* formidable. Or as we say back home, "*Donne, preti, e polli non son mai satolli.*" Women, priests and chickens are never satisfied. Nevertheless, just because she's even more beautiful than Sophia Loren and is determined to have every man in the room, *any room*, lusting after her within seconds, doesn't make her any less my Mama. In spite of her looks, I doubt she's even had a mild affair since she married my father. First, Papa would kill her and leave her without a penny, not necessarily in that order. Second, an affair would mean her leaving some young stud's room without a change of underwear. And that, for Mama, is out.'

Julia came rushing in, fresh from the showers and a rehearsal of *MND*, in which, after a second audition and a little soul-searching by Robert Penrose, she had landed the part of Helena.

In her haste she missed her footing, skidded and landed on her backside. Books, clothes and towel went flying.

Quick as a flash, Amanda carolled, 'Lo, fair Thespis, fresh from drama class, looks not where she's going, and falleth on her arse.'

'Cow,' said Julia, scrambling up unhurt. 'How long have I got?'

'Fifteen minutes.'

'Shit, can somebody dry my hair?'

'I'll do it,' said Amanda, fingering her own wayward locks, 'though you might wish you'd waited for Sweeney Todd.'

Dormitories had to be clear by noon on Open Days,

that was Mrs Gordon's rule. Beds made, lockers tidy, bits and bobs squared away. Beginning at five to twelve, House prefects were on the prowl to make sure everything was shipshape. Lunch was at twelve-fifteen, and the parents would start arriving from one o'clock.

There was no set pattern to the proceedings thereafter, no formal speeches as happened on Speech Day. Parents parked where they could, in roped-off areas of the school grounds for the early arrivals or in the avenue outside for latecomers. Then they made their way on foot to the Houses which were home to their offspring, where they were greeted by their children.

Those parents who wanted to were shown over dormitories, studies and classrooms and, in the case of first-year teenies, work in progress.

Heads of House remained in situ, while Mrs Gordon, her duputy and her curriculum teachers circulated, moving from House to House, making themselves available to answer questions, resolve problems. Each term's questions and problems were invariably identical to those of the term before. And the term before that, back to the beginning of recorded time.

How is so-and-so settling in?

How is my daughter's maths coming along?

Do you think so-and-so stands a chance of a scholarship to Cambridge?

She told me before she came to St Clare's that she was now a confirmed vegetarian, but I do hope you've driven that nonsense from her head.

She seems to get along well with Mrs So-and-so.

My daughter wrote to say she was having trouble grasping the fundamentals of German. All those compounds, I expect.

Et cetera.

These posers Mrs Gordon and her staff had no trouble fielding, thanks to long experience. For that matter, there was only one sentence all of them dreaded hearing!

Madam, my daughter has just informed me she's pregnant. What do you intend to do about it?

This had only happened twice in the past five years, and only half a dozen times in Mrs Gordon's entire career. She had accepted each pronouncement philosophically. After all, when one was dealing with hundreds of girls – thousands over the years – many of them very attractive, it was inevitable a handful would become pregnant. Privately – for Mrs Gordon was as human as she was academic – she had a few stock answers, which she always kept to herself.

What can we do? Well, I suppose we can supply a bottle of gin, a hot bath, and a long knitting needle in the hands of the school doctor.

What can we do? I'm sure the cooks can cater for a wedding.

What can we do? Tell Jane (or Jo or Jenny or Jackie) that, in future, her knickers should remain firmly on.

In reality, what she usually said was something like, 'This is as much a shock to me as it must be to you. I always viewed Jane (or Jo or Jenny or Jackie) as a most sensible young lady.'

After an hour or so parents were gently ushered in

the direction of the relevant Head of House's study, where drinks were served for those who wanted them. Jocasta's mother didn't, preferring instead to stroll around the grounds with her daughter, in spite of the fact that summer was now over and the weather turning cold. Heads turned to follow her incredible figure and dancer's legs. For once she seemed totally unaware of the stir she was creating.

'Stripe me,' said Ben Fisher from the steps of Napier House, 'now that is some woman.'

Fisher's parents had been unable to make it, along with the parents of many other pupils, male and female, who either lived too far away or abroad, were otherwise engaged in business activities, or who just couldn't be bothered, reasoning that paying close on £10,000 per annum to have their children educated ended their responsibilities.

None of the boys around Fisher disagreed with his assessment of Mrs Petrillo's desirability, not even Henry Morton.

See, he said to himself, I can look at her and find her beautiful. I can't be gay, I *can't*.

Henry was another Open Day orphan, though in his case it was his own choice. He had telephoned his mother two days after the invitations were sent out, saying it wasn't essential for her to make the trip.

'Lots of the chaps' parents aren't coming, half a dozen at least. We're planning a day out,' he lied.

'Anywhere interesting?'

'We'll follow our noses.'

'I do have rather a lot of work on . . .'

She ran a fashion house with a partner, had done for over a dozen years since his father died. Very successful she was too.

'I'm sure you do.'

'And it is only for a couple of hours.'

'Precisely.'

'But you'll be home for half-term?'

'Almost certainly.'

'Let me know the exact date and I'll put it in my diary.'

She already knew the exact date. It went out with various other documents during the long vacation. But, thought Henry, she'd probably forgotten. Still, she led a hectic life: Paris, Rome, Milan, New York. If she didn't, there wouldn't be any money for school fees. It wasn't her fault she'd lost her husband when she was a comparatively young woman, though it sometimes puzzled him that she'd never married again. Not disappointed him – he knew he would have found it very awkward to accept that she was sharing another man's bed – but perplexed him. She was an attractive woman only just on the downside of forty.

He'd put it to her once, not long after the au pair incident.

'Henry, Henry, I loved your father, and one love in a lifetime is as much as anyone gets. And now I love you.'

He supposed she did, though how anyone could love the face and body he saw in the mirror each morning beat him. He expected she had affairs, which depressed him. He would doubtless never meet the men she went to bed with, and he was sensitive enough to know that, when in bed with someone, any love she had to give would not be directed at her only son.

Ah well.

'What do you think, Henry?' someone asked. 'I'll bet even you could get it up with Jocasta's mum.'

'Lay off him,' said Fisher, quietly but with menace.

The same questioner was about to riposte, 'What, are you turning queer too, Ben?' but the look on Fisher's face made him think again.

'OK, OK. No offence, Henry.'

'None taken.'

Jocasta, aware of a certain tension in her mother, asked, 'Is everything all right between you and Papa?'

'Of course,' answered Mrs Petrillo. 'I told you, he's busy with his new restaurant.'

'No, it's not that,' said Jocasta. 'I understand that. It's just that you seem a little *distrait*.'

Hardly the word for it, thought Jocasta's mother. Bloody livid would be a better description, and murder the outcome if she got her fingers around the throat of the blonde bimbo Claudio Petrillo was spending all his spare time with.

He'd denied it, of course.

'Don't be ridiculous. She has to come with me when I travel.'

'*Come* being the appropriate word.'

'I don't like dirty talk.'

'You like it well enough when we're fucking, not that we do much of that any longer.'

123

'If you continue to be foul-mouthed, I refuse to listen.'

Typical Italian, she thought. Great lovers when it suited them, but puritanical mother's boys underneath it all.

If he was straying – and she had no real proof yet – she partly blamed herself. He'd wanted battalions of children, as they all did – *Keep 'em pregnant, barefoot and in the kitchen* – but she'd been adamant that there would be no more after Jocasta's younger brother was born. Damned if she'd be a brood mare and ruin her figure just to please Holy Mother Church.

They'd fought about it, of course, and he was livid when he discovered she had been on the contraceptive pill for almost a year before he found out. But she thought he'd accepted it and was proud of the way she looked.

Evidently not.

And if there was a blonde whore on the scene now, how many more had there been that she didn't know about? What irked her – what really irritated – was the number of propositions over the years she herself had turned down, the number of groping hands she'd pushed away. Not one affair, not even one, in almost eighteen years.

You must get lonely, what with the children at school and Claudio away all the time.

I've got this pleasant little cottage in the Cotswolds.

Come on, you know you want it.

My wife and I don't get along any more.

Huh!

And what depressed her unutterably was that his mistress was about twenty-five, if that, and she was forty. She might look ten years younger, but there was no escaping the calendar. When her husband's whore was her age, she would be moving inexorably towards sixty.

She had come down to see Jocasta with the intention of telling her daughter her suspicions, talking it over woman to woman, because there was no doubt they were very close, more like siblings. Now, she realized that was foolish. It was one thing to exchange makeup secrets with one's daughter, accompany her to their doctor when she, too, wanted to go on the Pill, consult over fashion and underwear – it was another to confide that, in her view, Papa was seeing another woman.

No, let sleeping dogs lie.

She could be wrong. Even if she wasn't, it could all be over by Christmas.

But, if she *wasn't* wrong and it *wasn't* over by Christmas, Claudio Petrillo had better watch out. Two could play at that game.

'Who was the teacher you introduced me to earlier, the pretty blonde woman?'

'Miss Lee? Lavinia? She takes us for Lower Sixth German and French.'

Like Kate, Amanda and Julia, Jocasta was studying English, French and German at Advanced level. Mrs Gordon had tried to persuade her to sit Italian also, but Jocasta had declined, doubting she would be able to handle all the work. In any case, she spoke fluent Italian.

'You've met her before,' added Jocasta.

'Yes, I know. Her name escaped me, that's all.'

For Freudian reasons, no doubt, thought Jocasta's mother. Give or take a little in height and years, Miss Lee resembled Claudio's bimbo.

Perhaps it was true, after all, that blondes had more fun. Perhaps she should dye her own tresses that colour.

She smiled at the thought. No, even though she was English as far back as she could trace, her looks were Latin, which was what had attracted Signor Petrillo to her in the first place. When men – it was usually men – compared her looks favourably to those of Claudia Cardinale, she was realistic enough to accept that they were not simply trying to flatter her into bed. She rejected the comparison with Sophia Loren, but only just. At five feet nine, she was taller than the actress by an inch.

'Something amusing you?' asked Jocasta.

'Not exactly. Don't grow up too quickly, will you, darling? These years are the good years, whether you know it or not. There's no substitute for youth.'

'Well, if it's youth you're looking for, I can introduce you to several.'

'I'll bear that in mind.'

Like Claudio Petrillo, Kate McNamara's father had not been able to make the Open Day due to business pressures, and only her mother had turned up, wearing an outrageous wide-brimmed hat.

'God, Mummy, this is St Clare's, not Ascot!'

Mrs McNamara had met Richard Carson briefly, before Carson had had to dash off to greet his own parents, and pronounced him to be 'a very nice young man'.

'Though I trust he behaves himself with you.'

'Mummy!'

'It's a mother's perfectly natural reaction, dear, especially . . .'

Kate completed the sentence for her.

'Especially after what happened in America. I thought we agreed to forget all that, start afresh.'

'We did and we are.'

'It doesn't sound like it.'

'Just my clumsy way of expressing myself, I expect. Still, you can't help your father and I being concerned.'

'There's nothing to be concerned about.'

Providing, thought Kate, you exclude my violent orgasm after witnessing a bout of lesbian love-making, an overwhelming desire to get laid, and the fact that I've been offered a smoke of good hash by the school's most aggressive dyke if I allow her into my pants.

Providing you exclude all that.

'Nothing to be concerned about at all,' she repeated, linking arms with her mother. 'What happened in the States won't happen again.'

Nor would it, she vowed. Nor would anyone at St Clare's ever learn about it – she hoped. At least they wouldn't from her lips.

'Of course, there is a condition,' she added slyly.

'What is it?' asked her mother, looking worried.

'For God's sake take off that damned hat!'

With the official two hours of Open Day at an end fifteen minutes since, but with few of the parents showing much inclination to leave, Lavinia Lee found herself boxed into one corner of Mrs Clinton's study. Fortunately, smoking was permitted here on Open Days and, even more fortuitously, the drinks table was within reach. Even so, and even with the windows open, a cirrostratus layer of blue-grey tobacco smoke hung from the ceiling, and the crush, with an overspill into the corridor, was comparable to rush hour on the Piccadilly Line.

Near the door, Robert Penrose, talking to Julia Hastings and her parents, caught her eye, and raised an empty glass. Lavinia shrugged her shoulders – no way through this mob – and held up a near-full glass, miming, 'Tough luck.' He mouthed something that could have been 'Bitch' but which was probably, knowing Penrose, 'Bother'.

Felicity Coggan had also set up camp by the drinks table and was busily making inroads with Mrs Clinton's whisky decanter, Mrs Clinton being one of the few Heads of House to offer a variety of stimulants and not just sherry, this being, no doubt, why Churchill House was proving so popular with the staff. Of Mrs Clinton herself there was no sign, neither tail nor whisker.

Probably totting up the damage on her credit cards, thought Lavinia.

Chips Chippendale, he with the penchant for the plump rumps of pubescent girls, was also close by, surreptitiously lifting the corners of sandwiches to find something he liked.

Felicity was holding a conversation with three or four parents, but plainly her brain was in neutral. Lavinia, too, had got this trick down to a fine art during her previous six terms. It wasn't necessary to actually *listen* to anything mothers and fathers had to say about their offspring, or any queries they had about their children's progress. With practice, it was possible to offer stock answers to what were, in any event, stock questions while simultaneously thinking about something completely different: a new dress, a skiing trip in January, the First Law of Thermodynamics, whatever that was.

Yes, she's coming along splendidly.

No, I wouldn't think she'll have any trouble at all with examinations.

I agree her class position at the end of last term left something to be desired, but I've had a word with her about that and I'm sure we'll see an improvement.

Flatter them, flannel them, and pray to God they'd soon be on their way. Though not before they were convinced that the £10,000 a year they spent on fees and extras was a solid investment.

The motto of St Clare's was a quotation from Cicero: *Interest omnium recte facere* – 'It is for the good of all to do right.' Lavinia could think of a more appropriate one, of Ovid's: *Auro conciliatur amor* – 'Even love yields to gold.'

She became aware that Mr and Mrs McDonald, Amanda's parents, were about to leave. Indeed, for no apparent reason, there was suddenly a general exodus towards the door.

Amanda's parents – of their daughter there was no sign, though she'd been in the vicinity just seconds ago – were grown-up facsimiles of Amanda: round and jolly, and with a slight trace of an Edinburgh accent though they had lived in the Home Counties, as far as Lavinia could recall, for many years. They owned two highly successful hotels, again as far as Lavinia could remember. Well, it was virtually impossible to keep up with everyone's occupation.

'Thank you very much for your time, Miss Lee,' said Mr McDonald, holding out his hand, which Lavinia shook. 'You've set our minds at rest.'

Really, thought Lavinia, now what the devil did I say?

'I'm glad to hear it,' said Lavinia. 'As long as Amanda continues to put in the hard work, she should have no trouble with her A levels when the time comes.'

Only a half lie, thought Lavinia, remembering words spoken by a mistress to a fellow pupil during her own schooldays, a student who'd been slacking throughout the academic year and who was then in a state of panic with examinations looming: 'Well, young lady, if you work very hard from now until the exam, forswear junketing and weekends off, keep your shoulder to the wheel and your nose to the grindstone – you'll just fail.'

Everyone had hooted with laughter at the time, but in many respects the homily applied to Amanda

McDonald. She would have to pull out all the stops to obtain grades good enough for university entrance. Still, no point in worrying the McDonalds with that at this stage, not with five terms yet to go before Advanced levels.

Or, as Mrs Gordon would doubtless reason, £15,000.

'We'll rely on you to keep her at it,' said Mrs McDonald, who, of the two, was slightly less round and jolly than her husband, and who had eyes like flint. An ideal hotelier. Surface bonhomie and a mind like a steel trap beneath it all, with an ability to spot a guest likely to sneak out with the towels on first meeting.

'I'll do my best,' said Lavinia, which she sincerely meant. 'I think I see Amanda beckoning you.'

Amanda was now with Julia's group surrounding Robert Penrose by the door, though whether Amanda was trying to hustle her parents back to their car or across to say goodbye to Penrose, Lavinia had no way of knowing.

'I'll drive,' said Mrs McDonald, glaring pointedly at her husband's now-empty glass.

'Perhaps that would be as well,' said Mr McDonald.

Felicity Coggan got rid of her group, with much handshaking, just as the McDonalds were leaving and turned to Lavinia and the drinks table, with a swift glance over her shoulder to see if there was any sign of Mrs Clinton. There wasn't.

She helped herself to another whisky, her third to Lavinia's knowledge, though she was a woman who could take her drink.

'No point in letting it go to waste,' she said, 'not if what I hear about salary reviews are more than the idle chatter of quidnuncs.'

Pay hikes were usually discussed in January, to take effect from the following Michaelmas Term.

'Hey, Chips,' added Felicity, 'leave some of the smoked salmon for the rest of us.'

'What did you hear?' asked Lavinia.

'That there'll be precious little in the pot, what with the recession making it impossible to increase fees without further student withdrawals.'

Ten girls had failed to return after the summer vacation, and in every case bar one, their absence was due to parents tightening their belts. Ten girls equalled £90,000 as a baseline figure and another 10,000 in extras.

'Damn,' said Lavinia. 'I hope you're wrong.'

'So do I, my dear, so do I. If it goes on like this I shall have to find myself a rich lover among the parents.' She gave Lavinia a broad wink. 'Or among their sons, for that matter.'

Lavinia remembered the unsubstantiated rumours about Felicity's divorce involving her adultery with a much younger man, and was inclined to give them credence. She was certainly attractive enough in her figure-hugging suits to entice an inexperienced youth into an affair, though she'd probably eat the young man alive, literally and figuratively.

'Plenty of those around,' said Lavinia non-committally, 'if you like that sort of thing.'

'Some of us do, some of us don't. Now, Chips,

what did I tell you about the smoked salmon? Any more of that and I'll tell Mrs Bartlet that your interest in the junior girls' hockey practices has less to do with *mens sana in corpore sano* and is more connected with frottage.'

Lavinia had to look up the definition of frottage – an abnormal desire for contact between the clothed bodies of oneself and another – when she got back to her study, but it was plain Chips understood the meaning. His cheeks turned bright red.

Lavinia left them to it and made her way across to where Penrose had finally bid farewell to Julia's parents and Amanda's. Julia, becoming more 'stagey' with every day that passed, now that she had landed the part of Helena, was saying to her mother, in a loud voice that everyone, including Penrose, was meant to hear, 'Isn't he just dreamy, Mr Penrose? You can't begin to understand how lucky I am to be working with him.'

Lavinia handed her half-full tumbler to Penrose. Whisky. Neat.

'Here, you look as if you need this more than I do.'

Penrose accepted the glass gratefully and swallowed the contents in a single gulp.

'My God,' he said, 'why do we do it? You can't believe what the last fifteen minutes have been like. Julia did nothing but talk about the play and our – note *our* – interpretation of the way she'll portray Helena. Her parents, naturally, believe she's found a vocation. Forget English, French and German. RADA even came up, and I shall have to swiftly disabuse her of that idea. God save us from stage-struck kids. I'm starting to think I made a mistake in listening to you about casting her. Talk about unlocking Pandora's box. I've let loose a monster.'

'Look on the bright side,' grinned Lavinia. 'She thinks you're dreamy.'

Penrose was not amused.

'She's not meant to think I'm dreamy. Giving her the part of Helena was designed to get rid of all that nonsense.'

'Not exactly, if you cast your mind back. It was a damage limitation exercise: better to have an infatuated teenager in the play than a resentful one, though still enamoured, on the sidelines. Anyway, don't tell me you're not the teeniest bit flattered.'

'I'm not, and that's an end to it.'

'Too young for you?'

'Don't even think it, not even as a joke.'

I wasn't joking, thought Lavinia. Fiona Acland couldn't have been much older than Julia when she was sharing Penrose's bed.

'At least she's not turning up to rehearsals dressed like a vamp,' said Lavinia. 'And there's safety in numbers. As you said yourself when you persuaded me to assist you, there are a lot of characters in the play.'

'There's that, I suppose, but I'll wager you an even tenner that, long before dress rehearsal, Julia will be approaching me for private coaching, complaining she's having trouble with Helena's motivation, or whatever new theatrical buzz word she's picked up by then. Do you think anyone would notice if I snitched another drink out of Mrs Clinton's decanter?'

'Only Felicity and Chips and half a dozen others, including Sybil Heilbron over there, looking transfixed. I've never actually subscribed to the theory of the eternal wandering Jew, but I do expect them to move occasionally and not look as if they're under heavy sedation. Whatever happened to all those jolly people one used to see in *Fiddler on the Roof*?'

Penrose raised his eyebrows.

'Racist comments, you?'

'Mildly unkind, I acknowledge, but I have to work with her, you don't.'

Outside, Julia and Amanda waved their parents off. Mr and Mrs McDonald appeared to be having a minor altercation, though it was pretty much one-sided with Mrs McDonald as the monologist. Daddy having one more drink than he should have, no doubt, thought Amanda, though, for her mother, a virtual teetotaller, one was one too many.

The rest of the afternoon was a free one, and Amanda asked Julia if she had any plans.

'I want to go over my opening scenes, try to get my lines word perfect,' said Julia, flicking back her hair with one hand. 'Mr Penrose doesn't expect us to know them for weeks yet, but I'd like to surprise him.'

'Is this how it's going to be until the end of term,' asked Amanda, pulling a face, 'every spare moment taken up with that wretched play?'

'I expect so,' answered Julia nonchalantly. 'I don't want to ruin my big night by being unprepared.'

Lord preserve us, thought Amanda, allowing Julia to skip on ahead.

She saw Jocasta climbing into the passenger seat of her mother's Lamborghini, and Mrs Petrillo drive off with a racing start that scattered gravel. Tea somewhere in town, probably.

On the steps of Napier House Kate McNamara was laughing and chatting with Richard Carson and one or two other boys. After a moment Kate and Carson went off together. Oh well, good luck to them.

At a loss, Amanda strolled over to the sixth-form commonroom, which was unoccupied. Taking advantage of their free afternoon and what was likely to be, now that autumn was here, one of the last fine days of the year, most people seemed to have decided to leave the school grounds.

She shook the coffee percolator, but it was empty and would remain so until someone from the kitchens topped it up for the evening.

After a while, she walked back to Churchill House and went up to her dormitory. No-one there, either. Even Julia had evidently decided to study her lines elsewhere.

She lay on her bed and closed her eyes. She was surprised, a few seconds later, to find tears in them.

7

We Have Heard the Chimes at Midnight, Master Shallow

Heavy rain and high winds affected the whole county the second Saturday in October, and from the windows of the now centrally heated dormitories and studies pupils and staff of St Clare's watched while leaves were ripped off trees and umbrellas turned inside out. In two weeks the clocks would go back, signalling the official end to the summer. Time now to dig out all those winter clothes: raincoats, Barbours, anoraks, thick sweaters. Time now to get accustomed to classroom lights being switched on during the afternoon. Time now to experience all those primordial, atavistic fears of winter's onset. Time now to feel depressed without really understanding why.

Well, not quite.

It was Saturday, after all, hebdomadal feast of excesses. With games out of the question because of the weather, the afternoon could be used to deodorize for the evening. Off with the old, on with the new. School's out, kids.

For those in love, or about to be, the last hours of

daylight were used to plan the night. *What about this eye-liner, do you think it suits me? These Doc Martens have just about had it, but my parents will kill me if I ask them for any more money this close to half-term. Can I borrow your Levis, we're about the same size.*

For those merely 'in lust', similar preparations – and a few prayers to St Jude. *Please let me score tonight and I won't ask for another thing ever. Promise. There's this club where the townie girls go. Believe me, three double vodkas and you can't fail. Oh yeah? And then their fucking boyfriends, straight out of* Terminator, *beat the holy shit out of you.*

And a nervous joke or two.

'There's this new bar opened in town, I only just got to hear about it. You go in, order your first drink, and after that drinks are on the house. Not only that, they buy you dinner – free. And directly after that, cut my tongue out if I'm a liar, they take you in a back room and get you laid. Honest. My sister's been back three times.'

For those who were neither in love or lust, different preparations.

Well, I suggest the four of us go out together. Oh, Christ, you're not thinking of inviting her, *are you? She's OK, you'll see. We can't leave her by herself, in any case. Of course we can. She'd better get used to it, it's going to be the story of her adult life.*

Petty jealousies, the in-crowd protecting their kraal, circling the wagons; the outsiders for ever remaining beyond the pale.

'Trust me,' Dutch Paula said to Sappho Peters, 'I've

got it all figured out. Jennifer Langley won't know what hit her.'

'And Phoebe?'

'Fuck Phoebe.'

'Promises, promises.'

'Listen to me, you slag. Mary Donaldson and Jackie Thorpe are going up to London on the three o'clock train. They've got permission from Mrs Clinton to catch the midnight back, which means they won't be in House before one. Which also means their study will be unoccupied for ten hours.'

Mary and Jackie were not sinistrals but knew perfectly well that Paula and Sappho were. Their study was two along from Paula's, and they were not averse to sharing the occasional joint.

'Directly after tea, fiveish,' said Paula, 'I'll invite Phoebe up here to listen to some tapes. She'll understand what I mean by that, of course, but she'll complain – she's a right little complainer, our Phoebe – that there will be too many people around at that hour for us to get down to serious business. I'll agree. I'll then suggest, to make everything look a lot more innocent, that she brings along a friend.'

'Jennifer,' said Sappho.

'Jennifer. And tapes we shall listen to for a couple of hours.'

'Which brings us up to seven o'clock,' said Sappho, 'even later. Which also means they miss dinner.'

Paula shook her head in dismay.

'Christ, Saff, how many years have you been at St Clare's? How many people attend Saturday-night dinner? A handful. Just about everyone prefers to scoff cake and buns in their studies or dorms or in the TV rooms. By seven, too, this corridor will be deserted. Everyone will be out on the town.'

'Do we have cake and buns? The teenies don't like missing their fodder.'

Paula reached behind her and flung open the provisions cupboard door. Inside there were cakes and pies and fruit, tinned and fresh, in abundance.

'The teenies have to be tucked up in bed, in their dorms, by ten o'clock, Saturday or no Saturday,' said Sappho, playing devil's advocate.

'And you can't make it with Phoebe in two and a half, three hours?'

'I can,' said Sappho, eyes shining with lust, 'but a lot depends on the young lady herself. I take it I get Phoebe?'

'Jennifer's mine,' said Paula severely.

'OK, OK, point taken. But what happens if Phoebe gets miffed – at you because you're making eyes at Jennifer, at me because she prefers you?'

Paula smirked, and reached under her bed, producing three one-litre bottles of supermarket red wine.

'Secret weapon time. A few glasses of this, and maybe a pull on a joint, and we're off to the races. I keep Jennifer here, you take Phoebe along to Mary and Jackie's. If you don't get to fuck her, that's your problem. If I don't hack it with Jennifer, that's mine. Once we've made it – and we *will* make it – we swap them between us as the mood arises.'

Sappho appraised her study companion admiringly.

'You may weigh ninety pounds soaking wet, and I could break your neck if I put my mind to it, but I take my hat off to you.'

Paula grinned.

'It's called forward thinking, Saff. You'll learn all about that at Oxbridge – if you get that far.'

In her rooms, Lavinia Lee concluded that tonight was the night as far as Robert Penrose was concerned. She was midway between periods, and that always made her as horny as hell. Doubly so, now, as she'd been without sex since the first day of term.

Not entirely without some prompting, Penrose had invited her out to dinner in town.

'If you have no other plans.'

'I haven't. I accept.'

His nervousness, or perhaps she should say diffidence, didn't entirely surprise her. Since the publication of Greer's *The Female Eunuch*, way back when Lavinia was only a toddler, men had become wary of professional women, particularly good-looking ones with Oxford Firsts. Which was how it should be, in Greer's book and Book, but it could become very tiresome, having to make the running, and rarely exciting after the first thrill of being the chaser rather than the chased wore off.

Men, in Lavinia's experience, either fell into the category of the late and slowly becoming unlamented Peter Hennessy, who didn't give a tinker's cuss for Greer or Simone de Beauvoir or Betty Friedan; or the hairy machos, 'hearties' as they were known at Oxford, who believed the zenith of sophistication was to drink twelve pints of lager and grab the nearest woman's tits. A third category was the so-called 'new man', regularly seen in television adverts nowadays, who looked after the house while his wife/girlfriend, invariably a doctor, tended the sick. This type would get up in the middle of the night to feed or change the baby, be au fait with the washing machine and tumble drier, and generally need to shave about once a fortnight.

They kept their balls somewhere close to their cookbooks, and Lavinia had no time for them.

The fourth category was that of Penrose, who would make sure it was *de rigueur* to hold the door open for a lady before he did so, think twice before offering his seat in a train, and agonize over whether it was politically correct to flash his American Express card and pay for the whole meal.

This category needed coaxing, but Penrose must have something to have lured Fiona Acland under the duvet.

Lavinia dressed carefully, black from head to foot to set off her blond locks. Black underwear with just a touch of lace, black slip that ended mid-thigh, black stockings, naturally, and a black Jean Muir – to hell with the expense – that stopped at knee-level. Two-inch heels and a single strand of pearls completed the ensemble, apart from dabs of Arpège behind the ears and knees, and a swift squirt of feminine spray underneath her dress.

There.

Irresistible.

Of course, there remained the slight problem of what to do, whose rooms to go to, when they returned to school, but the mood she was in, and damn the weather, she'd settle for a good bonk in the back seat of her car.

Except, of course, she wasn't taking her car.

OK, then, the back seat of the taxi.

'Keep facing front, driver, this won't take long.'

The hell it wouldn't!

Much to his surprise, Julia had accepted Ben Fisher's invitation for a Saturday night out. After seeing how she'd looked on the occasion of that first audition for *MND*, he'd read for the part of Oberon. Then Bottom, Flute, the entire cast. But he was hopeless, and knew it. He couldn't act his way out of a paper bag. Then Penrose had suggested the task of stage manager. As a natural organizer, this he could do, and he'd jumped at the chance.

Julia ignored him for two solid weeks.

At first he put this down to embarrassment – hers, because she'd raised her dress for him after her failed audition. Soon, however, he learned otherwise: Julia was a 'player', he was 'behind scenes'. She was an officer, he was an other rank, an enlisted man as the Americans said.

He could not, however, forget how she'd looked all tarted up, and he was nothing if not determined. She was a virgin – so Dick Carson surmised – and so was he. She didn't like being a virgin – Carson again – and he was damned sure he didn't.

It was an elementary problem in pure logic: alone, tab A is incomplete. So is slot B. Therefore fit tab A into slot B.

Result: harmony.

So he asked her out the day after Open Day.

'That's very sweet of you,' she said, 'but I don't think so.'

Sweet. Sweet? Fucking *sweet!*

He asked her again two days later.

'I really do have a lot of work, but thanks anyway.'

And again.

'Ben, you get an A for effort, but no.'

Carson said, 'Wrong approach, old son. Treat it as an exercise in tactics. What do you have that she wants?'

'Bugger all, it appears.'

'Incorrect. She has a leading part in this poxy play you're both involved with. She wants to look good, star, name in lights. Today St Clare's, tomorrow Broadway.'

Fisher thought about it.

Part of the stage manager's function was to record the 'blocking' of the play, note down the cast's physical moves in his prompt book. Actors and actresses, because they were so wrapped up with performance and remembering lines, frequently forgot where they were supposed to be on stage from one rehearsal to the next. So did the director.

If Helena and Demetrius, for example, were facing one another in one scene, on one day of rehearsal, but chose to turn their backs on each other the next time, causing Penrose to say, 'That's not how we agreed it,' it was up to the stage manager to point out how they'd done it before.

Fisher chose not to help Julia from his notes.

'She was upstage right last time. She was down left. She didn't sit on the chair.'

Julia became bewildered. Twice she burst into tears. Fisher had a word with her.

'Look, I'll pay twice as much attention to your moves as I do to anyone else's. I'll show you my notes afterwards. That way, there'll be no mistakes.'

'Thank you, Ben. You're very kind.'

'Think nothing of it. Only too happy to help.'

Julia's performance improved. Even when she was wrong, made a mistake with a move, Fisher made sure it came out in her favour.

Fisher had heard about the old Hollywood casting couches. He'd simply updated the technique.

'I don't know where I'd be without you,' Julia said.

'Good grief, don't even think about it. You're the one with the talent. I'm just a valiant yeoman, a hewer of wood and a fetcher of water.'

'Heavens, you're saving my life. Do you really believe I have talent?'

'You make most of the others appear third-rate.'

'That's a really beautiful thing to say. Mr Penrose hardly ever praises any of us.'

'He can't be seen playing favourites. Of course, there are one or two areas where there's room for improvement.'

'Such as?'

'No, it's not my place to criticize.'

'I'd appreciate any help you can give.'

'Well, perhaps we could discuss it in detail on Saturday. I know I'm not the director, but sometimes the spectator sees more of the game than the referee. For example, in that scene with Lysander and Hermia, when you say, "Lo, she is one of this confederacy," I think you should attack Hermia more, go on the offensive. Otherwise, Hermia steals the scene.'

'Do you think so?'

'I do indeed.'

'Saturday, you say.'

'Well, Saturday night. We could take the bus into town, get something to eat or anything else you fancy doing.'

'I could bring my script.'

'Of course.'

'Saturday it is, then.'

Thank you, Carson, thought Fisher.

Henry Morton planned to spend the evening at the smaller of the town's two cinemas, the art house, which was running a Fellini season. This week's offering was *Amarcord*, which he had seen twice before, but he could find no takers to accompany him.

'Are you kidding? Jesus, Henry, you must be hard up.'

Going alone didn't bother him. He was used to it, and in many ways he preferred his own company. Especially at the cinema, where he could lose himself in the drama taking place on-screen. And particularly when the offering was someone like Fellini, an acquired taste that only the serious-minded could be bothered to sit through. Three hours in semi-darkness, with no-one to answer to or make fun of him, was as close as he ever expected to come to real happiness.

He caught the six-thirty single-decker from the school gates. Three seats in front Dick Carson and Kate McNamara were unashamedly holding hands. Across the aisle Jocasta Petrillo and Amanda McDonald had their heads together.

Amanda called across to Kate, 'Will we be seeing you in Flanagan's later?'

Flanagan's was a disco club that catered largely to the under-twenty-fives. No-one under sixteen was admitted, proof of age required. No-one under eighteen was supposed to buy or consume alcohol, but that was a rule almost impossible to enforce. Sixteen-year-olds like Amanda and Jocasta, if refused service by the bar staff, merely approached the nearest eighteen-year-old male and got him to buy. The club was a pick-up joint, pure and simple, which was why everyone went. St Clare's girls' scalps were highly prized by the 'townie' men, and no girl went short of a dancing partner for long. The trouble came later in the evening when propositions for straight sex flew thick and fast. The townie males knew that curfew for St Clare's students was eleven o'clock, which meant the girls had to be out of Flanagan's by ten-thirty at the latest. From around nine-thirty onwards, therefore, there was no beating about the bush.

'Come on, darling, how about a quick knee-trembler outside?'

Jocasta had succumbed once, in the summer before the end of last Trinity Term, after having had far too much to drink. She'd accompanied the boy outside to the car park with the idea, even in her semi-befuddled state, of indulging in no more than a little harmless petting. Then, before she knew it, she was wedged against a car, her skirt was around her waist, her knickers were off, and she was being humped royally.

It was all over in about a minute, she didn't enjoy it at all, he hadn't used a condom, and she sweated for a whole month afterwards in case she was pregnant. And then for a further few weeks for fear she'd picked up some unspeakable disease.

Thereafter she was very careful about how much she drank, though she never found her knickers.

'Maybe,' Kate replied across the bus aisle to Amanda.

'Because if you are,' said Amanda, 'we could all share a taxi back. It's not much more than the bus fare split four ways.'

Jocasta nudged her in the ribs.

'What, what?' demanded Amanda.

'They won't want us with them, fathead,' said Jocasta. 'We're the kind of luggage that's labelled Not Wanted On Voyage.'

'Oh, right, right. I wasn't thinking. Sorry,' yodelled Amanda. 'Scratch that. We'll organize our own transport.'

'For this relief much thanks,' murmured Carson.

''Tis bitter cold and I'd be as sick as a parrot. *Hamlet*, Act One, Scene One.'

Kate giggled.

'I don't remember the bit about the parrot.'

'Few do. Actually, some scholarship contends that for "parrot" read "carrot", but I think the advocates of "carrot" are confusing *Hamlet* with *Macbeth*. "Is this a carrot I see before me?" Much more acceptable.'

'Idiot,' said Kate.

Kate was happy. In fact, it was ages since she could remember being so content. Even though their physical relationship, hers and Richard's, hadn't progressed any further, she wasn't in a hurry. It would soon, when she was a little more confident that he had more in mind than a convenient lay to get him through the long winter evenings. This he evidently did, because he never tried to force her to change her mind when she took his hand off her thigh, no blackmail, moral or otherwise. He did say, regularly, 'Christ, Kate, this is driving me mad, you have no idea,' but that was as far as his protests went.

In any case, she *did* have an idea. It was as bad for her. But soon, soon. One day soon.

She wondered if she was falling in love. She thought she might be. Her feelings were certainly different from those times in America, those dreadful times, and that one particular time she refused to think about and prayed Richard would never learn of.

They were already discussing Christmas, how often they could see each other during the three weeks between the end of Michaelmas Term and the beginning of Hilary. And he wasn't seeing anyone else, not while he was at St Clare's anyway, she was sure. How could he? They were together every spare hour they had.

Naturally he had to have girlfriends back home in Surrey, and she'd heard stories that, before her advent, he'd had something of a reputation with the 'townie' girls.

She'd asked him about both.

'Well, Surrey, you know – at least my part of it – is Babylon South. We have a toast down there: "Here's to our women and our horses, and the men who mount them." Surrey girls do everything the fabled Essex girls do, but with a superior accent. For protection during sex an Essex girl uses a bus shelter, whereas a Surrey girl uses her father's Jaguar. An Essex girl worries that her dress might get soiled during sex on the golf course. A Surrey girl buys the golf course and re-lays it with Astroturf. As for the townie girls – well, you wouldn't expect me to tell, would you? If I did, you'd wonder who I'd be telling about you some time in the future. In any case, what about your adventures in America?'

'There weren't any. Many.'

'Kate, you've already told me you're not a virgin.'

'Let's drop the whole subject, shall we?'

'Fine with me.'

'Are we going to Flanagan's later?' asked Kate.

'Do you want to?'

'I've never been.'

'Lucky you. Hordes of sweaty peasants, like the

chorus from *Cavalleria Rusticana*, gyrating madly to some zonked-out pop group. A fiver apiece to get in, and drinks double a pub tariff. The men's accents are indecipherable, and the women would make the aforementioned Essex girl appear regal.'

'Sounds like you enjoyed yourself.'

'Love the place. It's a cross between downtown Bangkok and *Coronation Street*. But let's eat first. My father sent me fifty quid in anticipation that I'll skate the Oxford entrance . . .'

'Which you will.'

'. . . And I propose to blow the lot somewhere exotic.'

'We agreed Dutch.'

'Not with my father being so extravagant.'

'Even so.'

'Kate, before he left the army to pillage an unsuspecting Civvy Street, my father was a brigadier. Not the dizzy heights of rank, agreed, but not making the tea, either. As a colonel, in one of those places we used to call colonies, there was only one barber's shop on base, shared by officers and other ranks alike. Two chairs, wait in the queue. As it happened, my father and a corporal were alongside one another, and both of their haircuts finished at the same time. The barber who was dealing with my father said, "And would the colonel like some of this on his hair?" My father took a sniff of the proffered bottle and answered, "Good God, no thank you. My wife will think I've been in a Turkish brothel." Quick as lightning, the corporal in the adjacent chair said, "I'll have lots, sprinkle it on. My wife's never been in a Turkish brothel."'

Kate laughed.

'But is there a point to that anecdote?'

'There is. Never look a gift horse in the mouth. My father, his money, our treat. Agreed?'

'OK, but I buy the cab back.'

'Deal.'

At approximately the same time as Henry Morton was standing in line to see the Fellini film, Dutch Paula was uncorking the second bottle of wine. She and Phoebe were seated on Paula's bed. Sappho was perched on the windowsill. Jennifer Langley was curled up in an armchair. Rod Stewart was belting out 'Baby Jane'.

Sappho was pissed off.

It was already seven o'clock, Phoebe and Jennifer had been in the study for an hour, and Paula van der bloody Groot hadn't made a move. What was this, charity week? Or was Paula trying to keep both of them for herself?

If so, she was dead. Never mind that Paula was the most aggressive dyke in St Clare's, she was tiny. Sappho had known lesbians who kick-started their vibrators.

Jennifer Langley looked enchanting: bright-blue saucer-sized eyes, red hair that many a film star would kill for, and delightful freckles. And those tits. My God, those tits.

In the old days, when she and Paula had been having

a ring-a-ding-ding, and she, Sappho, had strapped on what they always referred to as 'the thing' or 'the machine', she'd squeezed Paula's breasts to enhance her pleasure when coming. But Paula had such tiny breasts. Not so tiny as to be unattractive, but nothing compared to Jennifer's. Sappho would have given a year of her life to screw Jennifer, who was undoubtedly a virgin.

Christ, those tits and a virgin to boot!

But Jennifer was Paula's, and it was better not to cross Paula, in spite of her size.

Still, Phoebe was also a beauty, if a petulant one. The trick was – and it had to be Paula's trick – how to get Phoebe, clinging like a vine to Paula, out of Paula's clutches and into the presently unoccupied study of Mary Donaldson and Jackie Thorpe. Before bedtime, their bedtime, the teenies.

Sappho attracted Paula's attention and made a smoking gesture with her fingers.

Paula took her cue.

'You kids ever tried pot?'

'You asked me that before, ages ago,' said Phoebe.

'And you turned it down, darling, I know,' said Paula.

'I have,' said Jennifer. 'In Cyprus, during the summer.'

'Did you enjoy it?' asked Sappho.

'It was good,' said Jennifer, 'really woozy.'

Woozy, mouthed Sappho to Paula.

'Help yourself to more wine,' said Paula.

Jennifer shook her head.

'I'm not that fond of wine.' She batted her eye-lashes at Sappho. 'But, if you were serious, a smoke of something seems an interesting idea.'

Sappho was off the windowsill like a flash.

'I know what's going on here,' said Phoebe, over Rod Stewart. She blinked up at Paula, the wine already getting to her. 'You want Jennifer. You're being unfaithful.'

'Darling, I'm not.' Paula petted Phoebe like a rabbit. 'You know I'm not.'

'Hang on a tick,' said Jennifer. 'Don't treat me like a piece of meat to be tossed to the nearest hound. Jennifer gets a say in who gets Jennifer – if anyone.'

Sappho and Paula exchanged glances. Jesus, thought Sappho, was I that confident, that precocious, at four-teen? Yes, I guess I was, and the teenies are much more mature than they were four years ago. And – and it wasn't just her imagination – much more available, ready to experiment sexually with another woman whether their natural proclivities were lesbian or not. Neither Phoebe nor Jennifer were gay in the true sense of the word, not the way she and Paula were. Oh, they'd indulge and enjoy it for a term or two, then they'd revert to type and be screwing boys before their sixteenth birthdays.

Still, four years ago fourteen-year-olds had really to be coaxed into bed. Four years ago there were no more than eight or ten dyed-in-the-wool sinistrals in the whole of St Clare's, and someone like Jennifer – maybe even Phoebe – would have run screaming to the Gorgon if an older girl had so much as touched her hair.

Different now, and thanks be to God for it.

She and Paula had a theory about the change of attitude: AIDS. A young girl feeling the first frisson of sexual desire wanted to do something about it, but was scared stiff of catching something fatal from some yobbo who'd been sticking his dick in God knows who. Another woman, they reasoned, was a safer bet. Not entirely true, but there it was.

'Sorry,' Sappho apologized to Jennifer. 'No-one was meaning to imply anything.'

But hell, thought Sappho, you wouldn't be here, you little bitch, if you didn't know the score. Even if Phoebe hasn't told you she's getting it on regularly with Paula, you've seen enough of their relationship in the last hour to recognize that, when the pair of them are together, they're not discussing world events.

Jennifer smiled angelically.

'Just as long as we understand each other.'

Sappho started to roll a joint from their stash.

'I'll never say I don't like cornflakes again,' said Jennifer.

'I feel sick,' said Phoebe.

Paula groaned inwardly.

'Take her to the loo, Saff. I'll finish rolling the joint.'

'I want you to take me,' said Phoebe.

God, thought Paula. She caught sight of Sappho grinning. *Just you damned well dare*, she mimed.

'Don't start anything before we get back,' she

said aloud, helping Phoebe to her feet.

'Wouldn't dream of it, dear, would we, Jennifer?'

'I'm sure I don't know what you mean.'

Shortly after the lights went down in the cinema, Henry Morton, seated in the back row, left of the aisle, three seats in, was irritated to be forced to stand up to allow a middle-aged man to pass him. The man was polite enough, mumbled something about, 'Terribly sorry to trouble you,' but that wasn't the point. Admittedly it was a small cinema, room for two hundred patrons at the most, but it was less than a third full. There were dozens of empty seats all over the auditorium.

The curse of the English, he thought, the same in cinemas as they were on beaches. You could bet your life that, if you set up your deckchair on an otherwise deserted stretch of sand, within five minutes some English family would have parked themselves not ten feet away. Herding instinct.

What was the old joke? If you got three Germans together they would form an army; three Frenchmen a restaurant; three Italians a political party; and three Englishmen a queue.

Still, the latecomer hadn't elected to sit directly next to him, and at the time Henry thought no more about it.

Unexpectedly so far as Lavinia was concerned, Penrose hadn't booked a table in one of the town's two good restaurants. Nor would he tell her where they were going when the taxi whisked them away from St Clare's.

'It's a surprise.'

And so it proved to be.

It wasn't a pub, either, but what could probably be generically classified as a country house hotel, eight miles the other side of town. She'd never even heard of the place, but it was delightful, suited her mood perfectly.

The bar where pre-dinner drinks were served had a huge log fire, the fireplace fifteen feet long if it was an inch; an ideal place to sit on a wet and windy October Saturday. The restaurant, observable through an open door, had seating for around thirty, and each table was candle-lit. Most tables were for two. This wasn't the sort of place one brought one's parents. It was a restaurant for lovers, young or old.

Goodbye, Peter Hennessy, she thought.

'You're right,' she said, 'it is a surprise.'

A waitress hovered, crisp and smart in a white blouse and black skirt.

'What would you like to drink?' asked Penrose, accepting a menu.

Two minutes earlier Lavinia would have settled for a large gin and tonic. Now she felt skittish, celebratory.

'Champagne,' she said to the waitress, 'Lanson. Chilled but not Arctic. And I'd appreciate it if that could be put on a separate bill, to be handed to me later.'

Penrose knew better than to protest.

As close to the fire as she could possibly get without

roasting, Lavinia kicked off her shoes and stretched her legs.

Bliss.

Julia and Ben were dining less splendidly.

Ben had put the bite on everyone he knew, raided his own piggy bank, added up the cost of buses, taxis and so forth, and arrived at twenty-three pounds and a few pence. This was a pub night, no mistake.

As promised (or threatened, Ben thought), Julia had brought along her copy of *MND*, and, sipping Coke, was going over scenes with him while waiting for their baked potatoes plus trimmings to arrive.

'But when Helena says this . . . If I do this when Hermia says this . . . And in that scene . . .'

Christ, thought Ben, does everyone have to go through this to get laid? No, only if you had red hair and a physique best suited to holding up black-currants.

He remembered a quote of Marlon Brando's, applied to actors but which, double, should be applied to actresses *manqué*. Brando said: 'An actor's a guy who, if you ain't talkin' about him, ain't listenin'.'

Richard Carson and Kate McNamara were getting along much better.

Like Henry Morton, they too were in a cinema, but viewing a film much more suited to their mood. Fuck Fellini, this one was *Basic Instinct*, with Sharon Stone proving to three or four hundred people that she was, without doubt, a woman.

Remembering, Kate whispered, 'Do you find her attractive?'

Carson wanted to answer, 'Does the Pope wear a funny hat?' but restrained himself. He was carrying an erection that, prodded in the right place, would have sunk a frigate, what the American writer Joseph Wambaugh called a diamond-cutter.

'A little less so than you,' he managed.

They were in the back row. This cinema, unlike Henry Morton's, was three-quarters full. Even though most of the patrons must have seen *Basic Instinct* before, as Kate had, this was Saturday night, after all. Work, or school, was over for the week, Sunday, indolent Sunday, lay ahead, and the world was just right for hedonists.

Kate glanced left and right. The nearest couple was four seats away, and they were deep in each other's mouths. The man – well, youth in actuality – had his hand far up his girlfriend's dress. Kate couldn't see where the girl's hand was.

Kate was also moist where it counted, and hurting, but her turn would come later. Time, now, to see what Richard would do.

She put her right hand on his lap, feeling his erection through his jeans. Carson shuddered.

'For God's sake, Kate . . .!'

'Ssh.'

She took a wad of Kleenex from her pocket with her left hand and, with right, unzipped his flies.

'*Kate!*'

'Watch the film.'

As she was.

She recalled all this from another time, another

place, and as his cock sprang free, she took hold of it, worked it.

Lovely, she thought. Oh, how lovely!

'You'd better take some of these tissues.'

Carson obeyed, in a trance.

'Leave it to me,' she murmured, and then stage-whispered, 'Sorry, I've dropped my bag.'

With everyone intent on Sharon Stone, no-one paid her a blind bit of attention.

She bent down, apparently to recover the non-existent purse, taking Carson's penis briefly into her mouth. Carson almost cried out as, simultaneously, she stroked him with her long, slim, cool fingers.

He bit his tongue. Not even the townie girls had gone this far in a very public place.

He knew they were going to be discovered. Some-one would bellow a protest, someone else would flash a torch, and they would both be in a police station and, shortly thereafter, out of St Clare's.

Goodbye, St Clare's. Goodbye, Oxford.

But he hadn't the willpower to stop her.

Then Kate's head was beside his again, though her hand was still on him. She covered her movements with her Barbour. Sharon Stone was in front of him, thirty feet tall, and he was going to die.

But before that he was going to come. The threat of sudden death couldn't have stopped him.

He had sufficient presence of mind to keep the Kleenex handy and just about managed to keep his moans under control as he shuddered into violent orgasm.

Kate managed a minor orgasm of her own – not brilliant, but acceptable.

When both were finished, Carson re-zipped his flies and pocketed the tissues.

No-one in the cinema audience had, it appeared, even glanced at them.

'Found it,' said Kate, referring to the bag that she hadn't dropped in the first place.

Carson gripped her hand very hard.

'Let's get the hell out of here, back to school.'

'No, let's see the rest of the film.'

'I've lost the thread of the plot.'

Kate giggled softly.

'Maybe, but everything else seems to be in working order.'

She glanced across to where the same youth still had his hand under his girlfriend's dress. Kate couldn't see what the girl was doing with her hand, but the girl was looking at her.

Even though her gesture probably couldn't be seen in the darkness of the cinema, Kate had the confidence, and impudence, to wink at the girl.

Oh, shit, she thought, here we go again.

In Flanagan's Amanda and Jocasta had teamed up with two local builders, both four or five years older than the girls. One was called Fred, the other Ossie. Both appeared to have money to burn, and Jocasta, at least, was more than willing to feed the flames. Rich people – of which Jocasta was certainly one – in Jocasta's view had an obligation to make sure that everyone spent money other than them. That was how the rich stayed rich.

Amanda was boogying away on the dance floor to some disco number with Ossie – or it could have been Fred – while Fred – or it could have been Ossie – was trying to spike Jocasta's Coke with dark rum. But, remembering the last time, Jocasta kept declining.

She didn't turn her back for one second on Ossie or Fred. The bastard would stick a rum in her cola quick as ninepence if she took her eyes off him. He would stick a damned sight more than that in her if she got drunk, and she did not have an inexhaustible wardrobe of knickers.

Amanda and Ossie or Fred came back after an energetic display on the dance floor. Jocasta checked her wristwatch. Not long, now, before it was time to go.

Amanda wiped her damp forehead with a handkerchief.

'I'm sweating.'

Jocasta corrected her.

'Horses sweat, dearest, men perspire, ladies glow.'

'Excuse us a sec,' said Fred – or Ossie.

'Note the "sec",' said Jocasta, 'which is otherwise dry wine. To us, that is.'

'You're a snob, Jo.'

'No, only *arrivistes* are snobs. The rest of us have breeding.'

'As I said, you're a snob.'

'Oh, well, have it your way, as long as *he* doesn't get his way. Not that that's likely tonight.'

'What are you, clairvoyant?'

'Just someone who can tell the time.'

'Spoilsport.'

'Amanda, you're not cut out for the role of Connie Chatterley.'

'That's all very well for you to say. You're so beautiful you can take your pick. Or leave it, as the case may be, knowing there'll be other times. My opportunities for dalliance don't happen that often . . .'

Sappho had one eye on the clock, the other on Phoebe, who, denim-skirted, was squatting on the floor of the study at Paula's feet, flicking at her blond hair. Phoebe was wearing white Knickerbox panties. Thrusting against the fabric was Phoebe's inchoate bush, penumbraed.

Sappho would have given ten years of her life to nose among that deliciousness.

At least Phoebe wasn't complaining of feeling sick any longer, though she'd switched from wine to coffee. She also continued to decline even the tiniest puff of a joint, seemingly content to lie with her head against Paula's knees and listen to whatever mindless crap was currently being played on the music centre.

Sappho wasn't happy. There was no way Paula was going to give up her Saturday-night sex, and if Jennifer Langley wasn't going to succumb, Paula would settle for Phoebe. Which would leave Sappho out in the cold.

Jennifer was devouring most of the second joint – which neither Paula nor Sappho objected to because it might loosen her up – but so far, though she was smiling vacantly and singing quietly to herself, she still seemed to have her head together. Certainly when Paula reached across Phoebe to caress the nape of Jennifer's neck, she pulled away.

'I'm not going to bed with anyone tonight,' she announced.

Oh yes you damn well are, thought Paula.

'And . . .' said Julia . . .

Fuck it, thought Ben, I'll go to Paris, find a hooker . . .

Midway through the excellent bottle of Chambertin which, on top of the champagne, had the effect of suffusing Lavinia's entire body with a warm glow, she said, 'Robert, I do believe you're trying to seduce me.'

Penrose was also feeling relaxed.

'What gives you that idea?'

'Don't be obtuse. Answer the question.'

'It wasn't a question.'

Lavinia frowned. 'Then I'll make it a question. You don't find me attractive?'

'You know damned well I do.'

'Well, then?'

'Well what?'

'Was kostet das Zimmer mit Fruhstuck? Benutzt den Augenblick.'

'You've lost me.'

'How much is bed and breakfast? And the German equivalent of the Latin *carpe diem* – seize the day, seize the moment.'

'That's the wine talking.'

'To hell with the wine.'

'Lavinia, we're not booked out for the night with the porter's lodge, and Dobbs saw us leave together in the taxi. How's it going to look if we don't come back together or at all until tomorrow?'

'There's nothing in school rules to say members of staff can't have affairs.'

'Agreed, but we don't have to trumpet it from the rooftops.'

Lavinia pushed her glass away.

'You're so bloody logical.'

'Mind you,' said Penrose, 'I do have some rather good brandy in my rooms at Napier.'

Lavinia thought about it. 'I'll be seen.'

'Now who's being logical?'

'On the other hand,' said Lavinia, 'it doesn't matter if I'm seen going in providing I'm not seen coming out, does it?'

'Have some more wine.'

'I think I will, but perhaps we can skip the coffee stage. Suddenly I feel like an early night.'

'So, what did you think of *Basic Instinct*?' asked Kate when the cinema let out.

But Carson was having no more of this.

'Kate, are we going to bed or not? I use the term bed loosely, of course, because you can't come to my study and I think we might raise a few eyebrows if we shacked up in your dorm.'

'Tonight?'

'No, Pancake Tuesday.'

'Don't be cross, it's immature. Where?'

'I know how to get into the hockey pavilion.'

And probably not for the first time or even the second, thought Kate, but who cared? She wanted to screw Richard Carson's brain loose, her own too, and if that had to be on a changing bench in the hockey pav, so what?

'Let's go,' she said.

Henry Morton was one of the last to leave the cinema when *Amarcord* finished. He never had seen any point in dashing for the exit the moment a film ended. He liked to sit there for a while, luxuriate in the images he had just witnessed. Besides, he had nowhere to go other than back to St Clare's, and that was a depressing thought.

He needed to relieve his bladder on the way out. Just as he was finishing, someone joined him at the adjacent stall. Henry kept his gaze averted.

'An excellent film, didn't you think?' said the new-comer chattily.

Henry recognized the voice of the middle-aged man who had been sitting a few seats away from him throughout the performance.

'Yes, it was.'

Henry washed his hands. The middle-aged man stood alongside him. Henry caught sight of him in the mirror: about fifty, well-groomed, iron-grey hair.

There was only one hand-drier working, and while Henry used it the man stood behind him, waiting his turn.

'You're at St Clare's, aren't you?'

'That obvious, is it?'

'Just a lucky guess. Do you have a film society at school?'

'A small one. Not much interest in Fellini, though.'

'No, he's an acquired taste. It's the same in the circle of people I mix with, a cultural wilderness. Perhaps you'd care to come for a drink and we can talk about some of his other work. I do mean my treat, naturally.'

'I'm afraid I have to get back. Curfew, you know.'

'But not until eleven. You have forty minutes.'

Before Henry could evade him, the man reached around Henry's waist and grabbed for his crotch.

'Please. It won't take long.'

Henry leapt away, unfortunately the wrong way, away from the door. His cheeks were aflame with rage and embarrassment, but, although he was shaking, he managed to keep his voice steady.

'I'm giving you five seconds to get the hell out of here, and then I'm yelling for the manager, who will undoubtedly, at my insistence, call the police.'

The man smiled, part sadness, part amusement.

'Don't be foolish. Besides, you know what you are. If it hasn't happened yet, or if it doesn't happen tonight, with me, it will one day soon. Don't deny your own sexuality.'

'Fuck off!' snarled Henry, and left the cloakroom at something between a hobble and a run.

Outside it was still raining, but Henry didn't care about the soaking he was getting as he made his way to the bus station. Fortunately the rain obscured his tears.

What is it about me, he thought, what is it? What is it about the way I look or walk or talk which makes someone like that think I'm gay?

'Hey, you're not going, are you?' said Ossie or maybe Fred.

'Sorry, we have to,' said Jocasta.

'Ten more minutes, five. We've got a car outside. We can drive you back.'

'Where's the harm, Jo?' asked Amanda.

Jocasta lowered her voice.

'The harm, Amanda, is that they would not be taking the most direct route. We'd find ourselves in some lonely road with the options of either putting out or getting out.'

'We'll walk you to the taxi rank or bus station, then,' said Ossie or Fred.

'No, thanks.'

'Well, fuck you.'

'Not tonight, darling.'

'I've had a really lovely evening, Ben,' said Julia. 'Thank you very much.'

They were in the shadows away from the entrance to Churchill House, sheltering from the wind and the rain under Julia's umbrella.

Lovely, thought Ben, *lovely*? I wonder what the hell she does for kicks?

'Well, so have I. I hope we can do it again.'

'Me too.'

Ben wondered if he should attempt to kiss her, but Julia pre-empted him. Far from a chaste kiss it was too, though it started out that way. Soon, however, Julia's tongue was in his mouth.

Then it was over as quickly as it started, and Julia was running up the steps.

Still, thought Ben, it was a start. He couldn't expect to touch all the bases first time out. Where the hell could he have taken her anyway?

Certainly not to the hockey pavilion, where Carson had forced the catch of a window he'd used before and was now sitting naked on a pile of clothes next to Kate, who was also undressed. Naked and miserable as far as Carson was concerned.

'I don't understand it,' he lamented. 'Nothing like this has ever happened to me before. Christ, I want you like mad, but nothing's functioning.'

Kate had given up trying to bring him anywhere near full erection five minutes ago, when Carson had pushed her hand away. Even her mouth hadn't worked the oracle, but the sexual tension had left her. Women could adapt much more easily to this sort of setback than men. There'd be other days and she was willing to wait.

'It's too bloody cold in here, that's the problem. Don't worry about it.'

'That's easy for you to say. Christ, I feel an absolute failure.'

'It's not a competition.'

'Even so.'

'Look, let's get dressed. We're going to be late as it is. There's nothing wrong with you, think of what happened in the cinema.'

'I'll be thinking of nothing else for weeks.'

'Good. Just don't be angry, that's all. It's counter-productive.'

No doubt anger is a negative emotion, but that didn't stop Paula and Sappho being beside themselves with rage.

An hour and a half ago, just when it seemed that Jennifer Langley was about to become more receptive – to a little mild foreplay if nothing else – and when even Phoebe was starting to view Sappho more kindly – who should turn up two-and-a-half hours before schedule but Mary Donaldson and Jackie Peters.

Paula's study door was held shut by a chair, but Mary called through the panelling, 'Sorry, ladies, we caught an earlier train.'

There was no chance of action after that. Phoebe and Jennifer had to be back in their dorms in thirty minutes, which would have given Sappho and Paula plenty of time, now that the kids were more relaxed, had Mary's study been unoccupied.

There was nothing for it but to pack the teenies off to bed, after which Paula stormed along the corridor to Mary and Jackie and gave them a full five minutes of colourful abuse.

Later, back in her own study with Sappho, when she had calmed down, she said, 'We're going to have to handle this differently in future. No doubling up. Christ, I'm horny.'

'I suppose we could . . .' started Sappho, but Paula shook her head.

'No, forget it. When my appetite's whetted for caviar, I don't want lumpfish.'

'Thanks very much.'

'Sorry, but you know what I mean. Is there any of that wine left?'

'A whole bottle.'

'Then let's get good and drunk. It's the only way I'll be able to sleep.'

Lavinia was surprised and thrilled at the quality of lover Robert Penrose turned out to be.

They had got back to St Clare's long before the students' curfew, knowing full well that the girls and boys of the Upper and Lower Sixths would not dream, on a Saturday night, of returning before the appointed hour of eleven. That being so, Lavinia could safely accompany Penrose to his study without trepidation. If anyone asked, they were going to discuss *MND*. It was early yet for adults.

There was no question of going to his bedroom, of course. That would have been taking too much of a risk. But the study was fine. It was warm, the floor was carpeted, and there were a couple of thick-armed armchairs that had interesting possibilities.

To start with they were slightly uneasy with one another. The intimacy of the restaurant had been fragmented during the taxi-ride back, and even the effects of the champagne and Chambertin were beginning to lose their edge.

Penrose broke the ice by putting on some soft music, dimming the lights, and pouring each of them a large slug of the promised brandy. Before long they were back to their earlier mood and lusting for one another's bodies.

A first kiss led to a second, deeper one, and Penrose slid his hand beneath Lavinia's dress, ecstatic to discover she was wearing stockings and not those wretched passion-killing tights so many women went in for.

Lavinia pulled away.

'I think I'd be more comfortable without the dress. Besides, it cost a fortune. Will you unzip me?'

With her back to him, the dress fell to the floor. She stepped out of it. He attempted to unclasp her bra, but she gave a little murmur of disapproval – 'Not yet' – and insisted on folding the dress over a chair before facing him.

'You could do with fewer clothes, too.'

He allowed her to undo his tie and take it off, thinking, Christ, she was gorgeous. Black underwear was made for a woman with that colour hair. His erection was hurting, but Lavinia knew all about that. She could feel it thrusting against the material of his trousers.

It was her turn to unzip him, feel for him, panting as she took hold of him, delighting in his size and thickness. He was as hard as a rock. Uncircumcized, too, which she preferred. And the glans was already beautifully wet under her busy fingers.

'Get out of those damned trousers,' she muttered hoarsely.

Still standing, he pulled them off in a hurry. Then his underwear, shirt and socks. His erection rose like a missile. Lavinia toyed with him, teasing him, while Penrose, with Lavinia unprotesting on this occasion, removed her bra. Her milky-white breasts cascaded free. He put his other hand under her slip, groaning when he felt the coolness of her thighs after the heat of her stockings. Then his fingers were beneath her briefs and inside her, probing among the liquid.

'Take them off, pull the fucking things off,' she commanded.

He wanted her slip off too, but she shook her head fiercely.

'No, no, I like it like this, stockings and all. I'm a whore, Robert, a street-corner whore. Fuck me like a whore.'

'Give me a minute.'

He fumbled for a condom.

'Let me do it,' said Lavinia.

She eased the condom on, rolling it down to the base of the shaft, quivering with anticipation.

She guided him towards one of the armchairs, making him sit on it, legs outstretched. When he was in place, she hiked her slip to her waist and straddled him, keeping him outside her for those last few beautiful seconds, until he could stand the torment no longer and pulled her roughly on to him. Which was what she had wanted him to do anyway.

Then he was massively inside her, much larger and thicker than she'd imagined when she'd simply had hold of him.

She did most of the work, using her hands as levers on the arms of the chair to raise herself until just the glans was touching her clitoris, before plunging down to accept his entire length. His head was buried in her breasts, his tongue licking her nipples.

'I – don't – think – I'm – going – to – be – able – to – hold – this,' she heard him say.

'Don't then, don't. Let it all come. Just fuck me.'

She bucked her hips faster and began whinnying with excitement. Even though he was as hard as she thought he could be, she felt him grow even harder as his spasms started. And through the condom she felt him coming in huge spurts.

Then she was coming, fighting for her orgasm. Her hip movements became quicker. She leaned back as her own spasms grew in intensity, pressed both her hands against his shoulders and flung her head from side to side.

'Oh Christ Christ Christ fuck me fuck me fuck me,' she whimpered.

Penrose gripped her buttocks hard, keeping himself tight inside her, as the last of his orgasm left him, wishing that the fucking world had never heard of AIDS and that it was into her beautiful body that he was ejaculating.

When their breathing returned to normal and Penrose's erection had subsided, she slipped from his lap and hunted for her cigarettes and her brandy glass. When she next looked at him he had disposed of the condom somewhere.

'That was bloody marvellous,' she said, curling up at his feet.

They grinned at one another, absurdly pleased with themselves for doing no more than a million other couples throughout the kingdom were doing this Saturday night.

'I hope that wasn't your only condom,' said Lavinia.

'It wasn't, but you'll have to give me a break. I'm not eighteen.'

'You'll do.'

They fucked twice more. Neither of them, privately or openly, thought of their actions as 'making love'. That would have been an imprecise definition. Perhaps love-making would be part of another evening, when they knew each other better. For the moment it was just sex, and none the worse of it for that.

Lavinia removed her slip the second time, but still wanted to keep her stockings on. Penrose was all for that idea, and he took her from behind, with Lavinia standing but bending from the waist over the arm of an armchair. Before they started she said, 'Wait a minute, wait a minute. Let me put my heels on.'

The heels gave her two inches in height and, just as important, raised her wondrously muscular vagina by the same degree. With her arms outstretched like a crucifix, her fingers gripping the armchair wings fiercely, she felt as she wanted to, like a ten-dollar whore.

Being the one in control on this occasion, Penrose

delighted in exciting himself by rubbing his free hand against the silk of her black stockings.

He rammed into her again and again, all long strokes, withdrawing until he was almost outside her before thrusting forward with all his power, making her whimper and beg for release.

'Please please please.'

His tightening scrotum slapped against her bare buttocks as he strained to get that extra fraction of an inch inside, and he could feel the juices pouring out of her, dripping on to her stockings, on to his inner thighs.

Her head thrashed from side to side and her fingers tore into the fabric of the chair as she began to come. And then he was coming in her like a rutting stallion and leaning forward to bite and nuzzle the nape of her neck.

'Whore whore whore,' she moaned as she felt, again, the sudden extra hardness as he exploded. 'Oh Christ fuck me for ever.'

He liked that in a woman, the dirty talk. Fiona Acland had once said she was a whore when he was fucking her, but she had genuinely thought she was. Lavinia was just acting out a fantasy.

They made it finally on the carpet, facing each other, with Lavinia's legs entwined around Penrose's neck, opening her up so deep and wide that he thought he'd be lost in there.

When they'd exhausted themselves they had another glass of brandy apiece while Lavinia smoked a further cigarette. She had no wish to get dressed and return to her own rooms, but she couldn't stay here all night. More was the pity.

'Play rehearsals are never going to seem the same again,' she said, 'and you'll have to restrain me if I start trying to unzip you when Julia is being especially tiresome.' Lavinia chuckled throatily. 'Dear Julia, what would she think if she could see us now?'

'I don't think I'd have the willpower to stop you. Still, we'll just have to hold on until we're alone.'

'Yes, we haven't considered that, have we? I mean, was this just a one-night stand? Where do we go from here? Do we become an item, or what?'

'I like the item idea better than the "or what".'

Lavinia thought about it and found that she did too. Where and how often they could get it together was a problem for another day, though clearly they couldn't meet like this on a regular basis without tongues wagging.

'Christ, look at the time,' she said. 'Do you think I'll be safe getting out of Napier?'

'Well, just in case somebody's still wandering around, I'll get dressed too and escort you to the front door.'

'You'd better leave me there. I'll make my own way across.'

Lavinia didn't bother with her stockings. They were ruined anyway. She handed them to Penrose.

'Souvenir. Keep them under your pillow, to remind you.'

'I won't need any reminding, but I will keep them.'

No-one was about in the hallway, but, even so,

it was always possible someone was on the prowl. Therefore Lavinia thought it prudent not even to give Penrose a gentle peck on the cheek.

The House door closed behind her.

The rain had eased, but it was still very windy and a sliver of moon was peeking out from behind some scudding clouds. The school clock played its overture prior to striking twelve.

We have heard the chimes at midnight, Master Shallow.

That we have, that we have. In faith, Sir John, we have. Oh, Jesus, the days that we have seen.

8

She's Not the Pheasant Plucker,
She's the Pheasant Plucker's Daughter

There were scholarship kids at St Clare's, girls whose IQs were almost too high to be measured accurately on the Stanford-Binet scale, whose parents couldn't afford the fees but whose presence within the school enriched it academically. Girls who would gain Oxbridge Double Firsts and who would, one day, be in line for Nobel Prizes. Gifted children.

By their very nature such girls were often difficult.

It didn't help much, either, that often these girls didn't speak with cut-glass accents, that frequently their clothes were of poor quality, that their table manners and other social graces left something to be desired.

Such students had hardly ever travelled abroad except on package holidays to the less fashionable parts of Spain and the Greek islands, scarcely knew one end of a horse from the other, and thought squash was a drink and not a game played with racquets.

Despite Amanda McDonald accusing Jocasta Petrillo of snobbery, there was very little of it at St Clare's, not even among the titled ladies like Fiona Acland or the immensely wealthy. Certainly they knew they were different from students who attended state schools, privileged, even, but as they were all privileged in the same way, it hardly mattered. Neither did they look down on the female shop assistants who served them in town, nor the mechanic who serviced their parents' cars back home. They would not have wanted to share a dinner table with either shopgirl or artisan, naturally, but that was less to do with snobbery than a lack of common interests. It wouldn't be easy to hold a conversation with someone who had just returned from two weeks in Benidorm bearing raffia donkeys and outsize sombreros when one had spent the long vacation high up in the Andes with one's cousin, who just happened to be the daughter of the ambassador.

No, it had nothing to do with feeling superior. God knows, a girl with an IQ close to 200 should feel superior to *them*.

Mrs Gordon and the St Clare's governors were all in favour of scholarships in rather the same way that Victorian mill-owners were proponents of charity, though the candidates were always vetted carefully, to ensure they would fit in with the school's ethos. It was not the slightest use having a genius on the premises if she was going to be disruptive. Regrettably they made a terrible mistake with Patsy Kelly.

Or Patricia Margaret Kelly as she had been baptized.

There was no doubt that the fourteen-year-old daughter of a Basingstoke butcher and poulterer was a prodigy. Every test known to humankind and psychologists, not always the same thing, proved it without fear of contradiction. She could read before she was two, and was devouring novels before the age of six. Algebraic equations were a doddle and she'd mastered differential calculus long before her eighth birthday.

A paternal uncle possessed an old violin, passed down through the family from God knows where. No-one could scrape more than the odd jig out of it, but Patsy picked it up one day, found some music from somewhere, and, within three weeks, had solved the fingering. Within six she was tackling Bach's Brandenburg Concerto Number One.

Backgammon was too easy, and she abandoned the game when she realized she could not control the luck of the dice, but chess became a fetish. Before her age was in double figures, she was the best player in her county.

At bridge too she was a phenomenon. Most adults never learn the rules and subtleties, and most husbands spend most of their lives being scowled at by their wives for overbidding and going down on a contract. Patsy could look at her own cards, estimate from the point-count what her chances were, and, after the first round of bidding, be pretty damned sure where any sort of strength lay.

Clever, yes; a future contender for a Nobel Prize, certainly; perhaps even a composer or Poet Laureate.

Unfortunately she was a little shit.

And if that wasn't enough, and if it wasn't enough

that her accent contained the flat vowels of Hampshire with a touch of London's East End thrown in for good measure, she also looked funny.

Before these days of political correctness, where the short are 'vertically disadvantaged' and the fat are 'horizontally challenged' and the myopic are 'sight hindered', Patsy would have been called a dumpy, four-eyed midget.

Which is what she was, whatever labels were put upon her.

To labour an old joke, an Englishman, a Frenchman and a German were discussing definitions and the worth of each national's language. The German insisted that his country's tongue was that of business and philosophy. 'Look at the Bundesbank, examine Nietzche, Schopenhauer, Hegel.' The Frenchman ridiculed the German; his land was the home of Romance. 'Never mind our great writers such as Voltaire and Molière, see the screen actors we have produced: Jean-Paul Belmondo, Delon, Signoret, Moreau. Romantics all.'

The Englishman was unimpressed. As they were dining, he held up a knife.

'You see this? In Germany you call it *Das Messer*, in France *le couteau*. But in England we simply call it a knife, which, when all's said and done, is precisely what it is.'

No, Patsy Kelly was a dumpy, four-eyed monster.

She'd been through the usual routine, of course. Mensa had found out about her, tested her, discovered her IQ was off the scale. The Society for Gifted

Children had nurtured her, shown her options. Or rather, shown her parents options.

Her parents were bewildered as to how they had produced such an *enfant terrible*.

Eventually she wound up at St Clare's, quite a catch for Mrs Gordon when Roedean and Cheltenham would have been more than willing to accept her and waive the fees.

To call her short was not strictly accurate. Not all fourteen-year-olds are leggy and five feet five. She was about five feet tall, but God, she was fat. With a father in the butcher's and poulterer's business, it would have been thought she had not lacked for red meat or game throughout her childhood; *ergo*, that she would not have to consume everything in sight at the dinner table. Except she did, cramming sausages, potatoes and salad into her mouth as if there was no tomorrow. Two or three helpings of pudding, also, just for good measure.

Her first fight – so much for the pacifism of the intellectual – that Michaelmas Term, her first, was with an inoffensive little girl, also a newcomer of fourteen, named Annie Belton-Bray, nicknamed instantly Annie Belt-and-Braces. It was over strawberries.

Annie was a weedy little mouse of a girl who normally wouldn't say boo to the proverbial goose. But she did want her strawberries, even if she was taking her time eating them.

Then Patsy grabbed for them.

'You don't need those, you're not eating them.'

'I'm not a p-pig,' stammered Annie, shocked at the freebooting ways of Patsy.

'So I am, am I?'

'If the pig cap fits, wear the pig cap,' said Annie defiantly, holding on to her strawberries.

Patsy snatched them.

'You're not eating them, you can't have them.'

Annie tried to retrieve them, failed, and began to cry.

Patsy leaned across and slapped Annie's face.

'Cry-baby.'

Patsy was brought before Mrs Gordon.

'Look, Patsy,' said the Gorgon, 'I realize this is all very new to you, but we do have our standards at St Clare's. You must not steal another girl's pudding.'

'Wasn't pudding,' said Patsy scornfully. 'They were strawberries.'

Mrs Gordon sighed.

'Even so.'

'That's not a complete sentence,' said Patsy.

The next fight was a knock-down, drag-out, hair-pulling affair in which Patsy kicked her way to victory, losing her spectacles in the process but deciding the contest by planting twelve stones of strapping endo-morphy on her opponent's chest.

'Patsy, this has got to stop,' said Mrs Gordon, 'and I also have to caution you that repetition of this sort of behaviour may force me to take sterner action.'

In this context, 'sterner action' meant expulsion, a step Mrs Gordon was reluctant to take because it would mean that she and the governors had made a mistake by offering Patsy a scholarship in the first place. Secondly, she was a whiz in the classroom and, to begin with, teachers loved tutoring her because she was so fast and receptive to new ideas. But some of them began to dread classes in which she was a participant before the term was more than a few weeks old.

The first to feel the full force of Patsy's venom was Chips Chippendale, who taught English and history to the teenies. Chips had given her an alpha minus for an essay Patsy thought deserved an alpha plus. Another teacher might have given her the higher grade, but Chips had never awarded anything greater than alpha minus throughout his career.

Patsy stamped her feet.

'It's not fair.'

Chips thought it was, and said so. And Patsy vowed to get her own back.

As in most closed societies – monasteries, convents, army battalions or boarding schools – some secrets just cannot be kept, and Patsy learned that Chips had a penchant for patting the bottoms of young girls. Though sexually inexperienced, she wasn't naïve, and she asked Chips if she could stay behind after a certain class, in order that he could explain where she had gone wrong with her essay.

Chips agreed, and they were alone in the classroom for fifteen minutes. Fifteen minutes after that, Patsy sought out a prefect and complained that Chips had 'touched' her.

'Show me where, Patsy.'

Patsy pointed to her ample bosom, but was cunning enough to guard her back.

'Of course, it could have been an accident.'

185

Mrs Gordon shook her head in despair when the matter was brought to her attention. She too had heard rumours about Chips during last year's play, but now Mr Penrose and Miss Lee had taken that over, for this year, she thought that was an end to the matter. Chips was due to retire before long and surely he wouldn't do anything so foolish, especially not with someone so physically unprepossessing as Patsy.

However, she couldn't afford to overlook the accusation which, if justified, was a matter for the police and a black mark for St Clare's.

She had Chips on the carpet first. Tired eyes brimming with tears, the old man denied everything. Mrs Gordon was convinced he was telling the truth.

Next came Patsy, with whom Mrs Gordon elected to fight fire with fire, cunning with cunning, the satanic with the more diabolical. Young Miss Kelly might be a genius, but that was no substitute for age and experience. Besides, Mrs Gordon wanted to give Patsy the benefit of the doubt. She might genuinely believe Chips had tried to molest her.

A long shot, true, but academics were taught not to jump to conclusions.

'This is a very serious charge you're making against Mr Chippendale, Patsy, and just before I telephone your parents, and thereafter the police, I'd like to hear your version.'

Patsy stiffened at the mention of the police and her parents, and she was quick enough to recognize she had only two options. To pursue the accusation would doubtless lead to a formal charge being laid against

Chips, followed by a court appearance in which she would be expected to give evidence. She had no experience of police procedure or courts, but she did know her mother and father, who would be merciless on Chips if the verdict went in her favour, but pitiless with her if it was proved she had lied.

No, involving the police and her parents placed the matter outside her control, and she didn't fancy that.

To say that she *could* have made a mistake was the better alternative. She had doubtless given Mr Chippendale an uncomfortable few hours, and that would have to suffice.

'I've been thinking about it all, Mrs Gordon,' she said, apple-dumpling cheeks creasing in what she hoped was a sweet and winning smile, but which resembled more a Hallowe'en pumpkin put together by the Marquis de Sade, 'and I could have made a mistake. On reflection, it was probably an accident. I'm sure Mr Chippendale meant no harm. I was just shocked to begin with, that's all.'

Mrs Gordon felt like shocking Patsy with something like a garrotte, but that was not her function. However, she was not about to let the girl get away with it that easily. She was a vindictive liar, and that was all there was to it. She had taken the scholarship place of someone who would have been, doubtless, more deserving and grateful.

Ten thousand pounds a year plus clothing allowances. Really, expulsion was too good for the little minx, but one could not use the ultimate sanction without hard proof.

Still, she made her displeasure apparent.

Patsy could have destroyed a long-serving master's career, not to mention his life. Mr Chippendale could have ended up in prison. In future, Mrs Gordon trusted Patsy would think long and hard before speaking out, on any subject.

Patsy left Mrs Gordon's study in tears – of rage, not remorse – vowing vengeance but knowing the headmistress was unassailable. Very well, there were more ways than one of skinning a cat.

She selected her next victim with care: Sybil Heilbron, who taught lower school French and German. Miss Heilbron, as not only Patsy but all the juniors were aware, was a knowledgeable teacher but a poor disciplinarian whose classes were easily disrupted if a handful of determined girls set their minds to it. If Chips was off the hook and Mrs Gordon impossible to get at, at least Patsy could make life miserable for an easier target.

As Lavinia Lee had discovered to her chagrin, Sybil Heilbron was shy and reticent, hardly ever originating a conversation and finding it difficult to make a contribution even when someone else was doing most of the talking. She sparkled but rarely, and only then in small-group tutorials. For her, handling classes of twenty-odd was sheer hell and, in a kinder world, she would have joined the Civil Service, found a desk and a job where nothing much was expected of her, and sat it out until pension or husband arrived.

Sadly for her, she enjoyed teaching when it worked well.

She also enjoyed doing *The Times* crossword, which Patsy soon established. Further, she discovered that Miss Heilbron normally saved the puzzle to complete during mid-morning break and located the table on which the young teacher's newspaper was placed by Dobbs each day.

Patsy had been completing *The Times* crossword without much difficulty since she was twelve. To begin with, therefore, she was up with the skylarks in order to get to Miss Heilbron's *Times* before Miss Heilbron did. Taking the newspaper to a lavatory, being careful not to make the paper look read, she raced through the clues, filling in the answers in heavy block capitals. Then she replaced the newspaper.

It was annoying that she couldn't see Miss Heilbron's dismay in the staffroom when she discovered that the grid had already been filled, but there was nothing Patsy could do about that.

After two mornings of completing the puzzle, she judged Miss Heilbron would make other arrangements for the delivery of her newspaper and didn't try to steal it. When the bewildered teacher found that her puzzle was untouched for a week, the old arrangement with Dobbs resumed and the newspaper appeared on its usual table.

Once it did, Patsy resumed her early morning ablutions, again taking the newspaper, but on these occasions simply snipping the crossword from the back page with scissors.

This happened twice before Sybil Heilbron cancelled *The Times* for a week. But by then Patsy had wearied of the game anyway. Miss Heilbron was too easy a target.

Patsy made her biggest mistake by selecting, as her next victim, someone who was not easily intimidated. Like many geniuses – Napoleon upgrading the Peninsular War while he attacked Moscow, Hitler fighting on two fronts, Salman Rushdie believing that a *fatwa* was Arabic slang for an overweight wife – she made the basic mistake of believing that, just because she was clever, everyone else was dumb.

It was not entirely an accident, on either side, that she wandered away from the crocodile one Saturday afternoon when the teenies were taken en bloc into town. When she slipped away, none of the other fourteen-year-olds could be bothered to tell the mistress in charge that she'd gone. If Patsy got it in the neck, good luck. As for Patsy, she'd fake her way out of it somehow.

In the shopping precinct, she saw Felicity Coggan, who taught geography to Patsy and whom Patsy hated. The feeling was mutual.

Keeping fifty yards behind Mrs Coggan, Patsy followed her, hoping that the teacher was a secret kleptomaniac about to steal lightbulbs from Woolworths.

No such luck.

Mrs Coggan didn't even slip so much as a toffee from Pick-n-Mix into her handbag.

But there was something about the geography

mistress's demeanour that intrigued Patsy. When she found out what it was, she thought Christmas and her birthday had arrived all at once.

Felicity Coggan entered a café. Patsy peered through the window. Mrs Coggan sat down opposite a boy Patsy had seen around school but whose name she did not know. A member of the Upper Sixth. Patsy saw them clasp hands intimately. The young man could have been Mrs Coggan's son or nephew and, at the beginning, Patsy was not sure he wasn't. They were certainly very close whatever the relationship.

Patsy sought out the crocodile, apologized profusely to the mistress in charge for losing it, and accepted her telling-off with good grace. After all, she now had bigger fish to fry.

Back at St Clare's she made some discreet enquiries. The sixth-former's name was Guy Young. He was no blood kin of Felicity Coggan, and it didn't take long for Patsy to conclude that Guy's relationship with Mrs Coggan was of a sexual nature.

She didn't care that it didn't make any sense, to her, that a good-looking eighteen-year-old boy was involved sexually with a woman more than twice his age. Or that a woman in her late thirties wanted to bed someone young enough to be her son. It was a fact, she was convinced, and that was all there was to it.

She approached the geography teacher after first period Monday morning, even giving the slight curtsey-bob that juniors were expected to perform when looking for favours, and something that, normally, Patsy was loath to do.

'Excuse me, Mrs Coggan, but I think you dropped this in the precinct in town on Saturday, near the café.'

Patsy held out a pound coin, something she could ill afford to lose if Mrs Coggan claimed it, but worth the sacrifice as an opening gambit.

Felicity Coggan didn't turn a hair though her insides described a somersault. Damn it to hell, of all the rotten luck. With only one minor lapse since her divorce, and none at all during her time at St Clare's, she had resisted her penchant for much younger men. Then Guy Young had caught her eye, and she his. With his beautiful blond hair and classic profile, he had reminded her instantly of the J.H. Thomas drawing of Rupert Brooke hanging in the National Portrait Gallery.

That was just before the end of last Trinity Term, before the start of the long vacation.

She had resisted it, of course, knowing that it was more than her job was worth to be caught in bed with a male student, but he kept seeking her out, practically demanding to know where she would be spending the summer holidays.

'France,' she told him.

'Funny,' he'd said, 'that's where I'm going.'

'Probably not the same part.'

'Oh, I think you'll find it is.'

Well, where was the harm? she'd asked herself, and not even the small voice of conscience had answered.

They'd spent an idyllic six weeks in the cottage she rented every year. He'd proved a gentle and caring lover, and what he lacked in experience she soon taught him. Naturally they couldn't give each other up when school started again, but they'd been ultra-cautious. Or so she'd thought.

'Thank you, Patsy,' she said, 'but I don't believe I did. However, I commend you for your honesty.'

'Then perhaps it was the young man's, ma'am.'

Oh dear, thought Felicity. For one brief moment she'd hoped Patsy hadn't seen her with Guy, but that of course would have been asking a lot of the gods of fortune.

'Perhaps it was, Patsy, perhaps it was.' There was nothing for it but to bluff it out. 'However, I doubt it. I suggest you put a notice on the bulletin board, without saying, naturally, where you found the coin. Just write that you found one and allow someone to tell you where they lost it.'

'If you say so, ma'am.'

'Oh, I do say so, Patsy, I do say so.'

Patsy stood her ground.

'I think the young man was Guy Young, ma'am, Upper Sixth. Perhaps I should approach him directly. I mean to say, it would save all the bother of the bulletin board.'

Felicity sighed inwardly. That this was blackmail, pure and simple, there could be no doubt, even though Patsy hadn't formalized her demands yet. And what was the advice usually given to blackmail victims in a thousand cheap novels and 'B' movies? Don't pay. The blackmailer is never satisfied.

Easy to say, harder to act upon.

'You see, Mrs Gordon, I'm having a passionate love affair with one of my Upper Sixth students, and Patsy Kelly has learned of it. I hope you don't mind.'

No, impossible. It would mean the end of her career at St Clare's for certain, and probably the end of her teaching career. Worse, Mrs Gordon would feel compelled to expel Guy, which would doubtless destroy his university chances and thus his future.

'What is it you want of me, Patsy?'

'Ma'am?'

'You heard me.'

'Why, nothing, ma'am.'

'Then I suggest you leave and act on my advice vis-à-vis the bulletin board.'

'Perhaps I will, ma'am. On the other hand, perhaps I'll think it over for a while.'

The evil little bitch, thought Felicity when Patsy had curtseyed and left. She thought, now, she understood the fourteen-year-old's motive, which wasn't for better grades: Patsy was a straight A student with no need to ask for favouritism. No, she just wanted to wield power, watch someone squirm, someone in authority.

Yes, evil was the *mot juste*.

To tell Guy or not? No, not yet, no point in worrying him for the moment, not until she'd decided what to do with little Miss Kelly.

The trouble was, what could she do? She could resign, plead personal reasons, that was one option. Go at the end of term. But her resignation would soon become common knowledge, and there were no guarantees that Patsy wouldn't do something appalling once she realized her victim was escaping. An anonymous note to Mrs Gordon was all it would take.

She could wait for the axe to fall and then deny everything, but that was scarcely acceptable. In the first place, it was putting her, and Guy, in Patsy's power, which was precisely what the malevolent creature wanted. Nothing might happen for a week, a month, or ever, but each day would be filled with fear. In the second place, she knew she was incapable, if challenged by Mrs Gordon, of lying. She knew very well that Guy – dear, sweet Guy – wouldn't be able to carry it off.

No, she was in a fix, there was no question. Her own stupid fault, but there it was. Her ex-husband had warned her, all those years ago during the bitter divorce proceedings, that she would one day find herself in trouble. Very well, that day had arrived.

In the tradition of all good boarding-school stories, however, help was coming from an unexpected quarter.

9

The Secret Three

Vanessa Maxwell grinned in the darkness at her two closest friends, Tina Johns and Lucy Harris. The school clock chimed the half-hour. By rights they should have been tucked up in bed long since, but tonight they had a mission.

'Got the mice?'

Tina held up a cardboard box, inside which tiny feet could be heard scampering.

'Poor bloody mice,' said Lucy. 'You might have come up with a better idea.'

'Oh, they'll be all right. Mice are survivors. I read it somewhere.'

They were in the dimly lit long second-floor corridor of Frobisher House, making for dormitory number two. The Frobisher Lower Fifth netball team had beaten Vanessa's side that afternoon, using unfair tactics in Vanessa's view, and this was the trio's way of taking revenge.

So far they remained undetected, but even if they were spotted they stood an excellent chance of getting away without their identities being uncovered, for all three girls were wearing dominoes, hooded cloaks with eye masks.

The three fourteen-year-olds had been at prep school together since the age of five, and had joined St Clare's the same first day of Michaelmas Term just over a year ago. They had based the idea of the Secret Three on characters called the Silent Three they discovered in a dog-eared girls' Christmas annual belonging to Lucy's mother, who hoarded such childhood memorabilia. They had made the dominoes during school holidays out of old blankets, dyed them black, and kept them hidden in their lockers. The society's sworn object, which Vanessa, having the best handwriting, had written out on a sheet of foolscap and which they had all signed and sealed in blood by pricking their thumbs, was to root out injustice wherever they found it, and set wrongs aright. Regrettably, it was a fact of life at St Clare's that school menials rarely had stolen diamonds planted on them by the wicked uncle of the school bully, and no crisis ever arose whereby, unless a piece of long-lost parchment, giving St Clare's absolute title to the land on which it stood, was found, the institution would be forced to close and the grounds turned into a Sainsbury's.

Still, they did their best, even if the best was rarely more than the occasional midnight feast behind the fives courts or scaring the living daylights out of Frobisher's Upper Fifth. They'd all tried cigarettes, of course, puffing at them furtively from behind the safety of their masks, but none of the trio had liked the taste so smoking as an act of devilment or rebellion became a non-starter. They openly campaigned to save whales and preserve the ozone layer, but so did everyone else. Soon, they all realized, without ever expressing it aloud, they would grow out of their games, and their cloaks and masks would be packed away for good. For the moment, however, the Secret Three existed, and it was quite fun to invent arcane handshakes and write to one another in code – even if, lately, the subject matter of the messages was less to do with ways out of school after curfew and more to do with the looks of certain boys.

Lucy stumbled over the hem of her domino, almost falling.

'Ssssh,' said Vanessa, making more noise in telling Lucy to be quiet than Lucy had to warrant the admonition.

'Sorry.'

Lucy was a lanky girl who wore her hair in bunches and who was privately dismayed that her breasts were apparently reluctant to develop. She wore a bra because school rules said she had to, but it was almost unnecessary.

Tina, clutching the mice box, was the tomboy of the trio, her dark hair a mass of unruly curls. If there was a wall to be scaled, Tina would be over it first; if there was a stream to be forded, Tina would lead the way. If there were mice to be caught and carried, Tina was the catcher and the transporter.

Although all three generally considered themselves as equals within their society, if ever a vote had been taken regarding a *primus inter pares*, Vanessa would probably have got the nod because she was the brainiest. And looked it with her straight brown hair brushed carefully back and plaited down to her waist, and her heavy-framed spectacles. She also had another, minor claim to fame in that her mother was an actress with a leading role in a long-running television soap opera, in which she played the divorced mother of a wayward teenage daughter. With a northern accent, to boot, though her natural tones were those of a well-bred Surrey matron. However, she was good at accents, Vanessa's mother, and frequently had her daughter and her daughter's friends in stitches by mimicking characters from Australian soaps, whose acting ability made the cast of the late and un-lamented *Eldorado* look like the RSC.

'Gimme a brike, Feenlie, and put a few tinnies in the Eski so that we can have a barbie before we go to uni this arvo.'

For her older friends she usually had to translate this as, 'Give me a break, Finlay, and put some cans of beer in the cooler in order that we may have a barbecue before we attend university this afternoon.'

When the other girls wanted to know what was going to happen next in Vanessa's mother's show, Vanessa usually gave them a mysterious smile and said she was sworn to secrecy. In actuality she didn't know, and neither did her mother more than a couple of scripts ahead, but that was not the sort of information one divulged.

'Ready?' said Vanessa over her shoulder when they were outside dormitory number two.

Tina held up the box.

'Ready.'

Vanessa flung open the dormitory door. Tina took the lid off the shoebox and scooted the mice inside.

'Mice!' yelled Lucy. 'Mice, *mice*, MICE.'

Vanessa slammed the door shut. The three girls legged it. Behind them they heard screams of panic.

The following afternoon, directly after classes, Lucy said, 'You know, that's not what we formed the Secret Three for, capturing and releasing a few harmless rodents.'

'Nonsense,' snorted Vanessa. 'Frobisher won the netball by cheating, and that's a form of injustice.'

'Yes, but . . .'

At that moment all three saw Patsy Kelly deliberately knock Annie Belt-and-Braces's books from the timid girl's hands and then, when Annie tried to pick them up, kick them away. Their form mistress, Mrs Coggan, had already left the classroom and did not witness the incident.

'Here, here,' protested Tina.

'Buzz off,' said Patsy, and barged past the trio.

The three helped Annie collect her books and afterwards, when Annie had gone, looked at one another.

'Now that,' said Lucy, 'is injustice.'

That Patsy was a monster the trio concurred, but it wasn't easy to deal with a monster.

'Cut one head off,' said Tina, vaguely remembering something from Greek mythology, 'and another grows.'

They discussed apple-pie beds, booby-trapping Patsy's locker, sabotaging her classwork, and various other nefarious schemes, but dismissed them all as either too tame or too vindictive.

It was Vanessa who finally came up with a stratagem so outrageous it left the other two dumbfounded.

Once a fortnight each class of teenies spent a double period at the school farm, to learn something of animal husbandry. Strictly speaking it wasn't the school's farm at all but a section of a nearby working farm set aside for use by the school, for a suitable annual fee – which pleased the owner because farmers are always pleading poverty.

For close on two hours, always the last two hours of the day, the girls mucked out the stables, fed the pigs and goats, and generally got thoroughly dirty. It was while throwing potato peelings at a litter of very pink Tamworths, all about four months old and not one larger than an average-sized dog, that Tina said, 'Who do they remind you of?'

'Patsy!' chuckled Vanessa and Lucy in unison, before Vanessa added as a solo, 'Troops, I have it.'

Back at St Clare's, after showering and changing, Lucy said, 'You're crackers, Van. We'll never get away with it. It's over a mile to the farm and pigs, especially young pigs, make a dickens of a racket. Even if we put the wretched animal in a wheelbarrow and pushed, one of us would have to sit on it.'

'Lucy,' said Vanessa severely, 'you weren't listening. The mountain is not going to Mahomet, Mahomet is going to the mountain. That is, for a dimwit like you, the pig is not coming to Patsy, Patsy is going to the pig. Or pigs.'

'And how do you propose to persuade her to do that?'

'Belt-and-Braces is going to challenge her to a paint-gun duel. You know, those things war-games enthusiasts are so fond of. They splatter you with colour but otherwise do no harm. We had a demonstration last Trinity. Outside school grounds, of course, and early in the morning, before classes, before breakfast, even. The clocks haven't gone back yet, and it's light at six-thirty. Six forty-five seems a good time.'

'We don't have access to paint-guns, remember,' said Tina. 'After last term's demonstration, Mrs Gordon and the governors vetoed the whole idea. "Unladylike".'

'Ah, but Patsy only arrived *this* term. She won't know we don't have access. Now, do you remember those face masks we all wore just before break-up last Christmas? They're with the drama group's props, I think. And who do we know that's got a Polaroid . . .?'

Annie Belton-Bray wasn't keen on the idea.

'She'll beat me up if I push her. She'll jump on me and squish me like a bug.'

'She won't, trust us,' said Vanessa. 'Just call her a fat cow and leave the rest to us. You want to see her humiliated, don't you? God knows, she's done it to you often enough.'

Annie's eyes glittered.

'Yes. Fat cow, you say.'

'Or fat pig,' giggled Tina.

'I don't understand,' said Annie.

'You will, B-and-B, you will,' promised Vanessa.

Annie waited until after morning classes one Thursday. The Secret Three made sure they were close by.

'You fat cow,' said Annie timorously, though on this occasion Patsy hadn't offended her.

'I BEG your pardon,' exploded Patsy.

'I said you're a fat cow.'

Patsy took a swipe at Annie, which would have knocked her head off had it connected, but fortunately Vanessa grabbed her arm before putting in her own twopenn'orth.

'Enough, enough,' she said. 'First the strawberries, then the books, now fighting. We don't do that at St Clare's, Patsy.'

'She called me a fat cow. Twice.'

'And she was wrong to do so. But you two are going to have to sort this thing out, in a civilized manner.'

'I'm going to splatter her with paint,' said Annie, sticking to the script. 'Yellow paint,' she added, improvising, 'because she's yellow like a . . . a . . .'

'Coward,' mouthed Lucy.

'Birds Eye custard,' managed Annie.

Lucy groaned audibly.

'God speed the plough,' she murmured.

'What paint, what's she talking about?' asked Patsy.

Vanessa explained about the war-game guns. Patsy's eyes lit up. There was no chance of a little pipsqueak like Annie Belton-Bray coming out of this without being covered, head to foot, in paint. Apart from that, she would find some method of retaining the gun, and then everybody had better watch out.

The 'duel' was arranged for the following morning. Accidentally on purpose, the venue chosen was on a direct route to the school farm.

'I'll need a second,' insisted Patsy, who'd read all the books and seen all the films.

'That's you, Tina,' said Vanessa.

'Why me?' protested Tina, before Vanessa shushed her with a finger to the lips. 'OK, so it's me.'

'It is I,' Patsy corrected.

'I'll kill her,' said Tina later.

'Let her dig her own grave,' advised Vanessa. 'And, just for tomorrow, the Secret Three are the Secret Two.'

Patsy couldn't wait to get at Annie Belton-Bray when Friday dawned, and she was up before the bell. She met Annie and Tina behind the tennis courts.

'Where's the squirt's second?' she asked.

'Meeting us there,' answered Tina.

Midway between school and farm, Patsy said, 'Haven't we gone far enough? And where are the paint guns?'

'Coming,' said Tina.

On cue, Lucy and Vanessa leapt out from the hedgerow, cloaked in their dominoes.

Despite her size, Patsy was overpowered before she could utter more than a few shrieks. A potato sack was placed over her head and shoulders, and her arms bound with rope. Wickedly but understandably, Annie kicked her fat tormentor's behind before Patsy was frog-marched the rest of the way to the farm, a matter of a few hundred yards. There she was placed against a sty of squealing piglets, and the loose ends of rope tied to the railings. A pig mask from the props' basket was put over her head, over the potato sack, and a sign around her neck read:

HERE I AM, PATSY KELLY
CLOSEST TO A FAT PIG'S BELLY
I OFTEN WONDER, WONDER WHY
HOW PIGS ARE NICERER THAN I.

Vanessa's grammar might have left something to be desired, but the sentiment was about right. She took several Polaroids of the scene before she, Lucy, Tina and Annie scarpered.

There was hell to pay, of course.

The farmer released Patsy when he found her, making as much noise as the sty full of piglets, called Mrs Gordon, and Patsy was returned to St Clare's breathing fire and demanding to call her parents.

'After you've seen Matron,' said the Gorgon, who had already viewed the Polaroids, photocopied in colour on the science lab's copier by Vanessa and rapidly circulated. She could hardly contain her laughter. Children, without doubt, had their own methods of dealing with school thugs, and superior it was, too, to anything headmistresses could mete out.

Mrs Natalie Howe, the matron, known throughout school as Auntie Natal, gave Patsy a clean bill of health.

'Shocked, that's all,' she advised Mrs Gordon.

Even so, and even though Friday was one of his busiest days, Patsy's father accompanied her mother to the school.

As it was close to half-term, Mrs Gordon suggested they take Patsy straight home.

'And it wouldn't distress me in the least if she didn't return for the second half of Michaelmas, or indeed at all.'

Mr Kelly, accustomed to rapid mental arithmetic, did a couple of calculations in his head. Half a term was £1,500. On her own authority, which she was certain the governors would support, Mrs Gordon agreed that £1,500 of scholarship money, in the form of a cheque, would be sent to Mr Kelly if Patsy found alternative schooling.

Patsy's parents jumped at the opportunity.

'But I expect you to find the culprits and punish them,' said Mr Kelly as a parting shot.

In Mrs Gordon's view, the flags should be put out and the bells rung for whomsoever had rid St Clare's of the turbulent Patsy, but, unfortunately, the system didn't work like that. Mr Kelly was right. The offenders had to be found and admonished.

As it happened, there was no need for a witch hunt. When news circulated that Patsy had more or less been sacked, never to return, Vanessa got an attack of guilt.

'We'll have to own up,' she said to Tina and Lucy.

The other two agreed.

'Might mean the sack for us too,' said Lucy.

'Still,' said Tina.

They went to their form mistress, Felicity Coggan, first.

Not much at St Clare's was a secret to Felicity, and the little that escaped her was illuminated by Guy. She knew all about the Secret Three. Nevertheless, she had to appear severe.

'Mice were let loose in a Frobisher dorm a little while ago, resulting in pandemonium. The culprits were never found, though I understand three girls in cloaks were seen running away. Wouldn't be you three, by any chance, would it? No, please don't answer. At St Clare's secret societies are not permitted. We are not Masonic, nor are we Jesuit. The dominoes will go, and I shall take the whole matter up with Mrs Gordon myself. Fifty lines for each of you, to be handed to me in Great Hall tomorrow afternoon. I know it's Saturday, but there you have it.'

Felicity went to see Mrs Gordon.

'Vanessa Maxwell, Tina Johns and Lucy Harris, correct?' said the Gorgon, who was also nobody's fool.

'Correct, Headmistress.'

'A hundred lines apiece?'

'Fifty.'

'You were too lenient. You would also not believe the things Patsy said before she left. She admitted lying about Chips, but said he deserved it. She said something about Miss Heilbron's crossword, about which I know nothing. And she had the effrontery to scream abuse about you and a member of the

Upper Sixth. Naturally, I paid her no heed. After all, we both know what a liar she is.'

'Mrs Gordon,' began Felicity, but the Gorgon held up her hand.

'No, Felicity, I prefer to think of the late Patsy as a teller of untruths. But do bear in mind that this is a very small world. And I do hope we've heard the last of the Secret Three.'

'You have my word, Headmistress.'

But in that, as in so much else in her life, Felicity Coggan was wrong.

10

Half-Term

The mid-Michaelmas break ran from Friday lunchtime to lights-out Tuesday evening, when all boarders were expected to be back. Some students lived too far away to make the journey worthwhile; others had parents or guardians who resided abroad or were out of the country on business; others still had no reason or desire to go home. To cater for these groups a skeleton staff had to remain on school premises. Robert Penrose was one of those who drew a short straw.

'Damn and blast it,' he said to Lavinia. 'I had our hotel already picked out: log fires, three-star cooking, and a king-sized bed. I guess I'll have to ring and cancel.'

'There'll be other times,' soothed Lavinia.

Secretly she was relieved. She had business to take care of in London and she had been wondering how she could explain to Penrose that she wouldn't be able to see him over the break. Now Mrs Gordon had solved the problem for her.

Others with an appointment in London were Paula van der Groot and Sappho Peters. Their cache of marijuana was almost exhausted, and they left on the one o'clock train. Paula's parents lived in South Africa, though her mother was English and an alumna of St Clare's. Sappho was a Londoner born and bred, her own parents having a house in Kensington. Neither she nor Paula intended using it, however; there was usually some action, somebody's bed to share, on a Friday and a Saturday, and if there wasn't that was no great loss. They were only making the trip to restock, and if they ended up back at St Clare's Saturday afternoon, well, so be it. Providing their supplier didn't let them down, and he never had, they would have everything they wanted within the four walls of their own study.

OK, perhaps not quite everything because Jennifer was still proving an elusive fish to catch, but that would happen in time. Not this weekend, though, because both Phoebe and Jennifer had gone home for half-term.

Amanda Panda's mother collected her from their local station late in the afternoon.

'You look different,' said Mrs McDonald.

Amanda was delighted her mother had noticed, but shrugged it off as a matter of no consequence.

'I'm trying to lose a little weight, that's all.' She had, in fact, shed six pounds in ten days. 'I'm also thinking of changing my hairstyle and perhaps dye-ing it a different colour. Darker.'

'That's silly,' said Mrs McDonald. 'Plump is plump and mouse is mouse. You can't go against your nature.'

'That's just idiotic,' retorted Amanda crossly. 'Like

saying you can't have your teeth fixed if they're crooked or an unsightly wart removed.'

'Don't address me in that tone, young lady,' said her mother.

Well, it is idiotic, thought Amanda, remembering how the men had flocked around Jocasta at Flanagan's, how they always did. Very well, she could never hope to compete at the highest level with Jocasta Petrillo, but that didn't mean she always had to be 'the other one' when out with Jo. Oh, yes, she'd heard boys talking. 'I'll take the cracking-looking brunette, you can have the other one.' There was no reason she couldn't change her hair-colouring and lose some of the horrible fatness that made her so miserable. Her weight, in any case, was largely due to her mother and the fact that her parents owned hotels, where there was always food available in the kitchens.

Oh, Amanda's always been big-boned. Yes, she does have a healthy appetite, runs in the family. No, darling, I'm sure another cake won't do you any harm. Better than throwing them out. Waste not, want not is what I always say.

It grew from there, and so did she. At the age of eight or nine, it was fun to have parents in the hotel business, satisfying to entertain her small friends and have parties where the tables were groaning with food. Far too late did she realize that weight put on at that age and in her early teens would be hell to take off, would make her life agony when boys stopped being horrid individuals who pulled her hair, and became objects of desire — desire that was not reciprocated because there were exotic creatures like Jocasta and Kate McNamara around.

Well, that was all over.

Mrs Petrillo picked up Jocasta in the Range Rover mid-afternoon and, as arranged, gave Julia Hastings a ride all the way home because Julia's parents lived only thirty miles from the Petrillos and it was on Mrs Petrillo's route.

'We won't come in,' said Mrs Petrillo, declining Julia's invitation. 'Give Jo a ring if you want a ride back on Tuesday.'

In truth, Petrillo *mère et fille* were glad to see the back of Julia, who had chattered interminably about her role in *A Midsummer Night's Dream* for the best part of an hour.

'Lord,' said Mrs Petrillo, 'is she always like that?'

'For the last few weeks, yes. How's Papa?'

'Well, as far as I know. He's in Brussels today, but he'll be home tomorrow evening.' And his bimbo will be spending Saturday night and Sunday night alone, because she had made it quite clear to Claudio that, if he didn't put in an appearance for Jocasta's half-term, he would be in serious trouble. He hadn't seen his daughter since the first week in September, for God's sake.

Mr Petrillo had meekly complied with his wife's ultimatum, which surprised her. Perhaps the affair with his secretary was winding down.

'And how's the brat?'

The 'brat' was Jocasta's younger brother.

'He's fine too. I spoke to him on the phone earlier

in the week. Unfortunately his half-term doesn't coincide with yours.' Mrs Petrillo smiled sideways at her daughter. 'He sent his regrets that he won't be seeing you before Christmas.'

'I'll bet,' grunted Jocasta.

'Have you any plans for the weekend?' asked her mother.

'To get some hard riding in and forget about schoolbooks,' answered Jocasta.

And a little sex wouldn't go amiss, either, she thought to herself. No, make that a lot of sex. It had been almost six weeks, and it was a great pity she didn't fancy any of the boys at St Clare's or feel able to take a chance with some of the horny young goats who frequented Flanagan's.

After ten minutes' chat with her parents, Julia excused herself and headed for the upstairs telephone. Her first call was to Teddy Hedges.

'I have to have dinner with my family tonight,' she said, after station identification, 'but I thought we might meet up tomorrow and do something, go somewhere.'

Teddy said something to the effect that there was only one place he wanted to go and doubtless Julia knew *precisely* where that was.

Julia feigned shock.

'Teddy, this *is* the telephone.'

Still, she felt the same way, or supposed she did. Teddy wasn't and never would be the great love of her life, but they had been as intimate as two people could possibly be without consummating their relationship, and she so desperately wanted to do 'it', free herself from virginity. She was, she thought loftily – her ideas becoming more literary since landing the role of Helena – like a climber twenty feet short of the Matterhorn's summit in a snowstorm. She could descend, try again with a different partner at a later date, or she could make one last effort and gain the top.

After she hung up, she wondered briefly if she were being unfaithful to Ben Fisher. No, that was absurd. There was nothing between her and Ben apart from a few wet kisses, though she had to admit, with every rehearsal that passed, she liked him a little more.

But Ben was at school, where she spent most of her time, and Teddy was at home. It was like one of those holiday romances she'd read about: always easier to have a fling a thousand miles away, where flinger and flingee abandoned inhibitions.

Ben would have been delighted to hear that Julia was beginning to like him a little more with each day that passed, had Julia expressed it openly. For that matter, he would have appreciated a few encouraging words from anyone, but the facts were, what with his duties as stage manager for *MND* and his preoccupation with Julia, his studies had fallen behind alarmingly this term.

At the beginning of Michaelmas, he had confidently expected, with Richard Carson and one or two others from Lavinia Lee's fast-track languages stream, to be sitting the Oxford entrance examination in November, the so-called Mode E method of application. Just before the break, however, Lavinia had made it clear that that was a non-starter. His work wasn't up to scratch. He would fail, and that would reflect badly on St Clare's. (And on her, though she didn't say that to Fisher.) Instead, he would have to apply via Mode N, which meant skipping the entrance examination and, instead, submitting some samples of written work before attending for the interview in December. Since admissions tutors were no fools, knowing full well that candidates preparing in private invariably received help, even if he passed the interview he would have to obtain minimum grades of A, A and B in next summer's papers or he would not be awarded a place. Candidates accepted via success in the entrance examination usually only needed two passes at grade E or better. In other words, Fisher had to get his head down and do some serious work this half-term, write several essays for Lavinia's scrutiny, and the place to do that was St Clare's, where the library facilities were far superior to anything he could find at home, never mind the time lost travelling. No junketing for him.

His parents were disappointed when he called and told them that they would not be seeing him for the break. Fisher was equally frustrated that he could not get away from St Clare's for a few days, but he owed his parents a lot and he was well aware they were not as wealthy as some. Paying the fees meant making sacrifices.

Miss Lee had also told him she was not happy that he was spending so much of his leisure time at rehearsals, and had threatened to get Penrose to relieve him of his stage-managerial chores unless he pulled his socks up. She didn't know the half of it, of course. If he could just once – please, God, just once – get his leg over Julia, much of the other pressure would evaporate.

Henry Morton was also staying behind, but for different reasons.

Henry, I'm so sorry, but I have to be in Milan that weekend.

His mother had evidently forgotten their earlier telephone conversation, just before Open Day, when she had asked him if he was coming home for half-term and promised to put the date in her diary.

That's OK. There's lots to do here.

If I could cancel it, I would. God, what must you think of me!

It's all right, really.

You could, of course, come home anyway. I'll probably be back late Sunday or early Monday. Naturally I'd have to go, assuming Monday, straight to the office, but we could spend Monday evening together. On the other hand, I expect you'd be bored in the flat by yourself.

I expect I would. And I have to be down here again on Tuesday.

Yes, there is that. I am so sorry. Still, we'll have Christmas together, and that's not so far off.

Of course. Have a safe flight.

There was, naturally, very little to do at St Clare's during half-term, the weather being what it was. Also, since the incident after the Fellini film, Henry had not even been to the cinema in town. It was crazy, he knew – he didn't want to become a total recluse – but he was feeling increasingly isolated, even paranoid. He wished he had someone he could talk to, but there was no-one.

After *Amarcord*, he had secretly read a few articles on male homosexuality, which didn't enlighten him one iota. Some authorities claimed it was genetic, some environmental, some a combination of both. All, however, appeared to be agreed that, providing the baseline conditions obtained, most male homosexuals came from homes where the mother was the dominant figure, or where the father was absent.

Or dead.

On a strict interpretation of the word dominant, Henry didn't feel his mother qualified. She was, however – and had been for years – the only adult role model in his life.

Kate McNamara could have done without role models of either gender this half-term, without parents, for that matter. Carson had had no trouble convincing his father that he had work to catch up on in view of the impending entrance exam, and that he should remain at St Clare's during the break. Kate's mother was having none of it when she tried the same tactic.

'Your father and I would like to see something of you. Either he or I will be collecting you outside House around one o'clock on Friday.'

'You still don't trust me.'

'That has nothing to do with it. Of course, if Mr Penrose or Miss Lee are adamant you remain in school – and neither of them seemed dissatisfied with your work when I spoke to them on Open Day – I'll call them and try to persuade them otherwise.'

'No, don't do that. I can bring my books home.'

'I thought you might be able to.'

'Sorry,' said Kate to Carson, 'she won't wear it.'

With the school being nine-tenths unoccupied for ninety-six hours, they had planned to pass a few of them in unrestrained debauchery, hopefully in Carson's study since Fisher could be relied upon to vanish. God knows, thought Kate, she needed some physical release even though they had finally managed to get it together on Carson's coat in the fives courts a couple of nights after the failure in the hockey pavilion. But what a disaster it had been! While Carson had managed a puny orgasm, Kate didn't even come close – as it were – and ended up even more frustrated than before they began, so much so that she was angry.

'Christ, you might have waited for me!'

'Jesus, I know, I'm sorry.'

'Seems to me that all you wanted was to get inside me, have a free fuck, and chalk up another scalp. Shit, *another* scalp? I'm beginning to wonder if you've got any outside your tepee. Talk about a two-minute wham-bam-thank-you-ma'am! Who the hell do you think you are, John F. Kennedy?'

'Jesus, Kate, have a heart, I feel bad enough.'

'*You* feel bad enough? Well, bully for *you*! How the hell do you think I feel? Or doesn't it matter?'

'Of course it matters. It's the circumstances. First the hockey pavilion, which was at least enclosed, and now here, virtually in the open, on concrete, and with the temperature in the middle thirties Fahrenheit.'

'At least you'd got me to lie on. Apart from your coat, I was on the fucking concrete.'

Eventually Kate calmed down. Richard was right, it *was* the circumstances. At least she hoped that was the case. He was funny, witty, and she suspected she was half in love with him, or as much in love as any sixteen-year-old girl can be. But if he proved inadequate as a sexual partner, there was no future in their relationship.

No, that couldn't be it. They needed a bed, that was all, or at least somewhere comfortable, and half-term would be perfect. So perfect, in fact, that when Carson suggested, two days later, that they sneak out after lights-out and try the pavilion again, she turned him down.

'No, let's wait.'

And now her mother had put paid to that little idea. Oh, well.

'Will you stay here or go home?' she asked Carson.

'Home, I suppose. No point in staying now. I'll give my father a ring and tell him there's been a change of plan.'

'Don't go screwing any of those Surrey wenches.'

'I won't.'

He meant it, too. It hadn't been a total lie when he told his father he could do with some revision prior to the entrance exam. A little extra work wouldn't do him any harm.

'Don't you go getting laid by any of those young bucks down your way, either.'

Fat chance, thought Kate.

*   *   *

Without exceeding the speed limit more than a couple of times, Lavinia was in the South Kensington flat she shared with her sister Rebecca long before dark. Rebecca, who worked in computers, often from home, had two stiff gins poured before Lavinia was unpacked.

Lavinia kicked off her shoes and stretched her legs.

'So, tell me about it,' said Rebecca.

'About what?'

'About the new man in your life.'

'What makes you think there is one?'

'Vin, do me a favour. You have that self-satisfied look that only comes with regular bedding.'

'*Bedding?*' grinned Lavinia. 'Did I hear you say bedding? Are you reading those Gothic romances again?'

'Never mind my reading habits, let's have chapter and verse.'

You'd be shocked, sister dear, thought Lavinia, if I gave you so much as an iambus.

Even though only two years separated them, they never – and never had, even as teenagers – discussed their sex lives in anything other than the most general terms. Lavinia had no idea what Rebecca got up to when she was with a man, what her fantasies were, and had no desire to. And she certainly didn't want her sister to know that she, Lavinia, enjoyed fucking in open places or playing the whore, or more outré pursuits which even Penrose hadn't learned of yet. But would when the time was right.

Lavinia shook her head.

'I don't think I'm quite ready for the confessional yet.'

'Not that special, then?'

'Half and half. No, a bit more than half and half.'

'So why are you here for the break, or does he have a wife?'

'He does, as it happens, but all that's over.'

'Ho-hum,' said Rebecca.

'No, seriously,' said Lavinia, with a touch of annoyance, irritated that anyone, most of all Rebecca, would think she could be taken for a ride. 'Don't you think I can tell by this time when I'm being *aufs Eis gefuhrt* – led up the garden?'

'You didn't with Hennessy,' said Rebecca maliciously.

'Ah, yes, Hennessy,' said Lavinia. 'Which is the real answer to your question about why I'm in London for half-term.'

Rebecca pulled a long face.

'Oh, Christ, Vin, not Peter fucking Hennessy.'

'Yes, Peter fucking Hennessy.'

'Why, for God's sake? No, don't tell me, let me guess. You have to see him to make sure it's finally over. Now who's been reading romantic trash?'

'It's not that at all,' said Lavinia. 'I just have to see him, that's all.'

He was surprised to hear from her when she phoned, but readily agreed to meet her for a lunchtime drink in a Hampstead pub they both knew the following day.

Lavinia was up early, checking the weather, which

would govern what she would wear. It was raining and windy and looked cold, which was a nuisance but only a marginal one.

She spent part of the morning shopping in the King's Road, buying just two items: a black lace-trimmed garter belt and black stockings.

Back at the flat, Rebecca was still in her robe at the kitchen table, reading the financial pages and drinking her third cup of coffee. Lavinia grabbed a quick shower, washed her hair, then retreated to her own room to dress – dress to kill.

First, on went the garter belt, stockings and four-inch heels, the highest she possessed. Otherwise naked, she paraded in front of the full-length mirror. Perfect. Then came the black Lycra mini and open-necked silk shirt.

Knickers, she thought. No, no knickers. She might freeze her ass off, but it would be worth it.

After drying her hair, she considered jewellery, settling finally for a thin gold neck chain and her wristwatch.

She rejected several perfumes before opting for an atomizer of Cabotine by Gres, which she sprayed liberally around her neck and under her skirt.

Finished at last she pulled a chair in front of the mirror, sat on it, and crossed and uncrossed her legs slowly. A brief flash of blond pubic bush, framed by the garter belt and stockings, told her that all was well. She'd drive Hennessy mad with lust.

To top off the outfit she selected a black cashmere overcoat that reached just below her knees. Ideal.

When she took that off she'd blow a few minds.

She gave a final twirl. Yes, perfect.

Rebecca's jaw dropped when she saw her sister.

'Christ, Vin, you look stunning.'

She arrived at the pub a few minutes after one. It was fairly full as it usually was on a Saturday lunchtime, but she found Hennessy sitting at a table below a stag's head. A sign underneath read: The Buck Stops Here. Hennessy had always found that funny, which, nowadays, told her something about his sense of humour.

She was chagrined at first to see he had a woman with him, a redhead about her own age. After he'd pecked her on the cheek and bought her a small whisky and soda – 'I'm driving, have to be careful' – it transpired that the redhead wasn't actually with him but merely keeping him company. Her name was Grace and she was a journalist on the *Daily Mirror* and, with him or not, she showed no inclination to go away in a hurry.

She and Lavinia did not hit it off at all. They sniped at each other from the word go.

'Public school teacher, huh,' said Grace, dragging heavily on a Marlboro, and drinking a large brandy. 'Teaching the class-conscious little bastards how not to participate in John fucking Major's class-less society. Well, Major's a jerk, no question, but we stand no chance of ridding this country of class distinction while schools like yours are still around. Which university?'

'Oxford,' said Lavinia, keeping a tight rein on her

temper. No point in letting this silly bitch upset her. 'You?'

'Sussex.'

'No so much a redbrick as a white tile,' said Lavinia.

'Jimmy Porter, *Look Back In Anger*,' sneered Grace.

'Circa 1956,' said Lavinia. 'Did you manage to see it first time round?'

'Ho-hum,' said Grace, eyes sparkling. 'I sense combat. I suppose you got a First at bloody Oxford.'

'Naturally.'

'Time to join your playmates at the bar, Grace,' said Hennessy, not unkindly, but making it quite clear that three was a crowd. 'Vin and I have things to discuss.'

Grace stood up, unsteadily.

'OK, I can see when I'm not wanted.'

'Where the hell did you find her?' asked Lavinia.

'Nowhere. She's a local, lives round the corner. And no, before you ask, I haven't been to bed with her.'

'I didn't ask,' said Lavinia.

Until now she had kept her coat on. Now she removed it and hung it over the back of a chair. Then she leaned back and crossed her legs, as rehearsed.

Hennessy didn't see what was on offer first time round. He was looking at her entire outfit as if he'd never seen her before.

'Vin,' he managed, 'you look beautiful.'

He wasn't the only one to notice. A dozen male heads had turned, some of them standing with Grace. Lavinia heard her stage-whisper, 'Forget it, she probably doesn't put out unless you've got a spare million.'

Lavinia shifted her position, putting Hennessy's body

between herself and the rubber-necks. Another time she would have got a sexual kick out of teasing a dozen men, but what she had to sell here and now she only wanted Hennessy to buy.

'Thank you. How are you, anyway?'

'Fine. And you?'

'Equally fine.'

Small talk occupied ten minutes and the remainder of Lavinia's first whisky and soda. When that had gone, Hennessy offered to buy her another.

'Perhaps just one more.'

When he returned from the bar, just as he was sitting down, Lavinia repeated her trick of slowly crossing her legs. This time, she knew, Hennessy did not miss the fact that she was wearing, under her mini, stockings and a garter belt and nothing else. His eyes damn near popped out of his head, but she could tell he wasn't absolutely sure what his next move should be. She helped him, leaning forward and putting one hand on his knee.

'Let's make this the last drink, shall we, and retreat to somewhere more intimate?'

'Christ, yes. I've missed you, Vin. I didn't know how much until you walked in.'

Bullshit, she thought. You've just spotted an opportunity to spend the afternoon humping your old girlfriend, who, let's face it, was pretty damned dynamic between the sheets even if she does say so herself.

'I've missed you, too.'

They finished their drinks in a hurry. A chorus of

wolf-whistles and sotto voce remarks, most of them
lewd, followed them as they left the pub. Only Grace
raised her voice.

'I'll wager she doesn't give blow jobs – spoil the
plum in her mouth.'

'Have you got your car here?' asked Lavinia.

'Of course.'

'Never mind, let's take mine. I'll drive you back
later.'

'What's the point if we're going to my flat?'

'No, I don't want to go there,' said Lavinia. 'Too
many painful memories. Let's drive to Highgate Wood
like we used to.'

'Vin, it's pouring with rain.'

'What's the matter, lost your sense of adventure? It
wouldn't be the first time we've done it in a car.
Why do you think I dressed like this? Peter, it's what
I've missed most, getting laid in the open where it's
dangerous. Still, if you're not game . . .'

Lavinia judged by the expression on his face that
he would have humped her there and then in the pub
doorway, given the opportunity. He wasn't going to
turn down an unexpected fuck, rain or no rain.

'Let's go,' he said.

Highgate Wood was about a mile and a half from
the pub. They had often used it for their alfresco
sexual adventures in the past because it was about the
same distance from Hennessy's flat.

Lavinia kept within the speed limit. After a quarter
of a mile she unfastened her coat and took hold of
Hennessy's right hand with her left. She placed it

under her skirt, felt his fingers enter her. She was wet, of course. Only a nun wouldn't have been.

'Christ,' he said.

With his free hand he unzipped his flies and brought out his cock, which was three-quarters erect. It became fully erect when Lavinia, keeping half-glazed eyes on the road and praying she wouldn't have to shift out of fourth gear in a hurry, took hold of it.

'No, no,' he said. 'You'll have me coming before we're there.'

Lavinia didn't want that, and didn't want his fingers inside her. She began to breathe heavily.

'Don't,' she said, 'or you'll have me coming too.'

It took them five minutes to reach Highgate Wood and another sixty seconds to find a deserted spot. Because of the rain there was no-one else around.

Lavinia eased off her coat and raised her skirt to waist level, so that Hennessy could see the goodies he was about to plunge into. She glanced across at him. The head of his cock glistened. Ah, Jesus, she thought, remembering.

'Get out of those fucking trousers,' she muttered hoarsely. 'I want to feel flesh against flesh.'

Hennessy struggled to do so, couldn't manage it with his shoes on, slipped them off, but still couldn't make it within the narrow confines of the car.

'Get out and do it. Come on, Peter, hurry. I need you to fuck me like I've never been fucked before.'

Hennessy opened the passenger door, stepped outside into the rain, removed his trousers and underpants, and flung them back inside the car.

Lavinia then snapped the catch on the passenger door, turned over the engine, engaged first gear, and roared off. Via the rearview mirror she saw him leap up and down with baffled rage and then, realizing he was half naked and sporting a massive if soon to be wilting erection, race for the cover of the nearest trees. It was going to be a long walk home.

A mile down the road Lavinia wound down the window on her side and tossed out Hennessy's trousers, underwear and shoes.

'One-nil, one-nil, one-nil, one-nil,' she sang at the top of her voice.

To get back to South Kensington she had to pass the pub where they had been drinking earlier. She had a thought, and drove into the car park.

Grace the journalist was still at the bar, swigging brandy as if there were no tomorrow. She and the men around her were surprised to see Lavinia again so soon. And alone.

'What happened?' sneered Grace. 'Lover boy couldn't get it up?'

Lavinia beckoned her to one side with a forefinger.

'Look,' she said, 'I'm sorry we got off to a bad start a while back, and I'd like to buy you a drink if you'll have one with me.'

Grace was startled but, being a typical journalist, was not about to turn down free booze.

'Well, if you're paying, mine's a large brandy and soda.'

Lavinia ordered a Pepsi for herself.

'How much soda?' she asked, holding the syphon.

'Top it up, Oxford, top it up.'

Lavinia paused before doing so.

'You really should drop that Oxford thing, you know. It's not funny.'

'Everything about Oxford's funny,' slurred Grace. 'The cream of society, I'm told, and you know what they say about cream: rich, thick and full of clots.'

Lavinia still had the syphon in her hand.

'Did you read English at Sussex?'

'As it happens, yes.'

'Remember how Hemingway defined courage?'

'No time for the chauvinist bastard.'

Lavinia gave her a full five-second squirt in the face from the syphon, drenching her and stunning the other customers.

'Grace under pressure,' she said as she made for the door, 'that's how Hemingway defined courage. Grace under pressure.'

The gales of laughter behind her made her feel that, so far, she was enjoying a thoroughly satisfactory half-term.

'Two-nil, two-nil, two-nil, two-nil,' she sang all the way back to South Kensington.

At around the time Lavinia was midway between Hampstead and her flat, Paula and Sappho were on their way back to St Clare's by train. They too were more than satisfied with the break so far.

The previous evening they had sought out and found their connection in a Notting Hill pub. He was a swarthy North Londoner, Cypriot by origin, and much given to heavy gold bracelets, the real McCoy. Evidently business was booming.

After they had completed their marijuana transaction, he asked them if they would like some coke.

'You know, nose candy.'

Neither Paula nor Sappho had ever tried cocaine, but they'd heard all the tales about how it enhanced sex and were not, in theory, averse to anything that would provide extra kicks. The practical side was money. They were not short of funds, either of them; they never were when they came up to London.

'How much?' asked Paula.

Now that they had enough hash to keep them going until Christmas, Paula was anxious to be away. Even though the pub was the kind where drug deals were conducted without much secrecy, it had, to their certain knowledge, been raided by the police on more than one occasion, and they didn't want to be swept up in the net if tonight was the night. Besides, Notting Hill was not the sort of area where public schoolgirls were thick on the ground. Mugging was a cottage industry, and the muggers would beat you to a pulp for your shoes and coat, never mind a pocket full of money and enough marijuana to make a lot of people very happy for the weekend.

The Cypriot was streetwise enough to know that the tinier of the two dykes was the leader of the pack.

'I can let you have enough for ten lines for a ton and a half.'

'Get lost,' said Paula.

The Cypriot laughed.

'OK, as you're new customers, and I want you to be regulars, make it a ton.'

Even after the marijuana deal, Paula had just about that on her. Sappho had roughly the same. Still, no point in letting this jerk know that.

'What about a free sample?' suggested Sappho. 'We've never tried the stuff before. How do we know if we'll like it?'

'You'll like it, stand on me.'

'Still,' said Paula.

The Cypriot thought about it. The price charged to him by his wholesale supplier was a fraction of what he sold it for on the street, and if he could hook in these rich bitches he had a source of income for the future.

'OK,' he said. 'There's a pad up Ladbroke Grove I sometimes use for occasions like this. It's a trick pad, though. You know, whores. Any objections?'

'A word in your ear, Saff,' said Paula. 'Excuse us a minute, will you?'

'Don't take all night. I've got a business to run.'

Paula and Sappho moved a few feet away.

'Fuck it, Saff,' said Paula. 'We get busted with coke, they chuck us in the slammer and throw away the key. A bottle of vodka and a couple of joints will have the same effect on us. We'll pass,' she told the Cypriot.

'Please yourselves, ladies, but you don't know what you're missing.'

Paula flagged down a passing cab.

'Sussex Gardens, and stop at an off-licence.'

Neither of them remembered much about the night the following day, not details anyway. Their hotel rate, payable in advance since the receptionist spotted they were each only carrying small overnight bags, was forty-five pounds for a twin double with private bath. Sappho thought the price outrageous.

'Leave it, Saff,' said Paula.

The marijuana was good stuff. Mixed with the vodka, they were soon in orbit.

After fifteen minutes, Sappho said, 'You know, I could pass that rotten Oxbridge entrance, no bother, right here and now if I had the papers. Left-handed, while my right hand would be doing wondrous things to Phoebe's blond snatch. Clitty, clitty, come here, clitty. Oink, oink, oink.'

Paula giggled.

'I could job Phoebe with my left hand, Jennifer with my right, and answer five Oxford – and six fucking Cambridge – papers with my foot. Oink yourself, porker.'

Sappho began singing. The words didn't make much sense, but most of them rhymed with hunt and duck. Someone banged on the wall.

'Shugar off, bitface,' shouted Sappho, in a phrase Dr Spooner would have envied.

But she quietened down anyway.

Paula said, 'God, I feel horny.' She removed her jeans and underwear and lay on her back, legs wide apart. Sappho got to work with her fingers.

'How does that feel, darling?'

'I don't know. Yes, I do. Do it again. Oh, Christ,

I'm coming. Jesus, am I ever coming! Your mouth, Saff, your tongue. Oh, Jesus, give it to me!'

Then there was a fierce pounding on their room door.

'Fuck off!' bellowed Paula.

'Right,' said a male voice, 'I'm sending for the police.'

On the train they went over events.

'I remember some of it,' said Paula, 'but mostly it's a blank.' She looked around, to make sure no-one was within earshot. 'And I also remember having the best orgasm ever. I think.'

'Maybe it's my weight,' said Sappho, 'but I didn't get turned on as maniacally as you. Some, but not out of my skull. I recall you telling that bastard who was pounding on our door to piss off, that this was a private party for mammals only. I also recall that it took me virtually every penny I had to stop him calling the cops, and he still chucked us out. We spent the night on Waterloo Station, remember?'

'Vaguely. Christ, I feel rough. Do we have any money left? I don't fancy calling Dobbs.'

'Lots,' said Sappho. 'At least you have.'

'Then another bottle of vodka to take back?'

'Hair of the dog?'

'Hair of the bitch,' said Paula.

Amanda spent the best part of Saturday afternoon in the local hairdresser's, having her locks completely remodelled in a shorter, more bouncy style, and dyed. At first she wanted them jet black, but the owner, who got a lot of hotel guests as customers on the recommendation of Mrs McDonald, a woman whom one offended at one's peril, talked her out of it.

'Not with your complexion, Amanda. What about this shade, Midnight Blue? It's close to black, as you can see from the model on the chart, but it will be easier to re-dye if you change your mind. I can also sell you some sachets of the colour for you to apply yourself when the roots start to show.'

Amanda was delighted with the outcome. Looking at her reflection in the mirror when the refashioning was completed, the image that stared back wasn't the old Amanda Panda at all but a sleeker, more soignée version. However, there was still something wrong and it wasn't just the extra few pounds she still had to lose.

'It's your makeup,' said the hairdresser, 'eyeliner and shadow. You need something more dramatic. Here, let's try this.'

The hairdresser dipped into her own handbag, produced brushes, boxes and an eyebrow pencil, and began the transformation. After five minutes, Amanda could hardly believe the result. She now looked like an older and more attractive sister – not that she had one.

Walking back to the hotel, a matter of only a few hundred yards, from the other side of the road two local youths wolf-whistled. She ignored them until she realized they were whistling at her, which had never happened to her before, not once, in the whole of her life, and she knew she would remember that moment, a few minutes before four o'clock on a Saturday afternoon in October, for the rest of her days.

Also a few minutes before four o'clock, though fifty miles away, Jocasta Petrillo was getting laid for the second time in half an hour across a bale of hay covered with a horse blanket in the heated tack-room of the estate's stable block. And making a lot of noise about it, as was her partner and regular boyfriend when she was at home, Paul Buchanan, whose parents farmed in the area.

Jocasta had reached that stage of incipient orgasm where her eyes were beginning to roll and race off to some secret place in the distance that only she had access to. Then, as Buchanan plunged ever deeper and ever faster into her, nuzzling her neck while she dug her fingers into his buttocks, pulling him on to her, and timed her upward thrusts to match his, a gentle smile, almost incongruous, with the demonic howls she was making, parted her lips as she knew she was going to get there.

Almost.

Now!

Yes!

THERE.

Oh, beautiful, a multiple, because she had come a few heartbeats ahead of him and was now coming again as she felt his spasms begin.

THERE.

'Phew,' she said a little later, sitting up, revealing by

the exclamation that, in spite of her sexual experience, she was still only sixteen.

Jocasta's riding breeches and the rest of her habit were scattered all over the tack-room, as were Buchanan's, who was four years older. Now he began to gather his up and get dressed. She watched, half amused, as he carefully wrapped the second condom in a handkerchief and placed it in his jacket pocket. Jocasta wondered if she loved him. No, she thought. He was very handsome in the kind of dark-haired, black-eyed way that Barbara Cartland heroes were handsome, but love? She thought not.

'Is that it, then?' she asked pertly, making no move as yet to get dressed herself. Her mother was not due back until six, and her father's flight didn't get in until eight or thereabouts.

'I have to get home, Jo. Are you invited to the Telfords tonight?'

'My mother did say something about it, but I don't think we'll be going as Papa's due back from Brussels. Don't blow your nose until you've got rid of the evidence.'

Buchanan grinned.

'What about tomorrow?'

'It'll be difficult, what with Papa home.'

'Now it's my turn to say: is that it, then? The earth didn't move for you, I take it.'

'No, but the bloody hay bale did that second time.'

Jocasta stood up and stretched. Outside the rain was hammering against the stable-block roof.

Buchanan looked her up and down admiringly as he finished dressing. God, she was beautiful, even more so than her mother.

'You should get dressed, Jo.'

'Worried one of the estate workers might wander in?'

'Well, yes.'

'The door's bolted from the inside.'

'You'd have to open it if somebody rattled.'

'They won't. I've groomed my own horses since I was ten. I'll see to Sultan after you've gone.'

Buchanan sat on the hay bale and produced a packet of cigarettes. Jocasta shook her head. Buchanan lit up, making sure the match was totally extinguished by grinding it underfoot with his riding boot.

'Something I've always meant to ask you,' he said. 'What do you do for sex when you're at school?'

'What a question!' said Jocasta.

'No, I mean it.'

'I'll bet you do.'

'So?'

'Do you mean me or the girls in general?'

'Both.'

'That's private information. What do *you* do when I'm not here?'

'Ah,' said Buchanan.

'See,' said Jocasta.

'OK, I'm no saint. Nobody ever said I was, least of all me. But the girls, women, around here can't match you for looks. I'll bet no-one else at school can either. It's only natural men, boys, would chase you, and you wouldn't be human if you didn't allow yourself to be caught once in a while.'

'Remember AIDS?'

'I seem to have heard of it.'

'Then there's your answer.'

Buchanan stubbed out his cigarette. He kissed Jocasta on the lips and, unable to resist it, ran a hand over her breasts and between her legs.

'Go,' commanded Jocasta, 'or you won't be going anywhere.'

She rebolted the stable-block door after he left and listened to him ride off. She then rubbed herself down with the horse blanket they had been lying on before wrapping it around her shoulders. She should, she knew, get dressed herself and see to Sultan, but she was in no hurry.

Since as far back as she could remember she had loved horses, but it wasn't until she was fourteen that she found other pleasures astride them apart from the thrill of leaping fences and galloping on the flat at thirty miles an hour. On that day, when she was fourteen, aboard Sultan's dam, she had had her first orgasm as a result of the friction between the saddle, her tight riding breeches and her body.

She hadn't known what was happening except that it was the most exciting feeling she had ever experienced. And, to begin with, the most shameful.

She had retreated immediately to her bathroom and scrubbed herself from head to foot. But she couldn't wait to climb on Sultan's dam again.

Nothing happened.

Nor did it the next time or the time after that.

Then it started to happen regularly, and she always wore several Kleenex inside her knickers henceforth.

Soon she recognized that there was nothing sinful in what she felt, and soon after that she freed herself of virginity's shackles. A short time later her mother had insisted that their doctor should prescribe the Pill for Jocasta, and gave her a stern lecture about the potential fatality of sexually transmitted diseases.

Boys were fun, she quickly concluded, but nothing compared to the orgasms she achieved astride a horse. Or with other things equine.

Come on, Jo, come on, she admonished herself: time to stop day-dreaming and get kitted up before Mama puts in an appearance. Then she spotted her riding crop where she'd tossed it. She picked it up, checked that she really had bolted the stable-block door, and lay back on the hay bale, the horse blanket beneath her. She began working on herself in earnest with the crop.

In Teddy Hedges's house, in his bedroom, with his father still at the football and his mother not due home until after six from her managerial job in the supermarket, Julia lay on her back and stared at the ceiling while Teddy, now off her and outside her and on her right, grinned idiotically and looked mightily pleased with himself.

Julia put a hand between her legs, on to the towel they were both lying on, and examined her fingertips.

There was no blood, or little of it. Everything she'd

ever read, or heard about, had told her to expect blood when she surrendered her virginity.

Surrender?

Surrender implied victory by superior forces, but there had been nothing of that here.

Was that it? Is that what everyone got so excited about?

Lord above.

OK, the actual penetration had been a shock. Like flying solo for the first time – she assumed – or taking one's first parachute jump, the emotions could never be repeated. You were on your own, and you had to get through it on your own.

But – was that it?

There are more things in heaven and earth, Horatio, than are dreamt of in your philosophy.

No, wrong play.

This is a slight, unmeritable man meet to be sent on errands.

Again, wrong play.

She felt terribly let down, annoyed with herself as much as being disappointed in Teddy. At the end of last summer, in the churchyard, she had promised herself that it would be someone like Robert Penrose, if not Robert himself, who would be the first. There could only ever be one first and she'd allowed it to be Teddy.

What a fool!

'How do you feel, honey?' asked Teddy.

Honey?

Honey!

'I don't know.'

'It takes a while, you understand, for women.'

And there speaks the voice of experience, Teddy Hedges, seventeen and a half years of age and pretending he was Richard Gere.

'What takes a while?'

'Finding out how to come.'

'I thought that was your job, to make me.'

Inwardly, Teddy felt it was too, though he remembered reading somewhere that it wasn't all down to the man.

'Well, you have to do your part as well.'

'There's a trick to it, is there?'

'Maybe not a trick.'

'A stratagem, then.'

'I don't know that word.'

'It's the same as trick.'

'Yes, then.'

'How do you find the trick?'

'As I said, it takes time.'

But how much time? Was it like examinations where, at sixteen, you couldn't possibly pass A levels? Was it like attempting three hard sets of tennis before you could scarcely run a hundred metres without getting out of breath?

It was all so confusing.

She had expected to be different, walking on air.

Would Robert have made love to her in that manner? No, he would not. He would have been caring, tender, given her something back for what he was taking, that could only be taken once.

What was it Helena said in *MND*?

O weary night, O long and tedious night, abate thy hours! Shine, comforts, from the east that I may back to Athens by daylight, from these that my poor company detest . . .

'Teddy,' said Julia, 'I didn't enjoy it.'

'You're not expected to, first time.'

'That's a rule, is it?'

He looked absurd, lying there with the condom still on his 'thing'. Her clothes, she saw, were sprinkled around his bedroom, and she wanted to get into them.

Get into them and out of his room, this house.

She wasn't unaccustomed to hearing the word 'fuck', particularly from Kate, and Teddy had just 'fucked' her, that much was history.

But where was romance?

Was that it?

Unbelievable!

'I must go, Teddy.'

'Already? I thought we might have seconds.'

Like pudding, at school.

'Not today.' Not ever if she had her way.

'You've changed, you know.'

Julia started putting on her clothes, her back to Teddy. 'In what way?'

'You seem older.'

'I am older.'

'But only by a few weeks.'

'Even so.'

Maybe it was the filthy weather outside or the single

light bulb showing up dust on the dressing-table, but she felt sordid.

Ben Fisher would never have allowed it to be like this, she thought. Ben would certainly have made her feel better.

11

King Herod Was a Much
Misunderstood Man

Amanda created quite a stir when she returned after half-term.

Makeup for the girls of the Upper and Lower Sixths wasn't forbidden during school hours at St Clare's, but, as 'young ladies', they were expected to keep it discreet, subtle, not stroll into class as if they were about to prowl Shepherd Market for the rent. Amanda turned up looking like a vamp from a silent movie. She had also resisted her mother's cakes and buns and four-course meals over the weekend and as a consequence had reduced her weight by a further three pounds.

First evening back she stood next to Jocasta in front of the dormitory cheval glass.

'Twinsies!' she said, beaming.

Even Jocasta had to admit there was a vague resemblance. Bizarre, she thought.

'If you ask me,' Julia said to Kate a little later, 'that is a very unhealthy trend.'

'It'll pass,' said Kate, 'given time. She'll be a blonde by Christmas.'

'And then you'll be her role model.'

'God, I do hope not. One of me's more than enough.'

Mrs Clinton, Head of Churchill House, asked Amanda to remove most of the eye makeup and the garish lipstick, which she privately baptized Placenta Pink. Amanda did so without demur. She had only wanted to see her friends' reactions to the new-look 'Panda', but it really wasn't for them, or even the Upper Sixth boys, that she was attempting the metamorphosis. The acid test would come at Flanagan's on Saturday.

She hardly missed a dance, so pressing were her suitors, and she even turned down several. One of the townie boys paid her the ultimate compliment while she was standing next to Jocasta. 'Are you two sisters, or what?'

Amanda was well-versed enough to recognize that rigid dieting could become obsessional and lead to anorexia. She had even read up on the subject in the school library's copy of *Britannica*. She didn't qualify as a potential candidate for the condition. Her obesity was genuine, not imaginary. When she reached her optimum weight, after losing another five pounds or so, she would stop and eat properly thereafter. The salad bar would henceforth be her friend. As a precaution she told Auntie Natal, the matron, what she was doing.

Matron weighed her and consulted her chart, where

height, weight and so on were recorded at the beginning of each term. Amanda had lost eight pounds since the first day of Michaelmas, and a further four or five would make her just about right for her height and build.

Natalie Howe sympathized with the podgies of the world. During her teenage years, in the Sixties, girls starved themselves to be able to wear the latest fashions. She had, and much good it had done her. She was now at least twenty pounds overweight. In Turkey or an Arab state, would-be husbands would have given fifty camels for her. In England she was another fat lady facing middle age.

Quasi-physician, heal thyself!

'Nothing wrong with what you're doing, Amanda, but be careful. If you experience any ill-effects – if you feel faint or your periods become irregular – come and see me at once. I shall, in any case, be keeping an eye on you.'

Neither the Upper nor Lower Sixths had examinations before Christmas, but some of the teenies did, form exams on which class positions were based and reports for parents made, bits of paper that were guaranteed to ruin some girls' Yuletide. The theory was, and had been since Flashman roasted Tom Brown, that parents springing £3,000 per term wanted to be assured they were getting value for money.

All nonsense, of course. Examination results, like graphs produced by pollsters, can prove anything you want them to prove.

If Mrs Gordon had had her way, all the girls in the

lower forms would have been first equal.

It was several years since Penrose had taught upwards of a score of fourteen-year-old girls on a regular basis, but in the middle of November Chips went down with flu, and Penrose was asked by Mrs Gordon to take some of the old master's junior English classes. He could hardly believe the racket they made just opening books. They seemed incapable of performing the smallest action without sounding like the denizens of a South American rain forest.

The second day, in the staff room during mid-morning break, he confided in Lavinia that it probably wasn't flu that had confined Chips but the onset of a nervous breakdown.

'He's got them reading *Julius Caesar*, and there are a couple of lines in Act One, Scene Two, where Cassius says, referring to Caesar, something about petty men walking under his huge legs and peeping about. You'd have assumed we were studying *Fanny Hill*. Talk about girlish giggles! In the same speech, a line or two later, are the famous words, "The fault, dear Brutus, is not in our stars, but in ourselves," and before I knew what was happening they got me on to astrology. Did I know when Caesar was born, what zodiacal sign he was? As it happens, that information is pretty well documented, with most authorities agreeing July twelfth or thirteenth, one hundred BC. "So that makes him a Cancer, doesn't it, sir?" said one of the little horrors, after which we spent ten minutes discussing the relative merits of various astrological signs.'

'No doubt Chips can find compensations,' murmured Lavinia, not realizing that Felicity Coggan was within earshot. 'Forget I said that, Felicity.'

'It's forgotten, dear. On the other hand, Robert's become spoilt, always teaching the sixth form, where the shrill soprani of youth mellow to mezzo contralto.' Puffing on the omnipresent cigarette, she continued, 'Until you've had the pleasure of teaching the pubescent on a regular basis, you don't know what a relief end of term is. Nor the efficacy of Valium, for that matter. I asked one of my little treasures the other day to give me three reasons why the Nile was vital to Egypt's economy. Yachting, water-skiing and scuba diving, she told me.'

Lavinia and Penrose chuckled. Felicity went on, 'I have another young lady who's a born-again Christian – you know, one of these people whose faces are permanently scrubbed clean and whose eyes sparkle with unnatural brightness. She holds no brief with conventional theories on geography and elementary geology. "That's all very fine and large, Mrs Coggan, but Genesis I, verses six and seven, tells us . . ." And so it goes on. Whenever I set them an essay she begins it in the same way. "When God created the continents . . ." Or the oceans or climate or rivers. I never dare give her less than a beta plus, whatever rot she writes. I'm terrified she'll accuse me of being the anti-Christ and have me burnt at the stake.'

Lavinia silently thanked whatever she held sacred that her days of teaching teenies were over, though she did have her own problems, mostly with Richard

Carson, whose mind, these days, appeared to be elsewhere.

They were discussing Beaumarchais's *Le Mariage de Figaro* during a one-to-one tutorial in Lavinia's study. At least, that's what Lavinia assumed they were deliberating, but Carson evidently believed it was Molière's *Le Misanthrope*, another of the texts in the syllabus.

'*C'est une folie à nulle autre seconde, de vouloir se mêler de corriger le monde.*'

'Translate, please, Richard,' said Lavinia, exasperated, though she knew he could easily.

'Of all human follies there's none could be greater than trying to render our fellow-men better.'

'And what does Beaumarchais mean precisely by that?'

Carson blinked.

'Beaumarchais? That's Molière.'

'Indeed it is, Richard, indeed it is. The trouble is, this tutorial is about Beaumarchais's *Figaro*. What on earth's the matter with you? You're going to fail at this rate.'

Something in Carson snapped.

'You're so damned superior!' he said in English, before switching immediately to perfect French and Beaumarchais's *Figaro* at that. '*Parce que vous êtes un grand seigneur, vous vous croyez un grand génie! Vous vous êtes donné la peine de naître, et rien de plus.*'

Translated this was, 'Because you are a great lord, you believe yourself to be a great genius. You took the trouble to be born, but nothing more.'

The insult was obvious and Lavinia was livid. She

held on to her temper, however, because she thought she knew precisely what Carson's trouble was.

'We'll leave it there for today,' she said coolly, 'pick it up when you're a little less distraught.'

From the door, Carson had the grace to apologize.

'Look, I'm sorry. I had no right.'

'As I said, Richard, let's leave it for today,' said Lavinia.

She asked Kate McNamara to stay behind after the following afternoon's Lower Sixth French class.

'A word in your ear, Kate.'

'I think I know what this is about,' said Kate, when the two of them were alone.

'Richard told you, then?'

'He mentioned something about behaving badly.'

'Oh, that, that's nothing,' said Lavinia airily. 'You probably believe me to be an ancient old wrinkly, but it's less than ten years since I underwent similar sorts of pressures myself before being accepted at Oxford. I do remember what it was like. No, the odd spat is inevitable, and it's not that that's worrying me. What is, is that since half-term Richard seems to have lost his powers of concentration.'

'And you think I'm the problem?'

'I wouldn't put it exactly like that, but I don't think either of you have made it a secret that you're an item. At least, I presume that's still the case, that you haven't broken up since half-term?'

'We haven't broken up,' said Kate, 'and I don't really think I can discuss this any further. You'll have to ask Richard if you want answers, but I don't think you'll get much out of him either.'

How could any young man of eighteen tell a rather beautiful woman – wrinkly indeed! – that he was suffering from impotence? They had tried to get it together three times since half-term – in the hockey pavilion – and thrice Richard had failed to perform. He had put it down, once again, to their insalubrious surroundings and also his worries about the forthcoming entrance exam. But then he had added something strange, turning the blame on her.

'It's not all my fault. You told me right at the start you weren't a virgin, but neither was I and neither are some of the other girls I've been with. None of them act like you. I'm beginning to wonder if you're not a damned sight more experienced than you let on.'

Because it was so close to the truth – in fact, because it hit the truth firmly and squarely on the head – Kate was furious.

'Maybe I am and maybe I'm not,' she stormed, 'but what happened in America has nothing to do with you.'

'I didn't mention America,' said Carson.

They kissed and made up after a couple of days, but it was an uneasy truce. Without ever saying as much to each other, they agreed there would be no more fumblings in the hockey pavilion or the fives courts in the foreseeable future, and they continued to make plans to spend some time together during the Christmas vacation.

'May I go now?' Kate asked Lavinia.

'Of course,' said Lavinia.

And here was I thinking I had it easy because I no longer have to deal with teenies, she thought. If anything, the sixteen- to eighteen-year-olds were worse. Some of them should have been strangled at birth.

12

Rehearsals

'Who's this?' asked Ben Fisher.

He darkened his eyebrows with greasepaint, puffed out his cheeks like a chipmunk, and intoned, 'The green shoots of recovery are just around the corner.'

'Easy,' said Julia. 'Norman Lamont.'

'This, then,' said Ben.

He sprayed some grey lacquer onto his hair and walked downstage, swinging his right leg as though he had an injury.

'Lewis, get in here!'

'Easier,' said Julia. 'Inspector Morse.'

'Right,' said Fisher, miffed, 'this one.'

He tilted his spectacles to an angle of forty-five degrees so that they were only just balanced on his nose. The right-hand lens was up by his forehead and the left-hand lens below his cheekbone.

'No idea,' said Julia.

'Picasso!' said Fisher.

Julia giggled. Fisher beamed.

Penrose clapped his hands for attention.

'Right, cast, let's have a bit of hush, please.'

Next to him, Lavinia murmured, 'I love it when you're masterful.'

'I know we don't have corporal punishment at St Clare's,' Penrose murmured back, 'but I'll see you in my study later for six strokes of the cane.'

'Promises, promises,' said Lavinia.

Penrose turned to address the cast. 'Tonight we're going to concentrate on Act Two, Scene One.' He held up a hand to stifle the groans. 'Yes, I know I promised you Act Four this evening and that we've been over Act Two, Scene One ad nauseam. But it's still not right and it's a key scene in the play. I am also more than aware that we have less than three weeks before the first performance. You'll just have to trust me to bring it all together. Ben?'

Fisher consulted his call list.

'Puck, Oberon, Titania, Demetrius, Helena, leading fairy and various other fairies.' Ben peered over his glasses. 'I'm afraid we're minus a few fairies, sir.'

'You should live where I live,' said Lavinia, not bothering to lower her voice.

She was rewarded with some appreciative laughter.

'I know about the fairies . . .' began Penrose.

'Glad to hear it, sir,' shouted someone, to more laughter.

'All right, all right, settle down,' said Penrose. 'I'll rephrase that. I've given the girls playing the junior fairies the night off because they're non-speaking parts in this scene and I'll be concentrating on principals this evening.'

Puck and the leading fairy occupied the whole of

the first quarter of the scene, being joined then by Oberon and Titania, King and Queen of the Fairies respectively. Penrose had been unable to persuade any of the Upper or Lower Sixth boys to play the King, and this 'he' was a fifteen-year-old 'she'. Fortunately she was tall and willowy, and not a bad actress at all. The Queen, too, was a fifteen-year-old with some talent. The unfortunate fact here was that, while she was built quite normally in all other respects, she had the most extraordinarily well-developed breasts. As Titania, with the emphasis on the first syllable, it was a piece of inspired casting, but the current joke was that she was more 'tit' than 'ania'. Penrose was dreading the dress rehearsal, when she would put on her costume for the first time. He would have to make sure – or, rather, get Lavinia to make sure – that there was not too much décolletage. Otherwise there was likely to be a riot among the male parents.

Puck was a delightful fourteen-year-old girl with a sweet contralto voice. Although, in the text of the play according to Shakespeare, Puck had no songs, the character had several long soliloquies which Penrose had asked if she could plain-chant. She had done better than that, and invented tunes of her own. Thus the lines: *Through the forest I have gone, but Athenian found I none* were sung, as was the most important closing speech of Puck's, the one where the sprite asks the audience to look kindly on the actors' performances.

If we shadows have offended,
Think but this and all is mended

That you have but slumber'd here
While these visions did appear.

Penrose planned to have the actress sitting cross-legged, centre stage, dressed in her green elf suit with a single pink spot illuminating her, while she sang the entire sixteen lines. The rest of the cast would be in darkness to her left and right and then, when the song came to the last couplet – *Give me your hands, if we be friends, and Robin shall restore amends,* – they would join young Puck, as she stood, and clasp hands.

Then he would bring up the lights, allow them a quick bow en masse, and pull the tabs.

A traditional walkdown would follow, beginning with the minor characters and ending with the major ones. After that, he'd get Puck to sing the valedictory song again and permit the entire ensemble as many curtain calls as the traffic would bear.

Not a dry eye in the house, he thought.

Guy Young, Felicity Coggan's lover, was playing Demetrius, Helena's lover – Julia's character – in the play. Felicity had encouraged him to audition for the part after the original Demetrius, tired of being ragged by his Upper Sixth friends, had dropped out. He was the only male in the cast, something that bothered him not a whit.

'With your looks, you'd be perfect,' Felicity said.

Felicity's motives were not entirely altruistic. Since the scare caused by the malicious Patsy Kelly and Mrs Gordon's veiled warning that she was not unaware of Felicity's relationship with a male member of the

Upper Sixth, their clandestine meetings had become rarer. But some of Felicity's juniors were fairies, which gave her a valid reason for attending rehearsals. Even tonight, when the fairies were not required.

Fisher wasn't so sure he enjoyed watching Guy being aloof from Julia's Helena infatuation. Julia pursued him with a little more ardour than was seemly. Then again, Julia was ambitious. But God, he'd dearly love to screw her.

'They look well together,' said Henry Morton from behind Fisher, as Guy/Demetrius entered followed by Julia/Helena.

'Who asked you?' growled Fisher.

Because he was unbearably lonely, Henry had taken to coming to rehearsals for the last two weeks, and Penrose, never one to reject an extra pair of hands, had dragooned him into being one of the scene-shifters and general dogsbody. Far from being dismayed at being a menial, Henry was overjoyed that someone seemed to want him for something.

'Mind you, I wouldn't worry about it,' said Henry.

'Come again,' said Fisher, one eye on Julia and Guy, the other on the prompt book.

'*I love thee not, therefore pursue me not,*' said Guy.

Fisher checked his script. Half a dozen lines to go before Helena's first. She'd give him hell if she dried and he wasn't there with an immediate prompt.

'You were saying,' he said to Henry.

'That I wouldn't worry, if I were you, about Julia and Guy or Julia and anyone else,' said Henry. 'She hasn't looked at anyone but you since half-term.'

Fisher lost his place.

'How do you figure that?' he asked.

'Just because I wear glasses doesn't mean I'm blind,' answered Henry.

'Line,' snapped Julia, forgetting her first.

'*You draw me, you hard-hearted adamant,*' stage-whispered Fisher.

'Thank *you*,' said Julia with heavy sarcasm.

'All right, all right,' interrupted Penrose. 'Julia, if you dry, accept the prompt and carry on. Don't thank him for it, or curse him. OK, continue.'

'Well,' grinned Henry, 'she *wasn't* looking at anyone else until ten seconds ago.'

'Bastard,' swore Fisher.

Felicity slipped away ten minutes before rehearsals ended. Today was Thursday. With any luck she and Guy would manage some time together on Saturday.

Most of the actors stayed behind to help Henry and the other dogsbodies tidy up. While the stage in Great Hall was used for theatrical performances and other major events in the calendar such as Speech Day, it also functioned as a platform for morning prayers if the chapel was otherwise occupied – for example, by the choir, who were presently involved, before school hours, practising the hymns that would be sung for the service marking end of term, now, like *A Midsummer Night's Dream*, less than three weeks off.

Guy Young and Julia, Henry Morton and Ben Fisher, Lavinia and Penrose were the last to leave. Guy was trying to convince Julia that on Helena's line, *You do me mischief. Fie, Demetrius!* that she should slap him. Julia disagreed.

'Helena's next line is, *We cannot fight for love, as men may do. We would be woo'd and were not meant to woo.* Which makes it ridiculous for her to slap him. She's just said that women don't fight.'

'But that's the delicious part of it, don't you see? First she slaps him, then she says that women don't fight. It's a joke.'

Penrose overheard their discussion.

'I've told you before,' he said, 'not to start inventing bits of business without my sanction. Bring anything you think of to rehearsals, naturally, and we'll try them if I consider they jell with my overall concept. But if each performer or duo begins acting in their own little circles, we'll wind up putting on a variety show with no leitmotif. Ragtag and bobtail stuff.'

'And other well-known rabbits,' said Lavinia.

'OK, point taken,' said Guy. 'Shall I walk you back to Churchill?' he asked Julia.

Julia glanced at Fisher.

'No, thanks. I've got a couple of things I want to discuss with Ben.'

Guy got the message.

'Oh, right. Henry, are you on your way back to Napier?'

'Sure,' said Henry, keeping his voice as casual as possible but secretly pleased that someone like Guy Young would desire his company.

Outside Great Hall Ben said, 'Sorry about the mix-up on the prompt. My mind was elsewhere.'

Julia linked arms with him and bent her head against the November wind.

'On me, I trust.'

'Well, yes, as it happens.'

'Good. What are we doing Saturday?'

'What would you like to do?'

'Oh, no doubt we'll think of something.'

She'd changed since half-term, thought Fisher, and wondered if what Henry said was right.

Inside Great Hall Lavinia said, just before switching off the lights, 'You know, we could hang around here for half an hour.'

Penrose shook his head.

'I'd love to, Vin, but I've got an hour's marking to do before I go to bed.'

'Going off me, huh?'

'You know that's not true. In fact – do you remember that hotel we were going to stay at over half-term, before I got landed with the babysitting?'

'Naturally.'

Lavinia wanted to keep him off the subject of half-term. He'd asked her what she'd done, when she got back, and she'd murmured something about spending a few relaxing days with her sister Rebecca, and doing some shopping. He hadn't had her, as yet, in the garter-belt and stockings she'd bought, and nor had he seen them. She was saving those little gems for a special occasion.

'Well,' said Penrose, 'I was thinking we might check in there Saturday until I had a better idea. A chap I was at university with, and with whom I spent part of the summer in France, as it happens, has a cottage in the Malverns, near Tewkesbury, which he hardly ever uses apart from the occasional weekend. I know he leaves the key with a local farmer, and if it's free on Saturday I thought we might go there. It can't be tomorrow, Friday, because we've got another rehearsal, and I don't fancy bowling up Monday morning. Go down Saturday afternoon and come back Sunday afternoon. The way you drive, we can be there in two hours.'

'Sounds fine. Why so diffident?'

'A hotel's one thing. It doesn't have the same ring of permanence. A cottage is another.'

Lavinia thought she knew what he meant, but made light of it.

'In a cottage, though, with no-one listening apart from a few sheep, I can scream as much as I like. Christ, that makes me feel horny. Do you have anything with you?'

'Yes, as it happens, but . . .'

'No buts, Robert. Just a quickie, up here against this wall.'

Lavinia was wearing a long winter skirt, which she hoisted to her waist. Penrose didn't even drop his trousers or remove Lavinia's knickers. Instead, he thrust them to one side, slipped on the condom, and, with one of Lavinia's legs curled around his hips like a ballet dancer's, he shoved up and in.

It was all over in under two minutes, but Lavinia came beautifully and so did Penrose, as she was well aware.

'That's better,' she said, when they'd both finished,

and made a mental note to pack the garter-belt and stockings for Saturday. Robert was in for a big surprise in more ways than one.

Saturday afternoon, with the wind howling and the rain lashing against the windows, Sappho said, 'I'm bored. What say one of us goes into town and hires a couple of videos?'

Paula was lying face down on her bed.

'What say you do?'

Paula was pissed off. Earlier Jennifer Langley's parents had driven down and taken Jennifer, Phoebe and two other teenies out for the day. The stash of marijuana was in the cornflakes box, but she didn't feel like turning on.

'I thought that might be the answer,' said Sappho. 'If I hurry, I can catch the two-thirty bus. Any preferences?'

'Anything with a bunch of dykes fucking another bunch of dykes, but something we haven't seen before.'

'I pick them up, you take them back – which means before seven Sunday.'

'Deal,' said Paula sleepily.

'I'll believe that when I see it,' said Sappho.

They were both regular customers at a town video shop called Blue Virginia, which sold and hired pornographic tapes as well as selling skin magazines. Most of the clientele was male, which bothered neither Sappho nor Paula in the least. For that matter, they got a kick from standing close to male punters and drooling over some beauty either parading her body or, on the special shelf, getting humped by a man or a woman and frequently both. Paula van der Groot and Sappho Peters were not intimidated in the least by the opposite gender.

Of course, most of the literature and videos were designed for masculine consumption, but, because of that, they all featured beautiful women, in their prime, with magnificent bodies. Neither Paula nor Sappho had ever figured out why lesbian videos and magazines excited heterosexual males, whereas tapes and photographs depicting male homosexual acts did nothing for women, gay or straight.

'If you want some money, it's in my bag,' said Paula.

'No, I received a cheque at the beginning of the week. Thank God for rich parents.'

'The lucky sperm club.'

'There's nothing lucky about sperm,' said Sappho. 'Nasty, dirty stuff.'

'You sound as if you know.'

'I read the paperback.'

At the wheel of her car with Penrose beside her, Lavinia saw Sappho walking down the drive towards the main gates, umbrella up and battling against the elements.

'We should offer her a lift.'

Their bags were in the boot. There was nothing to suggest they were off to the Malverns.

'OK,' said Penrose.

'Going far?' said Lavinia, winding down the window.

'Town,' answered Sappho.

'London town or town town?'

'Town town.'

'Hop in.'

It was on their way, and they dropped Sappho near the precinct.

'Thanks,' she said, as Lavinia waved goodbye.

Well, well, she thought, sensing that something was going on between the two teachers, lucky old Penrose. What a crying shame Lavinia's not one of us.

The manager of Blue Virginia recognized her, knew that she was at St Clare's, over eighteen, and not averse to spending money. He also knew she was a dyke, which was neither here nor there to him. All kinds of weirdos walked through his doors. He couldn't care less what their sexual preferences were as long as they didn't try to steal the stock. One day, though, he was determined to pluck up sufficient nerve to ask how many others like her there were at school and where they found the privacy to get their rocks off.

'We've got a few specials straight in from America via Amsterdam in the back room,' he said to Sappho. 'Check 'em out.'

'Thanks, I will.'

'Feel free.'

'I generally do.'

There were three men in the 'back room', flicking through magazines and studying video titles. They all looked sort of sheepish when Sappho pushed aside the beaded curtain. She chuckled to herself.

She went over the magazine rack first. There was one title she hadn't seen before, *Gut Feeling*, under a handwritten sign that read Just In. She turned over the pages. It was all hard-core material, mostly lesbians in twos and threes indulging in various sexual acts, but with a few layouts showing two women and one man and one woman with two men. The centrefold nude portrayed a magnificent-looking girl, and the pages either side the same beauty being humped royally by a stud who was hung like a racehorse while she was performing fellatio on a second man.

Once she'd seen these photographs in full colour, all thoughts of videos for Paula fled Sappho's mind.

Later that same afternoon, Fisher said to Carson, 'Are you planning on going out this evening?'

'No. The entrance exam is next week and I've got a hell of a lot of revision to do.'

'No Kate?'

'She got permission from Mrs Clinton to go home for the weekend.'

'No problems there, are there?'

'Of course not, why should there be?' answered Carson sharply.

'Sorry, sorry. I didn't mean to stick my beak in where it's not wanted.'

'That's OK. My apologies for snapping. Anyway, why do you want to know if I'm going out? Have you got something cooking with young Julia?'

'Anything's possible,' said Fisher lightly.

'You dirty devil, but be my guest. I can always use the commonroom. How do you plan to smuggle her in? Any information on technique would be appreciated.'

'Straightforwardly. The local amateur dramatic society is doing *The Comedy of Errors*, last night tonight, kick-off seven o'clock. It'll be all over by nine, and we should be back here by nine-thirty. Anybody spots us, we're discussing Shakespeare. One of the advantages of being part of the *MND* set-up.'

'Wish I'd thought of that. But it's still a serious offence if you're caught.'

'At nine-thirty on a Saturday? Be your age. Besides, Penrose is away. I saw him drive off with the delicious Lavinia earlier. Chips will be curled up in front of his television. Anyway, it's worth the risk.' Fisher put on his John Wayne voice, which was about as good as his Norman Lamont impression. 'A man's gotta do what a man's gotta do.'

'Say it with awe, Duke,' said Carson, encouraging a hoary joke.

Fisher accepted his cue.

'Aw, a man's gotta do what a man's gotta do.'

Carson grinned in spite of himself.

'That's the worst John Wayne take-off I ever heard.'

'You should see me do his walk. I look like Donald Duck. So, you'll give free rein until around, say, ten forty-five?'

'Consider yourself unfettered. You reckon she's ready, do you?'

'A gentleman doesn't discuss such matters. But, as I'm not one, the frank answer is I don't know.'

'You should be prepared. I can give you a packet of johnnies if you're not already equipped.'

'I'm not, as it happens, but I decline the offer. If

I get to first base tonight, I shall consider myself inordinately fortunate. Julia's no whore.'

Carson's mood changed again.

'Meaning Kate is?'

'For Christ's sake, Richard, I didn't mean anything of the sort.'

Hell's bells, he thought, talk about touchy.

Further along the Napier House landing, Henry was thrilled that Guy Young had invited him to the same play that Julia and Ben Fisher were going to attend.

'Got a spare ticket that's going begging otherwise, Henry. Shall we see how the *real* amateurs do Shakespeare?'

Henry realized, naturally, that he must be second or third choice for the spare ticket, though he had no idea for whom it had first been bought.

Felicity had told Guy, 'Darling, I'd love to accompany you, but it's a bit public, isn't it? Most of the cast of *MND* will be going along, if for no other reason than to see what the costumes are like. Take one of your friends – and I do mean male friends.'

Lavinia and Penrose dined at the Royal Hop Pole in Tewkesbury – early. Lavinia wore exactly the same outfit she'd had on when she took her revenge on Peter Hennessy, with the addition of knickers. The Royal Hop Pole wasn't the sort of place to be without them, the clientele being a mixture of City types in the country for the weekend and, mostly at the bar, rural oiks. Few of the males in either category could take their eyes off her, and all mentally undressed her. Without underwear she would have felt twice as naked.

Not that she objected. It was exciting to be the object of such undisguised lust. One day – something she'd never done but which had been at the back of her mind for years – she intended checking in to a hotel such as this, alone, selecting the best-looking man in the place and giving him the time of his life, a night to remember, without ever revealing her name and leaving before he was awake. These days, of course, with the ever-present threat of AIDS and so many weirdos around, it would be taking a chance, but what was life without risk?

Although they had taken a taxi there, and had ordered one for ten o'clock – sharp – back to the cottage they'd borrowed, Lavinia kept her drinking to a minimum. Like Ben Fisher all those miles away, she had plans for this evening. There was, in any case, champagne and brandy in the cottage, purchased on the way up. And – for a heart-starter on Sunday morning – a bottle of vodka, two cartons of tomato juice, a bottle of Worcestershire sauce, a container of celery salt, and fresh limes. Most essential, the limes. The Hemingway recipe for a first-class Bloody Mary.

Lavinia might yield to the night in a manner that would have shocked her parents and even Rebecca, but Oxford had taught her how to wake up.

After the taxi dropped them off, she asked Penrose to open the champagne. She was pleased to register that the cork made a gentle pop, that it didn't hit the ceiling as if he'd just won a motor race. A small thing, but important. Vulgarity had its place, mostly during sex. It should not be a way of life.

With her glass full, and his, she spreadeagled herself on the sofa. They had laid the fire before they went out, and put a match to it the moment they returned. The logs were now burning merrily.

She had insisted on dressing privately before they left for dinner, so Penrose had not seen what she was wearing under her Lycra mini. Now he did, the way she was lying. He sat beside her and ran a hand up her thigh. She didn't resist him, but neither did she encourage him. They had the whole night. There was no rush.

'Robert,' she said, 'do I occasionally shock you?'

Penrose had grown used to her ways.

'Sometimes. My wife never used the words you use when we're making love.'

'Fucking, Robert. When we fuck.'

'OK, then.'

'Say it.'

'When we fuck.'

She opened her legs and allowed his fingers to excite her a little.

'But we are friends, aren't we?'

'Christ, Vin, I thought we were a bit more than that.'

'You misunderstand me. What I mean is, are you screwing anyone else apart from me?'

'Who's got that sort of time?'

'Fiona Acland.'

'Ah,' said Penrose. 'In the pub, during the darts match, right? I thought she might have said something.'

'Actually, I tricked her into admitting it.'

'Whichever, it's all over and done with.'

'I know that, you gossoon. Fiona's a beautiful child, but a child she is. More champagne, please. And you might as well open the second bottle while you're on your feet.'

For a while they stared silently into the blazing fire until, well into their third glass and with Lavinia feeling deliciously sexy, she said, 'When I asked if we were friends a moment ago, what I really meant was: do you trust me?'

'I'm not sure I follow. God, don't tell me you're seeing someone else, or did at half-term in London.'

Naturally she hadn't told him of the incident with Hennessy, and probably never would unless she judged it would excite him. Some men liked to hear about a woman's sexual antics with other lovers.

'Wait there.'

She left him. When she returned, she was wearing a wig with a long ponytail that was the same colour as her own blond hair.

'Get undressed, Robert. Then undress me.'

He was out of his clothes in no time. As usual, he was three-quarters erect.

She lay back, sipping her champagne, only changing position when she had to, to help him, while he took off first her silk shirt and bra, then her black Lycra mini and underwear, kissing her all over as he did so. He was now fully erect.

He slipped on a condom and pushed her back on the sofa, opening her thighs, kneeling over her.

'Christ, I must get in you.'

'The stockings, Robert,' she panted, 'take my stockings off.'

He was puzzled.

'But you like it with your stockings on. So do I.'

'Do it, Robert. Take them off and strap them round my shoulders like horse-reins, then fuck me from behind. Pull at them while you're fucking me, take hold of my ponytail. Let me come like that. Make me!'

He turned her over roughly and forced her legs apart, understanding that she was half resisting him as part of her own fantasy. Her juices glistened on the insides of her thighs. She had kept on the garter-belt, which made her look sensationally whorish. He knotted the stockings and wrapped them around her shoulders, pulling tight.

She yelped with pleasure.

Then he thrust upwards and in.

He was almost beside himself with lust. The long strokes took only thirty seconds, during which, while he pulled frenziedly on the 'reins', he watched his thick cock plunge into her.

'No, no, no!' he thought he heard her say, but he paid no attention.

Then he got to the short strokes and began humping her with a fury, causing her to give out tiny grunts of surprise and lust and even pain which grew louder the faster his actions became. 'Uh-uh-uh-uh-uh.'

Still keeping the pressure on her shoulders with one hand holding the stockings, he freed the other, put it around her waist and repeatedly pulled her on to him. She matched her rhythm to his as he slammed into her. 'Don't, don't, oh Christ don't!'

Then he was coming, feeling the first thrilling spurts of the most wondrous orgasm he had ever experienced. His knees gave way, and he had to hang on to the feverishly bucking Lavinia for dear life. Lavinia who was emitting strangled screams and thrashing her head from side to side.

He did not relax his grip on her stockings even when he knew she was coming too, when he felt the sudden tightening of her vaginal muscles, and at that particular moment he couldn't have cared less if the world had ended and he and Lavinia with it.

The feminists were right, he thought inconsequentially, as he strained to get the last fraction of an inch inside her. Fucking was an aggressive act. Neither a million pounds nor the promise of eternal life could have stopped him coming. By the same token, Lavinia would have killed him if, by some means in his power, he had prevented her orgasm. Man and woman had crawled out of the primordial slime sightless with only the urge to reproduce. No, not reproduce, tell it like it is, the way Lavinia told it. Not reproduce, fuck. The greatest free show since Christians were tossed to lions.

The last of his orgasm poured out of him. The quantity seemed endless. As he finished he automatically relaxed his grip around her waist and on the stockings. Her head fell to one side and she appeared hardly to be breathing. For one terrible moment he thought he actually had hurt her, but then her fingers reached up.

He stayed inside her for some time, until her breathing and heartbeat returned to normal. And until his own did. He held her breasts and kissed her neck, bringing her down. When his cock, finally detumescent, slipped out of her, he turned her over on her back, parted her thighs, bent his head down and licked the juices. She held his head with her hands.

'That was the best ever,' he said at last.

'For me too. You were terrific. I really felt I was going to die there at the end.'

'I don't think it would have mattered to me.'

'Really?'

'Really. For a few minutes there I was out of control.'

'Good. That's how I wanted it.'

'Have you got any more bright ideas like that?'

'Oh, lots,' said Lavinia.

So far Robert hadn't humped her in a doorway, in daylight, as she'd enjoyed so much with Hennessy. But that would come, as would sex after smoking a joint or two. The beauty of it was – unlike Hennessy who would hump a snake if he could get someone to hold its head – Penrose had never met anyone like her before. He would do whatever she asked him to. He was hers to command, and that was a pleasing thought.

A little under two hours earlier Fisher had finally, and unexpectedly, had his way with Julia.

The town's amateur production of *The Comedy of Errors* had proved a little more unskilled than either of them could take. They left after Act Three and were back at St Clare's before eight-thirty. Although neither of them said as much, it seemed agreed that they should go up to Fisher's study. No-one saw them enter Napier House and Carson, as promised, had made himself scarce.

Fisher had uncorked a litre of Bulgarian red before setting out, and he and Julia each had a glass while sitting on the floor going through audio cassettes. Eventually Julia found something she liked and Fisher put it on the player.

He was nervous, and was sure it showed. Apart from the fact that he didn't know what his first move should be, there was always the chance, even if he made it, that Carson would come back for something he'd forgotten or that someone else would barge in, even though, as it was Saturday and still early, Napier seemed deserted.

Julia looked very pretty tonight, and knew it. Well, she'd tried hard enough. Over a full-length skirt she wore a sloppy sweater that reached below her hips. Her underwear was clean, her hair washed, and her makeup just right. All she needed now was for Ben to make his approach. When this seemed a long time coming, she moved a little closer.

'The girl playing Adriana didn't seem to know what she was doing,' said Fisher hesitantly.

'Girl!' scoffed Julia. 'She was forty if she was a day.'

'She was the wife of the producer, I read in the programme.'

'There you are then,' said Julia sagely. 'Nepotism. I suppose we are safe here?'

'I'm sorry?'

'I suppose Richard isn't going to walk in through the door?'

'He said he wouldn't,' began Fisher, then blushed.

'Ah,' said Julia. 'You've been plotting between you, have you?'

'Of course not.'

'Don't worry, I'm not offended. Still, it might be wise to put a chair under the door-handle.'

Fisher didn't know where all this was leading, but was happy to go along. This was certainly a different Julia from the one who'd gone home at half-term.

He placed the chair under the door-handle.

'You can kiss me, you know,' said Julia, when he returned to her on the floor. 'It's not as though it would be the first time.'

Fisher was astonished and a little scared at her passion. Her tongue probed his as they half-lay, half-sat on the floor. He was even more astounded a few moments later when, still kissing her, she took hold of one of his hands and placed it against her breast. Outside her sweater, true, but this was progress.

Emboldened by her actions and continuing to kiss her – because he felt he would be compelled to speak if he removed his mouth from hers – he slipped his free hand underneath her sweater, feeling for the clasp that secured her bra. Again she did nothing to stop him. If anything, her kisses became more intense.

It took him a little fumbling, but finally he had her bra undone. Then he moved his hand to caress her nipples. She exhaled a tiny sigh of pleasure.

They remained like this for several minutes, kissing each other, Fisher squeezing her breasts. His erection was beginning to hurt.

Julia pulled away momentarily, to take a breath and say, 'Not so hard, Ben, not so hard.'

He was gentler with her after that.

A few minutes later he took the next step. But this time they were lying flat on the study carpet. Fisher had one of his knees between Julia's thighs, and he slipped a free hand under her skirt. She was wearing tights and he put his fingers beneath the waist band, thrusting them down until they touched the wispy gossamer surrounding El Dorado. A moment afterwards and they were inside the city of gold itself.

Julia groaned and raised her buttocks. Fisher needed no second telling what that movement meant. Even though he had to remove his fingers from the delights they were exploring to accomplish it, Julia's tights were quickly off. With them came her knickers. Modestly she kept her skirt down.

Now Fisher found it easier to continue what he'd started, aiming upwards instead of down. Julia was very wet.

Fisher panicked. Could it be, was it possible, that she intended him to go 'all the way'? He cursed refusing Carson's offer of condoms, but he had to tell her he was unprepared.

'Just don't come inside me,' she murmured.

He was a virgin: there was no chance of him having any infection. Julia might not be – *something* had happened over half-term to change her – but

276

she could only have had one lover at the most. In any case, he was beyond caring.

He unbuckled his belt and lowered his trousers. His cock sprang free, straight as an arrow, perfect as a theorem. Julia eyed him.

'Um,' she said.

He couldn't wait to take his trousers completely off, frightened that this was all a dream that might disappear if he hesitated. He was also beyond caring if anyone rapped on the door.

He lifted Julia's skirt, hardly bothering to take note of the prize he was about to possess, and positioned himself between her legs. All the books said that Nature would take over from now, even for a greenhorn, but all the books were wrong. Julia had to take hold of him and place him inside her, but then he was there, really THERE.

Julia knew immediately that this was different from her experience with Teddy Hedges, and within seconds knew that she was going to come, *was* coming even as the thought occurred. The beautiful liquidity in her loins was everything she'd read about, heard about. It was sensational.

But then she recognized by Ben's urgent thrusts that he also was about to come, and commonsense, or self-preservation, took over.

'Not inside me, not inside me!'

Fisher pulled out of her at the last moment. That he had come there was no doubt. The evidence was everywhere. Her skirt was ruined, no chance of dry-cleaning there. The cleaning service would know at once what the stains were. She would have to trash it.

'Next time,' she said, 'remember the condoms.'

Fisher was beside himself with pride. There would be a next time! He hadn't screwed up. Screwed, yes, but not up.

He was on the scoreboard.

Several hours before that incident, Sappho Peters said to Paula van der Groot, 'Where the hell have you been all afternoon?'

Sappho had been back in the study they shared since three-thirty. Paula didn't appear until six-thirty.

'I went for a wander.'

'In the dark?'

'I like walking in the dark. Besides, I didn't expect you back so quickly.'

'I got a lift from Lavinia and Penrose in and, when you see what I've got to show you, you'll know why I came straight back.'

Sappho produced one of the six copies of *Gut Feeling* she'd bought at Blue Virginia, the only six the shop had possessed, and opened it to the centrefold and the photographs either side. Two of the captions read *Hard to believe this English beauty is only sixteen* and *This English rose can decorate our garden any time.*

Sappho said, 'Do tell me if my eyes are deceiving me, but isn't that voluptuous creature blowing the one stud while getting humped by the other our own beloved Kate McNamara?'

There was no doubt about it. The photographs were unmistakably of Kate.

'Got the bitch!' said Paula triumphantly.

They went down to the dormitory in search of Kate, but soon ascertained she had gone home for the weekend.

'Never mind,' said Paula, 'we'll get her Sunday evening or Monday at the latest. In the meantime, roll me a joint and let me drool over these pix. Christ, I had no idea she was built like that. Saff, I make you a present of Jennifer Langley. Kate McNamara and I are going to get laid before the week's out.'

13

Heteros Nil – Others Two

Kate was driven back to St Clare's by her mother and arrived just after dusk on Sunday. Paula had asked Phoebe, who was in another dormitory on the same landing, to let her know when Kate returned.

'Nothing that need concern you, darling. Just a little something I have to talk to her about.'

After Phoebe reported in, Paula strolled downstairs to Kate's dorm, where she was unpacking and telling Jocasta and Amanda about her weekend.

'Spare me a few minutes?' asked Paula pleasantly.

'Sorry, I'm busy,' answered Kate.

Paula had made no further plays for her since that first evening of Michaelmas Term, but Kate was always wary when, during the course of normal school or House business, their paths crossed.

'It really is rather important,' insisted Paula.

'Oh, very well, go ahead.'

'Important and private,' said Paula.

Kate accompanied her to the door.

'Fire away.'

'Not here, in my study.'

'No, thank *you*,' said Kate emphatically, turning away.

'It concerns some full-colour photographs,' said Paula, delivering the *coup de grâce*. 'Taken in America, I understand.'

Kate felt as if someone had hit her. Her knees buckled, and she had to clutch the door for support. All colour drained from her cheeks.

Oh Christ, she thought, no! How was it possible?

Recovering her balance and her composure, she attempted to bluff her way through.

'Photographs? What photographs? I haven't the foggiest idea what you mean.'

'Your face, my sweet, is as a book where men may read strange matters,' said Paula, misquoting Lady Macbeth. 'However, have it your way. I'm sure somebody will be interested in them, the photographs – Richard Carson, for example, or your little friends behind you.'

'You bitch!' hissed Kate.

Paula permitted herself a faint smile.

'Kate, Kate, is that any way to talk to someone who only has your best interests at heart? The photographs may not even be of you, just a girl who looks like you. Nevertheless, if they fell into the wrong hands . . .'

'Show me,' said Kate.

'Now what do you reckon that's all about?' said Jocasta, watching the pair disappear.

'Search me,' said Amanda, preening herself in front of the cheval glass.

She pinched her tummy. There was still a little

loose flesh there, but that would go with exercise. Otherwise her weight was perfect. As was her hair. She would have the styling and dyeing done again professionally during the Christmas holidays, not so far off now.

She sucked in her cheeks and patted the flesh underneath her chin. Yes, not bad at all.

'You're becoming vain, Amanda,' said Jocasta, watching her antics.

'Ah, that's just jealousy. The ugly duckling has progressed from cygnet to swan.'

No, it's a bit more than jealousy, thought Jocasta. It made her feel uncomfortable to wake up each morning and see, in the adjacent bed, what was looking more and more like a mirror image.

Still, the others were probably right in saying that Amanda would return for the first day of Hilary as a platinum blonde.

Paula had chased Sappho out of the study the minute she heard Kate was back. If, for now, Kate believed that only she, Paula, knew of the photographs' existence, that would be an advantage.

'But I want to see her reactions,' protested Sappho.

'Patience, dear, patience.'

Paula closed the study door behind them. Kate kept her distance, uneasy at being so confined.

'On the bed,' said Paula, pointing.

Gut Feeling was open at the centrefold. Standing, Kate stared down at the magazine, reluctant to touch it. And there she was, in all her naked glory, lips parted and moist, a come-hither look in her eyes.

'There are other, more interesting snapshots on the pages either side. Pick it up, it won't bite.'

Finally Kate did so. In spite of herself, she had to know which of the dozens they'd taken had been used.

She almost wept when she saw. Not out of shame or embarrassment, though both of these emotions were present to a greater or lesser degree, but because the obvious pleasure she was experiencing was now a matter of public record.

And she'd thought she'd left all this 3,000 miles away across the Atlantic.

Oh Jesus!

'That's not me,' she said, attempting and partly succeeding in keeping her voice steady. 'It looks a little like me, granted, but I assure you it isn't. What in God's name do you take me for?'

'That's what I said to myself when I saw them,' said Paula. 'What kind of girl would pose for those? I also said that, even though the model – is that what they're called? – resembles Kate McNamara of the Lower Sixth to an uncanny degree, it couldn't possibly be her. Our Kate, the St Clare's Kate, practically jumped out of her skin when I did hardly more than touch her thigh first day of term. That Kate could hardly be this Kate. Strange, though, that the names are the same. See, there, at the foot of the page you're on? No, not the picture where the caption reads something about an English rose, the one next to it, where you – sorry, the model – is lying with her legs wide apart, facing the camera, a chocolate bar in one hand and the stud's cock in the other. The wording is something like: *Kate evidently has an oral fixation, but we wonder which "bar" she's planning to eat?* No surname, of course, but that's quite common in magazines such as this.'

'It isn't me,' persisted Kate, though her words lacked conviction.

Still, Paula seemed to accept them. She had remained by the study door. Now she opened it.

'Good, glad we cleared that up. It's been bothering me since yesterday. However, now you've explained that it isn't you, if anyone else ever sees the photographs you can rely on me to support your story that the model is merely a lookalike. I recall reading that we're all supposed to have one somewhere in the world. I'll let you get back to your friends now.'

Kate sat down heavily on Paula's bed. With a sudden, vicious, despairing movement she tore the offending pages from the magazine and ripped them into shreds.

Paula made no attempt to stop her.

'I regret to tell you, Kate dear,' she said softly, 'that that wasn't my only copy. Still, I find your actions most odd for someone professing innocence.'

'You know damned well it's me,' said Kate sadly.

She remembered the occasion when the photographs were taken as if it were yesterday, though it had happened in May.

Together with two other girls and three senior boys from Choate, she had driven the fifteen or so miles from Wallingford, where Choate was located, down to New Haven, the home of Yale, where the parents of one of the Choate seniors had a house that would not be occupied for the weekend.

It was a bright, sunny afternoon and much beer and wine had already been consumed when two senior 'Yaleys' turned up bearing half a pound of good Mexican hash and a seemingly endless supply of amphetamines. Before long an orgy was in full swing.

Neither Kate nor the other two girls were virgins or unfamiliar with hash and speed, and a weekend of heavy sex and drugs had been expected and indeed anticipated eagerly. What was unforeseen was one of the Yale seniors producing expensive camera equipment and top-of-the-range lighting, but by this time everyone – the girls at least – were too far gone to care who was doing what to whom or whether they were being photographed. Kate couldn't have spoken then or now for the other two females, but she'd enjoyed every second of the experience. She was by far and away the most attractive of the three, and the knowledge that the men in the orgy wanted to be inside her more than inside the others thrilled her beyond words.

Then the bomb dropped.

When she came down from her 'high', she was naturally concerned about the photographs, but she consoled herself by saying that they would probably circulate among the Yale seniors for a while, and then be forgotten. She was, in any case, returning with her parents to England after the end of the semester in June. Goodbye, America, goodbye, photographs.

The weekend after the orgy, she received a plain brown envelope in her pigeonhole at Choate. Inside were a dozen or more eight-by-tens of herself and the three Choate seniors performing various sexual acts. It had to be the Choate boys because she had not been laid by either of the Yaleys, but the male faces had been cleverly airbrushed out or their bodies photographed in such a manner that only their backs or private parts showed. She was the one participant readily identifiable.

There was also a typed note.

I obtained these by a method that need not concern you, the negatives also. They obviously have a commercial value, which I judge to be $5,000. For this sum the negatives and all existing prints are yours. Please indicate your willingness to trade by returning to the location where the photographs were taken one week from today. DO NOT ATTEMPT TO ENTER THE HOUSE. You will be met and, in return for the aforementioned sum, will be handed a package. That will conclude the transaction and you will hear no more from me. If you fail to produce the money, I regret the negatives will be sold to an organization which specializes in such material.

Kate panicked. She had no means of raising $5,000 or even 500, but surely this was some kind of sick joke. If it wasn't, then the blackmailer must have somehow stolen the negatives. It was too horrible to contemplate that the extortionists were the two Yale seniors.

She sought out the other two girls who had been involved and, subtly, tried to ascertain whether either of them had received a communication threatening exposure unless they paid up.

That was some weekend, right? I wonder if we'll ever see those guys from Yale again. Those photographs must really be something.

After a while she was certain neither of the other girls was being blackmailed as she was. It took her some time to figure out why. The Yaleys – she was now convinced they were behind it – knew she was English and would be returning home in a few weeks. Whether they truly could sell the photographs to a porn magazine was neither here nor there. As far as the $5,000 was concerned, she would be beyond their reach. They could blackmail the American girls any time they wished.

She didn't bother approaching the three Choate seniors. Either they were in on it – it was curious that *their* faces were blanked out – or they would simply shrug and tell her they had no means of raising 5,000 bucks either. It was, in any case, different for men. Even if their faces had been revealed and the photographs published, they would become minor cult figures, heroes even, with their contemporaries. For a man to have a sideline as a porn stud was not only acceptable but laudable. The women were classified as tarts.

She cursed herself for her carelessness and stupidity, but resolved to do absolutely nothing and hope that it would all go away. She could not, in any case, lay her hands on the money.

The Tuesday after she failed to appear at the New

Haven house, she received a second envelope. On this occasion there was only a note.

You're being foolish, but that's your decision. No doubt your parents will be more amenable. Thursday, at the latest, at the New Haven house, or Friday morning your mother and father will receive a package similar to the one I sent you. Perhaps they would sooner pay than see their daughter as the centrespread in a hard-core magazine.

Kate had no alternative other than to request leave of absence from Choate and travel to see her mother. Better she learned the facts from her daughter than via the US mail.

'I've no wish to hurt you or see you hurt, you know,' said Paula, sitting beside Kate on the bed.

Kate edged away, keeping some distance between herself and the South African. She did not, however, attempt to leave the study. Whatever was to happen, it had to be worked out here and now.

Her mother became hysterical when she saw the photographs Kate produced. There was a great deal of, 'How could you? Oh my dear God, how could you!' Tearfully, Kate tried to explain that it was because of the drugs she'd been taking, which partly satisfied her mother – because a daughter acting like a whore under the influence of drugs was better than a daughter who played the harlot because it was in her blood – but which Kate knew was a long way from the truth. Without the hash and amphetamines she might not have gone that far, agreed, but the plain

288

unvarnished facts were that she'd enjoyed it. No way of telling a mother that, of course.

Mrs McNamara couldn't raise $5,000 virtually overnight, either, not without its absence from the bank account being noticed by her husband. No, it had to be faced. If the blackmailer was serious about marketing the negatives, Mr McNamara would have to be told.

'But it would be as well if you returned directly to school. You shouldn't be here when I talk to your father. Write down the exact address or location of this wretched house in New Haven.'

It wasn't until some time afterwards that Kate learned from her mother what happened that Thursday.

At first Mr McNamara wanted to bring in the police. His wife talked him out of it. There were no guarantees that, if one blackmailer was arrested, there wasn't another in the background with a duplicate set of negatives. The extortion money had to be paid.

Mr McNamara drove down alone. He was met, according to Kate's mother, by an unkempt individual who had several tough-looking accomplices with him.

None of them resembled students at Yale, but that was only to be expected. Either the negatives had genuinely been stolen or, more likely, the Yale seniors had hired some local thugs to make the collection for them. Whatever the truth, the money was handed over in exchange for a large envelope. It did indeed contain prints and negatives, which were duly burnt by Mr McNamara.

Within forty-eight hours Kate was removed from Choate and kept at home until her father could tidy up his American business affairs, several months before he'd anticipated. Then the family flew back to England and Kate was enrolled at St Clare's.

Mr McNamara only ever said one sentence to Kate about the whole matter.

'You disgust me.'

Kate understood. Her father had been compelled to look at scenes which violated the most ancient of taboos, that of a man seeing his daughter performing obscene acts.

He seemed to forget about it after a while, but the father and daughter relationship was soured for ever.

And might kill him, thought Kate, if he ever saw a copy of the magazine. Never mind her reputation at St Clare's, or with Richard Carson, it would destroy her father and probably her mother too.

Of course the foul bastards hadn't handed over all the negatives. They'd sold them on, as they'd first threatened. It was her bad luck that the magazine publisher's market was not limited to the States.

'What do you want from me?' she asked Paula dully.

'Want?' asked Paula innocently. 'Just to be your friend, that's all.'

She had Kate now, of that she was sure, but she didn't want her as an unwilling lover. There would be no pleasure in that. What she did want was to introduce Kate to the delights of gay sex between females, confident that her skills would soon make

Kate a convert. No, it was time to be tender.

'If you're offering friendship,' said Kate, 'you might begin by letting me have the other copies of this magazine.'

'Perhaps I will,' said Paula, 'soon. As I think I made it abundantly clear at the start of term, I find you extraordinarily attractive. I'd like us to get to know each other better.'

'You want to have sex with me.'

'Don't tell me it would be the first time. Looking at those photographs, I can't believe there's much you haven't done.'

Kate recalled that one of the Choate girls, during that afternoon in New Haven, had taken a fancy to her during the orgy, but they'd indulged in no more than a few kisses and some fondling. Whatever might have transpired didn't develop after she was seized by one of the Choate seniors. Those photographs had never appeared, not even in the original brown envelope. Perhaps none had been taken or had come out.

'I'm not a lesbian.'

'All women are, to some extent.'

'So you do want to have sex with me?'

'I'd be crazy to deny it.'

'And if I don't agree, you'll spread the photographs around.'

'Now, now, let's not start off on the wrong foot.'

Paula changed tack. The conversation was drifting too far away from her concept of tenderness, towards the threatening, which would get her nowhere. If Kate said, 'OK, damn you, do your worst,' she would be left with only two alternatives: back down or show the photographs around. Either way, she'd lose her chance at Kate's delicious body. If Kate said, 'OK, let's do it,' but reluctantly, through fear of exposure, that would be unsatisfactory also. She wouldn't participate eagerly, and Paula didn't want a passive lover.

'These photographs,' she said, picking up the remnants of those Kate had destroyed, 'under what circumstances were they taken?'

'I'm not going to discuss that.'

'No, you misunderstand me. It all looks very exciting and so on, but I can't believe you weren't smoking a little something or swallowing a little something throughout.' When Kate didn't answer, Paula went on, 'What I mean is, if you need something to relax you, help you unwind, well, I can provide that.'

Suddenly Kate could stand the study's atmosphere no longer. She got to her feet. Paula's eyes narrowed.

'You'll have to give me time,' said Kate. 'I . . . I can't just go into something like this without giving it some thought.'

'How much time?' asked Paula suspiciously, all sorts of images flashing through her mind: Kate feigning illness and going home early for Christmas, perhaps never to return; Kate just running away. Kate even going to Mrs Gordon to complain of being threatened. Dangerous for her, true, but not out of the question.

'A day or two. But I warn you, if I come back, I'll need whatever relaxant you can lay your hands on.'

'You need have no worries about that.'

Paula offered one further sop before Kate left the

study. She opened her locker, took out two further copies of *Gut Feeling*, and gave them to Kate.

'Here, do what you like with these, to prove what I meant about friendship.'

Kate peered inside the locker. There were no other copies in evidence, and she wasn't to know that Paula had the remaining three well hidden elsewhere.

'Is that the lot?'

'Let's just say it's a token of things to come.'

During the Monday lunch break a minor incident took place that was to have far-reaching effects.

In the run-up to the end of Michaelmas Term, it was part of Algy Hicks's job as gardener's assistant to remove from trees any branches that appeared dangerous, that might fall off and injure someone when the harsh weather of December and January arrived. There was one such branch on a birch close to Churchill House.

It was only fifteen feet from the ground and looked an easy job, so easy that Algy couldn't be bothered to trudge the 300 yards it would have taken to get a longer ladder, even though the one he had with him was only twelve feet in length and he would have to stand close to the uppermost rung to reach the branch with the chainsaw.

The inevitable happened. The chainsaw sliced through the wood faster than he had anticipated, and he lost his balance and fell.

He was a sturdy youngster, however, and the fall hardly hurt him at all. But the safety mechanism on the saw failed to cut out instantly, and some of the teeth bit into his wrist as he hit the ground.

Even here he was lucky. The wound was only superficial, though the blood made it look worse.

Julia and Jocasta were returning from lunch and saw Algy fall. They raced across to help. From her years of riding, and falling from, horses, Jocasta had more than a beginner's knowledge of first-aid. She wrapped a clean handkerchief around the wound, then she and Julia helped Algy to the building where Auntie Natal had her rooms.

Algy kept saying, 'It's all right, miss, really, I can manage,' but secretly he could hardly believe his luck that the girl he dreamt about almost every night had her arm around his waist.

Jocasta and Julia waited while Auntie Natal examined, bathed and bandaged the cut. Stitches, she judged, were unnecessary, but she gave him a tetanus booster to be on the safe side.

'Light duties for you for a week, my lad,' she said heartily, 'and take the rest of the day off. I'll give you a note. You should also come and see me tomorrow morning.'

Before leaving, Algy shyly offered Jocasta her handkerchief back.

'I think it might be an idea if you had it laundered first,' said Auntie Natal.

Algy blushed. Of course, how stupid of him to offer a lady a filthy, bloodstained handkerchief.

'It's all right, Algy,' said Jocasta, who had no wish to see the handkerchief again, 'keep it.'

★ ★ ★

Directly after rehearsals on Monday evening, Julia and Fisher disappeared in a hurry. Lavinia and Penrose exchanged glances.

Penrose said, 'This place is getting more like Babylon every day.'

'I'm glad to say,' said Lavinia. 'Anyway, what can you expect when you put a bunch of sixteen- to eighteen-year-old boys and girls together? On the other hand, there are probably no more than eight or ten serious affairs going on, a maximum of, say, twenty people. Considering the size of the school, I'd judge we were way below the national average.'

Guy Young was hovering to say something to Penrose about his part, so Lavinia made herself scarce. Henry Morton was the last to finish cleaning up the Great Hall stage, by which time it was gone ten o'clock and he was filthy. But he was used to this by now and always brought his towel and soap with him. Couldn't go to bed without a shower.

He was leaving as Guy was leaving. Penrose still had things to do. In any case, it was his responsibility to make a final check of the windows and lock the doors.

'Is that a towel I see, Henry?' asked Guy. 'I wish I'd brought one. I seem to have sweated buckets tonight.'

'You can share mine,' said Henry generously.

Hot showers were always available at St Clare's in the winter because the system which governed the central heating also took care of the water. In the summer, when the heating was off, there was an electronic override which kept the water boiling. The lights in the shower blocks, however, male and female, were switched off by the school porter from a master panel at ten-thirty sharp, the cost of electricity being what it was.

'Better hurry,' said Guy.

They showered in adjacent cubicles, Guy, much taller than Henry, reaching over for his turn at the soap. Guy finished first and was towelling himself down when Henry emerged, keeping his back to Guy because he was sporting a semi-erection. OK, that happened fairly regularly, what with the effects of the soap and the hot water and the friction created by rubbing himself clean. But it was embarrassing.

'Here,' said Guy, throwing him the towel.

To catch it, Henry had to face Guy, who saw immediately the part-tumescent state Henry was in.

'Well, well,' he said, 'perhaps we should do something about that. Here, let me.'

Before Henry could protest or make any other move, vocal or physical, Guy reached forward and took a firm hold on Henry's penis. Henry experienced something like an electric shock. 'Hey,' he began, but Guy said, 'Ssh,' and seconds after that Henry had no further wish to complain, because under Guy's fingers his penis hardened to full erection right away.

Guy began moving his hand, gently at first, standing close. Henry was ecstatic and horrified simultaneously, but God, it felt good, and felt even better when Guy's own cock, bigger and thicker than Henry's, rose between their bodies. No thoughts that this was the homosexual experience he had feared for years entered Henry's mind. This wasn't the man in the cinema or the furtive fumblings with Alan from the village two years ago. Guy was someone he admired.

'Come on, Henry, fair's fair,' grunted Guy throatily. 'This shouldn't be all one-way traffic.'

Henry knew what was expected of him. Fingers trembling with nervous excitement, he gripped Guy's thickness with his right hand and began the movements. Now that he was doing to Guy what Guy was doing to him, he became even more aroused. He'd never have believed that anything could be as erotic as this. Guy's penis seemed made of iron, yet iron that throbbed and pulsated.

Guy towered over Henry's five feet five and, it seemed to Henry, was looking down intensely at him. Henry couldn't find it within himself to return the look. He didn't want to see Guy's eyes, just hold him, feel his excitement mounting.

Guy was now pumping Henry's penis with a vengeance.

'Faster, faster,' he urged, his voice hoarse.

Henry obliged, listening to Guy's fevered grunts. Anyone could have walked in and caught them at it, but neither could have stopped what he was doing.

'I'm coming, coming,' moaned Guy. 'Tell me when you are.'

'Now, now,' panted Henry, feeling his orgasm starting.

Then Guy did something that practically made Henry swoon. He put both his own hands over

Henry's one, bringing Henry's cock directly in contact with his own, so that, facing each other, their penises were crossed like swords, and matched Henry's frantic jerking with his own until, with a sob, he ejaculated over Henry's hand and his own hands and on to Henry's still-wet stomach. No more than a beat behind, Henry too was coming into Guy's eager fists. He almost fainted with pleasure.

When it was over and they pulled apart, Guy said, because Henry's eyes were lowered, 'There's no reason to feel ashamed. I'm not. It was good, that's what matters.'

Guy Young was not homosexual or even bisexual, but he was of an age when he needed regular sexual release other than by his own hand, and he couldn't always get that from Felicity because of their circumstances. He had no desire to sodomize Henry, but this was intoxicating. Besides, he had aspirations to write, and a writer should experience everything. It was also illuminating to compare the lust he'd just felt with Henry to that with Felicity. They were similar but also very different. The way Henry had been so willingly and eagerly seduced – though this was a first at St Clare's for Guy also – and would no doubt be again, made him a little like a slave. In fact, that was an interesting thought.

The following evening Guy made sure his study mate, Marcus Bryant, would be absent after arranging for Henry to pay him a visit after nine.

Henry had scarcely been able to sleep the previous night, the image of Guy always before him. That these were the homosexual thoughts – no, now they were acts – which had always caused him panic, there was no doubt, but somehow Guy was right: shame was absent. He realized he was in danger of becoming infatuated, but it didn't worry him.

When the call came to visit Guy in his study after nine, therefore, he could hardly contain himself and was there on the dot.

Guy was lounging in an armchair, in his dressing-gown. There was an open bottle of wine on the table, and two glasses.

'Help yourself,' said Guy, 'or perhaps you'd rather . . .'

He untied the cord of his robe. He was wearing nothing underneath, and his penis was in the early stages of tumescence, in anticipation.

'Do it, Henry. Put a chair under the door first.'

Uncomplainingly, Henry did as he was instructed. He didn't question that, this evening, Guy wanted his own pleasure first. Or exclusively. If that was Guy's wish . . .

He sat on the arm of Guy's chair, alongside him, and stroked him, making him hard.

'That's fine, Henry, fine,' breathed Guy, head far back, eyes closed. 'Not too quick, not just yet. I want to make it last.'

Henry concentrated, only partly aware of his own erection beneath his clothes. He couldn't take his eyes from Guy's marvellous penis. Under the rather dim wattage of the shower-block lights last night, and the way they'd been facing each other, he hadn't been able to take in the full splendour of Guy's cock. Now he could, which must be Guy's intention, letting him see completely what otherwise, mostly, he had only felt.

'A little faster now,' panted Guy. 'Oh Jesus, this is really good. Faster still. I'm just about starting to come . . . at the bottom of the shaft . . . going higher now . . . higher . . . higher . . . just about . . . NOW. But don't stop. For fuck's sake keep moving your hand . . . oh Christ . . .'

Right at his climax, Guy produced a handkerchief from nowhere and, while Henry kept up his hand movements and watched with fascination that bordered on love, ejaculated into it with a loud cry.

The next evening, Wednesday, the same thing happened again. Guy summoned Henry to appear at nine o'clock, and Henry duly appeared. This time they had a glass of wine before Henry brought Guy to orgasm, but Guy didn't seem in the least interested in returning the favour. It didn't entirely bother Henry: just seeing and feeling Guy's pleasure was reward enough. But he didn't want to be taken for granted.

Over a second glass of wine, he asked timidly, 'Aren't we going to go to the showers again if you're worried about us being discovered here?'

'One day soon, perhaps. We can't have everything, can we? Besides, I thought you liked making me feel good, but if you don't, of course, maybe we should forget about the whole thing.'

'No, no,' said Henry hastily. 'That's not what I meant at all.'

'Excellent,' said Guy, and there, for the moment, the matter lay.

Also on Wednesday, Richard Carson and the other select few examinees sat the Oxford entrance papers in a classroom set aside for that purpose. Carson, Lavinia was sure, would sail through with flying colours, and she was pretty confident about one or two others from her languages stream. She did, however, offer them all a final piece of advice.

'Read everything carefully and don't put pen to paper until you're sure.'

When it was all over, Carson immediately sought out Lavinia.

'A piece of cake. As long as I don't blow the interview next month, I'm in.'

He told the same thing to Kate McNamara later in the day.

'I won't hear officially for a week or so, but I know I've passed.'

'I'm very happy for you,' said Kate. 'I knew you'd do it.'

'Maybe we could go out and celebrate tonight. I know it's only Wednesday, but with the end of term coming up they generally relax the rules. I'll come with you to see Mrs Clinton, if you like.'

'Sorry, I can't.'

'Can't?'

'I have other things to do.'

It sounded like a brush-off to Carson, and his heart sank.

'Look, Kate, I accept that everything hasn't been

perfect between us recently, but now that damned exam is out of the way . . . What I mean is . . . OK, what about Saturday?'

'I'll have to see.'

'Are you giving me the elbow? If so, I wish you'd tell me. What about the Christmas holidays, the plans we made?'

Kate couldn't think as far ahead as Saturday, let alone the Christmas break. Unless she sorted out Paula van der Groot, she might not even be at St Clare's on Saturday. And where she would be at Christmas, God only knew.

14

Betrayal and Its Aftermath

The first day of December fell on the Thursday. End of term was less than two weeks away. The teenies had completed their Nativity scene, which was on display at the rear of Great Hall. Christmas decorations were permitted for those classes which wanted them.

Everyone hoped it would snow before the break.

The two performances of *A Midsummer Night's Dream* were to be held on the evenings of the 12th and 13th, and the annual carol, and closing, service on 14th December.

Vanessa Maxwell, Tina Johns and Lucy Harris – the Secret Three – were planning one spectacular last coup before they put away their dominoes for the holidays, possibly for ever. Up to now, they hadn't decided what it should be.

Phoebe was disappointed that Paula seemed to have lost interest in her. Paula was getting angrier by the hour that Kate's 'day or two' had now become four.

'I tell you,' she said to Sappho, Thursday afternoon, 'she's for the high jump. The remaining three magazines, or her part of them, get pinned up on the bulletin board before the weekend unless she comes across.'

'Thus slitting your own throat, as opposed to her throating your own slit.'

'Very humorous. She's got until this evening.'

Kate had made sure she was never without company since Sunday, but it couldn't go on for ever. Paula was bound to catch her alone some time.

There was no way out. She either had to go to bed with Paula or take the consequences.

Was sleeping with her such a repugnant notion? After all, she'd witnessed the tiny South African having sex with Phoebe and it had excited her, and she would almost certainly have had sex with one of the girls down at New Haven if the Choate boys had not needed her more urgently. If she was a slut – and that had to be called a possibility even if she would have used a different definition – where was the harm? Paula had promised 'exotic substances' to help her relax, and there was little doubt that the South African had them hidden somewhere.

So what did it matter?

Well, it mattered because joining Paula between, or on, the sheets one time would not be the end of it. There would be others, and Kate wasn't sure she could take that.

There had to be a different way. Perhaps there was.

She waited for Paula after classes.

'Tomorrow night,' she said. 'But I hope you've got plenty of hash.'

Paula rubbed her hands.

'Make yourself scarce tomorrow night, Saff. I need the study,' Paula said later.

'You've cracked it?'

'Let's just say that, after tomorrow, I shall do everything within my power to get you and Jennifer Langley together.'

At six p.m. Thursday evening, Henry Morton vowed not to obey Guy's summons to be in his study at six-thirty. At six-fifteen he changed his mind. At six-thirty he was knocking on Guy's door.

Guy was fully dressed. There was an open bottle of champagne on his desk.

'Henry, I've been selfish and I'm sorry.'

Felicity Coggan had bought the champagne. Or rather, she had provided the money, and Guy had taken a taxi there and back into town the minute classes ended.

'This chap's got a crush on me,' Guy had said.

'Well, that can happen,' said Felicity. 'You're a very handsome man.'

'But the thing is, I have to put him off gently. He's a sad individual and I don't want to hurt him more than necessary. I was thinking a bottle of bubbly and a quiet chat might do the trick.'

'For which you need money.'

'I'm afraid so.'

Felicity gave him thirty pounds.

'You wouldn't care to tell me his name, would you?'

'No, no more than I'd reveal your name if someone accused me of having an affair with a member of staff.'

'Just as long as you're not turning gay.'

'Wouldn't you know?'

'I'm not that wise,' said Felicity.

Henry accepted a glass of champagne.

'There really wasn't any need. Besides, I don't know what you mean by selfish.'

'It was an aberration, Henry, in the showers on Monday, the last two nights here. I repeat, I'm sorry. I'm not gay, and I'm sure you're not either. It was just – well – I liked you and I think you liked me.'

'Past tense?' said Henry, feeling his reason for existence evaporating.

'Of course not. I still like you. But I sense that you're unhappy with the arrangement. I mean to say, I lie there and you give me great pleasure. But it's all so one-sided.'

'You could change that.'

'Not within me, Henry, old son. I'm greedy. Of course, if the shower scene ever happens again, purely by coincidence, I'd be happy to oblige. But it's unlikely.'

Henry felt himself go cold. He was being eased out, that had to be it. Unless, of course . . .

'You want more of me?'

'More, Henry? Such as what? Buggery. Not my style, old son. I prefer women.'

'There are other ways,' said Henry, not looking at Guy.

Right, thought Guy, right, understanding immediately what Henry was reluctant to voice. Felicity enjoyed fellatio, but he'd never done it with a male before. Nor was he sure he wanted to. However, there were still 'other ways', other means of generating sexual excitement, that Henry had undoubtedly not considered.

Play it carefully, though.

'Do you recall the story of the lion tamer who had rather a specialized act?' Henry said he didn't. 'Well, this lion tamer, instead of doing the usual trick of putting his head in the lion's mouth, put his cock in there. The lion didn't bite it off, to huge applause from the audience. Then the lion tamer issued a challenge: anyone with nerve enough to do the same would win a hundred pounds. There were no takers, except for one tiny, skinny chap who came forward. "You're going to take up the challenge?" said the lion tamer, amazed. "Yes," said the little fellow. "But I'm not sure I can open my mouth that wide."'

Henry didn't laugh.

'I'm a joke to you, aren't I? But if that's what you want . . . Just don't leave me alone, that's all.'

'As if I would. But look, not here and now. It's still early. God knows who's wandering these corridors. Make it eight-thirty. The champagne won't be flat by then. We can have a party – if you're sure.'

'I'm sure.'

'No, I meant, if you're sure you don't mind doing things to please me, things you wouldn't normally do.'

'I am,' said Henry, and, even though he was far from

being so, he returned to Guy's study a few minutes before eight-thirty.

Guy was in his dressing-gown, standing by his desk, two glasses of champagne already poured. Henry gulped one nervously.

Guy fixed the door, though the chair didn't fit tight under the handle.

Returning to his customary armchair, Guy unfastened his robe. His penis was already erect, his breathing laboured. At this point, usually, Felicity, on her knees, stared at it with awe.

'God, that's lovely.'

Then she went to work with that splendid mouth.

Which Henry didn't, seeming not to know where or how to begin.

'There's no hurry,' said Guy, though from the sound of his voice there obviously was. 'Just do your usual, to start with.'

Henry sat at Guy's feet and got to work with his hand. Perhaps, if he didn't think too much about it, using his mouth wouldn't be so terrible. He adjusted his position and moved closer.

Then the door-handle was rattled, the chair fell to one side with a crash, and the door was pushed open. Marcus Bryant, Guy's study mate, came in.

'Is this a private party or can anyone join in?'

Horrified at the sudden intrusion, Henry leapt to his feet and sprang away as if stung, his face beetroot red. Guy appeared irritated but otherwise totally unperturbed.

'You might have given us a bit longer,' he said to

Bryant, pulling a face but making no attempt to cover himself.

'Sorry, my timing's always been a little suspect.'

'What is all this?' said Henry, though he got the words out only with difficulty. 'What does he mean about timing?' he asked Guy.

'It's what we were discussing earlier,' said Guy, 'about you doing things to please me. I've been talking to Marcus about you . . .'

'You've WHAT?'

'. . . and it occurred to us both that you might like to extend your repertoire. You know, do for Marcus what you've been doing for me. After all, you obviously enjoy it, and what's one more?'

'You BASTARD!' screamed Henry, and launched himself, fists clenched, at Guy, who was out of the armchair, robe flapping, in a flash.

He fought Henry off without difficulty, pushing Henry to the floor. Henry lay there, catching his breath.

'What's the matter with you, for Christ's sake?' bellowed Guy, seeing his comfortable sexual relationship with Henry disappearing out of the window. He hadn't wanted to frighten the little creep off, just heighten the excitement by changing the *ménage à deux* to *à trois*. 'OK, forget Marcus. It was just an idea, that's all.'

'You unfeeling bastard!' Henry struggled to his feet, fists still clenched. Then he dropped his hands when he realized he stood no chance of inflicting any damage on Guy. 'How could you? How could you!'

He raced from the study, the tears already starting to flow.

'Looks like you haven't got him so well trained after all,' said Bryant, helping himself to champagne.

'Looks like I haven't, bugger it. You don't suppose he'll go squealing to Penrose or Chips or someone, do you?'

'He's hysterical enough to do just that.'

'God, I hope not.'

'You're probably safe. How on earth would he tell the tale? He'll just bury his head in his pillow for a couple of hours. He'll have forgotten all about it by tomorrow.'

'Yes, that's what he'll do.'

But in this they were both wrong.

Henry didn't even stop to collect a coat from his study. He ran down the stairs, out of Napier House, and on down the drive, not conscious of where he was going, oblivious to the cold. It began to rain, which hid his tears even though he was hardly aware he was crying.

Dobbs was on duty in the little cubby-hole attached to the porter's lodge, especially vigilant now Christmas and the end of Michaelmas Term were so close, because it was not unknown for sixth-formers to try to sneak out during weekdays, to see what was going on in town. It wasn't forbidden, not for the Upper Sixth, at least, but they had to sign out and sign back in, for the eleven o'clock curfew only applied at weekends.

'Here . . .' he began, but Henry, whom Dobbs didn't recognize in the darkness, ran straight past.

Dobbs picked up the phone to call for the duty master, for it was obviously a boy who had escaped the net, but then he put it down again. It was his job, Dobbs's job, to prevent that sort of thing happening. To raise a stink now would land him in trouble. He would collar the boy on the way back, give him a severe ticking-off, threaten to report him unless he had an adequate explanation.

It had happened many times before.

Sorry, Dobbs, but I had to see this girl. Will a fiver cover it?

Yes, leave it until later, that was best.

Henry's mind was in a turmoil. Even though he wasn't aware of it, his direction, once outside the school gates, was towards town.

How *dare* he? How *dare* he?

Oh yes, he could see it all now. Guy had toyed with him. He could just imagine the conversations Guy had had with Marcus.

This little weed of a chap – Henry Morton, you must know Henry though, God knows, he's easily overlooked – is infatuated with me. Does anything I want. Can't resist my cock, you see. I'll get him to service you, if you like. Queer as a two-headed llama, but he doesn't know it yet.

And he'd loved Guy, genuinely loved him.

Half a mile down the road, the rain started in earnest. He was beginning to get really wet when the town bus rounded a corner and pulled in to its stop, fifty yards away. Henry ran for it and caught it, one of those single-deckers where the driver also took the fares as a passenger boarded.

On the running-board, Henry checked his wallet. He had around thirty pounds in notes and another couple in silver in his pockets.

'Bad night to be walking,' said the driver.

Henry brushed the rain from his face. No-one would be able to tell he had been weeping.

'It certainly is,' he said, handing over the correct fare.

Alighting from the bus at the terminus, Henry made for the nearest pub. He ordered whisky, which he hardly ever drank outside his mother's flat.

'You look a bit damp,' said the barmaid who served him.

Henry glanced in the mirror behind her. Yes, he looked a wreck.

He retreated to the cloakroom to comb his hair and try, insofar as was possible, to dry himself down on the roller-towel. When he re-emerged, he didn't look much better, but there was a slight improvement.

He added soda to the whisky, drank it, and ordered another.

'And I'll have a half-bottle to take with me.'

He paid for that also and slipped it into his side pocket.

Like most public houses in England, as with bars in America, those close to bus and rail terminals attract the sort of customer who doesn't care much about his surroundings, who simply wants spirits and beer at a cheaper price than more upmarket establishments charge. Boys, and girls, from fee-paying schools do not usually frequent such places. Unless they're slumming, or feel at rock-bottom.

Which Henry did.

He retreated to a table with his third double whisky, needing to sit down.

Everything that Guy had told him, about them being close, was a lie. God, had it only begun on Monday? Guy saw him as a male whore, to be passed on to Marcus Bryant, spread around Guy's friends as Guy saw fit. Henry Morton? Sure, he'll service you providing you're nice to him. Show him your cock and tell him you like him. He's not bad at it, either. Better than self-abuse, anyway. He's a mug, Henry, for a thick cock, seeing as his own doesn't measure up to much.

He's gay, Henry.

Yes, Guy was probably right.

If it wasn't true, why had he been so willing? Why had he got so much pleasure out of masturbating Guy?

Why, why, why?

But – he didn't want to be gay. He didn't want to spend the rest of his life being taken advantage of, masturbating men and, later – he was sure – fellating them and possibly permitting them to sodomize him.

It wouldn't happen overnight, but it would happen. There'd be another Guy, someone he'd trust, someone who'd let him down. Then another. And the day would come when he wouldn't care whether he had feelings for the man or not.

Just because he was lonely.

'That's our table, mate.'

A couple of burly truckers loomed over him. Emboldened by the whisky, he stood up for himself.

'Who says so?'

'We say so. You're underneath the dartboard.'

'Then move the dartboard.'

'We've got a comedian here, Del,' said one of the truckers.

'But he doesn't mean it, does he?' said the other. 'I mean, a wimp like him. A little poof like him.'

The word 'poof' triggered off something inside Henry. He hurled what was left of his whisky in the second trucker's face.

'Right,' said the trucker, and grabbed Henry by the collar.

'Outside,' shouted the barmaid.

'Done,' said the first trucker, and lifted Henry off his feet.

They beat him senseless in the car park. For good measure, since they were unlikely to pass this way again, they relieved him of his twelve or so remaining pounds and his wristwatch, making certain they did so well away from the lights. Miraculously they missed the half-bottle of whisky in his pocket, and nor did it break.

Then they took off. With a watch worth upwards of a hundred pounds, plus the cash, they could find other pubs.

Thursday was a slow night for pubs in this part of town, which catered mostly to the weekly paid who would not receive their envelopes until Friday. No-one saw Henry bundled up in a corner or, if they did, looked the other way.

When he came to his senses, he ached all over. It was also raining more heavily.

The pub lights were still on, but he had no intention of returning there. What for, more humiliation? What was the point in reporting the robbery – for he soon ascertained that he was minus his folding money and his wristwatch – to the police. What would they say? Another queer-bashing, that's what.

He checked his pockets. His assailants had left him the silver and the Scotch, but the coins were nothing like enough for a taxi back to St Clare's. And calling the porter's lodge for help was out of the question.

So he walked, getting wetter as the miles fell behind him, taking regular swigs of whisky from the neck of the bottle.

It was after midnight when he reached the main gates. He didn't care if Dobbs spotted him, so depressed was he by now, but Dobbs was off making his late-night cocoa, having assumed that, somehow, the earlier runaway had made it back into the grounds undetected.

'Sorry if you get into trouble, Dobbsy,' muttered Henry.

In spite of his soaking and the long hike back, the regular sips from the bottle meant he was quite drunk as he made his way to the shower block. The lights were out, of course, and he had some difficulty in finding the pair of stalls where he and Guy had had their first sexual encounter.

Yes, I'm queer, he finally admitted. Yes, I'm gay. Don't want to be, but there it is. Guy thinks I am, so what's the difference?

He shook the bottle. From the sounds he judged it still to be half full, and he drank the remaining liquor slowly, sometimes talking to himself, sometimes giggling, sometimes crying.

When the bottle was empty, he hurled it away and unsteadily got to his feet. He untied his belt and looped it over the shower-head. Then he made a noose of the belt and wound it round his neck. That done, he stepped up on to the tiled shelf.

Then he let himself go. It was all so easy.

The police were called in the following morning, naturally, but they quickly concluded that there were no suspicious circumstances, as the saying goes in British jurisprudence. As if a young man hanging himself does not arouse a faint suspicion of something.

The absence of a suicide note was not considered sinister, not after the smashed whisky bottle was found and the post-mortem established huge quantities of alcohol in the bloodstream.

Henry's mother was in Paris. She was traced via her office, flew back, and the body was released to her. Under Coroner's Rules, Henry could not be buried until after the inquest, but that was regarded as a mere formality.

Henry Morton had killed himself while the balance of his mind was disturbed.

Felicity Coggan knew there was more to it than that.

'You'd better apply to Mrs Gordon to go home, Guy, before the end of term.'

'I'm not quite with you.'

'Don't be dense. That was the young man, was it not, who had the so-called crush on you?'

'Nonsense.'

'Apply to go home, Guy. Illness in the family or whatever. The police seem to have finished asking their questions, but that's no guarantee they won't be back.'

'I had nothing to do with Henry Morton's suicide.'

'I don't believe you did, not directly. If I thought otherwise, I'd be phoning the police myself.'

'What about the play?'

Felicity held on to her temper. 'I never realized you could be quite so cold-blooded. A young man is dead. Whether he was *your* young man or someone else's, or whether his death is entirely unrelated to his feelings for you, is immaterial. Apply to go home.'

Guy thought about it. It made sense. Although he in no way blamed himself for Henry's death – good God, a tiny incident such as the one that had happened in his study didn't send a *rational* person over the edge – getting out of school early made sense.

He saw Mrs Gordon, and was granted permission. Felicity wasn't sure she would see him, or wish to, again.

Before he left he had a quiet word with Marcus Bryant.

'I don't think for a minute that what happened when you barged in had anything to do with Henry topping himself, but it might be as well if you didn't mention it to anyone.'

'Mention what, old lad?' said Bryant.

One bonus, if it could be called that, out of Henry's death was that Kate could refuse to bed Paula. At least for the time being.

'I'm upset, damn it, and if you had any feelings you would be too. Henry was a friend of Richard's, who is a friend of mine.'

Paula accepted the argument reluctantly. 'But don't think this lets you off the hook. Before the end of term, or you know what will happen.'

15

Two Little Girls in Blue

Term had to go on.

It was a tragedy, Henry Morton's death, but Mrs Gordon concluded she could not close down the whole school with still almost two weeks to go until the end of term. There were other parents involved, other students. The governors agreed with her.

An ungenerous outsider might have suggested that many of the 'other parents' would not take kindly to having their offspring dumped back on them two weeks before the agreed date, and that two weeks as a percentage of a term's fees of £3,000, multiplied by the number of disgruntled mothers and fathers, would amount to a small fortune if rebates were demanded, but this was only partly true. For everyone's sake, it had to be business as usual.

After a service in chapel on Sunday for Henry, Mrs Gordon addressed the entire student body in Great Hall on Monday morning, 5 December. The tenor of her message was simple: if anyone, *anyone*, had problems with which they felt they could not cope, they should approach their Head of House without delay.

Kate McNamara thought about it, then dismissed the idea. She was unlikely to receive a sympathetic hearing for *her* sort of dilemma.

You see, Mrs Clinton, there are some photographs in existence of the hard-core pornographic variety which show me getting laid by several men. Now, Paula van der Groot has obtained copies of these and is threatening to distribute them to all and sundry unless I have sex with her.

No, impossible.

Although he was even less involved in Henry's suicide than Guy – if Guy had been in any manner responsible – Marcus Bryant heaved a quiet sigh of relief after listening to Mrs Gordon. Obviously no-one knew why Henry had taken his own life.

After Mrs Gordon had dismissed the school, Robert Penrose caught up with her in the Little Quad.

'About the play, Headmistress, *A Midsummer Night's Dream*.'

'It will go ahead, surely. The tickets have been sent out.'

'Yes, but Guy Young, my Demetrius, went home over the weekend, I understand. Family worries or some such.'

'So he did, so he did. But you have an understudy?'

'Guy was the understudy, or at least second choice when the original Demetrius dropped out. I have some cover in some of the parts, of course, in case of illness. Regrettably, Demetrius isn't one of them.'

'You are not suggesting, I trust, that we cancel the performances because one boy cannot appear?'

'I was hoping for your advice on that.'

Mrs Gordon had a lot more on her mind than a wretched play, important though it was for the good of the school.

'Mr Penrose,' she said in her most magisterial voice, 'I'm afraid *this* problem is yours. Is there no-one else?'

'No-one knows the part.'

'Apart from yourself.'

Oh Christ, thought Penrose, going in search of Lavinia.

'You'll look great in tights,' said Lavinia. 'What colour have we chosen for Demetrius? Blue, wasn't it?'

'Fat chance,' said Penrose. 'I'll get one of the seniors to do it.'

'Robert, be sensible, in a week? Today's the fifth. We perform on the twelfth and thirteenth. It's poss-ible, just possible, that someone with an excellent memory could learn the lines in that time. They'd stand no chance of learning the moves.'

'Fiona Acland could. She's got almost total recall.'

'I'll cut your balls off first. No, it has to be you. You know the moves inside out, the lines as well. You're nominated.'

'Or someone else who's been to every rehearsal.'

'One of the stage crew? Forget it. They're backstage because they didn't have what it takes to be in the cast.'

'I wasn't thinking of one of the stage hands.'

Lavinia saw how he was looking at her and sud-denly twigged what was in his mind.

'Oh no you bloody well don't! I came into this all those weeks ago because you practically begged me to be your assistant. But you don't get me up on that damned stage in doublet and hose!'

'You've got superb legs. You'll be perfect.'

'To hell with my legs. I'm not flashing them for every lecherous male parent to ogle, much though the idea would appeal under other circumstances.'

'You've been to every rehearsal.'

'So has the school cat. No.'

'Demetrius has his big scenes with Helena,' Penrose reminded her gently. 'And we know who's playing Helena, don't we?'

'Julia,' groaned Lavinia.

'Precisely. And if I remember correctly, you were the one who pointed out she had a crush on me.'

'That was weeks ago. She's involved with Ben Fisher now.' She brightened. 'There you are, use Ben. He knows all the moves. He plots the damned things, for God's sake.'

'And he's also hopeless, if you recall. We auditioned him.'

'I'll be worse.'

'But you'll look gorgeous. We'll stick with blue, but get a smaller costume. It's either you or me and, apart from everything else I've got to do, there are some pretty tight clinches between Demetrius and Helena. I don't fancy kissing Julia, for obvious reasons . . .'

'Nor do I, damn it!'

'. . . in case it all gets out of hand.'

'No,' said Lavinia, 'I'm not doing it if you tie me

up and whip me – or rather, if you threaten not to. No, no, a thousand times no.'

'I feel like a damned freak,' said Lavinia.

An hour before rehearsals that same Monday evening, Lavinia was examining herself in the full-length backstage mirror. Although dress rehearsal for the rest of the cast would not be until Sunday, Penrose knew that their costumes were ready and that they'd all tried them on for size. He wasn't worried that they'd be embarrassed when they walked out in them for the first time proper. With Lavinia it was different. She was a johnny-come-lately. She had to get used to striding the boards in doublet and hose, or there was a real danger of stage fright rendering her mute.

Penrose didn't want that for two reasons. The first would ruin the play. The second, Lavinia would never forgive him for exposing her to ridicule, and he would find it hard, now, to give up the sexual adventures they enjoyed together.

In the short time since the morning it had been impossible to find a costume to fit her, though they'd unearthed one that was close and it was being tailored for her by the girl who was acting as seamstress. For now, however, she was wearing Guy Young's doublet – far too big but there it was – over a pair of duck-egg blue tights she'd raced into town to buy straight after classes. They were thicker than any of the stockings she normally wore, but even that couldn't disguise the shapeliness of her legs. To stop the voyeurs having a field-day, she was wearing two pairs of heavy-duty knickers, bought with the tights, and her blond hair was tied back in a pony-tail with a ribbon.

Penrose thought she looked sensational.

'And I'm still not sure how you talked me into it,' she added.

'You look great,' said Penrose.

The few males who were helping out backstage thought so too, and Lavinia's entrance was greeted by wolf-whistles. She had thought she was a few years beyond embarrassment at masculine adulation, but she found herself blushing. These boys, after all, knew her as the woman who taught some of them French and German, a woman who dressed in smart business suits or tops and skirts with hemlines as decreed by Mrs Gordon. Right now she felt naked.

Penrose put an end to the catcalls with a few sharp words, though he had to admit that Lavinia was a fetching sight now that the spotlights were on her. God knew what Mrs Gordon would make of it all. Maybe he'd have to think again regarding her costume.

The rest of the cast were more or less word-perfect with their lines by now, but Lavinia was allowed to keep her script. She was surprised at how much she'd learned by osmosis, and after a while she began to enjoy herself. When Penrose finally called a halt, she was amazed at how quickly the time had gone. She was also gratified when several of the younger girls called out, 'Well done, Miss Lee.'

Even Julia congratulated her, though by the very nature of Helena's relationship with Demetrius, Julia had had to do quite a bit of adjusting to this new face and lighter vocal timbre reading Guy's lines.

'You were absolutely terrific,' said Penrose when everyone had gone and Lavinia was slouching in one of the backstage chairs, still in her costume, smoking a cigarette and wishing she'd had the foresight to bring a bottle of gin with her stage clothes. 'You also looked terrific.'

Lavinia detected sexual undertones in his voice.

'What, in these old things?' she said mischievously, and leaned forward to study herself in the mirror.

To get a better look, she stood and gave a twirl. No doubt about it, even in the thick tights her legs were excellent.

They had had sex in front of mirrors before, but not full-length ones. Before Penrose could say anything, she slipped out of the tights and the two pairs of knickers beneath and tossed them aside. She kept the doublet on but raised it, pushing up her bra, until her breasts were exposed. She faced Penrose, legs wide apart and inviting.

'Jesus, Vin.'

Penrose tossed a glance over his shoulder. The stage lights were out but the Great Hall ones were still on, as were those backstage. Nor was the Great Hall door locked.

'Take a chance, Robert. There, sit in that chair. No, with your back to the mirror. I want to see myself.'

She practically manhandled him to the straight-backed chair, sat him down, unfastened his belt, and lowered his trousers and underwear. Worried that someone might walk in at any moment, Penrose was far from erect, but Lavinia sat over him and moved against him until he hardened. Then she eased him inside her.

Neither of them mentioned condoms, or that this was the first time they'd got laid without one. Neither of them cared. For Penrose, the feel of being inside Lavinia without anything, however thin, in between, was exquisite. For Lavinia, it brought back the very first time she'd ever been fucked.

'Let me do the work.'

She held his shoulders and started moving her hips, all the while watching herself in the mirror, seeing her bare legs either side of Robert's around the sides of the chair, watching her mouth open and her eyes take on a glazed look.

This wouldn't take long. She could feel herself coming already and suspected, by his frantic breathing, that Robert was right there with her.

He tried to say something, but she knew what it was going to be, *Vin, I can't hold it,* and bent her mouth to cover his. *She* would make the decision to withdraw, not he. *She* would judge the precise moment he was about to come, which she knew, she absolutely knew, would be seconds after she had. *She* would take the risks. That was what it was all about, as was having sex in doorways, in daylight, or, the next best thing, having a marvellous fuck behind the stage of Great Hall, which she'd have bet a lot of money few had done. If anyone.

She felt her spasms starting, removed her mouth from Robert's, saw her head tossing in the mirror, and leaned back to feel Robert's hardness tight inside her.

There.

Now.

She whipped herself outside Robert just as he began to come. She pressed her belly to his, his cock between them, and came a second time as the heat of his fluid spurted upwards to dampen the underside of her breasts.

She could, she thought, get quite enamoured about dressing up in different costumes for sex.

Outside Churchill House, in the shrubbery, Algy Hicks was shivering in the cold December air. In his pocket, in a cellophane wrapper, was a freshly laundered handkerchief that had once belonged – and still did, in Algy's view – to Jocasta Petrillo. He had collected it on Saturday, the first time he'd been able to get into town since he'd presented it to the laundry for cleaning. The manageress had thought him mad for wanting a single handkerchief given the full treatment, and had charged him extortionately for the service. 'We have a minimum rate, see.' Algy hadn't minded.

At first he'd considered keeping it, as Jocasta had suggested, as a memento (although Algy would not have recognized that word) of the wonderful afternoon when he had touched, and been touched by, a girl he worshipped. Then he changed his mind. She had been kind enough to bind it round his wound. He had to return it, clean, as a way of saying thank you.

He hadn't seen her over the weekend and only once

today. But then she had been in the company of other girls and he was too shy to approach her. Besides, he wanted to see her when she was alone.

He had thought, if he waited outside Churchill for long enough after dark, she would emerge for a late-night stroll. Some of the girls did, no matter what the weather. But she hadn't appeared tonight, it was getting late, and he had no business lurking in the undergrowth outside any of the girls' Houses. Someone might get the wrong idea.

He would try again tomorrow, and the day and night after, until he caught up with her.

Among others, Richard Carson had sailed through the Oxford entrance examination, and his interview, the final hurdle, had been set for Friday, 9 December. Ben Fisher would not be going with him. Even with all the extra work, his submitted papers were not deemed to have come up to scratch.

Carson commiserated.

'Bastards,' grumbled Fisher. 'They might at least have seen me. I can't believe the work I sent in was *that* bad.'

'Yes, it's a bugger,' agreed Carson. 'Hard luck.'

Though it was far from that. Fisher knew, as Carson did, that the stringent standards set by the University, though fair, were designed to preclude wasting interview time on an applicant whose Advanced level results, next year, were unlikely to be high enough, based on the submitted papers' marks, to warrant admission. Much the same would have applied to Carson if he'd flunked badly in the entrance exam. He could still be turned down if he performed inadequately at the interview, but that he considered unlikely. Short of, God forbid, a bereavement in the family or some other trauma to put him off his stroke, he was home and hosed.

'You'll get into Durham, no problem,' said Carson.

'As long as it's not some ghastly redbrick. It'll be strange, though, won't it, to be heading in different directions next autumn after all this time?'

'Look on the bright side,' said Carson. 'Poor old Henry won't be heading anywhere. I wonder if we'll ever know what made him do it.'

'Probably not, as he didn't leave a note, not unless, when the autopsy report is made public, it reveals that he was suffering from some incurable disease.'

'Unlikely. We'd have seen some signs.'

'We didn't see any that he was going to commit suicide.'

Both boys felt more guilt over Henry's death than they were willing to admit. It was absolutely true that neither had seen any indications that he was a potential suicide, and they had no way of knowing that it was his treatment at the hands of Guy Young that had finally pushed him over the edge. It was also true that they had been too wrapped up in their own worries to be much concerned that Henry, during his short life, was virtually friendless. With Carson it had been the Oxford entrance, his affair with Kate and subsequent impotence problems. With Fisher, as well as submitting his Oxford papers, it was Julia.

329

No, Henry Morton had lived more or less alone and had certainly died alone.

Kate was genuinely happy about Carson's success in the entrance exam, and wished him the best of luck for Friday. She rejected his offer to spend some time with him before then, however. If Paula saw them together, hand in hand or even just deep in conversation, it might make her mad enough to release the magazine photographs and to hell with everything. Apart from that, Kate simply had too much on her mind.

Carson accepted her decision. She insisted it wasn't all over between them, but he had his doubts.

The *MND* seamstress had worked hard on Lavinia's costume, and she looked even more sensational in it at Tuesday's rehearsal than she had on Monday. The doublet had been cut very tight and showed off the upper half of her figure to perfection. The blue hose was thinner than the tights she had previously worn and, in them, her legs were displayed to considerable advantage.

News of how she had looked on Monday had spread throughout the school by Tuesday, and practically every male member of the Upper and Lower Sixths wanted entrance to that night's rehearsal. So did some of the sixth-form girls, Paula van der Groot and Sappho Peters among them.

'Christ,' said Sappho, 'will you take a look at that! Doesn't it make you as horny as hell?'

'Don't remind me,' drooled Paula, making up her

mind there and then that if Kate McNamara didn't come across by tomorrow evening there would be no further chances.

Usually Penrose didn't bother about barring visitors from rehearsals, providing they didn't make too much noise or interrupt the proceedings in any other manner. People were free to come and go as they pleased. Few wanted to attend, in any case. Even for professional actors the stop-start business of rehearsals was boring; for amateurs it was even more so. And for spectators at amateur rehearsals it was like watching paint dry.

So when thirty-odd people turned up on Tuesday evening, Penrose was surprised, though it didn't take him long to figure out their interest. Lavinia's first entrance confirmed his suspicions: whistles, gasps of admiration and some applause greeted her. After a few minutes when, even with the script in her hands, she stumbled over her lines, it became apparent that she was too self-conscious to concentrate.

Penrose cleared Great Hall of everyone who had no business there.

Lavinia's costume was going to be a problem, that was clear. He wasn't worried vis-à-vis the audience that it was far too revealing. She was playing a man. He couldn't put her in a dress, and if he tried to cover her with a long frock-coat, she'd die under the lights. What did bother him, however, was Lavinia's reactions. If a handful of people could put her off, God knew what would happen when she had to face several hundred.

He had an idea.

Though it seemed manifestly incongruous in such a high-profile business, he knew many professional actors were shy individuals offstage. They were only confident when in costume and makeup. They could hide their real personalities, the shy ones, behind the characters they were playing.

Lavinia was in costume, true, but it was the costume that was causing the trouble. Everyone could see it was Lavinia up there onstage. Her blond hair made her unmistakable.

He suggested a dark wig, cut in a different style from her own hair. In the props trunk they found a jet-black one in a page-boy bob that just about fitted. With a little modification, and with her own hair tucked up, it would be perfect.

Lavinia felt completely different with it on, more the character of Demetrius, or at least not Lavinia Lee.

She also suggested, in a quiet moment during rehearsals, that it would be a nice change for Penrose to screw a brunette for a change.

'And maybe a redhead tomorrow.'

On the morrow, Wednesday, after classes, Kate showered and, in her robe, lay on her bed. Paula had caught up with her during the day.

'This evening, seven o'clock, my study,' the South African had said.

There was no escape. There was, however, a way to deal with Paula once and for all, even if it meant that she, Kate, went down with the same ship, as it were. With any luck, though, Paula would not blame her and therefore not release the photographs.

'What are you wearing to the party on Saturday?' asked Amanda who, as usual these days, was admiring herself in the mirror.

Traditionally on the last Saturday of term, the Upper and Lower Sixths held a thrash in the sixth-form commonroom. Wine and beer were permitted in moderation and loud music was mandatory.

'Party?' said Kate.

'Come on, sleepyhead, wake up. Party, party!'

'Oh, that party. I don't know, I'll dig something out.'

'Are you OK?' asked Amanda. 'You seem pre-occupied.'

'Just a little tired. And I can't stop thinking about Henry Morton.'

This wasn't true, as it hadn't been when she'd made the same excuse to Paula the previous week. But it would suffice to distract Amanda.

'I know what you mean. Terrible, wasn't it?'

Julia came rushing in and dumped her books on her bed. Members of the cast of *MND*, because of the pressure of rehearsals, were permitted to dine early. But if you weren't there on time there was a good chance everything would be eaten by the greedy teenies, whose appetites were gargantuan.

Julia hadn't been the same since Lavinia had taken over Guy Young's role. It wasn't so much that Lavinia didn't, as yet, know the moves or her lines, which was throwing Julia's performance, the continuity of it, because Penrose had to keep halting the flow to correct Lavinia; it was more that Lavinia, with her sensational looks in that body-revealing costume, was upstaging Julia.

When it had just been Julia and Guy, a man and a woman, Julia hadn't felt threatened. Guy had been something of a scene-stealer, but at least he was a *male* thief and she, during her speeches, knew that the audience's attention would be on her and not Guy. Now, she was pretty damned certain that no-one would even know she was on stage when she was sharing it with Lavinia, whether Lavinia was speaking or not. All eyes would be on those gorgeous damned bloody legs. She might as well wear a sack over her head and whistle Dixie for all the approbation she'd receive.

Bitch.

Julia was also aware, as was the rest of the school, that Lavinia and Penrose had something going between them. They had been seen together, here and there, often enough in recent weeks. Not that that bothered Julia. She now had Ben – dear, redheaded, freckled Ben – and it was hard to recall the first day of term when she'd lusted after Penrose.

Still, if Lavinia was not only staggeringly beautiful but the producer's girlfriend to boot, it made life damned hard for everyone else.

'See you later,' she called over her shoulder.

Jocasta was asleep on her bed, a copy of *Horse and Hound* covering her face. Amanda tugged her toes to wake her when it was time for the school in general to dine.

Jocasta tossed the magazine to the floor, rubbed her eyes and stretched.

'Christ, my mouth feels like the bottom of a parrot's cage.'

'You're one up on me,' said Amanda. 'I've never tasted the bottom of a parrot's cage. Is that what the very rich do for kicks?'

'I was having such a lovely dream, too.'

'With a man in it, I'll be bound,' said Amanda.

'Two of them, actually.'

And some rather marvellous activity with a horsewhip, thought Jocasta, but kept that to herself.

'You'd better hurry and get dressed, Kate,' said Amanda.

Kate was still in her robe, still on her bed.

'I think I'll skip dinner this evening.'

After the dormitory emptied, Kate dressed slowly, putting on a pair of blue jeans and a blue cashmere sweater. She recalled the first evening she'd met Paula, and how the South African's hand had been under her skirt before Kate had known what was happening. Well, she wasn't going to make it easy for her tonight.

At a few minutes before seven she trudged along the landing and up the stairs to Paula's study. The door was open and Sappho was there also. Christ, were they planning a threesome? She hadn't bargained for that.

Sappho was eating a meat pie, but it quickly became apparent that she was excluded from the evening's proceedings.

'Just curious to see if you'd turn up,' she said as she left the study.

Paula put the customary chair under the door-handle.

'I wouldn't like us to be disturbed.'

She looked Kate up and down, admiring her outfit. She also smiled to herself at Kate's transparentness in wearing jeans. As if that was going to help!

But she wanted the younger girl at her ease, and Kate was self-evidently tense.

'Look, come and sit down, relax. Saff won't be back for hours and everyone else on this landing knows better than to barge in if my door's closed. We've got all evening. Have a drink. I've got wine, vodka, beer.'

'Vodka, I think. And tonic.'

Kate accepted the glass and sat in an armchair. Paula occupied the other, sitting with her legs crossed under her and looking for all the world like a malevolent pixie.

'You know I'm here against my will, don't you?' said Kate.

'You might think differently later.'

'I won't. Even if I were an out-and-out dyke, which I'm not, nobody likes to be forced to do something.'

'We'll see. Force can be fun, sometimes.'

'Not with me. And before we go any further, isn't there something you're forgetting?'

'Forgetting?'

'The other magazines you say you have. They'll belong to me after tonight.'

'Perhaps we should see what tonight brings first.'

Kate shifted in her chair, keeping her knees together, but pointing them diagonally away from Paula, not even conscious that her body language signalled 'unwelcome'.

'You mentioned something about hash.'

'Actually, I mentioned "exotic substances", but it is hash, of course. Do you want a joint right now?'

'Perhaps in a while.'

Paula was puzzled and irritated by Kate's attitude, apathetic, acquiescent without being willing, which was not what she wanted at all. If sex was to happen and Kate just lay there – well, that was worse than her not being here at all. Maybe a thick joint would liven her up, but not just yet. Drugs could only heighten an experience if one was eager for altitude.

She put on her most winning smile.

'Help yourself to another drink when you're ready and tell me something about yourself. All I know is that you're extremely attractive, have lived in America, and posed for a skin mag.'

'I didn't pose for it.'

'That's what it looks like.'

'Looks can be deceiving.'

'And the camera can't lie.'

'Don't try to be my friend, Paula. It won't work.'

'But I do want to be your friend. Obviously in more ways than one, but I want your friendship.'

'Huh.'

'You're sounding cynical.'

'I'm sounding pissed-off, manipulated.'

'Tell me about the skin pix, how they came about.'

'Tell me why you're a dyke,' retorted Kate.

Paula did not take offence. Even anger was better than apathy.

'Not much to tell. I was born that way. When I was thirteen or fourteen and other girls my age were starting to take an interest in boys, I couldn't be bothered. I was much more interested in *them*, their bodies in the swimming pool or showers, than I was in the bulges in boys' trousers. That didn't do anything for me. Then I was seduced, round about that age, by a woman of twenty-four. Fortunately she was a good teacher, knew her way around her own body and mine. Then it was my turn to teach.'

'Young Phoebe, for example.'

'That's no secret, not among those who need to know.'

'You could ruin her.'

Paula laughed.

'Rubbish! She was as eager to have me as I was to have her. She's not a lesbian and nothing will ever make her one. In a year or so she'll be dating boys, letting the filthy creatures put their hands up her skirt, paw her. But she won't forget me. And I won't forget her.'

'Seems like you have, me being here.'

'Grow up, Kate. Phoebe knows the score.'

'She'd be as jealous as hell if she knew what you were up to right now, as you're well aware.'

'Perhaps. I have been neglecting her lately, but you know full well the reason for that. I admit it openly, I haven't been able to get you out of my mind since I saw those pictures.'

'Girls of Phoebe's age, when they develop crushes, get angry when their love is unrequited.'

Paula raised her eyebrows.

'My, my – you suddenly seem to know a hell of a lot about it.'

'Not at all,' said Kate. 'If I did I'd be in bed with you right now, without need of coercion.'

'The image is attractive,' said Paula. 'Perhaps it's time for that joint.'

'Perhaps it is. You roll it, I'm not very good.'

'It? You're willing to share one?'

'No point in wasting the stuff.'

Good, thought Paula. Progress.

She got up from her armchair and removed the stash from the cornflakes box. She also took out a packet of cigarette papers.

So that's where it's all hidden, thought Kate, and wondered if the other magazines were there also. No, the space wasn't big enough.

With an expertise born of long practice, Paula rolled a thick joint on her knee, once again curled up like an elf in the armchair.

Kate sipped her vodka.

'You don't seem to think much of boys, men.'

Paula glanced up briefly.

'I told you, they were given cocks for something to hold on to when mummy took away their teddy bears.'

'That's a joke. It's not an answer.'

'Fair enough, here's one. Don't think I haven't been with men, boys – I have. Not many, but I have had that rather grim experience. OK, it won't make sense to you, necessarily, but all that huffing and puffing, that hair and body odour, made me want to puke. I've fucked three men, boys, to give you a head count. With the first one I did it because I felt I had to know what I was missing, if anything. I found I wasn't missing a thing. It was all over in about sixty seconds, he'd come but I hadn't – or got anywhere near – and afterwards you'd have thought he'd been the first to climb Everest or sail round the world single-handed. He was so ridiculously pleased with himself.'

Paula put a match to the joint, made sure it was going, and handed it to Kate.

Here goes, thought Kate, and took a deep drag. Then another. The drug took a few moments to hit, but when it did she started to feel much more relaxed. Careful from here on in, she cautioned herself, or I really *will* be joining her on that bed.

Paula studied her, watching for the effects. Excellent, she thought.

Kate passed the joint across. Paula inhaled, and held the smoke in her lungs for as long as she could. Exhaling, she blew on the glowing end of the reefer to make sure it stayed alight.

'But I'm open-minded,' she said. 'Just because one boy's a jerk doesn't mean the next one will be. How wrong can you get! He had a cock that, given fuel, could have put Neil Armstrong on the moon, but what the hell has size got to do with anything?

340

I can buy vibrators any length from Tom Thumb to Brobdingnagian. Is that what I need? Is it hell! Touch the trigger points and I'm away. A woman's erogenous zones are *terra incognita* to most men. And those ridiculous condoms filled with the most disgusting mess since tapioca! Here, have a hit.'

She passed the joint back to Kate.

'You said three men,' said Kate, inhaling. 'That's only two.'

'The third was a friend of my father. He was forty-odd when I was about sixteen, and back in South Africa for the long vac. By this time my mother and father – but especially my mother – were starting to suspect that I was, shall we say, differently inclined. My mother, therefore, saw no harm in my accompanying my father's friend – Henrik, his name was – down to Cape Town, where he had to go on business and where I was visiting a girl, not a dyke, I'd known since I was a kid.

'Well, we were no sooner in our sleepers on the train than Henrik was rapping on my door with a bottle of brandy in his hand. Some friend of my father, Henrik! It would have been obvious to someone with the naïveté of, say, young Phoebe, that what he wanted to do was fuck me. I mean, I'm not unattractive, am I?'

'No,' said Kate, her limbs beginning to float.

'So, I let him,' said Paula. 'I teased him a little at first, of course. "How dare you? You're my father's friend!" Then I let him get inside me. He probably doesn't know to this day that I was the one who seduced him. Men are such idiots. He kept telling me that I had the most marvellous breasts, which I haven't, and then he wanted to turn me over and hump me from behind. I let him, naturally. Neither of the other two jerks had even contemplated that.

'I'm a lightweight, as you can see, and he must have weighed fifteen stones, very little of it fat. It drove him wild that he could lift me off the bunk and hump me while he held me in mid-air.

'There was a mirror in front of me on the bunk in the sleeper. You know the sort of thing, or maybe you don't. I watched his face as he strained to come, the red ugliness of it, and all that great matted hair on his chest. No, sirree, I thought, this isn't for me.

'But I stuck him for a hundred rand. "I think I'll have to tell my mother about this." He offered fifty, but I held out. "Why, you're nothing but a little tart." "And what does that make you?" I asked him. Paid for an awful lot of beer on the Cape, that hundred.'

'You blackmailed him,' said Kate.

'Sure, why not? He'd got what he wanted, screwing a sixteen-year-old girl. What was wrong in getting what I wanted?'

'Just as you're blackmailing me.'

'Kate,' said Paula, 'it's not like that. A few more drags on that joint and I'll give you the damned magazines.'

'Promises, promises.'

Paula did not take the bait. The Mary Jane was

good and doing the job, but not that good. Not yet.

Kate glanced at her watch, surreptitiously she thought, but Paula spotted it instantly.

'In a hurry?'.

'Not me, though you know how I feel. Given the freedom of choice, I'd be out of here like a shot.'

Paula shook her head sorrowfully.

'Kate, you're not trying. For God's sake, get into the spirit of the evening.'

'And let you fuck me.'

'And let me fuck you. Believe me or believe me not, I'm very good. Ask Sappho.'

'Or Phoebe.'

'Or Phoebe. Here, give me a drag. You won't hear any complaints from either.'

'You're the best, right?' said Kate. She snapped her fingers. 'Let me have the joint back, if you don't mind. Shit, I've heard men talk like that. "Come on, honey, you don't know what it's like until you've had it from me." Big talk, and talk's cheap.'

'There's one copper-bottomed certain way of finding out whether I'm as good as my press releases.'

Paula leaned forward and put a hand on Kate's knee. Kate pulled away and, using the balls of her feet, scooted her armchair backwards, out of range of Paula's eager fingers.

'Push me and I'm out of here,' she said angrily. 'You can do what you like with the damned photographs.'

Paula frowned. The hash wasn't doing the trick

and it was already five to eight. Sappho was a co-operative friend, but she couldn't be expected to stay out of her own study for ever.

'Have some more vodka.'

'Why not?'

Kate swallowed the best part of four fingers neat and fought to keep her senses under control. Combined with the vodka, the marijuana was affecting her, no question, and her anger had been faked. She was also becoming uncomfortably hot, and wished she was wearing a flimsier top. But that would have sent the wrong signal to Paula.

She stood up on unsteady legs, taking her glass with her and collecting the vodka bottle on the way. She made for the window and tried to refill her glass. Much of the liquor ended up on the floor. Outside the school clock struck eight.

Kate returned to her armchair and sat down heavily. She attempted to sip her vodka, but somehow missed her mouth and spilt most of it down her front. Usually she would have cursed – specialist dry-cleaning for cashmere – but now she just giggled.

'Whoops!'

'Take the sweater off,' suggested Paula.

'Ha, ha, HA!' laughed Kate. 'No chance! First it'll be the top, then the jeans, then my underwear, which is silk, I'll have you know. A couple of minutes after that you'll have me spreadeagled on that bed of yours.'

'Sounds good to me,' said Paula, hoping to high

heaven that this was true. She was feeling very sexy. 'Anyway, I won't unless you want me to.'

'That's just the point, though, don't you see?' said Kate. 'I'm *beginning* to want you to.'

She got to her feet again and started pirouetting around the study, which was hardly the setting for a ballet production. She stumbled, collided with the table, and fell in a heap on the floor.

'And God bless us each and every one, cried Tiny Tim,' she gurgled.

Jesus, thought Paula, and was about to help her up – or join her where she lay – when there came a fierce knocking on the study door. Fists. Then the door-handle was rattled, the door pushed, and, when entry was prevented by the chair, a shoulder put against the panelling. The chair trick wasn't designed to bar ingress against such force. It gave under the assault and the door was flung open.

Paula turned sheet-white as Fiona Acland barged in, followed by Sybil Heilbron, who was duty mistress this evening.

There was no hiding the vodka, the remains of the joint, or the smell of marijuana, and Paula didn't try.

Kate couldn't. She stayed where she was on the floor, still giggling.

Earlier in the day, directly after Paula had instructed, 'This evening, seven o'clock, my study,' Kate had sought out Phoebe.

'You're a friend of Paula van der Groot's, aren't you?'

Phoebe had blushed.

'I don't know what you mean. I know Paula, of course, but . . .'

Kate lost her temper. She was close to the end of her rope. After all her promises to her parents, she was once again about to let them down. And all over an incident she had thought was a closed book.

'You know exactly what I mean. I wonder what your mother would say if she knew you went to bed with Paula on a regular basis.'

'I don't . . .'

'You do! I've seen you together.'

'But not recently . . .'

'Of course not recently. That's because she's found someone else.'

'Jennifer Langley,' pouted Phoebe.

Ho-ho, thought Kate, who knew nothing of the Jennifer Langley involvement.

'Maybe, maybe not. The thing is, she'll be with that "someone" at eight o'clock this evening in her study. I think you should tell the head girl to raid Paula's study at that hour. Better still, slip her a note. Here, I've written one for you.'

It was in a sealed envelope and its text said nothing about sexual misbehaviour. Instead, in block capitals, it read:

ILLEGAL SUBSTANCES ARE BEING
SMOKED AND OTHERWISE USED IN

PAULA VAN DER GROOT'S STUDY. BE
THERE AT EIGHT P.M. AND FIND OUT.

'I don't want to get Paula into trouble,' said Phoebe.

'What are you, a mouse?' demanded Kate. 'For
God's sake, child, are you going to spend the rest
of your life being used? Make sure Fiona gets the
envelope during dinner. Pass it up the table. No-one
will know where it comes from.'

'What's in it for you?' asked Phoebe. 'I mean, I
don't understand.'

'Because I've been one of Paula's victims, even
while she had you in her bed. Remember, get the
envelope to Fiona anonymously and keep your mouth
shut. After all, if your parents ever found out you'd
had a lesbian relationship . . . But I leave you to think
about their reactions.'

Kate spent the rest of the day hoping and praying
that a fourteen-year-old's jealousy would be enough,
but she had no way of knowing whether she was right
until Fiona and Sybil Heilbron burst into Paula's study.
And by that time she was beyond caring.

Mrs Clinton was summoned, who called Mrs Gordon.
Paula and Kate were escorted, or rather helped, to the
sanatorium, where Auntie Natal was brought in.

'Drugs or drink,' she pronounced, 'but from the
evidence I see in front of me it's obviously drugs.
Beyond that, I'm not qualified to comment.'

The school doctor was called. He didn't even have
to do exhaustive tests.

'Alcohol and marijuana,' he announced. 'I'm afraid it's out of our hands now. This is a police matter.'

'Jesus Christ,' exploded Mrs Gordon, startling everyone with her profanity, '*two catastrophes in a week!*'

Chaperoned by Auntie Natal, Kate and Paula were kept in the sanatorium, in separate rooms, until the police arrived. Then they were taken away.

Mrs Gordon had already telephoned Kate's parents. As Kate was a juvenile, they had to be present when she was questioned. This was not necessary in Paula's case, as she was over eighteen. In any event, her parents were thousands of miles away. Her nearest relative in England was an uncle in Kent, and he was informed. She would have to have someone to stay with when she was released, as she undoubtedly would be, on bail, and there was no way she was returning to St Clare's.

Although the formal paperwork would take several days to finalize, Kate and Paula were both expelled with immediate effect.

When she finally collected her wits, Kate wasn't too worried. She would get hell from her mother and father, naturally, but at least her expulsion was for taking drugs, not lesbian sex. Paula would never know that Fiona's *deus ex machina* appearance was the result of her, Kate's, discussion with young Phoebe. The pornographic photographs would not be made public.

But they were.

The police ransacked Paula's study and unearthed

the rest of the marijuana, but they didn't find the other copies of *Gut Feeling* because they were hidden behind a pile of books in the school library.

As the co-occupant of Paula's study, Sappho Peters was grilled unmercifully, first by Mrs Gordon and then the police.

You were obviously involved too. Even if you weren't, you must have known that Paula possessed drugs. Sharing as you do, it would be impossible for you not to know.

Sappho denied everything and, because there was no proof, she was given the benefit of the doubt. But when she emerged from the interrogation, she was shaking and as mad as hell. She had come that close, *that close*, to being expelled herself and gaining a criminal record into the bargain.

Kate McNamara had to be responsible for the sudden appearance of Fiona Acland and Miss Heilbron. Had to. It was stretching the bounds of credibility to believe otherwise. There were rumours doing the rounds about some sort of note but, note or not, Fiona and Sybil Heilbron had known where to raid and at what hour.

It was Kate, all right, even if she too had been swept up in the net. She'd probably thought that preferable to going to bed with Paula.

Poor Paula. Sappho was going to miss her badly, and the South African was no longer in a position to exact revenge.

But Sappho was.

She removed the magazines from their hiding place on Thursday morning and made sure they were found in the sixth-form commonroom the same day, where they were eagerly snatched up.

'How could she do this to me?' wailed Richard Carson.

He was an object of ridicule. His former girl-friend was a porno queen. Everywhere he went fingers pointed at him. The sniggers became intolerable.

A more mature individual would have laughed it off. *I knew it all along. Christ, why do you think I've been dating her? Did you get a load of those tits? She was keeping me nice and warm in these long winter nights, thank you very much.* But Carson wasn't a more mature individual. He took it all very personally.

'How could she do it?'

'Because she obviously enjoys sucking cock and gangbangs, you dumb bastard,' someone answered.

Carson flung a fist at his taunter, and a fist was flung back. He ended up with a bloody nose and a thick lip, and his Oxford interview was tomorrow.

Mrs Gordon soon learned that the photographs were doing the rounds. She dispatched school prefects and House prefects to collect all available copies. She was far too late, of course. The school's photocopier had been working overtime.

Mrs Gordon destroyed whatever was returned to her, though she couldn't resist looking at some of the pictures. Her thoughts were identical to Carson's.

How could a young girl do that?

Still, that was none of her business. Kate McNamara had been expelled for taking drugs. That was the official record. Obviously there must be other copies of this filthy magazine in circulation in other parts of the country, but the chances were Kate's parents would never see them. She prayed that was so.

A few lines of Juvenal came to mind, from his *Satires*. *Maxima debetur puero reverentia, siquid turpe paras, nec tu pueri contempseris annos.* The greatest reverence is due to a child. If you are contemplating a disgraceful act, despise not your child's tender years.

16

It's My Party and I'll Cry If I Want To

Carson failed his Oxford interview.

Nobody said as much at the time, of course, and formal notification would not be received by mail at his home address until just before Christmas, but he knew he'd come across as a sad, pathetic wimp without an ounce of mental vigour. Add to that a nose that was twice its normal size, a swollen lip, and what was going to be a beauty of a black eye, and he would have shown himself the door. He hadn't even had the wit to claim involvement in a car accident.

To be frank, right that red-hot minute, he didn't much care about Oxford or any other seat of higher learning.

It was all clear to him now, the reason why Kate was so sexually precocious, her nervelessness in the cinema that night. She'd doubtless been laid by half of Connecticut, probably at the same time. She was a whore and that's all there was to it.

He hated her guts.

As party time approached on Saturday evening, Ben Fisher tried to shake him out of his mood.

'Change your mind and come, you'll enjoy yourself.'

'Oh sure. "Hello, Richard, screwed any good hookers lately?"'

'There was nothing in the photographs to say she was a hooker.'

'You studied them carefully, then, did you?'

Fisher shrugged.

'Well, they were there.'

'You don't have to apologize. If they'd been of Julia Hastings, I'd have looked at them. But how do you think that makes me feel? She'll be the butt of every dirty joke and wanking fantasy for years.'

'Probably. Still, it all happened long before she met you.'

'But it *did* happen, that's the point.'

And it had happened, thought Carson miserably, with studs who were not only hung superiorly to him but who had probably never experienced an impotence problem in their lives.

No wonder Kate had lost her temper with him when he couldn't perform. She was no doubt wishing she was back in the States with men who could.

'Well, if I can't persuade you to come,' said Fisher.

'No, I'll sit it out here. Thanks, anyway.'

Checking her roots in front of the mirror to make sure her natural colour was not showing through, Amanda said, 'What I can't understand is why she showed us those porno magazines at the start of term. That was a bit close to home, if you follow my drift. I mean, for someone who's appeared in one to be carrying a stack of them around . . .'

Jocasta had the solution.

'She probably bought them in the first place to see if she was in them. When she found she wasn't she kept them with her, and showed them to us, for the same reason a reformed thief is more critical of robbers than the honest citizen. "Bloody crooks, I'd hang 'em all." That sort of thing. In Kate's case it would be, "Goodness me, look what these girls get up to. You wouldn't catch me doing something like that." That's my theory, anyway.'

The sheets and pillow cases had been stripped from Kate's bed, the mattress rolled up, exposing the springs. Mrs Clinton had supervised the emptying of her locker. Her belongings were now on their way home.

'You sound as if you have some sympathy for her,' said Julia, checking her hemline to ensure it wasn't too short.

'Is the Pope Catholic?' retorted Jocasta. 'Of course I sympathize. How do we know the circumstances under which the photographs were taken? Maybe she wasn't even aware they were. She was just enjoying herself, that's all.'

Julia was astonished.

'With two men at the same time? Or was it three? I forget.'

'Don't be such a prig,' snapped Jocasta. She recalled the pleasure she derived from her riding crop. 'Haven't you ever had a sexual experience, or imagined one, that you'd prefer others not to learn about?'

Julia tossed her head. It was one thing to have lusted after Robert Penrose at the beginning of term, and to have been more than prepared, the evening of her audition, to let him seduce her, but this was different.

'As far as I'm concerned, any of the girls in those magazines, *any of them*, are tarts. That makes Kate one in my book. I was never that keen on her, in any case.'

'Because she looks a bit too much like Lavinia, right?' said Jocasta. 'A younger version of? Lavinia who's stealing your thunder in *MND*, or will do when you perform.'

'Rot,' said Julia. 'Kate's still the closest thing to a hooker we'll ever meet, regardless of what interpretation you put on her actions.'

Jocasta took a deep breath.

'Jules,' she said, with as much quiet venom as she could muster, 'all these theatricals are going to your head. I never realized you could be such a cunt.'

'Well!' said Julia.

By nine o'clock the party was in full swing and more than a few bottles of wine had been consumed. The dancing was becoming wilder and, since there were not enough sixth-form boys to go around, many girls were dancing with each other. The music was deafening. Anyone over the age of eighteen could not have tolerated it for more than a few minutes.

At nine-fifteen Fiona Acland poked her head in,

shuddered, and left. Let them get on with it, she thought.

Around nine-thirty Lavinia and Penrose made an appearance, though at first no-one recognized the languages mistress. Earlier in the day she had driven into town and purchased an expensive auburn wig, and she now resembled Jill St John in the Bond movie *Diamonds Are For Ever*. Better legs than the actress, though, which she was displaying to considerable effect in a tight Lycra skirt over black stockings and two-inch heels. Compared to the female students, she looked like visiting royalty.

An hour before, she had enjoyed a highly satisfactory sex session with Penrose in his study while wearing the wig. To enhance his excitement, she had planted several of the Kate McNamara photographs on his desk while his back was turned. She had discovered them on *her* desk Friday morning, doubtless placed there by one of her sixth-formers to see her reaction.

She had folded them carefully, in front of her class, and put them in her briefcase without comment. Doubtless the culprit was expecting her to pass them on to Mrs Gordon for burning. Well, perhaps she would. Eventually.

'God,' said Penrose, when he saw them, 'that's a body and a half. And to think I've been teaching her English since September.'

'The men aren't bad either,' teased Lavinia. She pointed a finger. 'Especially that one.'

Penrose hummed and hahed.

'Do you fancy her?' asked Lavinia, 'Kate? Come on, you can be honest.'

'Well,' Penrose prevaricated.

'Then you shall have her, and Jill St John at the same time.'

Penrose screwed her from behind, with Lavinia bending over the arm of the chair, holding the Kate photographs up in front of her, where Penrose could see them.

It was beautiful sex, as good as anything they'd ever had, with Lavinia concentrating on the stud Kate was fellating as she reached orgasm.

Perhaps, she thought later, she and Penrose might try something like that one day, a threesome. There were lots of advertisements suggesting such arrangements in various magazines available in London. Whether the third person was a man or a woman, Lavinia wasn't sure she cared. Maybe they should try both.

God, life was good!

She and Penrose stayed less than half an hour at the party. Apart from the ear-splitting music, it quickly became apparent that, when various sixth-form males asked Lavinia to dance, they planned to get as close as possible to the body that topped those unbelievable legs.

Lavinia wasn't biting. She wanted to get back to Penrose's study. The night was still young and he hadn't screwed her yet in the black Demetrius wig.

Carson came into the commonroom as Lavinia and Penrose were leaving. Lavinia patted him gently on the arm. Carson understood, and appreciated the gesture.

Though whether it was because of his interview disaster, which he'd told her about on his return, or his courage – and it was a sort of courage – in attending the party after all that had happened, he wasn't sure.

'And I won't tell you what Jocasta called me,' Julia was saying to Fisher, trying to make herself heard above the din.

She was on her fifth glass of rough red, far more than her usual intake, but she was enraged, boiling, that Jo had dared to use that word – *that word* – as an epithet for her.

'What?' said Fisher, who not only couldn't hear Julia but had just spotted Carson's entrance.

'What Jo called me.'

'What did she call you?'

'I can't say it.'

'Then how the hell am I supposed to know?'

'I'll whisper it.'

'I still can't hear you.'

Julia repeated it, louder.

'I'm sorry, there's too much racket.'

'CUNT!' bellowed Julia – just as the music finished.

A loud cheer went up from the boys, followed by applause.

'Where, where?'

Julia hid behind her drink.

'I'll be back in a sec,' said Fisher, and pushed his way through the crowd to Carson.

'You made it after all.'

Carson shrugged.

'What the hell. There are four more days to the

end of term, and I've got another two terms. I can't hide for ever.'

'Got a drink?' asked Fisher.

Carson brandished a half-pint mug filled with something that looked vaguely like wine, though God knew what else was in it.

'I really loved her, you know,' he said mournfully. 'Kate, I mean.'

'I didn't think you meant Mrs Gordon,' said Fisher, recognizing that it was dangerous for his friend to be drinking and thinking of Kate simultaneously, and trying to lighten the atmosphere. 'Anyway, is that past tense?'

'Of course it is.'

Fisher mopped his brow. The heat was overpowering and he would have to watch how much alcohol he consumed or he'd be under the table before the party was over.

'Would you suddenly stop loving your parents if you found out they were – oh, I don't know – selling arms to Iraq?' he asked irrelevantly

'Probably.'

'Then you're a fool. Stop feeling sorry for yourself. So you blew Oxford. So what? I did too, remember. Maybe we'll both wind up at Durham. And think of what Kate must be going through right now. Christ knows if her parents have seen the photographs, but she's been sacked for taking drugs. What kind of Christmas do you think she's going to have?'

'Fuck her,' said Carson. 'Everybody else has, apparently.'

'You were a bit harsh on Jules,' said Amanda, sitting as close to the open window as possible and waving away a Lower Sixth boy who was asking her to dance, something she would never have contemplated doing before her loss of weight and change of hair colouring.

'To hell with her,' said Jocasta, taking a pull at a can of lager. 'She's become a pompous little oaf. A phoney.'

Jocasta was on her fifth or sixth can, she couldn't remember which, and was more than a little drunk. What the hell, she'd paid, or her parents had, vicariously, for half the booze here.

'And while we're on the subject of phonies,' she added, 'will you please, for Christ's sake, stop dolling yourself up to look like me.'

Amanda was dismayed.

'I don't know what you mean.'

'Fucking right you do! Even those townies in Flanagan's noticed it. "Are you two sisters, or what?" Remember? The change of hair style and colouring to look like mine. Christ, you look more like me than I do.'

Amanda stood up, almost in tears.

'If that's how you feel,' she said, and stormed off.

Shit, thought Jocasta.

'I really did love her, you know,' Carson was saying forty minutes later to someone he could barely see. 'But she screwed me up royally. No Oxford now, no nothing.'

In a public house round about now on a Saturday

night, a landlord would be calling, 'Time, ladies and gents. Don't you have homes to go to?' In the St Clare's sixth-form commonroom, the pub, for the patrons, was their home, or part of it.

'I feel such an idiot,' said Julia to Fisher, 'shouting out like that.'

Fisher wasn't listening. He was polishing his glasses, wondering if the haze in front of his eyes was wine, beer or myopia. He decided he didn't care.

'Shut up,' said Fisher, putting on his spectacles and trying to find Carson.

'I beg your pardon?' said Julia.

'You talk too much, and I've got to find Richard.'

Julia could feel the tears starting before he left her side. Men were brutes. Everyone said so. A girl only really had her girlfriends in the last analysis. But, of course, she hadn't. Jocasta had called her – that word.

'I honestly did love her,' Fisher found Carson saying, talking to an empty chair, tears streaming down his face. A chemist would have analysed them eighty per cent proof.

'Of course you did, of course you did,' consoled Fisher, feeling moisture in his own eyes.

Jocasta found Amanda outside, sitting on the steps shivering and weeping copiously. Jocasta put her arms around Amanda.

'I'm sorry, I'm sorry. I had no right to say that. You're my friend, I love you. I take it as a great compliment' – hic – 'that you want to look like me.'

Then Jocasta broke down in tears.

In the commonroom, Julia found herself all alone.

'Cunt,' she wailed. 'She called me a cunt.'

It was generally recognized the following morning, Sunday, that the party had been a huge success.

17

Amo, Amas – Alack, Alas

Quite a few awoke with thick heads on Sunday morning. Hardly any sixth-formers attended breakfast. In their absence above the salt, the teenies giggled, chuckled and shrieked, and waded into the extra sausages, bacon and eggs. Miss Heilbron was duty mistress, and she was no disciplinarian. Wisely, on a Sunday, most of the staff breakfasted later or in their own quarters. Between seven-thirty and eight-thirty the dining hall resembled a cross between the bird house at the zoo and a pig trough.

Vanessa Maxwell said, 'Tonight, OK?'

Tina Johns and Lucy Harris nodded their assent.

'Tonight,' they chorused.

'We'll show them what a dress rehearsal can really be like, right, troops?'

'Right!'

Julia had woken up several times during the night, twice to be sick, once to swallow copious amounts of water. She wasn't sure whether she and Ben had had sex after the party. She thought not. God, she hoped not. If she had been so drunk not to know the difference, that was dangerous. Why, anything could have happened and she would have had to plead ignorance.

The irony of her thoughts compared to her comments about Kate didn't occur to her.

Fisher was sure not.

After helping Carson back to their study, he'd passed out on the floor. When he came out of his dreams, Carson was sitting in the corner with the wastepaper-basket on his head, moaning, 'Oh Christ, I'm blind. I knew I'd be punished.'

For what crime he'd be punished he didn't explain, and Fisher wasn't in the mood to enquire. They were both still fully dressed apart from each missing a left shoe, which neither, later, could find anywhere.

Fisher crawled over to Carson and played a rapid tattoo with a couple of forks on top of the basket, with Carson's head still inside.

'Help, help,' yelped Carson, 'the devils are here.'

After five minutes under a lukewarm shower, they felt a little better, but not much. They both kept well away from the stall where Henry had met his end.

Jocasta surfaced, saw goblins, and went back under the blankets. Amanda pulled them off and dropped water from a sponge on her face.

'Come on, lazybones. The temperature's a couple of degrees above freezing outside. I thought we might put on tracksuits and run for a couple of miles.'

I'll murder her, thought Jocasta. I'll find the biggest knife in the world and carve the little slag into stroganoff.

'I'll kill you!' swore Jo, when Amanda squeezed further water on her.

She attempted to leap out of bed to carry out her threat, but Amanda backed away. In any case, Jocasta didn't get her feet any further than the floor.

'You said you loved me, last evening,' grinned Amanda.

'Now I hate you. And why the hell are you so cheerful at this hour, whatever this hour is?'

'Coming up to ten o'clock, with chapel at eleven, compulsory for the Lower Sixth unless that Carlsberg destroyed a few brain cells. I'm doing you a favour.'

'I still hate you.'

'Fickle, fickle. I knew it.'

Amanda threw the wet sponge at Jocasta. It hit Jo in the face, and on this occasion sheer bloody-minded rage got her upright.

Amanda ran for it.

Lavinia woke up feeling glorious. Her dark wig and her auburn wig were alongside her, like trophies from an Indian massacre.

Geronimo!

Come on, John Wayne, where are you? You should be here by now to rescue the maiden.

Trouble was, the Duke's wig would probably join the other two.

One of the Kate McNamara photographs was next to her bed, propped up behind the alarm clock, though Lavinia could not recall putting it there. In this shot, it was just Kate and one man. She was on her hands and knees, Lavinia's favourite position, being penetrated from behind. Penetrated? Excavated was closer to the truth, judging by the size of the man. The photographer had clicked his shutter, with Kate peering through her hair over her left shoulder, as the man was about halfway home. Kate's expression was one of wonderment and ecstasy.

Lavinia donned the Jill St John hairpiece and, partly watching her reflection in the vanity mirror while keeping one eye on the picture, brought herself to a shuddering climax.

I'm crazy, she thought.

But nice crazy.

After lunch there was a rehearsal in Great Hall, the last before the dress that evening, the last in which the cast were allowed to use their scripts, Lavinia included. She was the only one in costume.

Mrs Gordon attended.

'Somewhat revealing, Miss Lee's attire, don't you think?' she said to Penrose.

Penrose was hungover and tired, and in no mood for criticism at this stage of the game. After he and Lavinia had left the party the previous evening, they'd demolished three-quarters of a bottle of brandy before Lavinia had insisted on wearing her Demetrius costume, black wig and all, for sex. Then she wanted him to take it off, stripping her slowly.

'Another fantasy,' she said. 'You're attracted to me even though I'm dressed as a boy, but you're horrified to think you might want to have sex with a male. However, you can't resist me. Come on, don't tell me you've never fancied a boy.'

Penrose hadn't, and there was no way on God's earth that Lavinia could pass for one. Not even beyond the footlights.

'All right,' said Lavinia, seeing that the idea of her being male did nothing for Penrose, 'pretend that I'm faking being a boy but you don't fall for the subterfuge. You try to get my clothes off to prove it, but I struggle. When you finally succeed, you find I'm a woman.'

Penrose went along with that idea and humped her horse-and-mare, not even waiting for Lavinia to suggest that position.

God, the woman was exhausting.

'It's the way I see it, Headmistress,' he replied to Mrs Gordon.

Mrs Gordon didn't bat an eyelid.

'Yes, I'm sure it is.'

Lavinia felt skittish and kissed Julia smack on the mouth during their love scene.

'Yuk,' said Julia, turning away.

'Can we have a directive on that, please, producer?' Lavinia called out. 'Is that any way to treat one's lover? For that matter, is "yuk" in the script? Or were you ad libbing, dear?' Lavinia smiled sweetly at Julia.

'I thought she was going to put her tongue in my mouth,' Julia said later, lying on her bed, her script held up in front of her, earmarked at her own scenes. 'I really did. I mean, I know she's supposed to be a man and everything . . .'

Jocasta was staring gloomily out of the window. She

could have used a walk to clear her head, but it was raining heavily, sleeting even, and the forecast was for snow next week. Perhaps the rain would ease before the afternoon was out. Even if it didn't before the evening, she had to get some fresh air in her lungs before bedtime.

At home, now, she would be astride a horse, galloping the countryside, regardless of the weather. But at home, now, she wouldn't be suffering from a gigantic beer hangover. A champagne hangover, maybe, but not beer.

What was it George Bernard Shaw said?

When I said I was teetotal, I meant I was beer teetotal, not champagne teetotal.

Which reminded her of one of her father's dumb jokes.

You say you're an atheist, but what sort: Protestant or Catholic?

Roll on Christmas.

'Has anyone seen my blue velvet headband?' asked Amanda, rummaging through her locker.

'Probably in the same place you left your underwear last night,' answered Jocasta, brightening suddenly. She owed Amanda one for that damned sponge.

But Amanda wasn't the same overweight sixteen-year-old who had appeared at the start of Michaelmas Term.

'In that case, would you mind picking it up when you collect your own knickers from Napier House? Or don't you remember?'

'Weren't you wearing it last night?' asked Julia.

'As a matter of fact, you were,' said Jo.

'And talking about last night,' said Julia, glowering at Jocasta.

'All right, all right,' said Jo. 'You're not a See You Next Tuesday.' Besides, she added to herself, remembering something her friend Paul Buchanan occasionally said, when accused of something: 'I'm sorry I called you a cunt. You're not. A cunt's useful.'

'That's right, I was,' said Amanda. 'Blast, I must have left it in the commonroom. It's my favourite too.' She checked the weather alongside Jocasta. 'Well, I'm not dashing across in this. If it's gone, it's gone.'

Vanessa, Tina and Lucy plotted their evening's escapade with care. Dress rehearsal, they knew, had been called for eight o'clock. Shortly thereafter, wearing their dominoes (which they'd managed to hang on to, despite Felicity Coggan's best intentions), they planned to sneak over to Great Hall. The main light-switches were just inside the door, a whole bank of them. While Tina reached inside and doused the lot, Lucy and Vanessa would ignite fireworks, bangers left over from a Guy Fawkes party at their prep school, and hurl them inside. Then they would run like hell.

Penrose spent the afternoon fretting, thinking of the hundred and one things that could go wrong with his production and how, after tonight, there was no way to put them right.

Whether 'tis nobler in the mind to suffer the slings and

arrows of outrageous fortune, or to take arms against a sea of troubles and by opposing end them.

What the hell was he worried about? It was an amateur play, that was all. A school production. If the girls didn't do the job, so what? Who would blame him?

Every bastard, that's who.

They all knew their lines, that was one plus, even Lavinia, who had surprised him at how much she could take in, in under a week.

Christ, no, not how much she could take in! How quickly she had learnt her part.

Thinking of Lavinia, he made a mental note to raise the question of Christmas. They'd discussed it in general terms, but had made no firm plans about where and when they would be seeing each other. She had a sister and parents, and he, too, had family. OK, they probably couldn't get together on Christmas Day or Boxing Day, but they had to meet some time. He couldn't stand the thought of almost a month without her company.

Without her body.

Everyone connected with the play, as usual, dined early. Those who wanted to, that is. Julia went down but found she couldn't eat a thing, possibly the result of the previous night's excesses but more likely nerves. Christ, she thought, if I'm like this at the dress, what am I going to be like tomorrow and Tuesday?

Is this what real actors and actresses went through, when money was being paid? Maybe a quiet life wasn't so bad after all.

There was no segregation by sex or House for the early diners. Even Penrose and Lavinia shared the general table, but conversations were muted, with everyone going over their lines and checking the clock.

'You should eat something,' said Fisher to Julia, sitting opposite her.

'I'd be sick.'

Fisher tried to cheer her up. Made a mistake.

'You're not pregnant, are you?'

'How could . . .? God, you don't mean last night?'

'When you threw the condoms away, said that's what you wanted?'

'I couldn't have!'

'Shouldn't I have mentioned it? It was so good.'

'Ben, you're not serious . . .'

Fisher grinned.

'You're loathsome,' said Julia.

Penrose rapped the table with a spoon as dinner came to an end.

'OK, cast,' he called out, 'eight o'clock sharp in costume.'

'Do we change in House or backstage?' one girl wanted to know.

'Backstage,' said Penrose. 'You'd better get used to getting in each other's way, and that applies to makeup mirrors as well as dress. I know the changing areas are small and there are a lot of you, but at least there are no male members of the cast so it shouldn't be too much of a problem.'

Lavinia had a word with Penrose before they left.

'As your girlfriend, lover, whore, do I get special privileges?'

'Such as?'

'Such as, unless you have any serious objections, I'd like to change in my study. What I mean is, I'm ten years older at least than anyone else and fourteen years older in many cases. I can do without a bunch of giggling girls checking the brand of my underwear.'

Penrose had no objections.

'But wear outdoor shoes to get across in case this weather keeps up, which it looks as if it will. Ben, can I have a word with you about prompts before you leave . . .?'

Alone in his study before Fisher returned, Carson thought again for the hundredth time since yesterday about telephoning Kate. She couldn't know, of course, about the photographs having been circulated, because she had left before they were. And he had no wish to add to her worries by telling her. But he desperately wanted to hear her voice.

Except he didn't.

Is that it? Christ, you might have waited for me.

I'm sorry, sorry.

No, he wouldn't make the call. Whatever Ben said, she'd caused him a hell of a lot of trouble and anxiety, blown away his Oxford chances. He would forget about her in time, though it was likely to be a long time.

Damn her eyes!

Towards seven-forty-five Penrose went over to Great Hall, umbrella up. It was raining stair-rods and the wind was howling like a banshee. Inside the Hall, though, all was quiet. The theatre was fun, even *Lear* with all its gales. Outside was reality, uncertain endings of love and death. Here, one knew the outcome. There was a certain relief in that.

A few minutes later, the cast emerged from their various Houses, the younger ones talking among themselves, shouting at the wind and rain.

Always fatal in theatrical terms.

'Well,' said Julia, to Amanda and Jocasta, 'aren't you going to wish me luck?'

'*Hals und Beinbruch*,' said Jocasta. 'It's what we say in the theatre, dahling. Break your neck and leg. It's meant to fool the Devil, in your case, the critics.'

'Thanks very bloody much,' scowled Julia. 'In any case, I know the expression.'

'I'll just bet she did,' said Jo.

'How did you know it?' asked Amanda.

'My father owns part of a theatre.'

'Would you care to swap fathers?'

Lavinia took her time getting ready. Once the blue doublet and hose were on and she'd strutted her stuff in front of the mirror, she dealt with her makeup.

Being a natural blonde, the shades she normally used looked insipid with the black Demetrius wig on. Everything had to be exaggerated. For the spotlights she'd be under, even more so. Layers of the stuff. Put it on with a trowel. There would be proper theatrical makeup backstage, but she'd do what she could here and now. Touch it up later, as that beautiful phrase went.

There.

Kim Basinger, eat your heart out!

She checked herself in the looking-glass, and noticed a run in her hose. Damn it, but did it matter for the dress rehearsal? Yes, it did. To her.

The seamstress could take care of the run tomorrow. For tonight, she'd wear a pair of those thick tights she'd bought. She'd be late, but Robert wasn't going to complain about her tardiness, now, was he? She was on at line twenty, along with Egeus, Hermia and Lysander, but she didn't have anything to say until line ninety-one. Then she exited on line 127 and did not reappear until Act Three, Scene Two.

'It's still hammering down,' said Jocasta, peering through the dormitory window, 'but if I don't get a breath of fresh air I'm going to be tossing and turning all night. Fancy a stroll?'

'Thanks, but no,' said Amanda. 'I'll give it a few more minutes and then go over and try and find my headband, just in case some thief has missed it.'

'Can I borrow your Barbour, then? I loaned Kate mine and I think it must have been sent home with the rest of her things. I won't be long.'

'Sure.'

At the front door to Churchill House, Jocasta shuddered. Even though she needed to fill her lungs, this was ridiculous. There were a few spare umbrellas, as there always were, in the brolly-rack, and she took one. Just once round the block, she thought.

'Relent, sweet Hermia, and, Lysander, yield thy crazed title to my certain right.'

Filling in for the absent Lavinia, Penrose spoke Demetrius's lines.

Come on, Vin, come on. Where the hell are you? You're making me look idiotic. The girls know something is going on between us, and they think I'm playing favourites. This is meant to be a dress rehearsal, for God's sake.

Amanda took another look at the weather outside and wondered if she should forget about her headband. Six pounds, so what? But no, why should someone else have that six pounds?

That's some walk you're taking, Jo, where are you? I need my coat.

Or, thought Amanda, I can borrow one of hers. That long cashmere thing. Fair exchange was no robbery and if the cashmere got wet, it got wet.

'Call you me fair, that fair again unsay?' said Julia as Helena. *'Demetrius loves your fair, O happy fair. Your eyes are lode-stars . . .*

'This is ridiculous,' complained Julia. 'I'm talking to Hermia about Demetrius, and Demetrius isn't even here.'

'I know, I know,' soothed Penrose. 'But press on.'

Where the hell are you, Vin?

Vanessa Maxwell said, 'OK, troops, here we go.'

Their dominoes were getting soaked, but that didn't worry them. It was three days until the end of term. They would either lose their cloaks and masks, if drenched, or dry them out and take them home – to bring back next term, if they felt like it. If the Secret Three were to live on.

'Keep those fireworks dry,' said Vanessa.

Lavinia raced for Great Hall with her head down. Someone ran into her, knocking her over.

'For God's sake . . . !'

Then she heard the screams.

It was Lucy who cried out as a rain-drenched figure rose up before them, shouted, 'Noooh,' and sprinted away.

In front of the trio, where the fugitive had been kneeling, was what appeared to be a bundle of old clothing, or a Guy Fawkes dummy.

'Point the torch,' said Tina. 'For God's sake shut up, Lucy!'

'Let me,' said Vanessa.

She knelt beside the bundle. It wasn't just old clothing, not that warm and solid.

'She's drunk, or passed out. Shine the light this way.'

'It's that sixth-form girl, isn't it? Jocasta Petrillo?'

'I don't know. I can't see. No, it's Miss Lee, isn't it? In that wig she wears. And she's not drunk. She's . . .'

★   ★   ★

Please, Vin, where are you? thought Penrose – and then he heard the screams.

Algy Hicks had been loitering outside Churchill House since six o'clock, waiting to give Jocasta's handkerchief back to its rightful owner. He was soaked to the skin, but that didn't bother him. She was bound to appear, sooner or later.

Then she did. He would have known that dark hair anywhere. And that coat. He had seen her wearing it often enough.

But let her get away from the House. Even in this weather, there were a few other girls around. Let her walk, take her stroll. He would follow.

'Miss . . .'

Amanda turned and saw this ghastly figure, hair plastered to his skull from the rain. She didn't recognize it as Algy. All she saw was a man.

Her parents had taught her to open her lungs if threatened. Or if she thought she was being threatened. So had Mrs Gordon and Mrs Clinton.

Algy proffered the handkerchief. Amanda saw his gesture as an aggressive act.

'Go away. I'll shout.'

Algy panicked.

'Please don't.'

Then he saw that Amanda, in spite of the hairstyle and coat, was not Jocasta.

'But you're not . . .'

'Go away, go away.'

'No, miss, no.'

Amanda kicked out and shrieked, and Algy was frightened.

He was a strong if dimwitted youth. All those years of cutting grass and lopping branches off trees had given him muscles. It wasn't entirely his fault, therefore, that, when he put his hand over Amanda's mouth to stifle her cries, he used too much pressure.

But Amanda continued to struggle . . .

And Algy tried to stop her.

'Please, miss, it's a mistake. I mean you no harm.'

Amanda thought she was about to be raped, and fought. Algy put his hands around her neck. Anything to stop those horrible noises.

Anything.

Then three frightful apparitions in cloaks and masks loomed up, and he fled.

'It was meant to be me,' said Jocasta. 'Dear God, it was meant to be me.'

They were in the sanatorium. Amanda Panda had a bandage around her neck, and looked pale.

'It's all right,' she said, 'it's all right. Hush. Shit, my throat hurts and I could use a drink.'

'Now, now, Amanda,' said Auntie Natal.

'Serves me right, anyway,' said Amanda, 'for trying to be something I'm not. Thank God for those lunatic teenies in their stupid cloaks. If they hadn't decided to sabotage the rehearsals . . .'

'I didn't know he felt that way about me,' said Jocasta.

'You shouldn't be so beautiful . . .'

And one psalm, 119.

I will thank thee with an unfeigned heart . . .

There were some tears in her eyes when she read the lesson and led the congregation in the final hymn. She was very proud of St Clare's, *her* school.

Lord, dismiss us with Thy blessing
Thanks for mercies past receive
Pardon all, their faults confessing
Time that's lost may all retrieve . . .

'You were decent to give Julia the breaks,' said Penrose to Lavinia.

'I'm a decent person,' said Lavinia. 'Well, sometimes. On the whole, though, I prefer indecency.'

Amanda had already left for home. Jocasta hugged Julia. Each promised they'd see each other, and together visit Amanda, over the break.

Then Jo's mother hit the horn of the Range Rover. The snow was thickening. Time to get home.

Long after everyone else had gone, Carson stood on the steps of Napier.

'Goodbye, Carson,' called Chips. 'Have a good holiday.'

Snow covering him, Carson walked towards his father's car as it ran up the drive. His mother was there also. He'd tell them both about his Oxford disaster on the way home.

Yes, that was best.

And there was one other thing he had to do. Come what may, he was going to see Kate over Christmas, perhaps show her she wasn't alone, friendless.

Or unloved.

THE END

RIDERS
by Jilly Cooper

Set in the tense, heroic world of show-jumping, Jilly Cooper's novel moves from home-county gymkhanas through a riot of horsey events all over the world, culminating in the high drama of the Los Angeles Olympics.

A multi-stranded story, it tells of the lives of a tight circle of star riders who move from show to show, united by raging ambition, bitter rivalry and the terror of failure. The superheroes are Jake Lovell, a half-gypsy orphan who wears gold earrings, handles a horse – or a woman – with effortless skill, and is consumed with hatred for the promiscuous upper-class cad, Rupert Campbell-Black, who has no intention of being faithful to his wife, Helen, but is outraged when she runs away with another rider.

Riders is Jilly Cooper at her most outrageous, most hilarious, sexiest and delightful best.

'Blockbusting fiction at its best'
David Hughes, *Mail on Sunday*

'I defy anyone not to enjoy this book. It is a delight from start to finish'
Auberon Waugh, *Daily Mail*

0 552 14103 8

A SELECTED LIST OF FINE NOVELS
AVAILABLE FROM CORGI BOOKS

THE PRICES SHOWN BELOW WERE CORRECT AT THE TIME OF GOING
TO PRESS. HOWEVER TRANSWORLD PUBLISHERS RESERVE THE RIGHT
TO SHOW NEW RETAIL PRICES ON COVERS WHICH MAY DIFFER FROM
THOSE PREVIOUSLY ADVERTISED IN THE TEXT OR ELSEWHERE.

☐	13648 4	CASTING	Jane Barry	£3.99
☐	12850 3	TOO MUCH TOO SOON	Jacqueline Briskin	£5.99
☐	13396 5	THE OTHER SIDE OF LOVE	Jacqueline Briskin	£4.99
☐	13558 5	AMBITION	Julie Burchill	£4.99
☐	14103 8	RIDERS	Jilly Cooper	£5.99
☐	13264 0	RIVALS	Jilly Cooper	£5.99
☐	13552 6	POLO	Jilly Cooper	£5.99
☐	13895 9	THE MAN WHO MADE HUSBANDS JEALOUS	Jilly Cooper	£5.99
☐	13877 0	A DARKER SHADE OF LOVE	Anne Dunhill	£4.99
☐	13830 4	THE MASTER STROKE	Elizabeth Gage	£4.99
☐	13266 7	A GLIMPSE OF STOCKING	Elizabeth Gage	£5.99
☐	13644 1	PANDORA'S BOX	Elizabeth Gage	£5.99
☐	13964 5	TABOO	Elizabeth Gage	£4.99
☐	14104 6	LOVE OVER GOLD	Susannah James	£3.99
☐	13708 1	OUT TO LUNCH	Tania Kindersley	£3.99
☐	12462 1	THE WATERSHED	Erin Pizzey	£4.99
☐	13504 6	BRILLIANT DIVORCES	June Flaum Singer	£4.99
☐	13333 7	THE PRESIDENT'S WOMEN	June Flaum Singer	£3.99
☐	13523 2	NO GREATER LOVE	Danielle Steel	£4.99
☐	13525 9	HEARTBEAT	Danielle Steel	£4.99
☐	13522 4	DADDY	Danielle Steel	£4.99
☐	13524 0	MESSAGE FROM NAM	Danielle Steel	£4.99
☐	13745 6	JEWELS	Danielle Steel	£4.99
☐	13746 4	MIXED BLESSINGS	Danielle Steel	£4.99

All Corgi/Bantam Books are available at your bookshop or newsagent, or can be ordered
from the following address:
Corgi/Bantam Books
Cash Sales Department
PO Box 11, Falmouth, Cornwall TR10 9EN

UK and BFPO customers please send a cheque or postal order (no currency) and allow
£1.00 for postage and packing for the first book plus 50p for the second book and 30p
for each additional book to a maximum charge of £3.00 (7 books plus).

Overseas customers, including Eire, please allow £2.00 for postage and packing for
the first book plus £1.00 for the second book and 50p for each subsequent title
ordered.

NAME (Block letters) ....

ADDRESS ....

....